AN imPERFECT LIFE

Hills Are For Climbing

Charles P. Malone

AC Power Media, LLC

To those who have climbed the hills of trial and adversity only to find mountains on the other side... this book is dedicated to you as a reminder of the trust God has in you to FALL FORWARD, LOOK UPWARD, and know He is by your side, has your back, and is two-steps ahead.

Contents

Chapter One

MARIA

"Maria, where are you hiding?" came the angry voice of Guadalupe Portencia Luiz, the mother of nine-year-old Maria, as she threw open each cabinet door after door without success. No, Maria!" You know you cannot hide forever. You will soon get hungry! Thirsty! Then I will find you, and when I do, you, little wench, you will wish you were dead." The little girl thought to herself, afraid to breathe... *I already do wish I were dead!*

As if her mother could read her thoughts, her mother's hand reached for the cabinet door under the kitchen sink, pulling it open to expose the crying Maria, who now screamed at the scowling face before her. A firm hand grabbed Maria by the arm, followed by pulling her struggling body out from her favorite hiding place. How did her mother know? She would have to find another. The beating was swift, with no attempt to reconcile afterward.

Maria Felisa Luiz was the whipping post for her mother's anger issues, and this type of punishment was pretty much a daily occurrence. She was a curious sort and not particularly good at following rules set by her parents–not a good formula for happiness with very strict parents. However, Maria's parents were not just strict, they were over-the-top strict. They were both no-nonsense shift workers at a garment assembly plant or factory–known as "maquilas" in Guatemala City... and had little time or energy to put up with a child who did anything rather than obey their wishes.

Maria was the only child of Fabio Eliseo and Guadalupe Portencia Luiz, native Guatemalans caught in the cycle of poverty, forced overtime, and lack of opportunity to progress. The minimal education provided by the Guatemalan government was of little value because of the pressure put upon parents to provide for their children instead of seeking selfish opportunities elsewhere. The only "legal" opportunities available to agricultural and industrial workers with no education were the fields... or maquilas. There was little opportunity for escape.

Guadalupe had the day shift and her husband the night, returning home after his wife had already left to replace him. There was only one hour before the day shift workers were to be at a station and ready to begin their twelve-hour shift. The factory production schedule only allowed one hour of downtime to make the change of tired, exhausted workers for somewhat fresh ones. And twice a year, the equipment would be shut down for semi-annual maintenance for 48 hours each. Unless you filled a management or maintenance position with the employer, you were not allowed time off to rest and heal or spend time with family—if you were lucky to have one—before returning to work.

Guadalupe hurriedly put her lunch together for the day and made her way out the door onto the busy street, which was already filling up with shift workers headed to work. The day was cloudy, with continued threats of rain in the forecast, but her spirits were already damp as she carried thoughts of the beating she had just given her daughter. But instead of remorse, there was a growing feeling of.... what? Hatred? No, she didn't hate her daughter, but it was not a normal feeling of love either. It was not uncommon for parents to become overwhelmed with trying to make a living, with little time for anything else, including raising a family.

Abortions were common in Guatemala, and Guadalupe often criticized herself for allowing Fabio to get her pregnant. She vowed then never to let that mistake happen again. She should have aborted the pregnancy, but the stories that surfaced from young girls dying on the abortion table or whisked away to a place unknown—where the child would be sold and the mother never to be heard from again—kept her from making that choice. She looked at work as a reprieve from the constant challenges being a parent and wife thrust upon her. She was so tired. Death could not come fast enough. A burden... Yes, that is what she was feeling toward her daughter. A burden that would not be lifted until her daughter was married and gone.

When Maria heard the door slam, she knew she had but one hour to dress, eat, and clean, so when her father came home from his shift, she would have his breakfast waiting for him. If any part of that daily ritual were missing, she would receive her second beating of the day, but this time from her exhausted father, who didn't have much in him after a twelve-hour shift at the factory. But a beating was a beating, and her father could still swing a belt or willow branch or wooden spoon and make her regret her actions... or inactions.

So Maria set about to prepare herself for whatever lay ahead, hoping her father would be so tired he could not find much to complain about, so he would take his jug of whiskey into his bed and drink until sleep overcame the fatigue of work and the disappointments of life—but that was not to be.

Fabio Eliseo Luiz was not a big man in terms of height and weight, weighing only 165 lbs and standing 5' 7", but with age and the daily twelve-hour factory shifts, he did not look much like the man Guadalupe Portencia Ramos had married only ten years earlier. But Fabio was blessed with good looks. His strikingly high cheekbones, relatively uncommon of the Guatemalan people, reflecting his Mayan ancestry, helped him charm his way through Catholic school by endearing himself to the school nuns with his wit and good looks. Fabio Luiz would also use these characteristics to capture the attention of the charming Guadalupe Ramos, who sat only three desks away.

Life in the small town of Palencia during the first few years of the couple's marriage was simple at first, but once the big textile factory was built in Guatemala City, it seemed the simplicities of life changed dramatically. It only took the next drought to convince the majority of farmers to abandon their simple lives in exchange for a regular paycheck as factory workers.

Maria lay whimpering on her bed after her father had assuaged his anger with strong drink and sleep, as well as beating her once again. When he awoke, he would be hungry, expecting his food to be ready and waiting. But Maria was herself angry and hurt as she willed herself back to sleep to try and forget the beating that had just taken place. It was not only the pain of the kitchen spatula that caused tears to flow easily, but it was also the dark feelings of rejection and loss of hope she felt within.

Although Maria was only nine years old, the responsibilities placed upon her and the unyielding expectations set by her parents aged her dramatically. She would never enjoy a childhood free from pain and defeat. It was her life to serve and to be beaten. What had she done to deserve such a life? Why was she being punished so?

***

Seven years later... Blackness filled the little room as sixteen-year-old Maria peeked out from underneath the covers of her bed. She could hear the heavy breathing of her mother in the next room through paper-thin walls, signaling she was in a deep sleep and would unlikely wake until morning. A quick look at the tiny clock with illuminated numbers told her she had only ten minutes to freshen up for her arranged meeting with the village priest, a meeting needed due to her nightly *escapes* with her new friend Manny.

Maynard Ellington was the eighteen-year-old son of the new Factory Manager, Spencer F. Ellington. Manny (as he preferred to be called) and Maria had become fast friends. With little opportunity to socialize or to learn socializing skills, their friendship soon led to intimacy with one another... and an unwanted pregnancy.

Maria sat nervously outside the rectory at her parent's church. She had nowhere else to turn once she became convinced she was pregnant. She knew her parents would be furious... no, worse than furious once they found out she was pregnant. "Another mouth to feed?" She could already feel the hot wrath of her father yelling at her—coming closer with raised hand and with veins popping out of his neck in unbridled anger toward his daughter. The beatings had become less frequent as Maria aged, but the anger issues of the parents had not improved at all.

As Maria waited to be called in to meet with Father Morales, she dreaded even more than dying her eventual face-to-face confrontation with her parents over this child who was about to be born into the same horrible environment she was living. Why had she been so careless and fallen for the handsome Manny Ellington? She knew they were getting close to crossing the line when their playful teasing turned to passionate kissing. She should have stopped at that point, but the feeling of someone loving her, kissing her instead of beating her, was so welcomed... and needed–that she just became absorbed into the passion of the moment. And then it was too late. There would be no turning back once they had become intimate with one another.

Masked as true love, Maria had allowed someone other than her future husband to introduce her to womanhood. At the age of seventeen years old, Maria would become a mother. Her life was about to change forever. She had feared to tell Manny because she had become so dependent upon him emotionally she was now fearful of losing the only escape from her miserable life at home. Manny would not be happy to know he had fathered a child. He would blame Maria for not protecting herself better. His parents had superior social standing in the community and would not tolerate him being married to a girl from a family with neither wealth nor elevated social status to distinguish themselves from the lowest strata of society. She will lose him. She will lose the one love of her life–for another.

"Maria, Father Morales will see you now," a whispered voice drifted into Maria's consciousness. Sister Bella Montero stood a few feet from Maria and spoke tenderly to the child who sat nervously waiting for the Priest. With unsteady legs, Maria stood and pushed herself toward the closed door of Father Morales' office while Sister Montero knocked lightly on the spiritual leader's door. With only a moment's delay, the door slowly opened, and there stood the smiling Father Hector Morales, the parish priest and spiritual leader. He graciously invited Maria in and slowly closed the door behind him, ensuring complete privacy to what was about to occur. An hour later, red-eyed Maria Luiz slipped out quietly from the good priest's office, and without anyone's notice, she hastily made for the big front door leading out into the world. She was alone in this mistake and would have to face it squarely and accept the consequences of her actions. Father Morales would not intercede on her behalf. He offered forgiveness, prayers, and instructions to pray to the patron saint of chastity, St. Maria Goretti, light several candles begging God for assistance, and resist the urge to sin any longer... but she was alone to face her mother.

"I am with child," came an almost inaudible whisper from Maria's parched lips as her eyes darted almost uncontrollably from the floor to her mother's gaping mouth, then back to the floor. Her mother said nothing, just stared at her daughter as if she was seeing her for the first time.

"How?" "Who?" Only two words, but a powerful reveal into the mind of Guadalupe Luiz. She had lost touch with her daughter. She was but nine years old, the last she could remember looking at her daughter. And now she was with child?

"HH...how old are you?" her mother finally said after stunned silence filled the room in place of air to breathe. "How old are you, Maria?" This time, using her given name. "I am sixteen, Mama—almost seventeen. And 'who' doesn't matter. He wants nothing to do with my child... or me," Maria said softly, as her voice revealed the loneliness and shame she had brought to herself and to her family. Both women now stared at the floor, each unable to look at the other, both willing this to only be a nightmare from which they would soon awake. Maria's tears now flowed freely as she tried to prepare herself for her mother's physical reaction. It did not come in the way Maria expected it... but it did come.

"When?" Guadalupe asked, all the air in her lungs now exhausted. Maria raised her head slowly toward her mother's still bowed head. She could not see her eyes, and for that, she was grateful. She answered, "What do you mean, Mama?" Then, a glimpse of the volcanic turmoil that stirred in the stomach of Guadalupe Luiz revealed itself. "When did you conceive, you fool? When did you stop having monthly periods? Have you felt the baby move? Are you showing? "The familiar fire had returned to her mother's eyes, and now they were no longer hidden in tears that had exposed the fire that burned within.

Guadalupe reached Maria so quickly the young woman had little time to prepare herself. Her mother grabbed Maria's arms with hands so rough from years of factory work that welts appeared immediately as she forced her pregnant daughter to stand in front of her while she removed the large t-shirt Maria had become used to wearing to hide her growing stomach. Her mother let her hands fly... first to Maria's face and then grabbing, tearing at the cloth that bound her stomach until she had exposed Maria's bare stomach. A skin-toned corset or body wrap was first revealed, and within the soft fiber of the garment meant to hide the fact that Maria was showing, her mother saw the advanced state of Maria's pregnancy. Without the wrapping that both secured and hid the child growing within, it quickly became apparent to Guadalupe that her daughter was well beyond "just" pregnant... Maria was months along, maybe only a month or two before delivery, perhaps even sooner.

For long moments—moments that seemed to Maria to be endless hours—Guadalupe just stood there, not saying a word but staring intently at Maria's belly, as if trying to come to grips with the severe impact a baby unable to care for itself would have on the entire family, let alone the disgrace of having an illegitimate child in the house, not that it was all that uncommon these days. But the physical, emotional, and financial burden imposed upon a family already at the brink of exhaustion and defeat would be too much. It just could not be.

Still in her mother's grasp and unable to think of anything to say, Maria stood there in abject misery, silently weeping, tears streaming down her young face. "We cannot tell your father," Guadalupe said with urgency now building in her voice as she began re-wrapping the soft cloth around Maria's abdomen. She knew what to do. What she must do. It did not take Maria long to comprehend why her mother was so insistent she come with her immediately. Luckily, her father had the day shift and would not be home until later that night. They would make their way to la Clínica. Abortion in Guatemala was deemed illegal by that country's Constitution, but that did not stop the practice when such conditions warranted it... and many that did not.

Following her exam by a grim Dr. Lux, Maria sat in a chair her mother had occupied during the exam, reliving the Doctor's words... "The baby's vitals appear to be strong enough, Señora Luiz," but then, in a whisper, he added, "But the mother, not so good. If you want more than what a simple exam can reveal, it will cost." The doctor and Maria's mother then left together, leaving Maria alone and afraid. She was carrying a life—and how she would care for the child without her parent's help... and approval, she did not know.

Where had her mother gone? Maria wondered. *Was she making arrangements to pay the Doctor?* Maria continued sitting there alone, confused, miserable, and sick with worry. A masked nurse suddenly appeared and opened the curtain surrounding the exam room without explanation or introduction. Behind the nurse was a male nurse and a trauma cart. "Miss Luiz, the Doctor is going to take your baby now," a voice behind the mask declared, void of any emotion. "Please position yourself on the cart, and we will take you to surgery."

Maria could not believe her ears. *Were they going to take her baby? Now? But why? How? It wasn't yet due.* Her confused and fearful–but unasked questions–remained unanswered as the male nurse from behind the cart had repositioned himself at Maria's side, placing a band around her arm in preparation for the needle that was injected so quickly she didn't even have time to resist. And then all went dark.

"Maria! - Maria, wake up!" came a shrill voice cutting through the darkness to penetrate her personal abyss. Maria's eyes fluttered open, only to be greeted by... no one. *Was she dreaming again?*

Maria's mind drifted back to the images still playing with her mind—dark and foreboding. She imagined crying... no, *wailing!* Was this just a dream from which she would soon awake?

Maria blinked several times before looking around, trying to gain her bearings, but there was nothing but a blue curtain surrounding her. *Where was she?* At that thought, the strange, shrill voice returned; this time, it was accompanied by a form. "Oh good, you are awake! Maria, do you know what day it is? What is your middle name?" Not waiting for an answer, the form pulled the blanket from Maria's body, exposing her again to the chill she had felt since arriving at the Clinic. "Your mother insists on taking you home, but I must warn you not to work or lift for at least two weeks, or you will risk infection setting in and maybe even lose your life," said the form, who now had a face. It was the face of the nurse who had tied a plastic patient identification band around her wrist.

Maria then felt her stomach. "Where is my baby?" She said in a cry of anguish and fear, as the sharp pain of having her baby removed rose above the numbing sensation she still felt from the surgery. "What have you done with my baby?"

"The baby did not make it, Maria. I am sorry," came the emotionless reply. "What do you mean? Where's my baby? Where is my mother?" Question after question now rose from a frightened but determined Maria. *Something was not right. She had lost her baby? How?*

Just as the nurse was opening her mouth to perhaps answer Maria's questions, an imposing figure darkened the small space containing Maria and the nurse. She quickly whispered something to Maria and then left the room. "Maria, why are you not dressed? I am to be at work in a few hours, and it will take us that long to get you home. Put on these clothes, and we are going home," roared the unsympathetic voice of Guadalupe Luiz. Maria had brought this upon herself. There would be no sympathy, no rest, and no baby to take home... Not another mouth to feed! Not now. Not ever!

Maria could barely hold herself upright as she exited the doors of the Clinic, being pulled and sometimes carried by her mother's surreal stamina fueled by her determination to end this nightmare brought on by this selfish daughter of hers. But Guadalupe had succeeded in ridding herself of the extra burden, without her husband, so much the wiser. He would have handled things differently, but given the medical condition of the newborn taken from its mother's womb, this small particle of life with all sorts of maladies that even the best of hospitals would find challenging to address would only become a burden upon those who would be charged with its care.

This was the right thing to do! Guadalupe rationalized within herself. *It was the "only" thing to do!* She concluded. The records would show a stillborn baby boy, born to an unknown mother. No one would ever have to know about this terrible mistake.

But the Clinique ambulance slowly making its way through the little village of Antigua, carrying its small and very much alive package, would one day foil that plan as the white-washed walls of Sacred Hearts Convent and University came into view, its usual bright radiance now muted from the low-setting Guatemalan sun, projecting a vision of hope to all who entered its doors.

Chapter Two

PAULO

*T*welve *years later...* "Paulo, you know better than to hit girls, don't you?" came the commanding voice of Sister Ramos. "Ever since you arrived twelve *long* years ago, you have been a problem child, always fighting, always getting into trouble," She continued to rant. "You have seen your friends here at the school leave into happy homes... but you, my boy, are destined to grow old and die here unless you change your ways."

"I didn't hit her," came the defensive cry from young Paulo. "She took my drawing pencil and wouldn't give it back... so I took it," he said in a mocked, hurtful tone... sticking out his tongue at the older girl who had taken his pencil. Felicia Torres was only two years older than Paulo, but, in her way, she cared for the boy. She was the first to realize his potential, but his physical challenges just invited scorn and ridicule from his classmates. The fact that Paulo had a mean streak that radiated from his face in the form of a chip on his shoulder and that he harbored a grudge, a grudge that engendered deep-set hostilities, didn't help matters. Paulo was not a child one could easily love; he was angry and aloof and not given to showing tenderness or affection to anyone. But Felicia enjoyed her little games with Paulo in an attempt to get the boy talking to her. He was so private and kept to himself most of the time... drawing and reading or just staring out into space as if he was expecting someone or something to just fly down and rescue him from his captive state.

Felicia didn't understand Paulo's resentment against the school or the Sisters who provided care and schooling for the orphans who resided in this special convent. The Nuns were mostly kind and caring, but if you got out of line, which Paulo did on most occasions, then you paid the price for such behavior. This often meant having to repeat lots of prayers, penances of solitary confinement, reduced meals, and sometimes corporal punishment in the form of a pine board that was flat on one end, about 6 inches wide by 1/2 inch thick, and a handle grip cut into the wood, worn smooth from many years of use.

To show forgiveness and that there was no lasting animosity by the staff, the penitent children were permitted to sign their names on the board and place a mark by their name for each subsequent offense. Paulo refused to sign even once. The first Saturday of each month of June brought prospective parents looking to adopt a child from the convent. The money received for each child went to assist in paying the overhead of the small facility. It was not the goal of the school to raise these children to adulthood and bear the burden of expense in their change in eating habits, as well as their growing curiosity with the opposite sex as their hormones kicked in. In any event, regardless of the nun's efforts to assist Paulo in finding new parents, he was not the ideal candidate to be adopted. His right leg was slightly shorter than his left, causing a limp, and his lungs had not been fully developed at birth, so he was always wheezing and coughing when he exercised along with the other children. This last defect almost guaranteed him to be known to his orphanage peers by the nickname of "Wheezy." In Paulo's case, there would be no nicknames. At least not to his face, unless you wanted to join him in Mother Superior's office after being punched in the face or somewhere else. The other kids pretty much left Paulo to himself... except for Felicia Torres. "Maybe today, Paulo."

"What?" answered Paulo, coming out of the apparent mind-wandering he frequently indulged himself. He often allowed himself to wonder, "why?" Why was he discarded by his mother? His parents. Or were they parents? Paulo just figured he was what the other kids called him... an *accident*! Neither the man nor the woman who were his so-called parents wanted him. His resentment for not having been wanted carried forward into his youth, which, of course, embittered him and did not serve to make him a more likely candidate for adoption.

"I said, maybe today a family will come who will want you... who will love you, Paulo," repeated Felicia, trying to keep Paulo from losing hope. Felicia knew about losing hope, for she was now beyond the age most families would want to adopt. Brought to the convent as a result of losing her parents in a drug trafficking accident, Felicia was rescued before she was sold on the child-sex market and brought to the school for adoption. But there would be no takers for Felicia, the child of a drug smuggler. Most adoptive parents who come to the Catholic Convent want a perfect child. Their dreams of having children of their own, having been dashed over time, so now they must consider raising another's child as their own. So, if they must choose, they want the best. They have dreams that don't include a child who may be drawn to drugs by their birth parent's illegal activities or who was born with any physical defect or malady. The fear that an adopted child might be attracted to drug usage or prone to addictive behavior would almost certainly be attributed to drug usage by the biological parents. The reasonable fear is that the child's biological parents were both dealers and users of drugs, with all the possible problems associated with such behavior being passed on to the child they might adopt.

At exactly 12:00 noon, Sister Ramona Medina came through the classes to dismiss the students for lunch and to visit casually with prospective parents who may have an interest in adopting, as they, too, enjoyed the simple lunch provided by the school. "Come, come, children... lunch awaits! Do not keep the prospective parents waiting!" Sister Medina chortled. "Put on your best smiles and be on your best behavior, or you will grow old and senile here at the school, like me," she teased. Paulo just rolled his eyes at his favorite nun's attempt at humor. There wasn't much to joke about here at the convent, and most of the nuns were very strict. But Sister Medina always tried to see the best in her charges and tried to teach them that they are never alone if they will just let God into their heart and accept the atoning sacrifice of His son, Jesus Christ. But that was easier said than done when you carried a hurt so deeply, let alone taught to believe in a merciful God he could not see but who, supposedly, loves him. Being happy seemed well beyond his reach. Believing in God was not an entirely easy commitment for him, either.

So, where was this God when my parents gave me away? Thought Paulo to himself. Parading oneself in front of prospective tickets to freedom should not have been that difficult for Paulo, but continuous rejection time and time again brought with it a forecast that this would be yet another failed attempt at being someone he was not. Someone who would be a perfect child for perfect parents. This was not Paulo.

Sister Medina held the big door open and embraced each child as they entered the visitation area already crowded with hopeful couples. "Smile!" She would whisper into their ears as she hugged them. "This is your chance for a real life," she encouraged. Paulo and Felicia were last to enter the crowded hall, being the oldest. There was little attention directed their way as they slowed to close the door behind them, signaling to all that there would be no more children to pick from. Felicia kept close to Paulo as they walked toward the grandstand filled with prospective parents... three rows of chairs, each row filled with eager and questioning eyes–Paulo could not help but cast an eye of defiance at the crowd, being careful not to stick out his tongue in protest or challenge as if to say, "I dare you to be interested in me. I dare you to take a chance. . . to look past my age and my hurts and see my potential, my goals, my dreams. . . my heart." But eyes were already focused elsewhere as these last two brought up the rear.

Anticipating yet another round of rejection, Paulo sent a searing gaze over at the VIPs, only to be intercepted by the woman with big green eyes and reddish hair that seemed to cover her entire set of broad shoulders and a smile! Someone was smiling at him. With Paulo's eyes locked onto hers, he did not notice the parade had stopped before he plowed right into the back of Andrea, who in turn ran into the backside of Raul. . . eliciting cries of surprise and confusion as the rear rear-end collision worked its way up the line as a stack of dominos might do when lined up closely to one another. Now, "all eyes" were on the boy and girl bringing up the rear, and apparently, the cause of this little bit of entertainment aided in breaking up the stuffiness and tense atmosphere felt in the room. As if on cue, the spectators began to clap, one by one, until the room was filled with applause and laughter. Prospective parents rose from the chairs and began circulating around the room, meeting the children with grand anticipation.

Before Felicia could react to this embarrassing train wreck of a moment, Paulo had already started a string of apologies but stopped mid-sentence when his eyes once again caught the sight of the red-haired woman whose green, almost glowing eyes looked, it seemed, only at him. She approached him and said, "Excuse me, young man, may I speak with you a moment?" Paulo almost looked away to see who this woman might be addressing. But he knew it was him. And she was addressing him in English. In addition to their native language, all the children in the convent were taught English in case they were adopted into an English-speaking family. And, oh, how Paulo wished at that moment he had worked harder at speaking English so he could impress this woman who was now looking directly at him. "Uh, yyyes of course," Paulo managed to spit out.

"My name is Annette," the beautiful English-speaking woman said with an inviting smile. "My husband and I live in Utah, in the USA. We have three children of our own, but we came to the school today looking for an older brother or sister for our family." Paulo listened, uncomfortable at first, but as the woman's eyes sank into his, he felt his uneasiness begin to lift, and his heart began to beat rapidly with hope. Could such a family as this truly be interested in Paulo? A broken-winged child with anger issues and crude manners?

"Tell me about yourself, please," the woman asked politely as she bent down to look at Paulo, eye to eye. "What is your name?" asked the woman, warm sincerity evident in the tone of her voice as she leaned toward him as if to signal, "This is just between you and me. I will protect your secrets. I won't laugh at you or make light of your hurts. You are safe with me."

"I don't know much," Paulo answered quietly, after pausing for a few seconds before answering at all. "I was brought to the convent to be cared for by the Sisters shortly after my birth... wherever that was. I am called Paulo."

Now puzzled, Annette asked, "Why have you not accepted adoption, Paulo?" Now it was Paulo's turn to look puzzled... "What do you mean, Senora? I am disfigured from birth and carry the mark of an unwanted child. Who would want a child with one leg shorter than the other and who cannot smile without revealing pain of the heart? I am short of temper and cannot read well." Instead of thoughts of abandonment and rejection on her face, the lady from the USA only smiled.

"You sound like a very normal young man, Paulo," Annette said with sincerity in her voice as she stood to leave... but whispered over her shoulder, "Wait here, please, Paulo. I want my husband to meet you." And with that, she disappeared, leaving Paulo searching to find Felicia with his eyes. She was nowhere to be found. Had she gone back to her room? Why? A dozen questions now flooded Paulo's mind as he waited by himself, off to the side of all the activity going on between prospective parents and the child residents of Sacred Hearts.

Where was Felicia? He briefly searched the room again and saw her standing not far away from him.

If he were adopted, what would become of his best friend? *America?* Just the thought brought unwanted chills to his slim frame. *Utah?* Wasn't that where the American Indians lived that he had read about? *Is it safe there?* And with that thought, Paulo smiled to himself, almost laughing aloud at how any place could be more dangerous than his own country. In the middle of these questioning thoughts, a hand, followed by a slender arm, followed by a most pleasant aroma, draped around Paulo's shoulders. "Paulo, I would like you to meet my husband. Richard, this is Paulo," came the sweet voice of his new friend.

After their get-acquainted visit, Richard and Annette excused themselves, and Paulo immediately made finding Felicia once again his main priority. It did not take him long to find her–sitting alone at the big fountain in the middle of the courtyard where the guests were always brought to mingle and visit with their adoptive hopefuls. There sat Felicia... by herself. "I couldn't find you," Paulo said, almost in a whisper. Felicia answered in like tone, matching his.

"You were busy, Paulo. Getting acquainted with your new parents," she quietly said, not entirely laced with congratulations but with a subtle wistfulness that betrayed her heart to Paulo, who knew her too well to be deceived. She was about to lose her best friend. No matter the age difference, she loved Paulo. She felt her heart breaking at the thought of him moving far away and never seeing one another again.

"I will come back for you, Felicia. You will not be forgotten... that I promise you! Besides, I am not likely to be going *anywhere,*" he assured her, remembering the many times before when someone expressed interest but never chose him.

A month had gone by, and Paulo's hope of adoption had now slowly faded into a dream-like mode. Something to think about when he was having trouble sleeping. But his close relationship with his best friend seemed to never be the same after the experience with that couple from America. It was as if Felicia knew something he didn't, and she was being very guarded. Yes, that was it, guarded... afraid to get close again for fear they would come and take *her* Paulo. And they did!

One Saturday morning after breakfast, Paulo and Felicia, along with several other younger residents, were immersed in Saturday chores in the Courtyard when a member of the office staff, Sister Montero, whistled a shrill whistle with two fingers between her lips to get the groups attention. Of course, such a general and familiar sound brought everyone's head up to see who was being summoned. She pointed to Paulo, bringing both friendly and not-so-friendly jeers and "Oohs" from the others as if they knew the reason he was being summoned would lead to an impending punishment. To Paulo, the embarrassment this caused him to feel was far worse than raking leaves or cleaning the restrooms.

Being summoned to the office was one or two of the worst things the children under the care of the strict Sisterhood worried about. It was almost never good. It was rarely about "office" stuff, but mostly about compliance issues, grades, or an extemporaneous interview with one of the Sister counselors assigned to the child... This time, it was none of the above.

Paulo was led into the inner sanctum, reserved for those with special needs to be handled by Mother Superior. He was invited to sit across from the big walnut desk, usually occupied but now sat vacant. Rubbing his hands together from nervousness, Paulo's thoughts ran the gamut of deeds for which he might have been pulled into her office. Never in his life was he prepared for what was about to happen. When the door opened, in walked Mother Superior Mary Eunice. She rarely dealt with commoners like Paulo... especially those with anger issues and disabilities–especially like Paulo. *This must be huge*, thought Paulo, wringing his hands like trying to remove a tight glove. But before he could get another thought into his brain, Mother Superior held the door open as another person, a woman... and a man, were escorted into the room. Paulo gasped! The woman smiled, her eyes dancing with excitement... but no words were exchanged as they were seated across from Paulo while Mother Mary Eunice positioned herself to conduct this little meeting before sitting behind the desk.

Mother Superior Mary Eunice was a short woman, but she had learned over the years how to project her small frame into a larger-than-life image. In fact, it was rumored among the children that Mother Mary had built a small platform for her chair so she maintained an elevated air over those she was instructing in her office. Today, it would be Paulo... and Mr. and Mrs. Richard Tone from Utah, USA.

"Paulo, this is Mr. and Mrs. Tone from America. They have come today because they are interested in adopting you as their son." One of Paulo's premature birth health issues slightly affected his hearing. But there was no hearing loss today. Not today. Not at this moment. Someone loved what they saw enough to want to make him their son. And there was no deficiency in tears either, as moisture welled up in Paulo's eyes and began to spill despite the defensive banks that had been put into place by years of low self-worth and anger. Paulo wiped fiercely at his cheeks with the sleeve of his shirt, and without saying a word, young Paulo would finally have a last name. He would become a Tone... from America. Annette Tone didn't need any further proof that this boy was meant to become her son. He has feelings. And with proper love, he can learn to love back... and to trust.

"Paulo, is there something you would like to say?" almost whispered Mother Mary. Paulo's eyes were still moist with tears as he considered what to say. Does he speak words that are expected? Or should he speak words that reflect the feelings of his heart? How would he explain his departure to Felicia? How could he abandon her to grow old in this convent and perhaps live her life in poverty after her stay here while he becomes a prosperous American? He had no choice but to go, but he vowed to himself he would return for Felicia. How, he did not know, but she was the only family he had in the world, and somehow, he would bring her into the Tone family.

"I... Uh, I would be honored to become a member of the Tone family," Paulo managed. Then, in uncharacteristic style, he looked at Mother M ary... tears again welling up and threatening to burst through the years of anger and resentment still held inside his heart toward those responsible for creating him and then giving him away, but for a moment, letting enough sunshine into his heart to recognize those who had literally saved him.

"Mother... Uh," Paulo choked as emotion rose to cut off his air supply. "Mother Mary Eunice, you and the sisters here at the school saved my life. I will not forget you. I promise to make something of myself..." Then, looking at Annette and Richard Tone, he added with somewhat of a forced smile... "With the help of my new family." Annette could not stay seated any longer. As if ejected from her seat, Annette Tone lost her cool composure and practically leaped over her husband to hug this frail boy who had no worldly wealth but offered the promise of wealth of a very different kind. Paulo reacted to this show of emotion in a way that exposed the years of distrust and disappointment that he had known since birth. Although he knew nothing more than the convent as his home and the Sisterhood as the ruling authority, there seemed to be a piece of him that was never connected. Something inside him longed for a connection with who he "really" was. Not just to know who gave him away, but also who had hated him so much that they would just wish him dead–*But who am I, really?* Paulo searched within himself.

Annette stopped almost in mid-air, noticing the look of... what? Fear? – Confusion? – on Paulo's face. "Paulo, are you ok?" She quietly asked in her soft voice as she took a step back to look at Paulo squarely in the eyes. "Yyyes... I am ok," Paulo answered quietly. "I am ok!" as he opened his arms and heart to welcome his new parents.

While the Tones attended to the paperwork involved with adopting a child from Guatemala, Paulo made his way to his room to pack his meager belongings... and to find Felicia. How do you keep from having feelings of betrayal for a friend who has been your only lifeline since becoming conscious of where he was and who influenced his life the most? He only knew the Sisters as his caregivers. He never bonded with them in the way others at the convent had. He grew into his nine-year-old frame, a fragile and angry boy with built-in resentments against life even before he understood why he was at the convent. As a baby, he was nursed to health by someone from the nearby village until it was clear he would live, and then even she disappeared from his life, replaced by a bottle of baby food formula held to his mouth. He was nothing more than the means of attracting an adoption bounty–and he knew it. But then this tall woman with long black hair and dark eyes that could practically look into his soul appeared out of nowhere and began caring for him, protecting him, defending him, and–loving him. She would become the sister and sometimes mother Paulo never had... but now that Paulo was leaving the school, what would become of Felicia? Little did Paulo know the real reason Felicia had never been adopted. It soon became clear to the Sisterhood that Felicia was the only one who could reckon with Paulo when he became unmanageable and full of anger. It was Felicia who kept the boy from being tossed out onto the streets to fend for himself, becoming sure prey to child trafficking–or worse.

It was decided by the Sisterhood early on that Felicia must remain with the boy "until" he was adopted, if he ever was. And Felicia agreed. It was her calling, and one she accepted gladly. Paulo packed quickly, throwing what belongings he had into his small pillow covering, tied it together, and threw it on his bed. He needed to find Felicia... and he knew the first place to look. As Paulo entered the small chapel from the main entry he could see a figure kneeling in the second pew from the front. Even when she was kneeling, Felicia was tall. And this was "her" pew. Boys and girls were not allowed to sit together at mass, but Felicia had brought Paulo here many times over the years to help him understand what and where God was. But Paulo had resisted knowing a God who would desert him while he was just a baby in need of a family. Even now, he could not see that he *was* provided a family... and someone who loved him.

Without saying a word, Paulo slipped in beside Felicia, careful not to make a sound . . . except when he sat down, and the bench groaned, just ever so slightly. She did not move but opened one eye to catch who she knew was there and returned to her prayers. Paulo sat there observing Felicia in the attitude of prayer. Her brow was creased, and her small lips were moving in sequence with the movement of her brow. How could she sit here for what seemed like hours and pray to someone she could not see? This had been Felicia's daily ritual for as long as he had known her. And she had not changed one bit. Not even today. Crossing herself in the ritual ending of prayer, Felicia sat back on the bench... now looking squarely into her friend's eyes as if waiting for him to say something first. But Paulo was at a loss for words and just sat there taking in the face of this long-time friend, sister, mother, and protector, trying to memorize every detail, every curve, blemish, and single dimple on her right cheek, knowing this memory

would be all he would have to live by as he began his new life without
Felicia.

"Are you frightened?" she asked softly, with her eyes just daring him to
lie.

"Yyyes, I am frightened," he answered honestly. "But not for the reasons
you might think. I am frightened to leave you." This brought a chuckle
from Felicia.

"You won't have me there to clean up your mess–that's all you are worried about," she said with a wide grin. Both sat in silence, each in their own
thoughts about the future that lay before them. With her "assignment"
complete, Felicia would surely be adopted as a nanny or cook's helper. But
how would she survive without this scrawny kid she had grown to love?
The ageless principle that we learn to love those we serve was certainly
true in her case. She had become this boy's advocate, his defender, trainer,
and most certainly a punching bag for when his anger and resentments
reached a boiling point, and she stepped in to defuse his anger. She helped
him by discouraging him from reacting to his feelings in ways that would
surely lead him to punishment and, thus, add fuel to his already smoldering
resentments. Now he would be in someone else's care . . . and how would
they deal with his issues? They didn't even know him. They had no idea
what they were bringing into their perfect home. Here was an imperfect
child full of resentments and anger about the way he was dumped onto this
planet from who knows where, and he is now 'theirs' to deal with. Would
he disrupt their life as much as he is capable, only to rebuff him and bring
him back to the convent orphanage rejected and even more broken? And,
would she be here to pick him up, dust him off, and prepare for his next
onslaught of violent behavior until it had run its course and she could talk
him up and have him again believing–until next time?

"You cannot come back, Paulo." Although said in a whisper, Paulo
recognized the intensity of feeling in her voice.

"What do you mean?" He asked–now looking her way, his brows creased
in mild concern.

"You must succeed with your new family, Paulo. Every child here knows about your anger. Your resentments. Your heart. But they love you, Paulo, uh... as I do. We all love you, and you must not fail us." Tears were falling now... freely. But Felicia didn't try to hide her emotions this time. She looked Paulo straight in the eyes and challenged him one last time. "If you ever feel like quitting, like running away, I want you to remember this: 'Hills are for climbing.'" Confused, Paulo again looked at her squarely... "What do you mean? What hills?"

"You are so dense, little boy," she said with lightness returning to her voice. "What are you ever going to do without me?" she added, now wagging her finger in his face. Her comment brought a sobering sense of reality to this lighthearted bantering. What would he do without her? And with that last thought, his arms grew a mind of their own as they grabbed Felicia in a tight bear hug and let go before his mind even got to ask the meaning of her "hills" comment. He would have to figure it out for himself. And, in time, he would.

With his small bag held over his shoulder as a sailor returning home from sea, Paulo entered the office where his new parents and Mother Mary Eunice were huddled over a stack of papers being signed. Annette Tone was the first to sense his presence. She immediately stood and, with all the poise of a runway model, walked to him. "Paulo, is there anyone you need to say goodbye to before we leave? Our plane leaves in two hours and it will take us almost that long in travel time," Annette said softly. "But if there is..." "Th... there is no one," Paulo interrupted. "There is no one... else," he finished, eyes now looking over to Mother Mary, almost expecting her to comment. She said nothing, only looked at Paulo as if she were studying him–his features, his soul.

Paulo then did an unexpected thing, even to him. He crossed the room to where Mother Mary was seated, still holding the signed adoption papers in her hands, and held out both hands to hers. "Mm... Mother Superior, I want to thank you for saving my life... You and the Sisters here. I still don't know why I am alive or what I am supposed to do with my life, but if there is a God and He sent Mr. and Mrs. Tone here to rescue me, then I must work hard to find out why. I will never forget you!" And with that, Mother Mary stepped into Paulo's open arms... an experience he had never before felt while growing up. Richard Tone stood to join his wife as she tearfully observed the scene before them. He placed his arm around her shoulders and pulled him to her. Paulo was their son now. And the awkward but tender exchange between their son and his caregiver was enough evidence they had made the right choice.

"It is time, Paulo; we must leave or miss our flight to America," came the voice of Richard Tone as he began gathering the adoption paperwork and motioning to his wife that they had no more time to spare. The trio then made a swift exit to a waiting car, with instructions relayed quickly for the airport. This had all happened so fast. Only hours ago, Paulo was a resident of Sacred Heart... an unwanted child deserted by those who brought him into this world. Now, with the stroke of a pen, he had gained a new name, with parents who wanted him–and now headed to a new country he had only read about.

As the town car sped toward the airport, its occupants sat in silence as mile after mile passed, the setting sun creating beautiful silhouettes of the passing majestic mountains and valleys. *Somewhere out there was a mother who had given away her son because he wasn't perfect,* thought Paulo. *She didn't want me, but now I have someone who does. They want me enough to bring me to their home in America and treat me like their own son. I am now free to become.*

Chapter Three

KIDNAPPED

T he drive to the small airport seemed like a blur, helped in part by Paulo's eyelids falling shut several times, only to fly open when the vehicle hit a pothole in the road or slowed to a crawl. But when the bright lights of the airport terminal flooded the interior of the town car, Paulo's eyes opened wide and, he sat straight up in awe. Never had he seen so much light in one building. The school had such poor lighting run by an electric power generator that much of their study was moved outside during the day.

"We're here!" came the almost gleeful sound from the front seat where Annette Tone sat with her coat over her head. "Paulo, are you awake? We're here! Have you ever flown in an airplane? No, no, of course you haven't... what am I thinking? Anyway, let's get moving, or we'll miss our flight," Annette directed as she pushed open the door, shouting commands at anyone who would listen. Paulo sat still while everything seemed to be moving in slow motion around him. His eyes were still wide open, but nothing was transmitting to his brain. There was so much activity unfamiliar to Paulo that he couldn't get his legs moving in concert.

"Paulo! Hand me your bag," Richard directed over the maze of activity that flowed around him. Guatemala Aurora was the only airport in the region, other than Guatemala City, and every seat on every departing flight was full. Missing your flight meant extending your stay... and with three young children waiting anxiously for the return of their parents, there was no option but to make this flight. With Paulo in tow, Annette and Richard Tone made their way toward the ticket counter. Besides having to inch their way through the crowded isles, Annette kept hold of Paulo to keep him from being carried away by the crowd while staring at every person, sign, food counter, and smell associated with airport culture. The boy was literally absorbed and would have evaporated into the moving crowd if Annette hadn't put her arm and hand around Paulo's shoulders and hugged him as close as she could get him.

"Mrs. Tone, what does it feel like to drink from one of those bottled Cola's?" Paulo asked, pointing to a sign with a beautiful lady with red lips tipping the bottle into her mouth and smiling while she drank. Paulo's question stopped Annette right in her tracks, unsure if it was the reference to her as "Mrs."... or if she was stunned into reality over what may lie ahead for her new son adjusting to the American way of life.

"You have never tasted a Cola drink, Paulo?" she asked, almost in disbelief. Then, reaching out to pull on Richard's shoulder... "Richard, you go ahead to the gate. Paulo and I are stopping for a Cola." And with that, Annette and Paulo backtracked to where Annette remembered seeing a vending machine near the entrance to the terminal.

"Paulo, we only have a few minutes before they board for our flight, so we'll have to hurry," Annette prodded, trying to keep Paulo in front of her while she scanned the wave of bodies before her, looking for the elusive soft drink vending machine.

"I need to use the baño," Paulo cried, with a look of urgency on his face. "Is that a baño?" Paulo asked, pointing to a red sign that read *Hombres*, and not waiting for an answer before removing his hand from Annette's and moving toward his target with urgency.

"Paulo, be sure to use the one that says *Men*, and when you are done, just stand in front of the restroom door until I come for you. I'll get the colas and come right back for you," Annette said to a disappearing Paulo.

When he was out of sight, she turned to resume her search and was quickly rewarded as she spotted the lighted sign that spelled C O L A.

It only took Annette a few minutes to obtain the proper coins to pull out two soft drinks from the machine and head back in the direction she had come, but now panic started to mount in her mind until the sign over the men's restroom came into view... *Hombres*. But there was no Paulo waiting outside the door as expected.

Spotting a man heading into the restroom, Annette reached out and pulled lightly on his arm. "Excuse me, sir... ah, my... ah, son, is using the restroom but he hasn't come out yet. Could you please check to see if my son Paulo is inside? Then quickly added, in her broken Spanish: "Uh, ¿podría ver si mi hijo Paulo es por dentro?" hoping her language skills didn't fail her when it counted most.

The man entering the restroom only nodded, and with a "Si!" opened the door and disappeared... returning moments later shaking his head.

The words, "No hay nadie en el interior, Señora," stung at Annette's heart, causing it almost to stop beating. There was "no one" inside. And with that, Annette Tone started running toward the gate and to her waiting husband, hoping... no, praying–that Paulo had merely shown some independence of youth and made his way to the gate instead of waiting outside the door as instructed.

Annette had already decided not to make a big deal of the missing Paulo and save this training for another day when she spotted Richard... his back to her, talking to someone. "Paulo, I am so..." It was then she realized Richard was talking to the airline attendant and not Paulo.

"Annette, thank goodness you are here... where is Paulo?" His questioning eyes sinking deeply into hers. Without answering him, Annette moved past him, looking feverishly into the line of boarding passengers. "Where is he, Annette? Where is Paulo?" Richard questioned, his patience starting to fade, replaced by heavy dread.

"I don't know, Richard," she answered... now holding both hands to her face to shield her emotions from observers. "He went to the restroom. He was only out of my sight long enough to get these stupid sodas... And when I returned to where I told him to wait, he was gone." Richard then walked swiftly over to the airline attendant he had been visiting with before this grave news was laid on him and advised her that they would not be traveling today. Their son was missing, and they had to find him.

***

Paulo opened the door to the men's restroom... so anxious to find an unoccupied stall that he did not notice the dark figure standing still in the corner behind the door. After finishing his business Paulo was just tightening his belt when he heard a wrap on his stall door. "Su ocupada!" Paulo shouted as he slid the lock to open the door; the rancid smell of chloroform immediately assaulting his senses... before blackness enveloped his world.

"Wake up, kid!" came a rough man's voice before pain attacked Paulo's face. Then a hand grabbed him by the arm and jerked Paulo to his wobbly feet. Staggering, Paulo did the best he could to obey the commands given him to stand. *Where was his new mom? She would be worried!*

"Where are my parents?" Paulo asked in a shaky voice... as he was trying to get his brain and eyes to coordinate. "Shut up!" came the harsh reply. "I'm your daddy now, kid!" followed by insulting laughter. With that, chills went up Paulo's back and chest. He had been taken. Paulo knew of the child labor ring that operated underground in his country, profiting from the ever-increasing supply of homeless children; the local law enforcement most likely profiting from the bounty paid for young children who could work in factories where cheap labor costs were required to remain competitive in the western world market.

"How could I have believed my life was about to change?" Paulo beat upon himself as he felt his will to fight drain out from his limbs, leaving him practically useless. He even felt his limp return. He was unwanted, period. He had been foolish enough to believe there was a God who dealt fairly. There would be no fairness in his life. He was rejected at birth and would die without a mother to love him or a father to teach and protect him. Children who were stolen to work as enslaved people in exchange for food and a roof over their heads were treated little better than the animals who provided meager meals for the workers.

Although there are child trafficking laws in Latin American countries, the graft existing in almost every level of government and law enforcement makes it very hard to control the importation and use of children ranging in ages 5-18, many of which are transported between countries. Paulo was merely taken because he was an unsupervised Latino, alone and vulnerable. The bounty hunters did not know he was an adopted orphan... Or that he had a disability with limitations. They would be paid for a live body, period–More for a girl... but the boy would do.

Paulo found himself thrust into a back alleyway with no idea where he was. A metal door slid open, and Paulo was sent flying into the dark cavity, landing hard on what felt like a concrete floor. And then something... or someone moved and touched his leg. He was not alone. "Sorry!" yelped Paulo as he moved to find a clear space to lie down. Someone opened the door and threw him a blanket, and Paulo was out like a burned-out bulb.

Paulo's mind opened to dreams that kept him running most of the night, as short as it was. It was as if he had never gone to sleep when the metal door opened, and light poured in to reveal Paulo's worst nightmare. It wasn't a dream after all. He was lying in the middle of ten other bodies that were now starting to move in unison. The floor that moved during the night wasn't concrete but a metal floor in what appeared to be the bed of a large truck.

A child Paulo thought to be no older than six or seven started to whimper, but for the most part, all bodies were silent, with heads down, so it was difficult for Paulo to see who his captive brothers and sisters were. But from their size, he would guess them to be his age and younger, probably no older than twelve. "I've got to pee," came a weak voice somewhere within the confinement. Then another and another.

"Shut up back there!" blasted another voice from nowhere. "You can all pee once we stop! But until then, you better hold it, or there will be hell to pay," threatened the gruff voice.

"Where are we?" cried one of the female children. "Where are we going?" cried another, in Spanish. And then, as if on cue, the wails and cries stopped in concert. Without a word spoken in response to their questions, they all knew instinctively what had happened and what their life was about to become. The whimpering stopped, and a dark silence once again prevailed.

***

"What do you mean there is nothing you can do to find our son?" screamed a shaken Annette Tone as she placed her hands, knuckles down, on the desk of the security officer at the airport.

"What I mean, senora, is we have no way of knowing where your son is. He probably ran off... maybe back to his home at the orphanage? Who knows for sure? This is what I have been saying for the past thirty minutes," the officer pleaded, using his English the best he could while trying to stay calm since this irate gringo and his she-lioness burst into the station demanding they find their runaway son just purchased from the convent.

"It wouldn't be the first time a kid and the convent played dirty and bilked money from a nice gringo couple wanting a son or daughter from this country, only to lose the child and end up empty-handed," the officer whispered under his breath. "Perhaps your son will hide out for a time before returning to the orphanage to collect his reward? And life will resume as if nothing had happened once your family has stopped looking for your lost child!" the officer spoke... a little too frankly. "Your son likely returned to where he feels most comfortable... You should go there and look for him." And with that, the officer bowed his head back into his paperwork, having dismissed the gawking gringos who stood speechless at his inference that Paulo and the convent were somehow involved in stealing their money without ever intending to give them their son.

"We must return to the school and search for ourselves," offered Richard. "At least to see if anyone has heard from Paulo. To see if...." and with that, the dark hopelessness that comes when reality strikes overcame Richard, accepting the fact they were in a foreign country and totally at the mercy of circumstances and local culture. If Paulo did not want to be found, he was crafty enough to make that happen. Paulo was raised off the streets, but he possessed a street-smart mentality that allowed him to co-exist with the pain and bitterness of knowing he was rejected at birth. It was this anger that got him into trouble, but it was also this anger that drove him to succeed and become a leader amongst his peers at the school.

Annette wrapped herself into Richard's weakly encircled arms, holding his face in her hands and looking deep into his soul. "Richard, we must not lose hope. There is one person who knows where Paulo is and why he disappeared. God is aware of our hurt, and if we are to find Paulo, it will be with His help and not by our own doing."

"Then let's make our way back to the school in the morning and spend tonight praying and fasting," Richard suggested.

"That won't be hard," Annette smiled... "There is probably nothing open this time of night and likely no place to sleep," now cringing at the thought of sleeping in a chair at the airport. "At least there are other people here... and security," thought Annette out loud as her eyes scanned for a private area where they could spend the night.

***

Paulo tried hard to go back to sleep after the brief outcries of his fellow passengers entrapped in what appeared to be a flatbed truck with a prison-like cage equipped for transporting—whatever. There seemed to be only a little air in the cage, and what there was seemed to carry a heavy, rancid taste and smell... probably from stale body sweat and strong urine odor from the group of street urchins who were his fellow victims. Just then, the truck came to a jarring halt, causing the children to let out cries of the need for a restroom again. But this time, instead of being told to stay quiet, there was the sound of a steel lock being opened and light pouring into the cavity of the truck, now revealing its cargo. A familiar voice boomed aloud, "Welcome to your new home!" followed by a hearty, almost devilish laugh. "Your accommodations await you!" Again, followed by that sinister laugh.

The little band of children were led to restrooms and then gathered together as close as they could, as range cows would do when facing an upcoming storm. There was confusion and terror written into the faces of each of the children, and Paulo found himself comforting those who seemed to be almost out of control. He did not want to see these kids beat up for causing a disturbance. It was best to remain calm and wait to see what was next—his eyes already scanning what appeared to be a large room filled with some sort of equipment, likely looms to weave the colorful Guatemalan and Mayan clothing that tourists and locals alike found both stylish and protective against the area's often harsh weather conditions.

As if on cue, lights from above flooded the floor area as doors opened, followed by several lines of what appeared to be workers clad in white overalls and white tennis shoes. No one said a word as the stoic bodies were led to their respective positions in front of a piece of equipment. No one even gave the new arrivals so much of a glance as they entered the room. Given their size, Paulo figured that most of these workers were children, forced into child labor in exchange for life–if such conditions could be called a *life*.

For as long as they were able, these children would work 18 hours a day with little relief. Meals were provided, but the work was tedious and often sparked contention among the workers. Paulo had no intentions of becoming someone's laborer. He had to find a way out of this mess. He would just play along, giving the impression he was more frightened than he was... although he *was* upset, he was more angry than afraid now, as internal anger surged toward those who had stolen from him his new life. He had no papers, no birth certificate, or proof of adoption. He was a nobody once again.

Paulo stood where he had been placed, steeped in anger and hatred but determined to overcome the odds against him in such an awful place. Lost in his thoughts, Paulo did not sense the imposing figure coming up behind him. "Hey, kid! Come with me... now!" roared the voice of a large bearded man whom Paulo immediately identified as one of his captors. Paulo hesitated momentarily, then remembered his resolve to follow the rules and blend in.

The man led Paulo through an open door, telling him to close it behind him. "Sit, kid!" the man directed. "Ok, who are you?" the man quickly asked. "What were you doing with those gringos, back at the airport?" Paulo hesitated before answering. "They hired me to help them with their luggage and find their way around the city," Paulo lied. The man watched Paulo for any indication he was lying. He gave none. "How did you learn to speak English?" He asked. "I was raised in a convent," Paulo started to explain... but before he could continue, the door flew open, and one of the men who had helped contain the children in the truck ran in.

"Diego, one of the machines caught a girl. She is bleeding very badly," the man shouted excitedly. The man known as Diego did not waste any time heading for the door, yelling at Paulo over his shoulder to follow him. Paulo did as instructed, more curious to see who was injured than being obedient. But in pretended character, Paulo meekly followed the man into the floor area, where a crowd surrounded one of the machines. Paulo held his breath, expecting the worst.

As the men attended to the injured girl, Paulo had an impression wash over him that was totally unfamiliar. It was as if someone were speaking directly to his mind; the impression was so loud. *Run*, it said. *Run for your life!* Paulo stopped in his tracks, willing himself to become invisible. *How could I run?* He thought. *Where would I go, even if I could run? Where am I?* It was then Palo felt a *measure* of peace come over him to stay put until he could learn more about his location. Paulo had experienced conflicting voices in his head for years, sometimes becoming louder and even more direct as he aged. Still, he chose to remain in his current situation even though he had no idea what the future held. Had he listened... and obeyed his first impression, he might have left undetected and eventually worked his way back to the convent–and ultimately to his parents. It was a decision Paulo would soon learn to regret.

When the excitement had died down, and everyone was directed back to work, Paulo was lined up for inspection like the other new arrivals. Each child was interviewed and asked their age and place of birth, whether or not they had parents, and any particular skills that could be used to profit their new benefactors. After their interview, they were escorted to a barrack-style room filled with bunk beds, three high. A thin partial wall separated boys and girls. Paulo was amazed at how defeated the children had become. Of course, every child in his country grew up being warned never to wander off alone, always be alert to "friendly" strangers, and never accept a ride from strangers.

The child labor trafficking business had become a critical piece in the Country's economic stability, providing handmade clothing at much lower prices... which had caught the attention of big box retailers in Western countries. Of course, the "big box stores" had no idea... or at least they did not want to know how these private entrepreneurs from impoverished countries could produce clothing so inexpensive. They merely passed it off as lower overhead.

The fact was that there were **no** wages. When a child had proven to be a liability rather than an asset of value, they were sold to the sex trades. This was known to lead to drug use–and death. Although the children here were only exploited for their ability to provide labor, they had a roof over their heads and were fed sufficiently to keep up with the rigorous 18-hour workday schedule. They were given no day off. They would only cause trouble.

Paulo would break out of here the first chance he got–he resolved to himself–as he lay on the top bunk listening to the snores and lowly whimpers from several of his roommates. He *would* escape and regain his freedom, that much he was confident about.

There had been almost no talking between the workers, which is what they would now be called. With no regard given to their names, each worker was assigned a number. The higher the number, the more recent their capture and, thus, the less time on the job. Paulo had no idea when he had finally succumbed to sleep. His thoughts drifted back to his almost-parents... and then replaced by bitterness and anger welling up inside him once again, mixed with thoughts of his best friend, Felicia– back at the convent–being pushed to the forefront of his mind. What would he ever do without her?

***

Mirroring Paulo's sleepless night were his new parents. Richard Tone was determined to stand vigil over his wife while she slept or tried to do so, but the strain of losing Paulo and seeing his wife in such turmoil took its toil... and he also fell into a fitful sleep. When the sound of a vacuum hit his senses, Richard's eyes flew open to where Annette was sleeping. She was gone! Richard's heart almost burst the second this revelation connected with his brain, sending him to his feet in a panic. "Oh no! Not Annette, too!" he gasped out loud.

"Not Annette too, what, dear?" came a tired voice behind him. "I merely went to the restroom," she said casually, with lack of sleep still lingering in her voice. Richard spun around to find Annette still wringing her hands... "No paper towels," she provided. "Anyway, what were you saying, dear?"

"Never mind," Richard responded more forcefully than he had intended. "We should find a phone and call the school. My phone hasn't had service showing since we arrived in this country. Someone should be awake by now," he added as he started down toward the entrance to the airport, which was beginning to show signs of life.

Finding a pay phone, Richard deposited the coins he had saved to take home to the kids, feeling the need to contact the school as quickly as possible with the hope they had heard from their son. That was not to be the case. Mother Superior Mary Eunice was very convincing that she had not heard from Paulo, and she was seemingly terrified to think what might have happened to him.

"If Paulo was indeed taken, finding him will be impossible," Mother Mary advised. "He was likely smuggled through to another part of the country to serve as a laborer or work the streets for a street boss. With the police looking the other way because they are paid off, no one will concern themselves with finding one boy. I am sorry for your loss, Mr. and Mrs. Tone... but we will most certainly call you if Paulo shows up here." With that, the line went dead, and Richard just stood there holding the phone in his hand, eyes fixed as if he were expecting Paulo to call suddenly.

"We need help," Richard said rather blankly. Annette just looked at him, waiting for Richard to explain his plea. "We need to pray!" Richard added. "Heavenly Father knows where Paulo is. We need to ask Him what to do. After finding a quiet corner where they could pray together, Richard offered a heartfelt prayer while embracing Annette in his arms and feeling her shoulders shaking through sobs and freely falling tears, causing Richard to pause often to gain his own composure.

When Richard ended his prayer... and after a few minutes of silence, Annette spoke first: "Richard, what did you feel?"

"I don't know, Annette," Richard confessed. "I just don't know. Maybe we need to make contact with the police anyway. I know what Mother Mary Eunice said about the corrupt police, but maybe the Lord will soften some hearts for us. It wouldn't feel right unless we do everything possible to find Paulo. We took him away from the safety of the school, and I feel responsible for the terrible plight I fear he might be in."

Annette agreed with Richard's suggestion and began gathering her things so they could find transportation to the police department. "Richard, we don't even have a picture of Paulo. How will the police know if they were to find him?" Annette said with emotion filling her voice.

"Well, let's at least try," Richard said, trying to add a little hope in his voice. "Wait a minute; didn't you take a picture on your phone?" Grabbing her purse, Annette dug out her somewhat useless phone and turned it on, scrolling down to find what she hoped would be a photo of Paulo. And her efforts were rewarded.

Finding a photo of Paulo wouldn't be their biggest challenge of the day. It was trying to convince the police that Paulo was worth looking for once they found out he was being adopted out of the country to live a princely life... or that was the impression most people of this impoverished country had of the wealthy Americans. But at least now the police would have a photo of Paulo to help identify him once they were convinced he was actually stolen... so Richard and Annette hired a driver to take them back to the school first, to eliminate that possibility. They wanted to look Mother Mary Eunice in the eyes before they decided when to return to the States... and to their children.

Annette rested her head on Richard's shoulder and slept for most of the long drive to the convent. When they arrived, it was dusk, and Richard had no idea how to explain the purpose of their visit to the Sisters without offending them. *But who cares if they were offended if they were lying to cover up their little con?* With that assuring thought, Richard pushed the front doorbell... and waited.

***

Darkness filled in around him, his heart pounding rapidly and so loudly that Paulo cupped his ears in pain. Shrill cries pierced his brain. Paulo was trapped... no place to turn. He wanted to escape, but his legs would not move... fighting to break out of this confinement, to run, but there was no escape. The noise, the cries, were coming closer... "Wake up, kid!" came the sound, now piercing Paulo's senses. Light replaced the darkness... and a man's gruff voice replaced the shrill sound of crying. It was just a dream. Or was it? Paulo quickly followed the commands being shouted in the room as the children were awakened to another day of labor. "Breakfast in five minutes, so let's be up and dressed... NOW!" came the roar of a lion, or so it seemed to Paulo.

"What's wrong with that guy, anyway?" Paulo thought *out loud*. A rough hand came out of nowhere so fast that Paulo had no time to duck before a stinging pain lashed across his face, a hand grabbing his shoulders and sitting him upright in the bed before moving on to the next lifeless body.

"Ouch, what was that for?" Paulo cried out, holding his cheek and eye where the slap had landed moments before. All went quiet as Paulo's resistance seemed to permeate the spacious room and suck out the stale air in one intake of breath. The man stopped in his tracks and turned to face Paulo, who was now off the top bunk and shivering on the cold concrete floor.

"Boy, I realize you just got here, but rule number one is to keep your mouth shut. Rule number two is don't speak unless spoken to. You already broke rules number one *and* two!" The man shouted, looking like he was going after Paulo again–but hesitated a moment, as if considering his opt ions... then turned back around and shouted, "Everyone to the food court, Haha!..." a term he had obviously picked up from the States. "Except the rule breaker!" he added, stopping again but now turning around and glaring at Paulo. "He gets to start work early with no food in his belly. Now git... all of you!" Then, pointing directly at Paulo, "You, throw on these clothes and come with me. ¡Ándale! ¡Ándale! (Hurry up in Spanish)Paulo did as told and joined the man at the doorway. One glance at the man's face told Paulo he had created an enemy and to obey without objection, no matter the task. Something inside him, that voice again, warned him that this man was dangerous and wouldn't think twice about taking Paulo's life. He believed the voice this time, without question.

"While the others are stuffing their stomachs on the finest of pastries and bread this morning, you get to start by cleaning the toilets. That should destroy any appetite you might have had before you broke rules one and two," laughed the man. Paulo instinctively opened his mouth to object but quickly closed it," eliciting a sinister smile from the man. "You got something to say, kid?" There was no smile on his face now. Paulo just stared ahead. "Good idea! Now git to work!" The man slid a bucket on the cement floor toward Paulo, hitting his feet and spilling its contents on the floor. "Haha!..." came that sinister laugh again. "You better have this mess cleaned up and the toilets cleaned by the time I return," He threatened, laughing over his shoulder as he departed.

Paulo set about doing his chores as directed, but his mind was almost spinning out of control as he began scrubbing every inch of the toilet room... just like the Sisters had taught him at the convent. At the convent, Paulo had been trained early in his life how to scrub floors, wash windows, and clean toilets. So putting his all into his first assignment wasn't a difficult task... and Paulo could go without eating for long periods of time, having been taught the law of the fast by the Sisterhood. Going without food or drink for twenty-four hours at a time, two or three times a week, in the spirit of prayer, was not uncommon at the convent, and the orphans were expected to participate. Paulo had thought it was merely a way of stretching the meager food supply that always seemed to plague the convent. He had determined to fix that if he ever got to America and found his family. He would study at American schools, become very learned and wealthy, and then take care of those who cared for him. But first, he had toilets to clean.

Chapter Four

RICHARD and ANNETTE

After patiently waiting for what seemed like an eternity, the big door to the convent opened slowly, exposing two angelic figures dressed in white. Annette was slightly surprised at the white glow and just stood there, unable to speak, until one of the figures broke her stupor. "Good evening, Miss. How may we help you?" Richard, having just noticed his wife's blank stare, spoke first. "Uh, good evening, Sister. Would we be able to speak to Mother Mary Eunice? We have an urgent matter to discuss with her." The Sister in the front reacted quickly to Richard's plea and opened the door wide, exposing the look of displeasure on the face of the sister behind her, who didn't move to allow the Tone's entrance but rather leaned in to whisper something into the other Sister' ear.

"Mother Mary Eunice is in prayer at this time," came a voice behind the group standing at the doorway." Is there something I can do for you?" Everyone turned toward the voice of Sister Ramona Medina, who now stood smiling behind the group as she outstretched her arms in a gesture of kindness and welcome, an attitude these two younger nuns had apparently not yet acquired.

"I am Sister Medina. Won't you come in so we can welcome you properly?" Sending a quick side glance to the sisters now standing to the side of the doorway, in the attitude of humility. "What brings you to our home this beautiful evening?" Sister Medina inquired with sincerity. As Annette and Richard walked toward Sister Medina, now out of the dark doorway, a brightness flew over her face before Annette could respond to her question. "I recognize you... You adopted our Paulo!" Now glancing behind the Tones, as if looking for her Paulo. "Did he forget something? There isn't anything wrong, is there? You aren't returning him so soon, are you? I admit he can be a handful, so angry over being abandoned by his birth parents and all–but he has a good heart and... "Annette quickly placed her hand on Sister Medina's arm... "Sister Medina, Paulo is missing!"

"Missing? What do you mean?" she asked. "I mean, he disappeared before we could board the plane," Annette responded, without a trace of suspicion in her voice... feeling a little guilty for thinking these good people would participate in such a scheme as she let herself think.

"But how...?" one of the younger sisters asked, now fully engaged in the conversation. "We don't know how," Richard answered honestly. "I was at our gate, and Annette took Paulo to the restroom, but he didn't come out. She searched around, but there was no sign of Paulo. "We think he was abducted!" Richard added. "What other explanation is there?"

"Then how do we find him?" Annette asked, hoping there would be an answer there somewhere. "If he was abducted, then he is already out of the country," warned Sister Medina. "I am afraid there isn't much hope of finding him. But I know someone who would know if he wasn't abducted and just ran away," she added hopefully. "Felicia?" asked one of the younger sisters, as if reading Sister Medina's mind. "Yes! Felicia is one of the older girls who took Paulo under her wing when he arrived to us as a baby. She knows him as well... or better than anyone."

And with that, the two Sisters did an about-face and darted off down the darkened corridor. Sister Medina invited the Tones into a quiet parlor area where two comfortable chairs sat across from a plain couch. Annette and Richard sat together on the couch where they could easily comfort one another... and waited without speaking a word. Sister Medina excused herself and departed, most likely to attend to whatever it was she was interrupted from when the Tones burst in. They did not wait long. "Mr. and Mrs. Tone, I would like you to meet, Felicia Torres, a good friend to Paulo. I have explained to Felicia the... problem, and she said she would be willing to speak with you about Paulo." Then, turning to Felicia and gesturing to the empty chair, she sat in the other.

"Mr. and Mrs. Tone, I can only tell you that Paulo was so excited to go to America as your adopted son. He has issues, yes... but he is a good boy, and I do not believe he would just run away. Please tell me what happened," Felicia said, anxious to learn about her best friend. Annette spoke first, explaining in great detail as if she were hearing it the first time herself... as if she could not believe it and wanted to hear it spoken again so that maybe she would wake up from this dream... this nightmare!

"Paulo had to use the restroom before we reached the gate, so he ran ahead of me so he could take care of himself quickly and we wouldn't be late," Annette explained. "I watched him until he was out of sight, and then I stopped to buy some water and fruit. It was only a couple of minutes before I reached the restrooms. I waited until I grew impatient and then began to call out his name. There was no answer," she added solemnly. "I asked a man going in if he could look in each of the stalls for me. I heard him calling out for Paulo, but when he came back out, he was alone, shrugging his shoulders and shaking his head sideways.

"That was the last we saw of Paulo," Richard interrupted. "We found a quiet corner where we could still see people coming and going and prayed until we fell asleep. At first light, we looked through the airport again, with no trace of him, and so we went to the airport security office and reported him missing."

"That was a joke," Annette said dryly. "Once they learned he was adopted, we got the brush-off. They said he was gone, and there was nothing they could do about it. We then found transportation and made our way here, hoping against hope that...." Annette's voice began to trail off, her eyes breaking contact and lowering as if to hide her thoughts.

"You thought we had him." Responded Sister Medina more as a statement rather than a question. "You thought his adoption might have been a scam and that he would run away at his first opportunity and show up weeks later after you had gone home, ready to deceive again? Is that what you thought, Mr. and Mrs. Tone?" With her head still bowed, Annette pleaded.

"We just wanted to cover every possibility. We had heard stories and were counseled to be careful. When he disappeared, the thought did come to mind. But we were just hoping he got lost and would find his way here, somehow."

"We called yesterday and spoke with Mother Superior. She was a little short with us over the phone," Annette confided. "We wanted to come and see for ourselves... and now we have!" Richard covered her shaking shoulders with his arm and drew Annette close as she buried her face in his chest. It was over. Paulo was not here, of that they were certain. Their son was taken.

Chapter Five

PLAN TO ESCAPE

"**M**ucho Grande!" bellowed out the big gringo known as Big Jack. "I have never seen these toilets so clean," he laughed. "And the mirror and sink, too? What are you, a Machacha?" the big man laughed, making reference to the native term for 'cleaning lady.' And with that, he let out a bellowed laugh that almost shook the building. But instantly resorted back to slave driver. "Let's go, Amigo; you have real work to do."

Paulo was led back into what appeared to be the work area where an estimated fifty people, mostly youth, were busy at various tasks—some at sewing machines, some knitting with thread and needle, some repairing, pulling thread. But none were talking. Other than the noise coming from the machines, the room was silent. "Over here, kid," called out Big Jack to Paulo, pointing to a huge pile of fabric, boxes, and what looked like junk but was actually stolen equipment that could be repaired and sold through the black market.

"Kid, you are going to supply the sewing crew with fabric. Watch for when they are nearing the bottom of their pile, and before she runs out, you put another pile on top of the last piece. Remember! there is no time to waste, so there is no lag time between when they run out of fabric and when you replenish. If a hand goes up, you are already too late, she is out of fabric. Now go to it, boy!" Big Jack roared, pushing Paulo so hard he almost fell to his knees... eliciting another round of laughter from the man.

Paulo recovered quickly and did as he was told, fearing retaliation from Big Jack, who walked the isles shouting angry threats at the workers to keep working.

It quickly became obvious to Paulo that these men had no qualms about working these children until they could not stand it any longer and then they would find other uses for them out on the streets, broken of spirit and trapped in a life of misery. He had to find a way out of here before the same happened to him. Paulo began right then to make a plan. But his thoughts of escape would be put on hold for now as a stern pair of eyes seemed to bore right into his soul as if Big Jack could read his every thought.

"Yes, boss!" responded Paulo when he became aware that Big Jack had been waiting for an acknowledgment and was still waiting. Paulo took a quick look over the sea of hunched-over bodies, all busily at work... scanning their piles to get a feel for where they were in their need for fabric. He quickly spotted one... and then another. Paulo quickly grabbed two piles of fabric and reached the first before her hand shot up. But he did not reach the other in time, but only a brief moment had passed. But it did not miss the scrutiny of Big Jack, who was on Paulo like a shadow, refreshing the slap across his head he had sustained earlier. "You missed that one, kid!" And with that, the big man let out a bellow of laughter that revealed how much he enjoyed his job.

Paulo did not wait for another slap, but grabbed another two piles and headed to his targets, reaching them both before they ran out. He quickly set up a plan on how manage the flow of fabric. He would control the delivery of fabric before the worker ran out. Paulo observed that some of the workers were faster at their craft than others; those were the ones to supply first. The majority of the fifty or so workers were slow, but steady in their use of fabric... so Paulo worked out a routine by the end of the day that seemed to satisfy Big Jack, resulting in giving Paulo a little space between glares. Once Paulo had a system firmly in place he was able to observe his surroundings without fear of retaliation by Big Jack, who had now shifted his attention to the "thread pickers," a group sitting on the concrete floor, a huge pile of clothes of various shapes and colors in the center. These workers were responsible for dismantling the clothes that were apparently "donated" from sources unknown to Paulo. The clothes were mostly used hand-me-downs, amongst others that appeared newer... probably with defects. Paulo observed another pile in a five foot bin in which the workers filled the fabric parts after they were dissembled. This bin was then unloaded on a pallet and taken to where Paulo was stationed. He would then distribute to the machine workers who were creating the most colorful sarape'.

These private entrepreneurs must have captured a world market for this product because each day they repeated the same process... starting with truckloads of clothing being delivered, always at night. There were no windows in the huge ceiling that loomed over the workers, probably to keep them from knowing when it was night. Paulo guessed the normal workday started by 6am and ended eighteen hours later, with little time off for rest beyond a couple of short breaks for food. Every chance he got to glance at one of the "bosses," Paulo made a mental note, gauging time between breaks, dinner, and patterns of the workers. He learned who were the fastest workers... the most likely to draw ire from the boss, and which boss was the most intelligent... and the least.

Paulo passed the time by learning the work patterns of the bosses, and looking for any gaps in their attention to the workers. He had no concrete idea how he would escape from this rat hole, but he was determined to learn everything he could about this enterprise and somehow take it down and free these workers. Big plans for such a little guy. But Paulo was no ordinary boy. Paulo didn't try to make friends with the other workers. He didn't know who he could trust, so he trusted no one. He just went about his work, supplying workers with fabric and making certain they did not run out before the "boss" focused his anger on Paulo.

One night, as Paulo slept, he heard a ruckus coming from another part of the workers sleeping quarters. Muffled sounds and occasional cries caused Paulo to slip out of his bed to the cold concrete floor, sending deep chills into his core. Paulo knew that if he was caught sneaking around at night, he would be punished, and part of his plan for escape was to appear weak and afraid in order to avoid attention so his captors would develop a false sense of comfort around him. But this night, Paulo was drawn to a noise that had now ceased. No worker was allowed to cross into the adjoining partition, supposedly separating worker units from one another, meant to control the size of the worker population from knowing just how many children were kept there. And from possibly being able to combine efforts to break out of this prison.

But where would they go that would be any more secure? Paulo thought to himself. At least here, they are fed, dry, and have a bed to sleep on. No matter if they had no life or education. They would be robbed of their youth, and once they reached the age or size to pose a threat to the bosses, they would just disappear one night. No one would ask, but it was well known that they were then sold to drug and sex traffickers, who would pay a fine price for the right young person. These thoughts almost paralyzed Paulo in his tracks as thoughts of the life he might have had flooded into his brain. Anger filled his heart again... and he turned on his heel and headed into the restroom instead of trying to follow the sounds that had now ceased. It was none of his business anyway. Why should he care about others when God, if there was one, had deserted him? Thoughts of a mother who had hated him so much she would throw him away at birth, leaving him a hopeless cripple, invaded his mind.

Now wide awake, Paulo let his negative thoughts take root in his heart as he settled back onto his bunk. He would escape from this place somehow, search for his birth mother, and tell her how much he hated her. And then a light blazed into his closed eyes, signaling the start of yet another day of work.

Paulo's struggle at birth carried forward with him to the convent, but with the Sister's help and the tough love from his close friend Felicia, Paulo was not deterred because of his limp or his slight body. He used his disadvantage to disarm those who saw him as weak or mentally challenged.

He did not speak much, but his eyes and ears were always on and searching. And planning.

Days turned into weeks and weeks into months. The thought of escape never left Paulo's mind. His captors did their best to rob him of hope, as they were able to do with most of the other children. Paulo let them think he had lost hope, but for a fact, he let his anger and resentment over his imperfect life fuel his resolve to make something of himself. And that meant he would need to escape.

In order to keep the children confused and afraid, the "boss" kept moving them from one machine or job task to another, always on the lookout for friendships beginning to form. The boss wanted none of that fraternization between the workers and often took drastic steps to prevent such friendships from forming, which he saw as a possible threat to having complete control over his workers. If a worker was seen engaging in friendship with another, that worker was either put into hardship duty or shipped out and never heard from again. Paulo saw that as a possible exit opportunity instead of a threat. But he had no idea how ruthless things could get on the outside. He just knew in here he was no better than a trapped animal.

After two years inside this prison, Paulo was ready to execute his plan of escape. Although the food supply was sparse for the most part, consisting of fat-laden foods, flour, and lard... Paulo used his punishment duties as strength-building and endurance training. He already knew he could survive without eating for days at a time, but now he worked on his inner core, lifting heavy objects with the intent of repeating such activities as a bodybuilder would do to strengthen his inner core. Paulo was still hampered somewhat by his birth defects, but he was so determined not to let those things get in his way of surviving an escape that he mentally pushed aside that weakness and focused on what could be strengthened.

Adding two years of growth, plus his secret exercises to strengthen his muscles, gave Paulo the assurance he could survive. Paulo knew he would only get one chance at escape. The word among the workers was that "no one" had ever escaped other than by way of death or being sold to the sex and drug traffickers. No one had ever returned when sold. But even the thought of dying from dealing drugs seemed a more fitting end to this young man's imperfect life. He was not wanted at birth. How appropriate that he suffers a meager existence before death. Paulo did not believe in life after death, but in his heart, he occasionally felt pangs of a pull heavenward, as if someone was calling out to him. But his anger and resentment would always pull him back into his miserable state of mind. He did not belong anywhere. He had nothing to lose by dying in the process of trying to escape.

Chapter Six

HOME

The flight home was uneventful for Richard and Annette Tone the day after losing their son. Annette donned a pair of dark glasses in an obvious attempt to shut out the world and try to cope with the experience of losing a son she never got to know. Once on the plane, she only removed them to exchange with black-out blindfolds. Occasionally, Richard would feel the sobs coming from her seat next to his and, with his best efforts, try to console and absorb her pain. She was not Paulo's birth mother, but in the very short time she knew him, there was an instant bond between the two. She loved him every bit as much as if she conceived and bore him into this world.

A mother is built to love and nurture. It is in her DNA, and Annette Larsen Tone exemplified that legacy as a woman and a mother. Annette had good examples of that legacy from her pioneer ancestors who risked life and limb immigrating to America from their native homeland of Sweden, only to then travel across the midlands of America to join with other members of their new-found faith in the Church of Jesus Christ of Latter-day Saints.

Annette's forebears first settled in Utah before being dispatched to settle parts of the Wild West in Arizona and Mexico. It was in the Mexican Colonies where Annette's great-grandparents met and settled, raising Annette's mother until they were again called to support the growing church in Arizona. Annette was born in Mesa, Arizona, and met Richard Tone at a youth dance one summer at the Mezona... a Church sponsored dance hall where youth and families alike would gather on the weekends and learn social skills and dancing. *It was a magical time to grow up*, remembers Annette.

Richard Tone had a similar family background to Annette, with his own ancestral line emigrating from Ireland and Italy. His family were mostly farmers when they arrived, but they quickly developed their entrepreneurial skills in the service industries and helped settle the southwestern United States in Utah, Colorado, and Arizona.

Richard often teases Annette that once she got her "hooks" into him, she just wouldn't let go. Annette remembers it a little differently than that. "Richard was this long-legged cowboy who wore a bow tie to church," she laughs. "He did have cute dimples, which always invited a second look. It must have been that second look that caught me, but I wouldn't let others notice my interest in anyone... especially Richard, who always seemed to have this girl or that crushing about him." Whoever made the first move will always be debated between the two, but it was definitely Richard who proposed. It was Annette who accepted after Richard cleared the way with Annette's father, who was quite protective of his two girls and insisted on things being proper, including not dating until they were sixteen years of age...

In the early days of the Church of Jesus Christ of Latter-day Saints, conditions were not favorable for young girls remaining single past maturity. The Mormons, as they had become widely known, were not welcome in most communities they tried to settle in the east, and were driven first to the mid-west and then to the state of Utah, where they were able to inhabit lands no one else wanted. These lands did indeed "blossom as a rose," as the scripture in Isaiah prophesied, allowing those who belonged to the Church to develop the social culture they had always dreamed of.

***

Annette did her best to hold back the feelings of hurt and anger that welled up behind her self-imposed dam of will and character... hoping against hope that sleep would overtake her and, when awakened, she would realize this was but a horrible dream. But for each reprieve from the thoughts that drew her down into this darkness, there was no Paulo when she awoke. During these brief moments, she removed the eye mask and allowed light in for a brief moment while she glanced at the seat next to her occupied by Richard. The seat next to him, of course, was empty. Her heart broke again and again.

As the huge plane touched down at Salt Lake City International, the jar of the wheels making contact with the Tarmac brought Annette back to the reality of her dread, which immediately flooded her heart. Gathering their carry-on belongings, Richard and Annette made their way into the gate area, heading to baggage claim. The early morning activity of airport life was just beginning to emerge and greeted the Tones with familiarity as they descended to the baggage claim area below. No words were spoken between them. There was nothing to say that had not already been spoken. They had no plan, only grief at the moment... and a strong desire to return home and reunite with their family.

The Tone children would now be in school and would not be home for hours, leaving Richard to catch up on work and Annette to relieve the sitter and make plans for when the children arrived home that afternoon. "I must not let my disappointment show to my children," she thought. "They are still my rock and my anchor."

Among the many challenges of playing catch-up after being away were the phone messages and well-wisher visitors who had come to welcome the new addition to the family. Embarrassed and heartbroken, the Tone's bravely greeted friends and family as they came and went throughout the day until it was time for the children start arriving home after school. At that point, a sign was placed on the front door advising that the Tones were unavailable for visits and to please call before dropping by.

The six-year-old twins, Dae and Darin Tone, blew through the door without even noticing the sign, which was pretty common for their after-school entrances, Monday through Friday... and today was no different; the boys excitement to meet their new brother radiating in their voices as they ran in the front door, each trying to outdo the other. But when they saw their mother's tear-stained eyes, void of any smile or happiness that usually radiated from her face, they both picked up that something was wrong.

Dae was first to reach her mother... "Mother, what is wrong?" she asked. "Where is Paulo?" followed Darin. "Can he sleep in my room?" Richard entered the spacious living room, and seeing the twins, he opened his arms to receive them as they yelled in unison... "Daddy!" Richard hugged the twins and took one under each arm as he made his way to the couch where Annette sat, now inviting them to join her.

"Paulo is not with us," Annette stated matter-of-factly. "He did not come home."

"When is he coming?" little Dae asked expectedly. Annette ran her fingers through Dae's long blond hair while trying to respond to the question she had no answer for. "Let's find Michael and go get some pizza!" Annette changed the subject. "Yay! Pizza," yelled Darin... heading into his daddy's arms and then tugging him toward the door. For the time being, this little family was just happy being together again. There would be time later to mourn the loss of the son they never had.

***

Paulo lay asleep, waiting patiently for sounds that signal unconsciousness. He knew he had only a few minutes before the door was locked for the night, and he had a lot to do in the meantime but he could not afford to be seen by any of the children in his bunk area. Satisfied that he had to move now, Paulo eased down the bunk onto the cold floor, causing a brief intake of air that was quickly controlled by his steeled will to complete his task. He then moved swiftly down the center isle leading to the closed door, holding his breath as his hand covered the round handle... and turned. The door handle began turning in his hand as Paulo pushed the door out, careful not to open it wider than would be needed to accompany his small frame, in case there was light to expose him—there was none.

During many weeks of Paulo's unsupervised cleaning assignments he came up with an escape plan. He would set fire to the warehouse and divert attention so he could escape—and it had to be tonight. His regular guard had come down with stomach sickness and they would be one man short tonight. Paulo needed to make this work, now. This was his golden opportunity... or so he hoped. He had stashed a can of kerosene, used to clean the machinery, in a cabinet, and stole a match book from one of the bosses... and was now headed to complete his mission. He hoped he could be lucky enough to burn the place down... but he worried for the safety of the children. All he needed was to create enough smoke that he would not be detected as he slipped out one of the doors opened to let the smoke out.

Paulo entered the work area, sensing it was eerily silent. He did not like the dark, but he was grateful for it this night and felt somewhat protected as he walked slowly toward the pile of dried fabric piled high inside a cardboard container. Paulo needed to place his lighting material in strategic places throughout the warehouse, guaranteeing there would be enough smoke to cause disruption and confusion among the workers to allow Paulo to find an exit into the cold night.

Paulo carefully picked up the kerosene can and doused each cardboard container, and moved as quickly as he could in the dark to his next target. Once he had primed several cardboard boxes he ran back to each one and tossed a match. Nothing! The liquid either evaporated or sunk into the cardboard too quickly for a match to ignite it. Paulo would need to hurry, his hands now fumbling as he poured more liquid onto a box and immediately struck a match and threw it into the cardboard flap. It immediately exploded into a ball of light, sending Paulo scurrying to the next box. He knew someone would be coming anytime now... he had only seconds to make certain his efforts would create enough smoke for the bosses to unlock the door to let the smoke out... and Paulo.

Satisfied with the amount of smoke now billowing from the dry fabric and boxes Paulo had drenched in kerosene he positioned himself where he would not be seen, but close enough to observe the main warehouse door, which Paulo was betting his life would be the door they would open. He did not have long to find out. Hard footsteps accompanied by shouting and confusion soon entered the big warehouse... followed by two bosses looking totally stunned at the smoke filling the warehouse with grey smoke and flame. One shouted instructions to the other as he raced toward the big door. There was no thought to anything but containing this fire and giving the smoke a place to exit. But neither the men nor Paulo were experienced in fire control, and Paulo watched in utter surprise as the door opened and the fire exploded like a killer lion being fed a piece of meat after a long fast. The cold outside air brought life to the flames and soon it became obvious to Paulo that these two men would not be able to control it. His plan was working better than Paulo could have ever imagined. Smoke was beginning to settle down after the flames had been fed with air, and covered much of the work area... giving Paulo the chance he needed to slip out the open door into what, he had no idea... but he knew he must go.

Just when Paulo had decided to make his move, he heard sheiks and screams coming from behind him where the children were sleeping. Obviously they had smelled the smoke and heard the commotion going on in the work area and poured out from their bunks running wildly toward the open door. Paulo made his move by holding a piece of fabric to his face and crouched into the smoke as he made his way quickly through the door, leaving behind the sounds of children screaming and bosses trying to control them. It was raining and Paulo's feet were moving faster than his body and several times he slipped and hit the muddy road below him, but not feeling a thing other than to distance himself as far as possible from these monsters.

When Paulo was satisfied that he could not be seen in the dark he paused to look back... and what he saw caused him to smile for the first time in years. Children were pouring out the open door, followed by threats and curses from their pursuers, who had children under both arms and unable to do anything but yell or lose the prizes already in their grasp. Some children were so shaken to be exposed to cold air of freedom and rain and trauma that they literally laid down and sobbed, making them an easy catch for the bosses who ran after them, shouting threatening orders to remain where they were and not run or they would be killed. To a child who had been held captive for years and learned to obey, and now confused and shaken from exposure to fire and smoke, they would simply lay down in the mud soaked field... and wait as directed.

But Paulo would not be intimidated by the crazed threats of harm. He was already outside the range of view and within seconds he was unable to hear anything coming from the warehouse. The rain intensified and Paulo's adrenaline rush had subsided to the point he could now survey his position, and feel the cold that now made its way into the deepest part of his body. But he was free... and the warmth of that thought sent a reprieve through his veins; but only for a moment.

Paulo scanned the area, still very unsure of himself and staying in the shadows, making his way down a muddy street, listening intently to a barking dog, some distance away. He had no sense of direction, but Paulo had an interior compass literally pushing him further away from the direction of the warehouse from which he had just escaped. At least he hoped he was headed in the opposite direction.

Adrenaline had done its part spurring Paulo away from his captors... but now that rush had run its course and left Paulo staggering in the rain and blinded by the darkness. He didn't fight it at all when his legs gave out. He had succeeded in gaining his freedom, even if it meant his death from exposure. His captors would not benefit from his labors any longer, and just maybe some of the other children had escaped as well. He was a hero. "I am a he rrr o!" Paulo uttered as his head hit something hard following the descent of his body.

Paulo had no idea how long he had laid there, unconscious. But when he came to his senses, that same adrenaline began coursing through his body... but this time it was initiated by fear. How could he have allowed himself to be so vulnerable without first finding a place to hide? Without moving, Paulo opened his eyes to assess his location. It was barely light and with his dark skin and brown sleepwear, he breathed a sigh of relief that he was still invisible to passersby, if there were any.

Paulo's first thought was to get off the road, if that was, indeed, where he was. No doubt the bosses would be out scouring the area for escapees. He had to keep moving. He spotted a couple of shacks not far from where he lay. The rain had finally quit, but when he tried moving his body it did not cooperate. He felt waterlogged and his head hurt from the fall. But he was alive and free! That thought alone gave him the needed surge of adrenaline to push up from his muddy hollow and again scour the area for any sign of life. There was none.

Paulo was both relieved and disappointed at not seeing activity... someone who could help him find his way home. *Home? Where is home?* Paulo thought to himself. He had had a chance at a real life, but that was gone now. He was on his own and must make the best of it. Paulo knew that a child alone on the streets had no chance of long-term survival. He had to come up with a plan. And his first order of business was food. Anything to keep him alive.

Paula listened for any sound at all that might lead him to food. A dog barking! He had heard a dog barking just before he fell. He listened. Nothing. Then something inside him sent a warning... "Move to high ground!" was the impression. And Paulo heard it before seeing it. The sound of an engine. A truck! "They are already here looking for me!" Paulo muttered out loud. "Where am I to hide?" he spat to no one in particular. They would surely look in those shacks. He had to get out of sight and hopefully they would just drive by.

Paulo was already on his feet, but crouching when he heard the distinct sound of an engine. He remained crouching as he moved off the road to a large bush about 100 feet from the road. It was then he let out an audible gasp! As Paulo took position behind the bush he saw clearly, deep footprints leading right back to where he had come. There was also a deep impression of his body left in the muddy grave from which he had been raised. And the footprints led right to him. Paulo had no time to think about what the consequences might be before deciding to run... this time using his light weight to avoid making such deep impressions in the mud.

Using the word *run* to describe Paulo's flight might be an overstatement, considering one leg was shorter than the other... but spurred on by the thought of capture and torture before certain death, Paulo moved his feet the best he could, looking behind him, satisfied his path was not easily followed. But he knew it was a matter of time before his captors would be on his trail. He did not have long to wait.

An older-than-old, faded-blue Chev two-door truck rounded the curve down the road from where Paulo chose to hide. He had full view of the truck now. One man sat behind the old truck. He was staring straight ahead. He was not searching for footprints. He was not searching for Paulo. He was moving slowly through the muddy road just as an idea came to Paulo so forcefully that he reacted as if someone had just yelled at him.

Where do these thoughts come from? Paulo thought, almost out loud. But with swiftness he did not know he possessed, Paulo moved from his hiding place and ran toward the slower-moving truck, keeping one eye on the driver for any sense of danger... and the other eye guiding him flawlessly over the muddy terrain, until Paulo caught up to the truck and carefully hoisted himself into the bed from the tailgate, relieved to see sacks of onions and empty burlap bags he could slide under to keep out of sight. It wasn't a perfect plan, but Paulo did utter a relieved "Thank You," before closing his eyes and letting darkness prevail. "Why did I do that?" he thought for a split second before dozing off.

Paulo had no sense of how long he had been asleep, but when he did come to his senses it took him a moment or two to gain his bearings and remember the incidents which had played out just hours before. He had been able to escape a two-year ordeal and was still alive. But where he was and at what peril he might still be exposed, he did not know. But he was about to find out.

Then, the hunger pain hit him, along with the strong aroma of onions. Feeling for anything that resembled an onion, Paulo soon found what he was searching for and quickly bit into it. Eating a raw onion wasn't his preferred fare, but with nothing in his stomach for what seemed like days, Paulo wasn't choosey.

While he ate, somewhat silently... and still concealed inside his hiding place, Paulo peeked out to assess his surroundings. A bluish-grey sky overhead was void of any direct sun, so Paulo assumed it was now late afternoon. His eyes scanned just over the top of the truck bed and saw nothing, and he began to relax a little, hoping that he was alone and that perhaps the driver had left the keys in the ignition. That was a silly thought since Paulo had only once driven a car–and that experience did not end well. He was only eight years old and wanted to show off for one of his fellow orphans by stealing a set of keys from the wall-mounted keyboard in the Reverend Mother's office to the only vehicle owned by the convent–before plowing the car into bales of hay stacked just outside the barn where the vehicle was parked. Paulo was lucky that day, only having to listen to Reverend Mother' angry rantings for several hours... if that was truly considered luck.

After being punished by his captors and having to go without food for twenty-four hours with a raw onion now sitting in an empty stomach, Paulo began to realize this wasn't going to end well. He needed food–real food. Just then, Paulo thought he heard muffled voices, maybe still a long way off. He dared raise his head in the other direction and saw heads of people working in a field. They were harvesting onions. *I bet this truck is used to gather the small harvest from these workers and transport them to a holding area,* Paulo thought. He then buried himself deeper into the sacks of onions, now expecting the workers to start piling more sacks on top of him as soon as they finished their harvesting. And he didn't have much time to wonder before he felt "Incoming!"

Amidst laughing and some foul language, Paulo held his breath that no one would try to reposition the bags that were already in the truck exposing his hiding place. He was in luck. Although the weight of the additional bags of onions began to push the air out of Paulo's lungs, the elation that he was free of his captors kept him from screaming through the terror of being crushed. Paulo then felt the truck again come to life and begin to rumble down the road.

Feeling safe again, at least for the time being, thoughts of what he would do when the truck stopped to unload began to fill Paulo's mind. Dust from the open truck bed began filtering through his shelter, making breathing even more difficult. He needed water. He hadn't eaten in days, and he began to be nauseated from the crushing sacks of onions that lay on top of him and the bites of onion in his empty stomach. Paulo started to panic, feeling the need to vomit and purge his churning stomach. That need was followed by belching nothing but air and gut-wrenching pain as bile and blood were expelled. Paulo's chest heaved to gain a little air... as blackness fell in around him.

Chapter Seven

ESCAPE

P aulo lay asleep, waiting patiently for sounds that signal unconsciousness. He knew he had only a few minutes before the door was locked for the night and had a lot to do in the meantime, but he could not afford to be seen by any of the children in his bunk area. Satisfied that he had to move now, Paulo eased down the bunk onto the cold floor, causing a brief intake of air quickly controlled by his steeled will to complete his task.

Paulo moved swiftly down the center aisle leading to the closed door. He held his breath as his hand covered the round handle... and his heart jumped as it turned. Paulo then pushed out, careful not to open the door more than would accompany his slight frame in case there was light that would expose him. There was none.

During Paulo's unsupervised cleaning assignments, he had figured out how he could set fire to the warehouse and divert attention so he could escape. And it had to be tonight. His regular guard had come down with stomach sickness, and they would be one man short tonight. Paulo needed to make this work–now. This was his golden opportunity... or so he hoped.

Paulo had stashed a can of kerosene used to clean the machinery, and he had stolen a matchbook from one of the bosses, so now he headed to complete his mission. He hoped he could be lucky enough to burn the place down... but he worried for the safety of the children. All he needed was to create enough smoke not to be detected as he slipped through one of the doors opened to let the smoke out.

Paulo entered the work area, sensing it was eerily silent. He did not like the dark but was grateful for it this night and felt somewhat protected as he walked slowly toward the pile of dried fabric piled high inside a cardboard container. Paulo needed to place his lighting material strategically throughout the warehouse, guaranteeing there would be enough smoke to cause disruption and confusion among the workers to allow Paulo to find an exit into the cold night.

Paulo carefully picked up the kerosene can, doused each cardboard container, and moved quickly in the dark to his next target. Once he had primed several cardboard boxes, he ran back to each one and tossed a match. Nothing! The liquid either evaporated or sunk into the cardboard too quickly for a match to ignite it. Paulo would need to hurry, his hands now fumbling as he poured more liquid onto a box, immediately struck a match and threw the flame onto the cardboard flap. It immediately exploded into a ball of light, sending Paulo scurrying to the next box. He knew someone would be coming anytime now... he had only seconds to make sure his efforts would create enough smoke for the bosses to unlock the door to let the smoke out... and Paulo.

Satisfied with the amount of smoke billowing from the dry fabric and boxes Paulo had drenched in kerosene, he positioned himself where he would not be seen but close enough to observe the main warehouse door, which he was betting his life would be the door they would open. He did not have to wait long. Hard footsteps accompanied by shouting and confusion soon entered the big warehouse... followed by two bosses looking totally stunned at the smoke filling the warehouse with grey smoke and flame. One shouted instructions to the other as he raced toward the big door. There was no thought of anything but containing this fire and giving the smoke a place to exit. But neither the men nor Paulo was experienced in fire control, and Paulo watched in utter surprise as the door opened and the fire exploded like a killer lion being fed a piece of meat after a long fast. The cold outside air brought life to the flames, and soon, it became apparent to Paulo that these two men could not control it.

This was working better than Paulo could have ever imagined. Smoke began to settle towards the ground after the flames had been fed with air and covered much of the work area... giving Paulo a chance to slip out the open door. To what? He had no clue... but he knew he must go.

Just when Paulo decided to make his move, he heard sheiks and screams from behind him where the children were sleeping. Obviously, they had smelled the smoke, heard the commotion in the work area, and poured out from their bunks, running wildly toward the open door. Paulo made his move by holding a piece of fabric to his face and crouched into the smoke as he made his way quickly through the door, leaving behind the sounds of children screaming and bosses trying to control them. It was raining, and Paulo's feet moved faster than his body. Several times, he slipped and hit the muddy road below him, but he did not feel a thing other than that *voice* impression to distance himself as far as possible from these monsters.

When Paulo was satisfied that he could not be seen in the dark, he paused to look back... and what he saw caused him to smile for the first time in years. Children were pouring out the open door, followed by threats and curses from their pursuers, who had children under both arms and could not yell or lose the prizes already in their grasp. Some children were so shaken to be exposed to cold air and rain, with thoughts of freedom fueling an emotional trauma that caused them to lie down and sob, making them an easy catch for the bosses who ran after them, shouting to them threatening orders to remain where they were and not run or they would be killed. To a child who had been held captive for years and learned to obey, and now confused and shaken from exposure to fire and smoke, they would simply lay down in the mud-soaked field... and wait as directed.

But Paulo would not be intimidated by the crazed threats of harm. He was already outside the range of view, and within seconds, he was unable to hear anything coming from the warehouse. The rain intensified, and Paulo's adrenaline rush had subsided to the point he could now survey his position and feel the cold that now made its way into the deepest part of his body. But he was free... and the warmth of that thought sent a welcome reprieve through his veins–but only for a moment.

Paulo scanned the area, still unsure of himself and staying in the shadows, making his way down a muddy street, listening intently to a barking dog some distance away. He had no sense of direction but felt an interior compass literally pushing him further away from the direction of the warehouse from which he had just escaped. At least he hoped he was headed in the opposite direction.

Adrenaline had done its part, spurring Paulo away from his captors... but now that rush had run its course and left him staggering in the rain and blinded by the darkness. He didn't fight it at all when his legs gave out. He had succeeded in gaining his freedom, even if it meant his death from exposure. His captors would not benefit from his labors any longer, and just maybe some of the other children had escaped as well. He was a hero. "I am a he rrr o!" Paulo uttered out loud as his head hit something hard following the descent of his body.

Paulo had no idea how long he had laid there, unconscious. But when he came to his senses, that same adrenaline came instantly coursing through his body... but this time it was initiated by fear. How could he have allowed himself to be so vulnerable without first finding a place to hide? Without moving, Paulo opened his eyes to assess his location. It was barely light, and with his dark skin and brown sleepwear, he breathed a sigh of relief that he was still invisible to passersby if there were any.

Paulo's first thought after regaining his senses was to get off the road if that was, indeed, where he was. No doubt the bosses would be out scouring the area for escapees. He had to keep moving.

Paulo raised his head enough to survey his surroundings and spotted a couple of shacks not far from where he lay. The rain had finally quit, but when he tried moving his body, it did not cooperate. He felt waterlogged, and his head hurt from the fall. But he was alive and free! That thought alone gave him the adrenaline needed to push up from his muddy hollow and carefully scour the area for any sign of life. There was none.

Paulo was both relieved and disappointed at not seeing activity... someone who could help him find his way home. *Home? Where is home?* Paulo thought to himself. He had had a chance at a real life, but that was gone now. He was on his own and must make the best of it. Paulo knew that a child alone on the streets had no chance of long-term survival. He had to come up with a plan, but his first order of business was food–anything to keep him alive. So he listened for any sound at all that might lead him to food.

A dog was barking! He suddenly remembered hearing a dog barking just before he fell and passed out. So he listened. Nothing! But then something inside him sent a warning... *Move!* was the impression. And Paulo heard it before seeing it. The sound of an engine. A truck! "They are already here looking for me!" Paulo muttered out loud. "Where am I to hide?" he spat to no one in particular. They would surely look in those shacks. He had to get out of sight, and hopefully, they would just drive by. Paulo was already on his feet but crouching when he heard the distinct sound of an engine growing louder. He remained crouching as he moved off the road to a large bush about 100 feet from the road. It was then he let out an audible gasp!

As Paulo took position behind the bush... he saw deep footprints leading right back to where he had just come. There was a visible impression of his body left in the muddy grave from which he had been raised. And the footprints led right to him. Paulo had no time to think about the consequences before deciding to run... this time using his light weight to avoid making such deep impressions in the mud.

Using the word "run" to describe Paulo's flight might be an overstatement, considering one leg was shorter than the other. He was caked with mud and water... but spurred on by the thought of capture and torture before certain death, Paulo moved his feet the best he could, looking behind him–satisfied that his path was not easily followed. But he knew it was just a matter of time before his captors would be on his trail. And he did not have to wait long.

An older-than-old, faded-blue Chev two-door truck rounded the curve down the road from where Paulo chose to hide. He had a full view of the truck now. One man sat behind the old truck. He was staring straight ahead. He was not searching for footprints. He was not searching for Paulo.

The passing truck was moving so slowly along the muddy road that an idea came to Paulo so forcefully that he reacted as if someone had just yelled at him. *Where do these thoughts come from?* Paulo questioned himself, but almost out loud. And with a swiftness he did not know he possessed, Paulo moved from his hiding place toward the rear of the slower-moving truck, keeping one eye on the driver for any sense of danger and the other eye guiding him flawlessly over the muddy terrain until Paulo caught up to the truck and carefully hoisted himself onto the bed, from the tailgate.

Relieved to see sacks of onions and empty burlap bags he could slide under to keep out of sight, Paulo breathed a sigh of relief for the first time. It wasn't perfect, but Paulo did utter a sincere "Thank You" before closing his eyes–inviting darkness to prevail. *Why did I do that?* Paulo thought for a split second before dozing off.

Paulo had no sense of how long he had been asleep, but when he did come to his senses, it took him a moment or two to gain his bearings and remember the incidents which had played out just hours before. He had been able to escape a two-year ordeal and was still alive. But where he was and at what peril he might still be exposed, he did not know. But he was about to find out, just as a hunger pain hit him, along with the pungent aroma of onions. Feeling for anything that resembled an onion, Paulo soon found what he was searching for and quickly bit into it. Eating a raw onion wasn't his preferred fare, but with nothing in his stomach for what seemed like days, Paulo wasn't choosey.

While he ate, somewhat silently... still concealed inside his hiding place, Paulo peeked out to assess his surroundings. A bluish-grey sky overhead was void of direct sun, so Paulo assumed it was now late afternoon. *Had he been asleep all day?* His eyes scanned just over the top of the truck bed and saw nothing. Paulo relaxed a little, hoping he was alone and perhaps the driver had left the keys in the ignition. That was a silly thought since Paulo had only driven a car once. And that experience ended poorly. He was only eight years old and wanted to show off for one of his fellow orphans by stealing the keys to the only vehicle owned by the convent from the keyboard in the Reverend Mother's office and then plowing the car into bales of hay stacked just outside the barn where the vehicle was parked. Paulo was very lucky that day if having to listen to Reverend Mother's angry rantings for several hours was considered luck.

Having to go without food from his twenty-four-hour punishment by his captors and having a raw onion sit alone on an empty stomach wasn't going down well at all. Paulo needed food! Just then, he thought he heard muffled voices, maybe still a long way off. He dared to raise his head in the other direction and saw the heads of people working in a field. They were harvesting onions. *I bet this truck is used to gather the day's harvest from these workers and transport the bounty to a holding area,* he reasoned.

Paulo then buried himself deeper into the sacks of onions, now expecting the workers to start piling more sacks on top of him as soon as they finished their day of harvesting. And he didn't have much time to wonder about the outcome before he heard and felt "Incoming!" Amidst laughing and foul language, Paulo held his breath, thinking that no one would try to reposition the bags already in the truck, exposing his hiding place. He was in luck.

Although the weight of the additional bags of onions began to push the air out of Paulo's lungs, the joy he felt from realizing he was free of his captors kept him from screaming through the terror of being crushed. Paulo felt the truck again come to life and begin to rumble down the road, leaving the workers to walk to their waiting transportation. Feeling safe again, at least for the time being, thoughts of what he would do when the truck stopped to unload began to fill his mind. Then dust from the open truck bed began filtering through Paulo's shelter, making breathing even more difficult. He needed water. He hadn't eaten in days and began to be nauseated from the crushing sacks of onions that lay on top of him.

Paulo started to panic, feeling the need to vomit and purge his churning stomach. That need was followed by belching nothing but air and gut-wrenching pain as bile and blood were expelled. Paulo's chest heaved to gain a little air... as blackness fell in around him once again.

Chapter Eight

THE SECRET

Maria Luiz Cervantes lay quietly next to her husband, but her mind was not quiet. She had married well, a promising Doctor's wife at first, but then her husband had decided on a different career, a quicker means to wealth, and she had been blessed with a life of means.

Maria had kept secret her teenage pregnancy and abortion from her husband and everyone else in her life. This was *her* secret and one that she alone would bear. Although that horrible day happened over ten years ago, it still held a presence in her mind.

Meeting the handsome medical student Carlos Danté Cervantes in the market six years ago was Maria's ticket out of her abusive home. She and Danté fell in love instantly, followed by a year of on-and-off-again plans for marriage, but Maria was not going to let her ticket to freedom leave without her. When Danté quit medical school for better financial opportunities, he and Maria were married... and moved to a suburb in Guatemala City, the most populated city in Guatemala, far away from Maria's home... but not far enough to escape the memories of the abusive parents she left behind.

Maria, unable to go back to sleep, turned over... now facing her husband's slumbering face. She and Danté had been unable to have children. For ten years, Maria had built up anger against her mother and blamed her for forcing her to have an abortion. Now, God was punishing Maria, not her mother, as she would have wanted. But Danté had been patient with her, to a point–yet, he wanted children, and Maria began to feel that if she was not able to get pregnant, he would leave her. "What's up, my love?" came the sleepy voice next to her... attached to a form with eyes still closed. "What troubles you so early in the morning?" Dante' continued before Maria could answer his first question.

Maria just stared at her husband, no answers revealed in her blank stare. "What do you mean, Danté?"

"I mean, what troubles you this morning?" Dante' persisted. "And yesterday morning... and the day before that? What is the reason for your unhappiness, my love?" Danté now moving closer, hoping to find an ear lobe to nibble on.

" Danté, I have not been perfectly honest with you!" came the reply, surprising even Maria but halting Danté's advances in mid-sentence. He did not speak, but his dark eyes dug deeply into Maria's as if to dig out a confession as to the nature of her dishonesty. The look in Danté's eyes told Maria she had crossed the line and could not retreat her confession. She had to tell him.

"When I was very young, I was treated harshly by my parents," Maria began. "Actually, I was abused, to be honest," which declaration brought Danté up on his elbows, now looking closer at Maria... trying to anticipate what was coming next.

"Being factory workers, there was no home life for my parents," Maria continued. "It was a wonder they had any children at all... and unfortunate for me that they did manage to have one child," she said somberly. "I was relied upon to care for the house so that my mother could work right alongside my father at the factory. I was left alone for long periods of time and expected to complete a long list of chores before my parents came home. Because I was a selfish child and wanted to have a child's life, I did not always do as expected... actually, quite often," she finished, trying to show a slight smile. Dante' only stared into her eyes. Was that compassion she saw?

"I was... uh, punished for my laziness almost every day. Soon, I lost my childish behavior and submitted to a life without friends, fun, or even being just a kid. I was allowed to attend a local school taught by the nuns from the local parish, but there was no tolerance for misbehavior there either. When I was about fifteen and so starved to have a friend, one of the factory manager's sons noticed me. We struck up a friendship almost immediately. I snuck out of the house in the middle of the night quite often, and we just had fun together, running through the streets... just being kids–doing silly things. We would talk, mostly... he about life moving all over the country with his father's job as plant supervisor. How difficult it was to find friends and build relationships. I talked about how trapped I was and could do nothing about it. Our fun then turned into romantic behavior, and once we started down that road, there was no turning back. "I was so starved for attention that I was easy prey to an ill-intentioned young man, who, it turned out, was only in it for the thrill it provided.

When I told him I was pregnant and asked if he intended to marry me and hopefully rescue me from this life of hell, he just laughed. He just laughed!" Maria repeated, with more intensity than necessary. "I was left to deal with this nightmare on my own, and so I wrapped myself with a corset to hide my condition as long as possible, hoping against hope that the baby's father would change his mind and decide to be honorable about the situation we both were responsible for. But he did not... and whether or not he told his parents, he and his family moved shortly thereafter, leaving me with no support, no backup... and with no one to share the blame."

Maria was now crying profusely, her head buried in her pillow, wanting her husband's forgiveness more than anything right now. "Go on," he whispered into her ear. "There is more, Maria. Please continue," Dante' asked.

Maria grabbed for a tissue to blow her nose, and dry her eyes. She looked at Danté with sorrow in her eyes, pleading for forgiveness.... but that is not what she saw. "One day, when I was about seven months pregnant, my mother discovered my bulging stomach and tore off my wrap to reveal my condition. She was outraged. She..." Maria now began to cry again, but holding firm she continued. "My father was at work and would not return until late that night. My mother had just returned from her shift and should have been tired, but her rage overwhelmed her, and she pushed me out the door and dragged me to a place I had never seen before. It was a clinic of sorts for abortions." Maria now sat up and willed herself to continue, no matter the outcome. She had sinned, and God would punish her for that. And she had sinned again by keeping this from her husband. She would accept the consequences of his reaction but with a clear conscience that she held no more secrets.

"I was drugged by a nurse and unable to resist the procedure entirely, but apparently I did make it difficult for the doctor to do his job... but in the end," Maria paused now, reliving the horrible experience was not new to her, but telling it out loud was. "But in the end, the doctor said the procedure was successful. He had killed my baby." Maria could take the feeling of shame no longer and yearned for some sign of understanding from her husband as to why she was not forthright with him about being pregnant and having an abortion that was forced upon her. But there was only a blank stare as if he was waiting to hear that this was just a dream and actually never happened. "Neither the Doctor nor my mother would tell me what gender my child was, but a kindly nurse leaned down as she was cleaning up after the procedure and mouthed "boy." It appeared to Maria's blurry vision that she mouthed something else, but her mother turned away from speaking to the Doctor, commanding Maria's eyes to shift immediately.

Maria continued with her confession, now breaking eye contact with Danté and repeating, as if he had not heard it the first time... "They killed my baby! When I had not yet recovered fully from the anesthesia, and only minutes after surgery, my mother insisted that she take me home before my father returned from work, against the Doctor's insistence that I stay.

The bleeding had not completely stopped, and yet my mother grabbed my arm, sat me up, and dressed me like a rag doll, stuffing wads of absorbent between my legs and wrapping a bandage around my waist and between my legs so tight I could hardly breathe," Maria continued.

"I was then pulled through the clinic doors and onto the street, which was just beginning to show life. My father would be returning home from work soon, and my mother would not let him know of this disgrace, both on the part of her daughter and of herself." I did not remember much about being dragged along the back streets toward my home, only a couple of hours after having had an abortion," Maria remembered out loud, "but I knew when we arrived home that my mother would beat me. She needed some measure of relief from her anger towards me for allowing such a selfish thing to happen to me... to my family," her voice now trailing off. "But I had no resistance in me and collapsed on the floor after the first hit... a merciful blessing."

At this, Danté raised up from the bed unexpectedly and said, with weakness in his voice, "Enough! Please do not continue Maria. I cannot absorb one minute more of this. I am late for work and have meetings afterward. Please do not wait up for me." And with that, he was gone, leaving Maria to wonder who she had married... and if she had just lost her husband also.

Chapter Nine

ANGELINA

P aulo first became aware that the rumbling had stopped. Then he realized he could breathe... and took a deep, sweet breath. Next, he dared open one eye, then the other... and listened. His raspy breathing was all he could hear. Paulo worked to wiggle himself out from underneath the huge sacks of onions that had been his close companion for what seemed like miles and miles of bumpy road. He had no idea what time of night or early morning it was... how far the truck had driven, or where he was. But he was grateful for being rendered unconscious enough to actually feel somewhat refreshed.

As Paulo moved from underneath his last bag of onions hiding his whereabouts, he was totally exposed to the cool night air, blowing a gentle chill across his body. Blackness again enveloped him, but this time he was wide awake as his eyes were drawn to the heavens, filled with millions and billions of stars and galaxies far away from earth. The brightness of the light overhead almost frightened Paulo into thinking he could be seen, but he just relaxed back onto the sacks of onions and stared. *Could there really be a God?* Paulo thought to himself. *He remains hidden from view, yet He controls the universe from behind some curtain that we cannot see through? What would be the purpose of that?* Paulo remembered lessons taught by the Sisters at the school, teaching Paulo to read English from the Douay

Rheims bible and how Jesus Christ was born to a virgin named Mary by the power of the Holy Ghost.

Paulo had never quite been able to understand the concept of virgin birth, but he was intrigued about the young Jesus' life as a carpenter's son. Paulo loved working with his hands, making things, and could see himself as a carpenter when he became old enough to leave the convent and be on his own, earning his own money and helping the convent financially, as was the understanding of every orphan, in exchange for their schooling, shelter, and food... meager as it was.

It would be so easy to forget he was an orphan boy on the run, with no place to call home, as he lay there under the stars. But he had to think of how to conceal himself from being noticed as a stray or he would end up as somebody else's slave. *From one pot of oil to another*, Paulo frowned. Part of Paulo yearned to know if any of his fellow workers had escaped from the warehouse after he had set the fire. He hoped they would but knew he could not return to that area. He would be hunted–that is for certain.

Paulo forced himself back to the here and now by noticing a slight glimmer of light in the far horizon poking up over the hill to what he now knew was an easterly direction... But not knowing exactly which direction he had come from, Paulo began to fear that he might be heading back toward the warehouse. *Oh why couldn't I have paid more attention to my surroundings?* Paulo criticized himself. He then noticed the direction the truck was parked... and then followed a perceived angle to where a road might be. In the darkness, Paulo could see none. But he knew he must get out of the truck for fear of easily being spotted once the workers started unloading the payload. He was shocked that they had not unloaded last night. "Maybe the driver is waiting for other workers to help," he said out loud.

Without the benefit of light or direction, Paulo decided to stay close to the truck instead of exposing himself to the unknown. For such a young boy, Paulo had instincts probably bred in him from birth and life at the convent. It was survive or become like everyone around him who had just given up. Paulo wanted more. He wanted a life. To become productive–to contribute. This was not a perfect life, but as long as he kept trying, Paulo believed somehow he would get through this.

There has to be a way, Paulo thought to himself as he scanned the area around the truck. Then he noticed a small house sitting dark a few yards away. A fenced area behind the house gave Paulo the thought that it might be a garden. *Food!* he thought, almost out loud. Moving quickly, but watching for any sign of movement around him... Paulo slipped over the fence and dropped low into the waist-high corn stalks to better see what he might dig up to eat.

Carrots! Paulo pulled up what felt like carrots. One bite told him otherwise. *Bitter!* He never liked turnips when they were added to stew cooked for dinner at the convent... but now, he didn't care. It was food. Paulo ate one. And then another... before the sound of a door slam brought Paulo to attention as he dug himself deep into the garden foliage. Voices followed. Two men. An engine roared to life... And the truck full of onions moved down the road. Paulo moved to the end of the garden and watched the truck disappear in a cloud of black dust.

Now what? Paulo asked himself. His stomach answered his own question the minute his senses took in the aroma of a sausage smell coming through a screened window leading to what appeared to be a kitchen. Someone was cooking. Paulo slipped under the window ledge and peeked in... his eyes resting on a beautiful girl clad modestly in a brightly colored robe covered by a well-used apron. She was preparing breakfast. Paulo watched with interest as she cracked eggs into a bowl and grabbed a spoon lying on the counter. Her eyes moved from the spoon to the window... and then she let out a shriek, causing Paulo to fall backward onto the ground as his feet couldn't keep up with the descent of his body, landing hard in the otherwise soft mud. Paulo didn't even notice the big hands that were waiting for him as he jumped up from the ground and tried to run.

"What are you doin' kid? Spying on my daughter?" the big man yelled in his native tongue. Paulo was too surprised to answer, having allowed himself to forget his surroundings as he focused on the beauty of the young woman.

"I... I was only looking, señor!" Paulo said without thinking how stupid that sounded. "Of course you were looking, estupido; that is how it starts, peeping through windows, then stalking my beautiful daughter." With that, the big man grabbed Paulo's other arm and twisted it behind him, causing pain to shoot up Paulo's shoulder and neck. "Come on, boy, I'm calling the Sheriff. He will know what to do with you."

Before Paulo could object to the man's threat of calling the police, a voice called out from the window. "Papa, he was doing no harm. Please do not hurt him," the young voice pleaded. "He is just a boy!"

"I am not just a boy! I am practically a man!" Paulo challenged, speaking in English... again without thinking. *Why do I do that?* He thought. This declaration in English both touched the big man's funny bone and aroused his curiosity, and he released his grip on Paulo, who was in full alert by now and, sensing the relaxed grip, had struggled free and began to run away. The big man did not try to pursue but yelled out to Paulo as he fled..."Amigo, ham and eggs are on the breakfast table for an honest day's work!" Paulo kept running until he was a safe distance from the man and his house and then stopped to process what he had heard shouted at him. Instead of calling the police, the big man was offering him a job? Paulo and the big man stood about thirty yards from one another now... with the man opening his arms in a gesture that made Paulo wonder if this was just a ploy so he could again capture Paulo and turn him over to the Police. But there came this "feeling" again, giving Paulo a sense of peace about this man's intentions. But he would not let his guard down again.

How stupid of me to have not heard this big man come up behind me! I won't be so careless next time, Paulo silently vowed, his eyes darting toward the beautiful creature at the window now looking directly at him. Although he could not see her features perfectly because of the early morning sun filtering through the dust, now beginning to rise from the earth, Paulo was drawn to her countenance. She was smiling! How his legs took over his mind, Paulo could not know, but without resisting, Paulo allowed them to carry him back toward the house and to the delicious smell coming out of the kitchen window.

The big man had turned his back to Paulo and walked toward the house, yelling to the girl at the window to set another place for breakfast. He then turned his head toward Paulo and pointed to a round trough filled with water. "Wash up before you come into the house, Amigo! And hurry up! We have mucho work to do!" he announced, using part English. And over that last statement the big man let out a belt of laughter like he had just told the funniest story ever–and disappeared inside the house.

Paulo did as he was told and quickly covered his face and hands with the foul-smelling water that was probably shared with humans and animals alike... but it was cool and somewhat refreshing. By the time Paulo reached the front porch, most of the excess water had left his face and hands, leaving traces of a face showing through. He then waited at the open front door for someone to come and invite him in. No one came, but he could hear voices. Paulo knocked... softly. "Hello?" he announced, almost at a whisper. "Come in muchacho! And hurry, the harvesting truck will soon arrive to take us to the field. You will want to have some of my daughter's famous beef gravy and biscuits before you hit the fields."

Paulo nodded as he accepted the invitation to eat breakfast with this family but proceeded carefully, still very much on edge that this was a trap, and at any moment, the "bosses" would jump out and snare him. But the house was quiet, and Paulo walked into the kitchen, just off the small living room he had walked through. Two heads raised as Paulo appeared in the doorway, but as if on cue, those heads bowed down again, and a voice uttered the words of a prayer. Paulo did as instructed... sitting cautiously and without taking his eyes off the big man across the table–and the most beautiful señorita he had ever seen staring right back at him.

"What is your name, Amigo?" the man asked, not looking up to receive the answer. "P..Paulo," he finally got out. "Paulo." he said again, a little more confidently."

"And where do you come from, Paulo?" Paulo did not answer at first... not sure how much he should say.

"I am just passing through," he said, honestly.

"I did not ask where you are going, Amigo... I ask where you come from?" And this time, the big man looked up, still chewing his food but now looking directly at Paulo as he prepared his food to swallow.

"I do not know, señor! I was abandoned at birth... raised in a convent, adopted by a family from America... and stolen to work in a factory against my will." Both the father and his daughter now stopped eating and fixed their gaze on Paulo as if to determine whether such a story was a fabrication.

"And how did you escape from this... factory prison, muchacho?" The man asked, now clearing his dishes to the sink while his daughter and Paulo just sat there in silence.

"Do you know of such a factory close to here?" Paulo asked.

The man had his back to Paulo, but answered quickly, "No! There is no such factory in these parts," drawing a quick look from his daughter. That look was not missed by Paulo.

"They are late!" the big man cursed as he wiped his hands on a towel and threw it on the counter as he left the room. "Hurry and finish your meal, muchacho, so you do not cause us to be later than we already are."

"My name is Angelina," came the sweetest voice Paulo had ever heard. "My father does not mean to be so rough. But ever since my mother died last year he has been bitter against everyone."

"I know that feeling!" Paulo muttered out loud to himself... but then asked quickly before Angelina could process what he had said... "Why did she die?"

"She did not choose to die, chamaquito!" Angelina shot out, emphasizing little boy. "She was ill from years of working in the fields. She finally died there."

"Honk, honk!" announced the arrival of the harvesting truck and crew hanging on for dear life. Like a charging bull, the big man with the beautiful daughter tore past Paulo like a speeding train... "You had better catch him, boy! Or you will walk to the fields," came the sweet alarm... with just a hint of playfulness in her voice. Paulo had already put things in motion, but until now, his disability had gone unnoticed. Yet with one leg shorter than the other, Paulo sped down the steps of the porch using his longer leg like a pole, vaulting the other leg in front of him until he reached the truck. The big man was in the front seat watching Paulo's amazing display of agility. In fact, everyone was watching without saying a word until Paulo reached the truck.

"This is Paulo... our new hired hand!" shouted the big man from the front window. When Paulo didn't move, the big man said... "Are you going to walk to the fields, amigo, or do you want to ride?" And with that, the laughter exploded as someone extended a hand... and then another, and Paulo came flying over the side railing into the waiting mass of bodies.

The days came and went; the ritual never changing from early morning breakfast–catch the truck to the fields, work the morning, short siesta and lunch, then work hard till almost dusk. There were no playful sounds on the ride home... only snores and heavy breathing, and occasional low whispers. Angelina did not work in the fields like her mother. She possessed an amazing gift of art, and while the men were in the fields, Angelina tended to the livestock, fed the chickens and hogs, and watered and weeded the garden until lunchtime. She would start cooking dinner for her father and Paulo and do some house cleaning. When all was cared for, Angelina would go to her painting room and enjoy her personal time. *Her* time was what kept this little family afloat.

During the short winter months there were no fields to work, so Angelina's art that sold on the weekends in the marketplace to tourists and art collectors alike would be their income during the down times. Paulo learned from the men he worked with that his host, Armando Felix Estrada, was the field manager for the company that leased and farmed the land. He was well respected by those he worked with and had charge over... but it was also well known that he had changed since his beautiful Carmelita had died of cancer. Armando and his family had no extra money for insurance, like most who labored in the fields, and so he had no choice but to watch his wife slowly die as this dreaded disease took over her mind and body. And this caused an emptiness deep into Armando's heart; one which he found very hard to fill.

But even Paulo noticed a change in the big man's attitude from the first few days of meeting him. He seemed to be more at ease with himself and with the men, even found joking and an occasional bout of laughter. The men say it was Paulo who has made the big man laugh again. Armando and Carmelita were only blessed with one child, before Carmelita started showing signs of sickness. She could never get pregnant after Angelina, and once she was found to have cancer, which took all their savings just for the diagnosis, there was no desire to burden Armando with another mouth to feed. With the work schedule the big man had to keep just to provide the very essentials, there was little chance he would marry again and have more children. And he seemed to have become attached to Paulo... a son he never had.

One day as rain drenched the area in and around the little Estrada farm, Paulo and the others were unable to work in the fields, but not until Paulo was fully dressed for work did Armando inform him that he had a day off from the fields. A ray of hope burst through the cloudy day as Paulo raised his fist in jubilation... "Yes!" he said with maybe a little too much energy.

"Yes! Is correct, my son..." Words were spoken that neither man had uttered or heard spoken personally. "Uh, what I mean is... we have much work to do here around the farm, muchacho. You can start with the chicken coop. The wire fence is getting weak and an easy pick for a stray coyote down from the hills. And while you are in there, take a shovel and muck out the coop floor. We must please our little chicks so they will bless us with muy huevos!" Armando directed, now acting as if nothing had happened. "But today after your work, we will ask Angelina to bake us some sweet churros with extra sukar, while we take a long siesta!" And with that the big man turned on his heel and headed out the door into the rain, laughter again filling his lungs.

Paulo had the strange feeling someone was watching him, and before he, too, exited the door he turned around to see Angelina staring at him. "What?" Paulo asked quizzically. "You don't even know do you, boy?" Angelina teased. And before Paulo could scold her for calling him boy, Angelina asked again. "You are totally clueless about the feelings my father has for you, aren't you?" "What feelings?" Paulo responded. "You mean the pleasure he gets sending me to muck out chicken poop in the rain?" Paulo complained. But seeing Angelina's dark brown eyes fixed on him like this erupted feelings of his own... and he quickly smothered out all intentions of expressing negative thoughts about the man who had rescued him.

Angelina became uncomfortably aware of Paulo's reddened face and eyes that betrayed feelings of hurt and disappointment, and she fought the urge to go to him and console. But instead said, "You should go to the coop Paulo... and join your little family. They are waiting for you." And with that, she put her arms under her chest and began clucking and waving her arms like a chicken, causing Paulo to turn towards the door with sounds of laughter following as the door closed behind him.

Paulo found the wet chicken poop almost more than he could bear. It was bad enough when the air was hot and stuffy... but being wet seemed to unlock an acidic aroma that attacked his nostrils with a vengeance. Armando had given Paulo a red-checkered bandana to wear around his neck while in the fields. So Paulo had tied the bandana around his nose and mouth so that he resembled an outlaw.

If only I could find something to cover my eyes too, I would maybe survive this punishment, Paulo thought to himself, then allowing his attention to focus on Angelina making those delicious churros... imagining himself putting one in his mouth and savoring its warmth and sweetness on his lips–oh my! another thought came crashing into his mind–*Angelina's lips!*

"Oh my gosh, what did I just think?" Paulo said out loud as if apologizing to nobody in particular for reading his thoughts about a girl. All this time growing up with Sisters at the convent and other orphan sisters he lived with, he had never thought of them romantically. He wasn't even sure what that was… and as close he and Felicia had become, he hadn't even held her hand. Of course, she was older and thought of Paulo as her little brother… but she wasn't that much older. And she was very good looking. But other than watching out for one another and being almost inseparable from the day he first became aware of her, there was no romantic horseplay between them.

Paulo laughed at himself for remembering the scolding the sisters would give to anyone found doing anything inappropriate with a member of the opposite sex, and the words "Do not engage in romantic horseplay with anyone of the opposite sex" being drummed into the children's minds. "You are brothers and sisters," they would teach. "Act that way!" And yet, here was Paulo, again with a sister… and he had just allowed himself to notice her lips.

They were full and curved… "Stop! he cried out, scaring the chickens into flapping their wings just like Angelina had done earlier this morning.

Forcing his thoughts to finish the work at hand and an occasional thought of churros… Paulo finally reached a point where he could stop and survey his work. He had repaired the chicken coop wire so that no coyote could just walk in and take some dinner home without working for it. This brought a sense of satisfaction to him, working with his hands. Reflecting on how he might obtain training that would give him a chance to earn more than what a field hand will normally earn, Paulo sensed an unfamiliar noise coming from the main road which they took each day to the fields. It was a truck sound like the one used to transport the field hands. With the rain there was even less chance of a car making it this far… so this must be a truck, Paulo thought. But who would be out in the rain if they didn't have to? Paulo's skin began to crawl, like it had done most of the time when he was forced to work in the factory.

A thought so hot entered Paulo's mind that he wiped his face, feeling like sweat was streaming down it; except there was no sweat. Fear does different things to different people. Paulo's mind was reeling from the effects of what he was feeling. Different scenarios were playing out in his mind... Was it the factory boss, still looking for him? Was it the family from America who adopted him? Was it only Armando, returning from wherever he went earlier this morning?

But why was he feeling fear? Was this a warning from a God he had blamed for his imperfect life? For his disability? For his life without family? Angelina was alone in the house..! Another thought hit Paulo. What if whoever was driving the truck he just heard coming had evil on their minds and Angelina was left with no one to protect her? Paulo had only a few seconds before whoever was coming would see the small farm... and possibly him. He had to make a decision. He would hide and watch.

The red truck made its way slowly up toward the house, navigating the road ruts which were now filled with mud and water. Paulo hid himself in the coop, but kept a visual as he observed its driver pulling up only a few feet away. Paulo put his hand on the flat shovel he had used earlier to muck out the coop. The smooth wood of the handle fitting perfectly into one hand, and then the other... as a protective fear put Paulo into a crouch position ready to spring into action should Angelina call out.

Just then the front door opened with a slam and his beautiful Angelina, with her arms outstretched, and paintbrush in hand, welcomed the visitor with a shriek that should have brought the neighbors running to see who was being skinned... except there were no neighbors within earshot. And then something happened that stunned Paulo right through his heart, and for a moment it stopped as he watched the scene play out before him.

Arms intertwined, bodies met, and lips locked, as Angelina melted into the welcome arms of this... person.

This person was none other than Rodrigo Portelles, a good-looking young man, well-dressed and apparently Angelina's boyfriend. Because there was little time for courting and meeting new people, families would pledge their children to one another to marry when they had reached the age of maturity. This custom had been accepted in this village for generations, with little resistance on the part of those being promised. Love was never a factor. It was all about promulgating the future generation of the community.

There were, of course exceptions to this way of life... and Angelina was one of those. Although she was pledged to Ralfo Matez, a young man in the community when they were young, she had never accepted him. He was known for his bad temper and was often in the middle of fights between the field hands when conditions were so severe that tempers were easy to set off. And Ralfo was usually at the forefront. Angelina had met this handsome stranger one weekend in the marketplace. He had admired her paintings and actually purchased one to give to his mother. That act of kindness tugged at Angelina's heart and she was smitten, knowing full well she would bring down the ire of her father if he ever found out.

After Angelina had released Rodrigo from her grasp, leaving the young man wanting more, she glanced in Paulo's direction as if just remembering the boy was working in the coop. Their eyes met and in an instant Paulo let his feelings for Angelina show. And his broken heart left exposed for just a moment... and then it was slammed shut as he reeled around and threw the shovel in the mud and began running.

Fearful that her father would return, and somewhat unsettled by the look in Paulo's face, Angelina broke her embrace and quickly gathered in the white fabric she had placed over the porch railing; a signal that Armando was gone. An invitation only the two lovers knew about.

Rodrigo did not miss the sight of the crippled boy running across the muddy field, slipping and sliding as he went. He was quite a sight. "Who is the boy?" Rodrigo pointed out toward Paulo. "Has he been spying on us?" he asked, with emotion now filling his voice. "Who is he, Angel?" Now showing a bit of impatience.

"He's nobody," Angelina lied, trying to make it sound insignificant that a crippled boy was seen running from their home. "He may be nobody, but he has eyes... and it's my guess he saw us kissing," Rodrigo said, a bit more playfully. "Why don't we give him something to really open his eyes about?"

"Rodrigo, have you forgotten what my father would say... would do, if he knew we were... involved? Angelina said, resisting Rodrigo's attempt at pulling her back into another embrace. "And you had better go before my father returns. I have no idea when he might return."

Rodrigo used his retreat as an excuse for another kiss and backed off the porch, still smiling widely while his eyes scanned the beautiful señorita he had just kissed. *How would he ever live if he couldn't see her anymore?* he thought to himself, starting the truck and shifting it into low, as he slowly navigated back onto the muddy road. Angelina watched from the porch as the red truck did sort of a slip-n-slide back the way it had come. She stifled a laugh as she watched him go. *Paulo!* her thoughts of the warm kiss would have to wait. She had to find Paulo.

Paulo had run away from the farm after seeing Angelina embrace her boyfriend, and hid himself about a quarter of a mile from the farm, behind an old, abandoned car. But it didn't take Angelina any time at all to track his whereabouts and try to convince him to come back to the farm. Paulo would not look at her. He just kept staring at the ground.

"Paulo, what is the matter? Why won't you look at me?" Angelina pled, touching Paulo on his shoulder... only to have him pull away. "I am nothing but a cripple," Paulo said, with more certainty in his voice than seeking sympathy. And he stood up without saying another word and walked back down the hill to the chicken coop... and took up the shovel once again.

Chapter Ten

FEELINGS

Maria turned over and wiped at her eyes to clear her vision. The clock on her nightstand reflected 2:54 am... then 2:55 am. Maria raised her head to check the space next to her. It was indeed still empty–Dante' had not come home. Her eyes closed with sad resignation.

Maria awoke with a start as the sun's rays burst through the window. A quick glance confirmed what she already knew–her husband had left her. It was her punishment for holding back the truth of her pregnancy and abortion, and something she would have to live with for the rest of her life. She put on her robe and went downstairs, the shock of an uncertain future still hanging over her.

The house was still, signaling the death of a relationship. It was that quick. Dante' had wanted children. She was unable to conceive. She had lied to him. Ok, maybe not lied, but isn't it living a lie when you withhold facts that would be especially important to know in a relationship? Isn't a marriage about honesty and openness between a husband and wife? She had elected to withhold that information and, in essence, deceived her husband of five years into thinking she was something she wasn't. She wasn't a virgin. She wasn't truthful. She had been part of committing a sin, the taking of the life of another... even though it was against her will, she allowed herself to become party to it by her relationship with a boy. There would be no forgiveness for her. And with that thought, Maria covered her face with her hands and wept for her imperfect life and what was to become of her.

It was dark when Armando Estrada returned to his home. He did not utter a sound upon entering his little cottage but instead took off his boots and headed straight to the kitchen, where he found his daughter waiting for him, expectedly. "I will warm up your dinner, Pa-Pa," Angelina said without looking up. Armando sensed it immediately...

"What is wrong, my daughter? What troubles you?" Armando inquired, still feeling the weight of the day upon his shoulders.

"Who will care for you when I am gone, Pa-Pa? Who will warm your food when you return late into the night? Who will...."

"Enough!" he spat out before Angelina could finish her thoughts. He said nothing else but walked to the kitchen sink and washed his hands. Then, he sat down and prepared himself to eat what was set before him... knowing full well what his daughter was going to say–that she would marry one day, and he would be left behind—he and Paulo.

"Paulo! Where is Paulo?" Armando asked as his eyes scanned the small kitchen, expecting the boy to jump out at him any moment.

"He is with the chickens," Angelina announced. "He is struggling tonight with his, uh... physical condition."

"Why? What is wrong with him, Angelina? What is wrong with Paulo?"

"Paulo thinks he is a cripple of no worth," his daughter responded.

"Well, what did you tell him? Did you not tell him how special the boy is? How much he has blessed our lives by coming to us in the back of a truck? How much we need him?"

"No, I did not tell him those things... because he will not talk to me, Pa-Pa... Maybe you should go tell him."

"But he always talks to you, Angelina. What has happened between you and Paulo? Did you have a fight? Again?" he continued to prod, now in between bites of food Angelina had just laid before him.

Angelina remained quiet as her father then directed his focus on the beans and chicken and rice he wrapped in one of Angelina's tortillas... and, without apology, stuffed the remainder into his mouth, drips of grease and sauce escaping down both sides of his chin, leaving a smile that told Angelina she had pleased her father.

Maybe now would be a good time to tell him of her plans to marry Rodrigo, Angelina thought, just as the big man rose to leave the table. In an instant, a decision was made, and Angelina touched his arm. "Pa-pa, I need to talk to you. Could you please sit a while longer?" Angelina invited, trying not to let her shaky voice betray her confident composure.

Armando sat back down slowly, not taking his eyes off his daughter. "What is it, my love? Is something bothering you?" he asked, sitting back down without taking his eyes off his daughter.

Angelina removed the used utensils from in front of Armando, taking the used towel he always uses when he eats and dabbing a bit of remaining juice from her father's chin as she continued.... choosing her words very carefully. "Pa-pa, I have found someone to love." she started, noticing Armando's tired eyes coming to life and growing larger now, but he said nothing. "One day while selling my art at the market, a young man purchased two of my paintings... and he came back again, each time I came to market. We talked about everything." her voice was now gaining energy and life as she recounted the experience of meeting Rodrigo, getting to know him... and wanting to marry him.

Armando just sat there, no words forming–no questions. He knew his daughter's spirit and the unlikely chance she would ever settle for an arranged marriage. But the fear of being alone–growing old alone, grabbed his stomach and almost caused the delicious food he had just consumed to surge up... and out. Swallowing hard to keep his emotions from ruining this special moment for his daughter, Armando asked one question: "When will I meet this man who has stolen your heart?"

Angelina rose from her chair and practically flew across the table into her father's waiting arms. It had been forever since such emotion was shared between the two surviving family members. The premature passing of

Armando's wife had made him a lonely and bitter man. He was now faced again with loneliness... but he still had Paulo. Everything would be ok.

"Let's go find your brother," Armando said, causing Angelina to pause when she heard Paulo referred to as her brother. But now was not the time for worrying. She had just crossed a huge barrier with her father, and she wasn't about to weaken that moment... not even for Paulo. He would have to find out for himself how attached her father could become. But she was about to become free!

"Paulo, where are you?" Armando yelled into the darkness. There was no response. "Are you sure he was in the coop?" Asked Armando, holding tight to his daughter's hand as they walked together in the dark and with only the stars in the heavens to light their path. Doubt started to grip at Angelina as she and her father neared the coop where she last saw Paulo. Her breath quickened as the chickens began to cluck at their arrival. Where was Paulo?

"Paulo, where are you?" Angelina called out, loosing her hand from her father's grip and opening the closed door to the hen house. A dark figure lay in the corner but did not move at the intrusion. Armando was less patient and moved Angelina to the side as he passed.

"Come on, boy! Angelina has a delicious meal of warm tortillas, beans, chicken, and rice... your favorite!" There was no response to Armando's invitation, but the big man wasn't deterred from kneeling down and feeling for the boy. Compassion filled his heart as he placed his arm around Paulo's neck and held him close. At first, Paulo resisted... but quickly gave in to the man's embrace, and expression of love.

"Come, my son... dinner is waiting. There will be time later to feel sorry for whatever is bothering you. For now, let's get you cleaned up and this smell of chicken dung off you. You stink like a dead chicken... or worse!" And with that, Paulo allowed himself to be helped up and into the house, completely engulfed by the smells of home... and food.

After Paulo had cleaned himself up, he enjoyed the plentiful meal set before him as both Armando and Angelina sat at the table, watching his every bite.

"Whaaat?" Paulo asked when his last bite filled his mouth and before he could make room for a word. Armando was the first to speak, opening a door he hoped Paulo would walk through. What do you know of your birthplace, Paulo?"

Paulo didn't respond at first, but after a few minutes, answered with, "Nothing! I was told nothing of my birthplace or those who brought me into this place. For all I know, I was born at the convent to one of the sisters who raised me!" which brought a laugh from both Armando and Angelina at the absurdity of his comment.

"Wouldn't you want to know who your parents are, Paulo?" Angelina asked, hoping not to drive him away by inserting herself into the conversation.

Paulo looked at her incredulously... "I want nothing from those who gave me this miserable life." And then, after a short pause, added... "Except that they rot in hell!" Armando and Angelina both put on faces that showed their disbelief at what Paulo had just expressed. And of the hurt that must still be lingering inside him.

"I was abandoned! Paulo said with anger now showing in his voice. "How am I supposed to want anything to do with them now? And what difference does it make, anyway," he retorted, again radiating a long-held bitterness inside him.

"It makes a difference in who you are, Paulo, in whom you become. You can't carry this hatred in you without it affecting how you look at life." Armando answered.

Paulo had heard enough. His stomach was beginning to hurt as this conversation got too personal... and too deep. He wanted to shoot back at Armando., to tell him to mind his own business. But all he could do was cry... and he would not let them see him cry. With that, Paulo grabbed his plate and water glass and laid them on the counter, hiding his face as he left the room without another word.

"That went well!" smiled Angelina as she went to the counter to wash off Paulo's dishes. She would not let this mistake with Paulo ruin what she felt she had gained with her father. She returned to the table and paused without saying a word as she saw tears running down her father's cheeks.

"Pa-pa, it will be ok. Paulo will come around... just give him time," Angelina promised.

Armando glanced up at his daughter as she began wiping off tears–not from herself, but from her father.

***

It had been exactly two months since Paulo's unexpected arrival, and he had fit in well at the Estrada household, except for the occasional blowout when exhaustion and temper crossed paths. But as much as Paulo was beginning to enjoy his new family, he was equally agitated and anxious to get on with his life. He was surprised at how often he thought of his American family and the promise of education and a better life. Thoughts of how he might find them would not go away, which led to a growing discontent.

Then, one hot afternoon as Angelina was putting the finishing touches on her latest painting to sell at the marketplace that weekend... and thoughts of Rodrigo still glowing in her mind, a solid knock on the door brought her to her senses and nearly caused her brush stroke to flare out and cause a real mess. She sat a moment, thinking she should ignore the knock. *It could only bring trouble,* she thought to herself. No one ever came to visit during the day... unless it was Rodrigo. And with that thought, she quickly ran to the door... and disappointment.

Standing on the porch were two young men a little older than Paulo but with very young-looking faces. Angelina could see through the screen that they were dressed in white shirts... and ties. *Why...?* but her thought did not finish. Instead, it was interrupted by an enthusiastic greeting: "Buenas tardes, senorita! Would you have a few minutes to hear about Jesus Christ and his visit to the American Continent?"

Angelina was almost to close the door on them without saying a word, but something the young missionary said caused her to pause, giving the other one a chance to practice his version of her native language. "We have come from America to teach the people of your country about Jesus Christ and that He has restored His church upon the earth once again," struggled the other young American with his new language.

Angelina had a thought pass through her mind and would not let it go... "Can you come back in a few hours? My bro... er, there is a young man staying with us you may like to meet. His name is Paulo. He is about your age... maybe a little younger, and has a fascinating story to tell. Perhaps you would like to come for dinner?" This invitation was readily accepted, and the young men departed, each sporting a wide smile. Angelina knew she would catch a scolding from her father for inviting these young men to dinner, but as she watched them walk away, a little too enthusiastically, she couldn't help but second guess herself. "What have I done?" she muttered aloud as she returned her paintbrush to its watery container and, once again, began thinking of dinner.

The familiar sound of a truck engine bled through the front screen door, alerting Angelina to the arrival of the men. She prepared herself for what was about to happen when her father learned she had invited two strangers to dinner. She hoped he would be so happy with the special meal she had prepared that he would temper his attitude and at least treat these young men courteously while they got to know Paulo.

Bam! slammed the front screen door as the two tired workers entered the house without a word between them or to Angelina. But once inside, both stopped almost mid-step as the flavor of spice, grease, and sugar hit their senses. Angelina had made churros! Both men made a bee-line for the kitchen, where they were met with a smiling Angelina. The trap had been set, and the prey was easily attracted. Now, to execute her plan.

"Wait!" Angelina yelled with her hand in the air as if she was at a school traffic crossing. "You are filthy dirty, and I have just cleaned the kitchen. You know you must wash up and change your clothes before you eat."

Almost in a childish fashion, the two men halted their progression and looked in disbelief, first at the kitchen guard... and then at the long, twisted objects covered in spices and sugar lying on the kitchen counter, securely behind Angelina. "I have something to tell you. The way you behave after I have done so will determine when and if you might have one churro. Do you two hungry, tired men understand the terms I have laid out?"

Armando and Paulo's thoughts soared with possibilities of what Angelina had to tell them... None of the thoughts were good. But without even looking at the other, both men nodded in unison. Paulo was the first to break rank and try to dart around Angelina, only to be restrained by that guard hand, pushing him back to his place in line. "Not until I have told you what I have to tell you," she barked.

Armando was now growing very uneasy. Yes, he had given in a little when his angel had told him of her love for another, but he had not even met this boy who thought he could swoop in here and take her away and fill her stomach with babies. "I have invited two LDS Church missionaries to dinner tomorrow night!"

Armando and Paulo just stood at attention... neither man moving, as if trying to process what Angelina had just said had paralyzed their capacity to move–react–speak. Paulo was the first to come out of his trance. "What is a LDS?"

"You poor, sheltered boy!" Angelina poked back, but not wanting to provoke either man to anger. So she just answered sweetly. "They are from America!" Angelina answered quickly now. "When I am in the market-place I have seen these two young men dressed in white shirts and ties talking to anyone who would stop to listen to their message. They happened to knock on our door this afternoon when I was painting. I did not let them in, but when they introduced themselves as being from America, I thought of Paulo... and how he would enjoy meeting them."

Armando was uncharacteristically silent... *almost eerily so*, thought Angelina... But then she remembered how her mother became enchanted with this religion and their teaching of life after death. And especially how families can be together forever... after life on earth has ended.

Angelina remembered her mother's love for the book the missionaries brought–"El Libro De Mormón: Otro Testamento De Jesucristo"("The Book of Mormon: Another Testament of Jesus Christ"). *Where was that book?* She pondered, wondering where it was put after her belongings were disposed of. She would ask the missionaries for another copy.

Before Angelina could give it a second thought, Armando spoke from behind her, as if reading her thoughts: "Is this what you are looking for, my Angel?" He often called her that when in a rare mood of reflection. This must be one of those times, she pondered, turning around to see her mother's copy of The Book of Mormon held out to her by her father.

"Yes, Pa-Pa, how did you know?" Angelina asked, accepting the Book as her father skirted around her, placed a warm churro on a plate, and poured some milk to wash down the delicious churro.

"Hey, what about me?" yelled Paulo, still wiping his hands on a towel. Angelina stepped in front of him, anticipating his move, and held up the Book so he could see nothing else.

"This was my mother's book, Paulo!" Angelina spoke, her voice breaking. "She loved the teachings in this Book. I have invited the missionaries to come tomorrow night and teach us from this Book," she finished, now handing it to Paulo... and turning around quickly as if to block Paulo from getting a churro–enjoying a good laugh as the Book was placed on the kitchen counter, and forgotten.

The next morning, a police vehicle was seen approaching the fields where Armando and his workers were busily harvesting. Armando was first to see it, and a pang of fear hit him for no reason. He had nothing to hide, but a thought with Paulo's name *came to him: Hide Paulo!* A thought burst through to the top of his brain just as he turned toward the arriving police car.

Armando catches the eye of his foreman and walks slowly to where the man is now watching the roadway. Handing his shovel to the foreman, Armando's mouth forms the words... "Hide Paulo!"

Two police officers get out and slowly work their way over to where the men are working, taking time to survey the field and roadway stretching past. They have a picture of Paulo and start showing it around, explaining he is wanted for arson. They do not see the figure on his hands and knees working his way deep into the field.

Even after Paulo watches the police car drive away, he remains in the field until dark, then disappears into the night, missing his opportunity to meet the missionaries. He did not have to be told who the police were looking for.

It was well past midnight before Paulo dared return to the Estrada home. The large silvery moon had reached its apex and was sliding in and out of clouds, offering Paulo a measure of protection from easily being seen crossing the barren field toward his destination. He knew the Estrada household would not be asleep–they would be worrying about him, but Paulo wanted to remain silent in hopes he could gather his belongings and plan a route of escape without being seen. He knew the Estrada's would try to talk him out of leaving, but he also knew he would bring pain into their lives if he stayed.

Paulo opened the front door, careful not to make a sound. The house was cold and dark, without movement on the inside. He quickly removed his coat and laid it on the couch before heading into the restroom to wash up, closing the door softly behind him. He flushed water onto his face and paused a minute before looking at himself in the cracked mirror. "What's going to happen to me?" he uttered to himself, squeezing the water from his face as if doing so would wipe away the unknown future that lay before him. And before he could answer his own question... or give more thought to its resolution, he heard a rap on the restroom door, followed by a tender voice.

"Paulo, are you ok?" A moment's hesitation would only cause her to bang louder, so Paulo responded simply:

"Yes, I am fine," in a tone that revealed nothing of his true feelings.

"Pa-pa wants to speak with you, Paulo. He is worried about you," she followed.

"I am fine," Paulo lied. "Tell your Pa-pa that I am tired and just want to go to bed."

"You know that isn't going to work, Paulo. Please sit with us for a few minutes so we can talk," with a hint of tender pleading hanging in her voice. "They are looking for you, Paulo! The police, they are looking for you."

But Paulo did not answer nor show signs of movement. He just stood there, a doorway and a world separating them. He knew what he must do... and it did not include bringing danger to the Estrada household by remaining as their guest. He must leave–tonight! Before Armando joined his daughter in their quest to interrogate him.

With that thought still in his mind, Paulo opened the door only to find two figures standing in the doorway, causing his emotional reflex to try and close the door between them, but there was no escaping this pair. They were going to have their talk, so Paulo just shrugged and walked past them into the kitchen, pulling up a chair... and sat, hands open, then holding his face for support. "What?" he snapped, without looking up to see the two figures beginning to materialize in the light.

Armando was the first to speak. "Paulo, the policemen had a photo of you. They say you are wanted for arson. That you started a warehouse fire?"

Paulo just stared down into his hands and did not immediately respond. Then, as if someone had flipped a switch, he started to relive his imperfect life, being born to a mother who did not want him... being raised in a convent, and finally being adopted. He told of his abduction, being so close to freedom that he could taste it... only to have it snatched right from underneath him. Yes, he had started a small fire to obtain his freedom. He offered no apologies–no regrets. He hoped others had also escaped the brutal treatment.

Were those tears welling up in Armando's eyes? A sign that exposed his understanding that this young man he had come to love, even as a son he never had... would be leaving. There was no chance the boy could remain now with a price on his head for his return. His captors had made it clear by the way the police had interrogated Armando and a few of his men that they wanted Paulo back and would stop at nothing short of his return. He knew what he must do.

"You are not safe here... with us, Paulo," began Armando, his voice now shaking. "Once word begins to spread that there is a reward for your return, there is no telling who will betray us and turn you in for such a bounty. The workers... my men, are loyal friends, to a point. But they are human and weak when choosing friendship and loyalty over providing for their family. They will choose family every time."

Paulo was now sitting erect and fully alert to what Armando was saying, the emotion in Armando's voice no longer hiding the love he had for Paulo. Paulo glanced briefly at Angelina... then back to Armando, who was now lost in his thoughts of how he could help. He had to have a plan... and fast.

It was Angelina who first spoke: "I will take Paulo to market with me tomorrow," she said confidently. "He will act as my steward, and when the time is right, he could be smuggled out of town by Cousin Marcos." Noticing a blank look from Paulo, she added... "He is a fruit vendor," Angelina explained.

"Paulo will not be safe anywhere the police have influence," countered Armando. Softly now, almost a whisper: "He must leave our country."

Chapter Eleven

THE PLAN

Paulo sat silently as if invisible to Angelina and Armando... who were busily engaged in active discussion about the best way to get him safely past the border guards and out of the country. It was Armando who suggested the acceptable plan. "Paulo, we have a Cousin Francisco who owns a fishing trawler. He operates in free-trade areas and often docks inside U.S. coastal waters to trade with the Americans for supplies. We will have a passport made for you and ask Cousin Francisco to hire you for free in exchange for passage to America. He has done this before and will know how and when the best time will be for you to disembark. Probably unload with the fish!" And with that bit of humor, Armando dismissed his little family and returned to his thoughts of life alone.

Morning came quickly for Paulo, but the delicious smell of bacon and eggs frying in a skillet basted with used bacon grease hit his nostrils like a sucker punch to the stomach, causing him almost to forget he was not appropriately dressed to be seen by the opposite sex. This example of chastity was strictly taught... and enforced by the Sisters at the convent. Now able to regain his thoughts, Paulo changed into his field clothes and hurried to the kitchen where Armando had just come in from his nightlong vigil of putting things in motion for Paulo's departure... and now sat patiently waiting for Angelina to fill his and Paulo's plates. The worker truck would be coming soon, and he and Paulo must be ready. Angelina would prepare for the market... with her steward in tow.

With the men fed and out the door just in time to hear the single honk of the worker truck, Angelina still managed to smile as she thought of the joy this extraordinary young man brought into their home. Through the darkness of losing her new friend and brother... Angelina hurriedly began packing for the market. There was no telling when the men would be home, but knowing that Armando would be anxious to put his plan for Paulo's safety into action, she had to be ready for anything.

Armando had given his daughter strict instructions on what to do to prepare for their return. As he was going over those instructions in his mind to reassure himself he had not forgotten something, a sense of concern raised his heartbeat as he observed the behavior of one of the workers. He was a new hire and did not possess the loyalty to Armando as did the others. "Have you noticed Felipe watching Paulo today, as if he is afraid the boy will disappear?" whispered Gabe Soza to Armando, when the two men were close enough for a whisper to be heard. Armando just nodded but did not take his eyes off the subject of the warning.

"Should I do something to distract the men from Paulo and get him out of the field before someone does something they... and we, will regret?" asked Gabe... pointing to the new hire who continued his gaze toward Paulo, and then upward toward the road.

"Si, he is expecting someone, Amigo. The man is looking to the road, see? There, he is doing it again. He has betrayed us!" And with that declaration, Armando grabbed the hoe Gabe was holding onto and said with a low but menacing voice, "Find Paulo and get him in the truck ready for my return. We must act fast to keep this traitor from winning." But just then, another thought burst through Armando's mind. "Wait!"

With Armando's new plan explained to Gabe, he resumed his march across the field again. One of the younger-looking workers resembled Paulo enough to be mistaken for him... so Armando quickly found the young worker and explained his plan to put him into the row instead of Paulo, but with Paulo's hat and colorful bandana. Armando took his hoe and started for the man, hoping he could distract him sufficiently to make the exchange without the man noticing. Armando walked swiftly but not fast enough to give the man a warning so he could escape the confrontation. Armando was the crew boss, and it would not be out of line for him to critique the man's work style to conform with the more experienced workers. Armando would also take this opportunity to inquire about the man's family and relations... a very important discussion in their culture.

While the meeting between crew and crew boss was taking place, the exchange between workers was also in motion. Positioning himself so that the new hire could not see Paulo and with the hoe waving enthusiastically near the man's nose, Armando had no trouble keeping the man's attention riveted on him. When the signal came from one of the workers that they needed to drive the truck into town to get supplies, Armando gave the ok. He then resumed his discussion with the hire... knowing the exchange had successfully taken place and Paulo would soon be on his way with Angelina to town, and the new hire left holding an empty bag and to endure the wrath of the police commissioner for wasting his time. There might have been a tear welling up in Armando's eyes, but he did a masterful job of hiding it.

"Via Con Dios, my little friend... my son, until we meet again," whispered Armando before offering a silent prayer for Paulo's safety.

The ride from the field was bumpier than usual, with only a quick stop at the Estrada farm to gather Angelina and her paintings... and what few items Paulo considered of personal worth. He did not come out of hiding in the back of the truck for fear that someone passing by would notice them. The big truck continued its mission toward town with its cargo safely intact, only slowing down once and moving to the side of the road for a police car in a hurry... heading in the direction from where the big truck had just come, drawing a silent smile from the occupants in the front seat of the big truck.

Not wanting to call unnecessary attention to themselves, the driver of the big truck first drove slowly through the growing crowd of marketers, tourists, and townspeople, all seemingly headed to the marketplace where Angelina would set up for her day of selling her paintings.

Next, he would circle through the marketplace, and before settling at the local hardware store to pick up some tools, he would take an alleyway the driver knew would place Paulo within feet of where the fishing vessel, "Conquistador" was docked. A good plan, indeed. However, before his final destination was reached, the big truck slowed to a stop in the alley, where a door opened slightly on the driver's side, and an envelope flew through the narrow opening and up into the waiting sure hands of the driver. The truck started moving again toward the sunlit end of the alley, then made a left turn onto the busy roadway and a quick right into the fisherman's port. The driver quickly spotted the vessel, "Conquistador," and pulled alongside, where three men were untying lines and reading the big ship for departure.

The truck driver carrying Paulo did not stop directly in front of the boat but waved at one of the men preparing the ship for its departure and continued past, slowing almost to a stop but watching in his rearview mirror to be sure one of the men was following behind. When the truck was positioned behind a large dumpster, he parked briefly, went to the back of the truck, and climbed up. He grabbed some loose packing boxes and handed them to the waiting man, who placed the boxes into the dumpster in such a way as to avoid attention should someone be casually or intentionally watching as he uncovered Paulo from his hiding place.

After receiving a quick set of instructions along with the envelope received in the alleyway, Paulo turned to see the waiting worker, who said nothing as he turned to head back to the ship, carefully motioning Paulo to follow. The big truck once again came to life and resumed its mission to collect supplies, and then headed back to the fields, one passenger short.

Other than the clothes he wore, Paulo carried nothing with him but a couple of colorful reminders of his upbringing by the Sisters of the convent–two small, brightly colored bead chains and a simple copper cross lightly engraved with the words: "Que Dios esté contigo." May God be with you!

The two men casually strode across the street to where the line of fishing vessels had unloaded their cargo and were preparing for the next port, and when the man in front reached the ship, he ascended the passenger plank with only a quick glance at Paulo–with no word spoken, but to be sure the young man followed. Inside the hull, the two men descended to the cabin level, where the man pointed to a bunk. "This is yours, matey! Welcome to ye' new home!"

Chapter Twelve

THE DREAM

S everal days had passed since Maria had heard from her husband. Danté Cervantes was a self-made man in a country with few wealthy individuals, and those with wealth were recipients rather than creators.

Danté was intelligent and possessed street smarts as well. Half-way through medical school he had established contacts in the Western world and learned what products fed the appetites of the consuming class and provided them at prices hard to beat. Using his abilities to recognize opportunity, Danté put aside his medical studies and pursued importing. Some say Cervantes' suppliers for much of his products came from child labor... which is how he was able to compete, but nothing could be proven–not that there was anyone trying. He and others like him were part of the food chain; it was what it was. When Maria Luiz came into his life, he was a struggling med student with unbridled ambitions. It was that look of fire in his eyes that drew beautiful Maria Luiz in. She could not believe her luck when the handsome medical student from a neighboring village noticed her shopping for vegetables in the local marketplace that fateful rainy day. She saw a ticket out of the poverty she had been raised in and decided young Danté Cervantes would be her ride.

Maria pictured her life as the wife of a successful doctor, who was gone most of the time, leaving her with money and time... and distance from her family. She sunk her hooks into Danté, and he came along willingly. But she soon recognized a burning ambition in her new husband that would not be quenched while spending five more years in medical training. He was ready now. And success came quickly as opportunity and preparation met.

It was not easy for Maria to break away from her parents, who held her in a tight grip of guilt for deserting them. But when her new medical student boyfriend entered their lives, the parents loosened their hold on Maria. When young and soon-to-be Dr. Cervantes agreed to provide financial support to them once the couple had married and Danté was employed, their attitudes changed significantly.

Danté wanted to wait until he had finished medical school before marrying Maria, but she convinced him she might not be around that long, as she had other suitors. So they were married in a simple Catholic wedding, and Maria moved into a small apartment in the city closest to the medical school, promising her parents she would visit often... which she never did. She did send money occasionally, which kept her parents content. But she could never get past the abortion her mother had caused her to have. She knew Danté wanted children, and she refused to reveal the fact that along with an abortion, the butcher who killed her child also must have stolen from her any chance of having more children. What other explanation did she have for being unable to conceive after so many years? And she held onto the blame and hatred of her mother for causing that.

Sometime after Danté had disappeared, Maria started having dreams... likely due to the stress she had been under after confessing her deception to Danté. She began to see a young man in her dreams. He was bright and handsome. Perhaps this was Danté when he was young? She mused to herself. But that did not seem to satisfy her. Why would she be having dreams of a young Danté? But the dreams only got more intense as the days passed without any word from her husband.

One night, as she had barely gone to sleep, Maria gasped from an image in her mind that called out to her: Mother! She shot straight up in bed... and called out to Danté before she woke to the realization it was just a dream, and Danté was not there beside her. But, she was certain she'd heard the word *Mother!*

Maria took a sip of the water from the open bottle on her nightstand and laid back down, hugging her husband's pillow tightly to her chest. *Mother*, she whispered as her eyes closed to a most marvelous feeling of hope. *Mother.*

Awakening hours later, by the early morning sun streaming into her room, Maria was amazed at how well she had slept. She then remembered the image of the young man who appeared in her dream. *I never remember dreams,* she thought to herself. Why this one? Maria made no attempt to get up for the day, still relishing how good she felt after a good night's sleep. But then the thought of motherhood that came during the night began to unnerve her. Why would she see a young man in her dreams and not a sweet baby?

As Maria fluffed up her pillow and turned it to the cool side before laying her head back into its welcome softness, she began to explore what she thought she saw in her dream. The young man had dark hair, like Danté. And brown skin... like Danté. She couldn't remember his eyes, but... Wait! He was not smiling. Or at least she did not remember him having a happy smile, as she would have expected. Maybe this was young Danté showing his displeasure of his wife. But why is he calling me Mother? she pondered.

Maria fixed her breakfast and began writing down the details of her dream so she would not forget. She thought of calling Danté again, as she had many times, but no return call. She was worried that something may have happened to him, but when she reported his disappearance to the local authorities, they said they had easily found him and he was fine.

Of course he was fine! Maria wanted to blurt out over the phone. *He is probably the source of your and many others' Christmas bonus' for turning your heads to his "imports!"*

No, she had lost her husband and should begin to plan how she was going to take care of herself should he refuse to lend support, given it was her deception that caused the marital break, she now admitted to herself. Bills were due, and although there was plenty of money in her checking account to pay them, she wondered if she should use that money for bills or cash out the checking account and find herself an apartment. Or maybe move back to her parent's home? No! That idea was quickly scrubbed. She would not be reconnecting with those who had caused her such unhappiness. She would figure this out herself.

Then, a thought crossed Maria's mind that maybe she should turn to God for help in finding her way out of this mess, but human stubbornness and long-embedded bitterness toward her mother had kept her from entering the doors of a church for years. God had not protected her when she was young and vulnerable, and He allowed her mother to cause her to have an abortion.

She could not forgive either God or her mother for that.

Maria admitted that she had made a mistake in not telling her husband before their marriage about her abortion; she knew that now, but her desire to escape the miserable life as her parent's servant and her desire to not look at the person every day, who had killed her baby, overshadowed her sense of right. She had caused this. She alone had made the decision to hide this from her fiancé before their marriage. Now it was too late; the damage was done—and with that last thought, Maria returned to bed and the comfort of her pillow—eyeing the one lying empty next to her before she heaved a heavy sigh, willing her own eyes to close and remain closed until morning.

Mother... Maria awoke with a start; her baby was not dead! This was her baby, all grown up, calling out to her. *Wait a minute, how could that be? My baby was dead. Taken from my womb. Or was it? All these years, I never doubted the child was killed. I was so traumatized that morning that my mind could not even revisit the horrible experience for months... and then, only to rationalize my mother's actions as being for my own good. I had no means of supporting another mouth to feed. But I could have put my baby in an orphanage,* continued Maria's self-talk. *An orphanage!* Maria repeated silently to herself. *What if....?* The thought almost shocked her from the bed, pushing the pillows off her as if they were confining her ability to think.

What if... my baby actually lived? Maria continued with her thoughts. *What if he is now reaching out to me through my dreams? What if my baby was given to another family to raise or sold through the baby black market? How would I ever find him?*

Maria could sleep no longer with the thoughts of "what if" rolling through her mind. After her shower and towel-drying her shoulder-length hair, the natural curls taking shape once again, Maria began to think of the possibilities. Her eyes were brighter than they had been in months... maybe years, as thoughts of how she might find her son crowded her mind and took precedence over any hurtful thoughts of her husband's disappearance. She had purpose now, even if it was a long shot with little to go on. Maria had suppressed for years thoughts of that most agonizing morning when she was dragged into the medical center and drugged to unconsciousness while her baby was removed from her womb. She now tried to open her mind to that experience, hoping to discover a clue that would give her direction from which to start.

Maria tried to put the missing pieces together without allowing herself to succumb to the darkness surrounding her childhood. The thought of bright lights flooded her memory as figures with muffled voices crowded her mind, causing her not to think clearly and then have no thoughts at all. If her child survived the birth that night, what would be the most probable course of action to remove him from her life but also to care for him? She thought about the medical center staff who might still be working. She recalled only the eyes of the nurse who had bravely whispered, "It's a boy," without hardly making a sound, causing Maria to doubt herself later on that she even heard the announcement. But she did hear it! And this dream proved it, didn't it?

Maria would visit the medical center in her hometown and see if she could make contact with anyone who might remember her... and what had happened to her son. She would canvas the area for information about other children who had turned up missing. Maybe she could locate the source of the illegal transporting of children and put an end to their activities. *What am I thinking? That was twelve years ago!* Maria rebuked herself. Did she have any chance at all of finding someone who might be helpful in providing information about a birth that took place so long ago? Feelings of doubt and despair began to chase out the hope of ever finding her son. But Maria had grown strong during her years of living amid adversity. She knew this feeling of hopelessness was nothing more than Satan's tool for stealing hope. She would not allow this to happen. She picked up the phone, and with a credit card pulled from her purse, she began to dial.

Chapter Thirteen

REUNION

T hree hours later, the wheels of Airbus Flight 792 touched down on the Guatemala City International Airport tarmac. A car waited just outside the passenger pick-up terminal, its driver waiting expectedly, holding a sign that read "Cervantes." Maria approached the man, who quickly grabbed her two bags without saying a word and while Maria stood there waiting, he opened the trunk and placed the bags gently inside. Then quickly moved to the passenger side and opened the backseat door, inviting Maria inside. The long ride to the medical center in Maria's small village was filled with anticipation... and trepidation for what she might find. She stared out the window, images passing by one after another, with Maria looking for any recognition of what had been her home only a few years ago. Each recognition brought with it a memory, a story... a heartbreak.

After what seemed like hours, the small vehicle slowed, then pulled off the dirt road onto a paved parking lot in front of what she remembered as the medical center. The sign read, "Urgente." Maria asked the driver to wait while she went inside. The entry was well-lighted, with what appeared to be a reception desk a few feet inside. The figure behind the desk did not look up as Maria approached. A quick glance around and nothing seemed to jog a memory. A mother with two young kids sat quietly on three of the ten plastic chairs reserved for waiting patrons. Maria looked back at the woman behind the desk. She was still absorbed in the paperwork in front of her without acknowledging the arrival of a new potential customer.

"Excuse me, I was wondering if I could speak to whoever is in charge?" Maria asked politely in her native tongue. The woman started to raise her head but decided to finish the sentence, where she placed her finger to maybe save her place... then looked up with one glance at Maria and another quick glance at where her finger now began to smudge the white paper. "Sales calls are only on Fridays," she offered, again lowering her eyes to the placeholder.

"I'm not sales. I was a patient here a few years ago," Maria said, now pausing to see if this new information would cause a reaction from the receptionist. It didn't. Maria spoke again, still holding her patience in check. "I would like to see whatever information you have of my... procedure."

"What did you have done?" Maria thought for a moment and decided not to play this woman's game any longer.

"May I speak with whoever is in charge?"

The woman now raised her head, letting her finger fall off the page she was saving, and looked directly at Maria. "She is busy!"

Just then, a door on the other side of the waiting room opened, and a uniformed nurse carrying a clipboard announced, "Señora Comacho, the doctor will see your baby now!"

Maria moved swiftly to get the nurse's attention before the next patron reached the door and it closed again. "Excuse me, nurse, may I speak with you a minute?" Not waiting for a response, Maria continued: "I was brought here to this clinic years ago for a procedure. I need to see what records you still might have on me." By now, the receptionist had made her way to the open door and reached past Maria to grasp the free hand of the woman with two children at her side and pulled her through the door, giving Maria an icy look that communicated she would not be messed with. Maria returned to her place at the receptionist's window and waited for the woman to return.

"My name is Maria Cervan... I mean Luiz. I was fourteen years old when my mother forced me here to have an abortion," she said icily.

"I started to have contractions from the trauma and was drugged. When I awoke, I had no baby. I was told the baby was dead and to go home with my mother. I want to see if there are any records of my baby's birth or death."

"What was the date of your admittance?" the receptionist asked, with ice still in her voice. Maria gave the date as best she could remember and waited patiently while the woman made her way slowly to a filing cabinet protruding from an alcove just off the receptionist area. Maria watched while the receptionist flipped through the files, her mind recalling horrible memories of her experience here as a young girl.

"Please spell your name for me," Maria heard words spoken as if commanding the files to reveal the requested information. Pushing aside her unwanted memories, Maria did as she was told, then continued to hold her breath expectedly. And waited. Without saying a word, the receptionist shut the drawer and turned again to face Maria. "There is no record of your admittance," she spoke, ice still dripping from her words.

"I was not admitted," Maria returned quickly. "Then we would have no record if you were not admitted,"

"But you kept my baby," Maria pled... tired emotion sounding in her voice. "I was brought in by my mother to have an abortion against my will. The trauma caused my baby to be born before it could be aborted. You took my baby, and I want to know if he was born dead or if he lived.

"How do you know it was a he?" the icy receptionist questioned.

"Because someone whispered 'It's a boy' to me after I awoke.

"I am sorry, señora, but I cannot help you. We have no record of you even being here. And there is no record of the birth of a child with your last name." And then, in an almost repentant voice... "Maybe the last name of the father?"

Maria looked at the woman now, both seeming to understand the hopelessness that lay ahead. "No... but thank you for trying." And with that,

Maria turned slowly toward the open door as another patron entered with a crying baby in her arms. Maria glanced down at the child, weariness seeping through her limbs. It was all she could do to walk back to the waiting automobile where the driver waited with an open door. Maria let herself sink into the soft velour of the backseat, not wanting to admit the only option that lay in front of her.

The driver started the car and then looked in the rearview mirror before asking her the obvious question: "Where to señora?"

Maria gave the man the address and shut her eyes, dreading what was about to occur. Maria had not seen or talked to her mother since cancer had taken her father, and she was forced to attend the funeral out of family obligation, mostly because her husband had insisted. Maria had never spoken to her mother the way she knew she must now. Over the years following the death of her baby, she had accepted the horror that she experienced that fateful day as punishment for her sin of becoming pregnant. She had violated God's law and would stand accountable. But in her heart, she carried hope that one day she would meet her son, maybe after her own death, and would beg his forgiveness for denying him a chance at life.

The squeaking of tired brakes brought Maria to the here and now. Her mother still worked several days a week to support herself, and Maria hoped she would be home so she could get this over with before she lost her courage. Maria stood in the dust caused by the departing town car, hesitating at the curb to possibly gain inner strength before proceeding, her eyes scanning the front of the little house—looking for any sign of life.

The sun was beginning to set, and shadows played tricks on Maria's eyes as she moved toward the front door. The yard was well-kept, a sign that her mother could still care for herself. *But the wood on the home that wrapped its fascia was worn, and sun-bleached*, she thought. *Maybe when this is over, I will need to send over someone to paint her house*, Maria thought to herself as she knocked on the door, hoping for a response. There was none. Another knock... this one more determined. A sound from inside the home instantly brought Maria back in time. That loose floorboard a few feet from the front door always served as an alert that her parents were home.

The door to Maria's childhood home opened and there stood Guadalupe Portencia Luiz, hairbrush in hand–not even a change in her facial expression as the recognition of who was knocking on her door became clear.

"Maria? What are you doing here?" she asked, raising the brush to her hair and causing Maria to flinch from memories of where that brush had landed time and time again.

"MaMa, may I come in? I have come a long way to speak to you about something." Her mother's eyes darkened as she honed in on her daughter. "Why? Why do you now come after so long Maria? Are you in trouble? You have a fine husband now to solve your problems; why do you come to me?"

"May I come in, MaMa?" Maria asked again, without responding to her mother's battery of questions. Guadalupe Portencia Luiz had aged during her daughter's absence, the sun catching strands of gray and deep-set wrinkles that now coarsened the woman's once youthful features, as Maria observed from the doorway, still not invited to enter.

"I am tired Maria. I have been at work and need to rest. Cannot this wait for another time when you have given me notice of your visit, and then I could..."

"No, MaMa! This cannot wait." And with that, Maria stepped around her mother's still form and went immediately to the couch and sat down, her eyes still dancing, both with fear and anticipation. "I came because my husband has left me, MaMa! He has left me because of what you did to me." Maria let that sink in a moment before proceeding, noticing her mother was still standing in the doorway, hairbrush in hand, but now her hands held it like a baby, cradled in her arms as if seeking support from it.

"I was ashamed to tell Danté that I got pregnant as a child, but even more ashamed to tell him my own family killed my baby and stole away any chance I would ever have to bear him children!" Guadalupe stood motionless as words hurled in rapid succession toward her began to hit their target, bringing back to the surface the shame she bore for her acts committed out of desperation– to save Maria from humiliation and possibly physical abuse if her father ever knew she was pregnant.

Guadalupe knew her daughter would never forgive her, but strangely, she did not feel defensive at that moment... as she contemplated her reaction while mother and daughter stood gaping at one another... One the attacker–the other the target.

"Would it matter if I said I was sorry?" an almost whisper-like plea released from Guadalupe. "Those were desperate times, Maria... They still are. Since your father died, I haven't been well. I live with the knowledge of what I did to you. Not a day goes by that I don't feel your pain, but..." Before she could continue, Maria spat with dart-like venom.

"You feel my pain? You are sorry? You killed my baby, Madre! As if you took a knife and slit his throat!" The look on Guadalupe's face told Maria she had delivered a killer blow. But what came next was not what Maria was expecting.

"What do you mean *his*?" Guadalupe shot back as a return volley. Maria only blinked, the hot tears in her eyes now pooling over their banks and running freely.

"I mean 'his' as in my son, MaMa. I had a son."

"How...?"

"How did I know?" Maria quickly anticipated her mother's question. "Because a nurse was kind enough to tell me. I was so drugged I couldn't feel a thing, but I could hear. And she whispered into my ear what no one else could hear, that it was a boy!"

Guadalupe had moved to the couch now... motioning to Maria that she come and sit by her. "You had better be sitting for what I am about to tell you, Maria. You might as well know the full truth so you can hate me even more." Maria sat... but as far away as she could get and still be on the couch.

Her mother had now raised herself upright, trying to show a measure of
dignity but failing miserably as her voice began to quiver.

"Mm... Maria, your son... he is not dead!"

Maria did not move for fear she would wake up and discover what she
had just heard was a dream.

"Did you not hear me, Maria? Your son is not dead... at least he is not
dead by my hands," Guadalupe proclaimed weakly.

Maria turned to face her mother but said nothing, her mind racing
through the possibilities.

Seeing her daughter stunned, Guadalupe continued..."You went into
labor as soon as we reached the medical office. The doctor said your son
was too far along to abort... and told me he would find a home for the baby.
They put you out so you would not know."

The silence in the room was deafening... all air had been pumped out,
waiting for Maria to respond to this latest punch. Emotions ran wild
within her, unable to make sense of any of it. Her baby lived. Her son was
alive! Her hands started to tremble as she continued wiping across her eyes,
mostly out of reaction but feeling nothing.

"How much did you receive for my child, MaMa? You sold my baby...
How much was he worth to you?" Maria chided as she wiped at her tears
with her sleeve again, feelings of anger boiling and very much alive.

"I did not receive payment, Maria. I made the doctor promise he would
find a good home for your son. Your son was raised in the Convent of
Sacred Hearts, located outside of Antigua... over the mountain. He received a good education at the Catholic school there and was adopted by
an American family from the state of Utah. That is all I know, Maria... I
swear it!"

Maria's mouth just hung open as she tried to comprehend a lifetime of
loss, only to learn she had spent her life grieving for a son who was alive.
He was alive!

"When?" Maria asked.

"When?"

"Yes, MaMa. When was my son adopted?" Maria asked slowly. "How long ago?"

"I don't know exactly. Maybe a year ago? Maybe longer. When a child is raised by the Sisterhood, they become his family until he is adopted. There is no contact with his birth family until the child is at least eighteen years of age and is legally considered an adult in this country. That was the arrangement, Maria... or they would have tossed your son out of the school where he was gaining an education. You may not believe this, but what I did, I did out of love for you and the child."

"Love?" Maria screamed, now focusing her complete wrath upon her mother. "You call what you did love? You deceived me, mother. You lied to me. You allowed me to torture myself from the time I was a child–that I had had an abortion. That my child was dead. And you took away my ability to have children of my own! You call that love?" Maria was now standing over her mother; the roles reversed... she being the attacker, her Madre being the accused.

"It could not be helped, Maria. You went into labor as soon as the Doctor started to take the baby, which put you into cardiac arrest. The doctor said you were so anemic he didn't even want to chance it, but then he had to act fast just to save your life. He had no choice!" Guadalupe wailed, tears hitting the brim of her eyes, ready to explode.

Maria's rage of anger had hit a boiling point... and before she followed her instincts and hit this woman and made matters worse, she sat back down and hugged herself tightly, complex emotions coursing through her veins... causing her to shake violently. Guadalupe only watched, unable to reach out with a mother's love, afraid of the rejection that would surely follow. So she just watched and said nothing.

Minutes passed without a word spoken between the two figures on the couch. The only sound in the house was the low whimper of a mother grieving for a lifetime of missed opportunity to love a son she thought was dead. Her tears had long run out, and now all that remained was the raw hurt that punched and dug deep into her gut. There was little Maria could do about this now. Her child was practically grown and most likely never had any inkling that his mother was still alive. He was now in America, legally adopted by a family who loved him. Why would she try now to enter his life? *I am his mother, that's why*! Maria bit into those words as they coursed through her mind. Her own mother had taken her son and given him away to be raised rather than be inconvenienced herself. She says it was out of love, but Maria knew it was only out of fear of her husband and what he would do if there were another mouth to feed. Maria hated them both.

Without a word spoken, Maria stood and walked to the door. After a brief pause, perhaps to acknowledge her leaving her mother's home—only to have *that* thought sink into the fire of bitterness swirling within her, to be consumed and never spoken. She grabbed the screen door handle, turned it, and pushed outward, followed by the shell of a body that housed a dead spirit. There would be no forgiveness today.

Maria stood at the curb, her mind coming to grips with the news her son was alive... but dead to her. She was so consumed she had lost awareness of the fact that she had dismissed the taxi driver, and now, after leaving her mother in such a cruel fashion, deserving or not, Maria had no ride, no way to get away from this terrible place, to the comfort of her own grief. Still in a stupor of thought, she did not notice at first the black town car that had rounded the corner and slowly approached Maria. "How...?" she questioned, as her mind cleared to finally see a familiar face behind the wheel of the large vehicle now stopped in front of her. But without hesitation, she opened the door herself one second after the driver hurriedly put the vehicle in park... and instructed him: "To Sacred Hearts Convent, please," the driver now looking into the rearview mirror and answering without hesitation or question, "Si señora!" a smile revealing satisfaction of his instincts, as tires grabbed at the loose gravel sending clouds of dust and gravel into the air, blinding Maria from looking back and seeing the dark figure at the door watching the red tail lights carrying her daughter disappear from her life, forever.

Chapter Fourteen

SACRED HEARTS

Maria settled in but was unable to relax while the driver sped in the direction of the convent. As a young girl, when Maria's mother would lose patience, she would often threaten to leave her on the steps of the convent over the hill, telling her stories of what the evil nuns would do to strays left in their care. Maria had never wanted anything to do with that terrible place, and now she found herself facing another giant fear. The convent was over a hundred miles away... not that far from town in terms of miles, but because of the large hill and winding roads leading to it, it seemed like forever to Maria as she looked expectantly out the window at the passing scenery. The landscape around her little town mainly was typical desert, but lush trees and foliage quickly replaced the dry dirt as they gained elevation, and Maria found herself enjoying the ride despite the butterfly chorus churning around in her stomach.

Crowding out Maria's enjoyment of the passing scenery was the recent brutal scene between her and her mother, as well as the feelings of dread that now anchored deep into her heart. What if she can't find her son? Or, If she does find him, what if he wants nothing to do with a mother who deserted him... even unknowingly? Will he be able to live with himself and be successful in society, knowing he was born from an error in judgment? Maria shook her head from side to side and brushed her hands over her face to rid herself of those thoughts that only made her feel weak and hopeless.

She must remain calm and positive, especially as she confronts the evil Sisters who hold the key to finding her son.

An imposing silver cross peering over the ground below it, gleaming in the late afternoon sun, was the first welcome visitors to the convent saw as they pulled slowly up the steep last mile onto the sacred grounds. Below the cross stood a steeple made of weathered brass... mounted atop a castle-like crop of buildings set in a backdrop of lush, green grass.

It is beautiful! Maria thought to herself... at least she thought it was a private thought until a voice broke her spell.

"Yes, it is most beautiful! It was built in the sixteenth century by Pedro de Alvarado, who, with his mixed force of Spanish conquistadors, occupied this land after conquering Mexico in 1524," he explained, grabbing Maria's interest.

"After much bloodshed, the occupied Maya kingdom was trounced, and the Spanish remained in power. However, the property remained deserted for over a hundred years until the Catholic Church purchased the run-down structure and the land around it. It was the Sisterhood who saw a need for it. They occupied it and went to work, turning it into an oasis in the desert–a place of refuge... a place of healing. Thus the name Sacred Hearts."

"I was an hungered and ye gave me meat, I was naked and ye clothed me." Maria recited into her chest...remembering a verse of scripture that had given her comfort when she felt abandoned and alone as a pregnant teenager.

"When saw me, Lord?" joined the driver, with his own recollection of the scriptural verse. "I saw you when you served another, fed another, clothed another." That is the mission of the Sisterhood, señora... to offer a place of refuge to the lost. A sanctuary where the heart may heal. Are you lost, señora? Does your heart need healing?"

"Yes, I suppose I am," Maria answered slowly. "And I suppose it does."

Both driver and passenger sank into their own thoughts for the rest of the trip, with no words spoken, until the town car stopped, causing Maria to focus back on the task at hand. The chorus of butterflies began to rise and sing once again but quickly dispersed as Maria exited the car with purpose and strode toward the entry, taking a deep breath before pulling the lever marked "Enter."

Maria waited patiently but glanced nervously over her shoulder to satisfy herself that her ride was still within sight. A sound at the door told Maria her wait was about to end.

"Si, what can I do to help you?" came a voice from the other side of the door. It took Maria a moment to realize the sound was coming from a sliding peephole, now occupied by a pair of beautiful eyes. Maria was taken aback, not expecting beauty, but aged, cranky witches dressed like nuns.

"Uh, I am here to learn of my son," Maria announced, without any thought or plan of what she should and shouldn't say.

"What is his name, señora?" Maria remained silent, giving thought to how she should answer.

"I don't know his name," fell from her mouth. The next sound was that of sliding metal, closing the only portal to where the answers she sought were hidden.

Maria waited for some indication she would be admitted, but there was none. Seconds turned into minutes while she waited anxiously. Then another sound and movement... the door was opening. An older woman, not the one with the beautiful eyes, greeted Maria with a kindly smile and offered, "Good afternoon, señora, please come in, come in," the kindly looking woman invited, holding out her hands as an invitation to enter. "My name is Sister Romona Medina. Welcome to our home," she greeted.

Maria gazed in shock at the two figures before her but did as invited, warily. Behind Sister Medina was another nun, clad in a black and white skirt combination, much different than that of Sister Medina, who wore the traditional habit. The woman's eyes... It was the one who answered her knock to be let in. Maria's quick assessment was that there was no evil here. Strict, maybe, but no evil. At least the first three feet inside the darkened entry court only portrayed peace and tranquility, as the late afternoon sun quickly obscured itself behind the range of hills surrounding the estate.

A peace Maria had not felt in some time came over her, and she breathed out rather loudly, which caused Sister Medina to look behind her... and Maria to respond in embarrassment. "So, not as folklore would have you believe?" Sister Medina inquired, hiding her smile.

"Pardon me?" Maria responded with a little too much emotion still in her voice. "I mean, what do you mean?" knowing full well her concerns had been noticed.

"That is ok, my dear, we don't have much interaction outside these walls... and people will judge harshly that which they do not understand. That is all I meant by my question." Maria could feel a smile from the woman even though her back was now turned... and she felt one of her own smiles begin to form as a sign of relief.

Maria followed the two women into a large courtyard, beautifully adorned with the most beautiful flowers she had ever seen. They were everywhere. "What is the name of these flowers? Maria asked quietly, suppressing an urge to pick one and put it into her hair. It was a deep flower, with its petals shaped outward like a bell, as if it were announcing to the world just how special she was. Inside the bell was a golden tongue, the *stigma* of the flower. It was spectacular.

"It won't do you any good to know the plant's name, my dear. It is only grown within the sacred grounds of our school. We have very bright students here at the school," she said proudly.

"Our agriculture students are second to none," spoke an unfamiliar voice. It was the nun walking beside Sister Medina. Besides beautiful eyes, she had the voice of an angel, so young, Maria thought.

"But we call it Saint Rose," Sister Medina continued. Maria could not believe she was right in the heart of the dragon, so to speak, walking the grounds and being shown the magical flowers grown there. There were no wicked people here... at least none that Maria could see while walking among these beautiful flowers. At least there were no children tied to a stake in the courtyard and forced to eat their vegetables, as was rumored.

Maria was so deep into her thoughts as a child that she failed to notice the two bodies escorting her had stopped, causing an embarrassing collision into the back of the younger one, eliciting both a chuckle and laughter from the pair; Maria, not so much.

"Let's sit here in the garden, where we can visit and enjoy the beautiful evening scents at the same time," suggested Sister Medina as she motioned to a particularly beautiful portion of the grounds full of Saint Rose blossoms, inviting Maria and beautiful eyes to sit beside her, Maria in the middle. As Maria lowered her body to the bench below her, she felt a rumble in her stomach that almost brought the convent walls down. She quickly grabbed her stomach with both arms wrapped around her, hoping against hope that no one heard her. But neither Sister said a thing, acting as if such sounds were commonplace here.

"Now, my dear, what brings you to Sacred Hearts–on such a beautiful late afternoon?"

Without waiting for an answer, Sister Medina continued with another question... "Please tell us about yourself," and, without taking a breath, continued: "My aide this evening tells me you are looking for a son! Your son?"

Maria, nervously, had been unaware that she'd been holding her breath... and now completely exhaled. "Yes," Maria answered, wanting to hurry before the little woman volleyed more questions and before she could get the first one answered, but she was not sure how much of her past she should reveal. "I am looking for my son. He came to you as a newborn several years ago."

"How many years ago?" Sister Medina said, after a pause to let Maria clarify.

"He would be 16 years old." At this, Maria noticed both women grew tense... neither woman attempted to look at her.

"You say he came to us as a newborn? How did he come to us, Maria? Did you bring him? We often find abandoned children on our steps. Many die from exposure before we even know they are there."

"This baby was not left on your steps. My mother arranged for him to be brought to you by the doctor who tried to perform an abortion on me against my will." Maria felt her cheeks burning now as she began to radiate the wrath she felt for her mother and everyone who took part in the botched procedure. "My mother told me the baby had died. The doctor told me I went into labor, and they could not save the baby. Both lied to me. I lived with this lie for sixteen years until I lost my husband because I kept my illegitimate pregnancy from him. I could not bear to hold this lie inside me any longer. So when I told my husband why I could not have children of my own–because of the butcher who took my child–he left me."

Sister Medina and her companion only stared down at the ground below their feet as Maria took a deep breath, let it out slowly... and continued. "One night, I had a dream! In my dream, I heard a voice. It called out to me: Mother!" she whispered. "My baby called me Mother! I wanted to believe so badly that my baby was alive, but I dared not. But when the same dream repeated the next night, I knew it was time to find my son, if he was alive. I decided right then my mother knew the truth and had withheld it from me. I would not be denied. I flew to her home and confronted her. I think she had held onto this lie long enough because she confessed the deed–and where she had taken my son. He was brought here," Maria added, thrusting her hand down... pointing to the ground and looking straight at Sister Medina as she did so.

"My mother told me my son was adopted by a family from America... from Utah, in America," she shared.

"Paulo!" spoke an unfamiliar voice from one of the three women huddled together.

"What did you say?" asked Maria, excitement building in her voice, looking to see who had spoken. It was the other nun accompanying Sister

Medina. She was much younger than Maria, and her eyes were so beautiful, and... sad. Sister Medina was now standing, offering her hands to Maria. Sister Torres was, uh... a resident of Sacred Hearts before she committed her life to God. A young baby boy was brought to our convent to be raised about 16 years ago. He had health issues, a deformed leg, breathing problems... and he cried constantly. Felicia... I mean, Sister Torres took this little boy under her wing and practically raised him herself. She wouldn't leave his crib. Here was this little five-year-old girl holding a bottle up to the mouth of this sleeping baby... trying to get him to eat."

"Where is he?" Maria could hold back no longer, tears flowing now. "Where is my son?" her legs shaking wildly now. Her eyes also raced wildly from Sister to Sister, neither making a move to get her son.

"What?" Maria asked. "What is wrong?"

"Mrs. Cervantes, your son was adopted... that is true. But before his new family could leave the country, he was... uh, kidnapped!"

"Kidnapped? What do you mean kidnapped?" Maria shrieked! Causing both Sister's to stand now.

"Mrs. Cervantes... Maria! Please be calm. There wasn't anything we could do. His new family came to see if he had somehow been taken here..." Then, looking like someone had just insulted her, "They thought Paulo might have come back here as part of some scheme to keep both their adoption fee and the boy. I can assure you we do not operate that way here."

"Then where is he, Sister? Where IS he?" Maria's voice again gaining volume. "Has anyone gone looking for him? Do the authorities know about this?"

"Maria," Sister Medina spoke coolly, "Your son was likely sold into child labor or to work the streets in some other country. They would not keep him here, Maria. He is gone. If he survives the next few years, he will likely become dependent upon drugs or worse, put into prison for stealing or killing someone." Maria did not want to hear this...

"Stop! My son is not dead. He came to me in a dream. He called out to me! I will not accept that he is dead or in prison."

"She is right!" came the soft voice of Sister Torres. "I have been praying constantly for Paulo since he was taken. At first, my prayers fell to the ground. I was so forlorn and brokenhearted for him. He had happiness right in his grasp, and then it was taken. But then something happened. One day, my prayers took flight. They had life. I knew at that moment my prayers had been answered. At least I knew he was alive. Your son is alive, Maria. He is alive! I know it!" And with that declaration, Sister Medina took Maria in her arms.

"I believe if Sister Torres says he is alive, Maria... then he is! No one knows Paulo better than Sister Torres... Not even Paulo himself."

The emotions of the day had now caught up with Maria as she allowed herself to be swallowed up in the embrace of Sister Medina... and then Sister Torres, who gently beckoned to follow them to the dining room where dinner awaited. As they walked, the most enticing aroma filled her senses. It was the last thing Maria remembered before blackness struck.

The first sound Maria heard as her eyes fluttered open was a rolling thunder sound. Is it raining, she thought? The room was dark, except for a small candle flame on the nightstand by the small bed she was lying on. And just below the candle was a plate containing bread, fruit, and water. And a note: *Maria, you passed out before we could get you fed. Please eat this food to get you through the night until breakfast in the morning. You will know when it is time, so please relax and enjoy your sleep. -Sister Medina. PS. I sent your driver on and asked him to return tomorrow morning after breakfast.*

Maria first took the cup of water in one hand and then the other to keep her shaking hands from spilling its contents. *What is wrong with me?* She asked to no one in particular. *I have fasted before and never felt this badly.* Maria put her head back on the pillow and fluffed it up so her head was elevated, hoping the room would stop swirling. She reached over for the piece of bread. It was heavy, nutty in texture... and sweet, as if a piece of fruit was added to the mixture and began to melt and disappear, leaving a satisfying aftertaste.

Then it happened... a nausea that felt like it started under her feet and then grew with such strength that she was powerless to stop it. The only positive was there was little to spew... but spew it did before Maria could do little but cover her mouth as she made her way to the wash basin in the corner of the room left there by one of the Sisters for Maria to wash up before dinner. Maria's coughing and spewing sounds penetrated the thick door that was shut, meant to give her some privacy, but now reverberated with anxious knocks before someone finally turned the glass door knob and gasped at the scene before her.

"Mrs. Cervantes, what is wrong?" asked Sister Torres as she quickly noticed the soiled bedding and liquid gushing from Maria's mouth. She grabbed a towel, ignored the bed, and put her arm around Maria, who looked like she might fall at any moment.

"I ddont know!" Maria stuttered. "I was trying to eat a little bread and fruit, and then my head started spinning and... and it felt like my feet were being sucked up through my stomach and out my mouth. I couldn't control it. I am so sorry, Sister Torres. I am afraid I soiled the bed."

"What has happened?" came a familiar voice behind the pair, Maria still washing her face.

"Mrs. Cervantes has taken ill, Sister Medina. She needed some help, so I came in to assist."

"I am ok now," responded Maria, looking up for a moment before another wave of nausea hit, accompanied by dry heaves. Sister Torres and Sister Medina were both attending now, with one on each side of Maria. Sister Medina began rubbing her back while Maria remained bent over the wash basin for another few minutes before standing upright and staggering backward, held by the capable Sisters.

"You are too weak to stand, Maria, the older woman noted. "Sister Torres, please gather up her soiled bedding, and let's get her bedding changed and her back to bed. She is very ill."

While Sister Torres was gone from the room, Maria was helped to a corner chair, where she slumped down hard, without the strength to hold herself steady. "I have not eaten well since confessing my sins to my husband," Maria said to no one, her eyes now open but staring at the floor. "I forget to eat most of the time, and I think I must have allowed myself to contract some form of bug," she said, trying to explain her sudden illness.

"We will get your bedding changed, Maria, and get you back into bed. You are in no shape to travel," Sister Media said with great compassion in her voice. "We will care for you here until you regain your strength," she continued as Sister Torres returned with clean bedding and accompanied by another Sister, who eyed Maria cautiously at first but quickly attended to her task of gathering up the wash basin and placing clean towels on the table in the room. Before leaving the room, she went to the aid of Sister Torres, who was changing pillowcases.

When both Sisters had left and closed the door behind them, Maria tried to stand but was joined by Sister Medina, who aided her attempt to get back into bed.

"Here are some dry towels in case you have another bout. Sister Torres will bring in some herbal tea to calm your stomach. Drink just a little at a time and let your stomach accept it before drinking more. You will likely experience some more discomfort if it is the stomach flu."

When Maria's eyes opened later that afternoon, she heard bells faintly coming from somewhere on the premises–she would later learn they were coming from the inner courtyard, calling the young students to afternoon classes. Maria was lulled by their beauty as she snuggled herself into the soft comforter that lay beneath her. The warm tea was soothing, giving her stomach a much-needed break. Maria's thoughts turned to her son... then to her husband, and to her mother–and back to her son.

He was alive! She knew it! *These people knew him. Paulo, they named him. A strong name*, she thought. She wanted to know more about her son. She would never give up looking for him. She needed to learn all she could about him while she was here, where he was raised, from those who raised him. Maria then let her eyes close, enjoying the warmth of the comforter around her and the thoughts of... Paulo.

The sound of a creaking door hinge brought Maria out of her sleep, alert now to look at the doorway where a figure had entered. "Maria, I have brought you more tea," the familiar sweet voice of Sister Torres spoke softly. "How are you feeling?" she asked, replacing the cold cup of liquid on the nightstand with hot tea.

"Actually, I am feeling much better," Maria responded. "I think I just needed a little rest, that's all. And something I ate along the way must not have agreed with me."

"But your stomach was empty," Sister Torres said casually. "No matter, you are feeling better; that's all that counts. Please continue to rest, and we shall see if you are up to a small dinner later," she smiled, patting Maria's arm.

As Sister Torres turned to leave, Maria held onto her arm... and, looking up into her eyes, asked, "What was he like, Sister Torres? You knew him better than anyone; what was he like?" she asked tenderly, but her searching eyes revealed her determination to learn about her son. She wanted answers.

Sister Torres glanced at the doorway, then sat on the edge of the small bed, looking back into those wide, searching eyes. "Mrs. Cervantes..."

"Maria, please! Please call me Maria."

"Maria, it is," came the reply. "You need to know that when Paulo became old enough to understand why he had no last name, he was bitter–against the world, his birth parents in particular. There is nothing worse than not having answers, leaving only speculation as to why he was deserted as a baby and not wanted, even rejected," her words stinging Maria's heart. "Paulo was sure it was because he had a few physical defects... which affected his self-image–and often made him hateful to be around. He was mad at everything normal and good."

Maria had been listening intently, soaking up every word, placing images in her mind as Sister Torres spoke. "But how were you able to earn his friendship? I understand you were the only one he would let anywhere near him as a baby?"

"Paulo cried and cried from the day he was brought to us," Sister Torres began. "It was as if he knew he had been... uh, that he had no family," she quickly corrected. "I was drawn to him the minute I saw him. He was a little bundle of dark hair when they brought him into the nursery late one night. I was helping one of the Sisters clean the cribs after dinner, or I would never have seen him. He was crying, and the Sister was busy with another child, so she asked me to pick him up and hold him. The minute I did, he opened his eyes, and we connected immediately. He stopped crying until I put him back in his crib—then he started right up again. It was as if we knew one another in another life," Sister Torres said pensively. "Do you believe in a before life, Maria?"

"I don't know what I believe, Sister Torres. I haven't gone to church in years. Where was God when I was being abused in my own home?" She questioned. "Where was he when they took my baby? How could He let my parents live when they took something so precious from me?"

Sister Torres just sat on the side of the bed, staring at the floor but listening intently. "Did you ever try to reach out to God during those times, Maria?" Her tone was not judgmental but instead inquiring to understand better this woman who bore her best friend.

"Did I ask God for help? I don't remember," she finally answered after a long pause. "I know I cursed him," she said flatly.

Sister Torres reached for Maria's hand and covered it with hers. "I can only imagine the life you had growing up, Maria. And to lose your son the way you did... my heart breaks for you," as tears began falling down her already moist cheeks.

"Paulo was a very bright student," Sister Torres resumed, "but his anger at God... at you... and at life in general, kept him in trouble most of his growing years. I was... *assigned* to watch over Paulo until he was adopted." That comment brought Maria's head up!

"Assigned?" Maria asked incredulously.

"He was in such trouble with the Sisters, and they just could not change him. He would not be changed. So I was assigned to never leave his side, which wasn't hard because I loved Paulo." Noticing Maria's quizzical look, she altered her declaration. "Uh, like a brother! When prospective parents came to choose which child to adopt, Paulo always seemed to be overlooked. Probably because he most often was in detention," she laughed... drawing at least a flicker of a smile from Maria. "Paulo was very self-conscious about his appearance. Did you know he was born with one leg shorter than the other? He had breathing problems that scared the Sisters to death when he first stopped breathing. As his lungs developed and got stronger, he grew out of his earlier symptoms, but occasionally, when he gets really tired, he starts wheezing."

Maria said nothing, but it was apparent by her moist cheeks that she was grieving over not being with her son during his most challenging years of growing up. Instead of being there to support and love him, he was forced to be paraded about like horseflesh. *No wonder he was never present for these 'adoptions,'* Maria thought.

Sister Torres continued... "But when the Tone family came, it was different. Mrs. Tone and Paulo connected instantly like he and I did when he was a baby... and ever since. I watched Paulo light up when Mrs. Tone spoke to him. I did everything I could to keep Paulo positive about himself and not run away, but Paulo will be Paulo no matter what, and when the Tones left without choosing him, he was devastated. He was quite unmanageable for a time. He can be challenging," she laughed.

"A few weeks later, the Tones returned," Sister Torres continued. "It was the sweetest thing... and frankly the hardest, watching Mr. and Mrs. Tone ask Paulo if he would be their son. The look in Paulo's eyes... first concern for me and then the fire of excitement that shone in his eyes. I had never seen him like that. When he left a few short hours later, I could not say goodbye. It was too hard. But he found me." Tears now streaming again. "That is why when the Tones arrived later that night without Paulo, thinking he may have run away, I was so certain he hadn't. He wanted this family, Maria. He would have a chance at an American education with a beautiful family. He would not have run away from that. He was frightened, yes... but Mrs. Tone already loved him in a way no one else had, and I think he felt that from her. That was evident in her eyes when they returned to bring Paulo home with them. She was beaming and never left his side... like she was afraid he would change his mind and run away. She was brokenhearted when he disappeared."

Silence filled the little room until the bells calling all to dinner rang in the courtyard. "Oh my gosh, I missed my prep assignment... I must go, Maria... are you alright? Do you want me to bring dinner to your room? Are you hungry?" The questions left her mouth without her even looking back as she reached for the door and closed it behind her. Then the door opened again almost immediately, and Sister Torres just looked at Maria in anticipation of her answers to her rapid-fire questions—but now smiling.

"Yes! I am hungry, thank you! Yes, I will come to dinner," she smiled just before the door closed again. *I can see why these two bonded so well,* she thought. Maria washed her face and dried off with a small towel left at the foot of the bed. She placed it back... Just in case, she thought. And with a quick glance in the mirror, Maria opened her door and followed in the direction of the hungry crowd.

Several tables were set up to accommodate maybe fifty children; each seemed to eye Maria cautiously as she sat among them—the Sisters at the head tables served first. Maria sat between a boy who blushed every time she looked at him and an older girl who paid little attention at all and kept her head bowed to keep from looking at Maria.

"What is your name?" Maria asked the girl.

"My name is Omar, I'm five," came a boy's voice from her *other* side.

"I bet you are," Maria shot back with a grin that caused the boy to turn tail and blush again. Then, looking back to look at the girl, Maria asked, "What is your name, sweetie?" Maria asked more directly.

"Clara," she finally answered. "My name is Clara," spoken in flawless English. Maria was astounded.

"H-how did you learn English so well? You speak..."

"like a gringo?" Clara finished, now smiling broadly.

"Yes, exactly like a gringo!" Maria smiled back.

"English is our first language here at the school," Clara explained. The Sisters prepare us to be adopted by parents who mostly live outside our country, and being able to speak two languages is very helpful," she finished, now picking up her plate. "We need to get in line, or nothing will be left."

Maria could not take her eyes off this young girl, who carried herself so well and spoke like a poster child for the orphanage. *She is smart too!* Maria thought. Then, as if someone had turned on a switch, the smells of the evening meal of pork and beans and warm cornbread hit her nostrils... and her stomach. Maria grabbed at her mouth to cover it as a dry heave hit her and almost knocked her down; she was so weak. The next one left her hands moist, but Maria quickly dashed to the exit door only to find herself lost in the large hallway. A small hand slipped into hers and tugged.

"Let me take you to your room, señora, so that you may rest." It was Clara. Another heave brought Maria back to the here and now as more moistness hit her hand. "Here, take this," offered the young girl, holding up her napkin for Maria to use. And use it she did, just before another wave of nausea hit. Clara went straight to the guest room and went to work settling in her nauseous guest, who was now bent over the wash basin with unashamed gasps and groans in between punishingly painful, dry stomach convulsions. Clara was right by her side, rubbing her back and speaking softly to her.

As the nausea began to wane, the relief brought a vision of humor to Maria's mind, "If I ever get pregnant again, I want you with me," Maria whimpered, in kind of a groan- laugh. *What did I just say? Pregnant! How ridiculous to even say that!* She thought. Clara helped Maria over to the bed to lie down, where she placed a cool cloth on her forehead. "Where did you learn such tenderness skills at your young age, Clara?"

"I am not so young, señora!" she said rather sharply. I am twelve... almost thirteen... in nine months," that last part trailing off to a whisper.

"Yes, you are *so* old, 'mi tierna flor'"(tender flower).

The door creaked open, and Sister Medina and Sister Torres stepped in, both showing a look of concern on their faces as they took in the scene before them. "Clara, what are you doing here? Why aren't you eating with the other children?" Sister Medina chided.

"She is taking care of me," came the quick reply from the patient. "I have had another bout of nausea. Just when the smells of dinner had reached my senses, I lost it... again! Clara was by me and quickly escorted me to my room and has been caring for me. She is amazing!"

The look between the Sisters did not go unnoticed by Maria, but she tucked that away for later as Sister Torres gently guided Clara off the bed and out the door.

"Thank you, Clara! Thank you so much," Maria said in a whisper.

"It is time for you to see a doctor, Maria. This... condition is not likely to go away anytime soon," offered Sister Medina as she took Clara's place at the side of the small bed.

"Wwhat do you mean? What do I have?" Maria asked weakly, not able to open her eyes to see the glint of excitement and not pity radiating from Sister Medina's eyes. Sister Torres observed the change in demeanor and asked cautiously: "What do you see, Sister?"

"I see a woman. I see a woman with child!"

It took maybe a full second for Maria to comprehend the words that were spoken... Her eyes opened first as if she had to see who had spoken them. And then, with the same intensity as the dry heaves had delivered, "What? What did you say?"

"I said... I see a woman with child!" Maria, I think you are pregnant!"

"No! That cannot be! How?... When?"

"Well, only you know the answers to those questions, Maria..." Sister Medina said with a coy smile, glancing at the blush in Sister Torres' countenance. But, having seen these same symptoms in women of the village, she was quite certain Maria would soon be bulging in the middle with some form of life just waiting to get out.

Maria laid back down on the bed from which she had just risen and let her head fall into the soft feather pillow under her. She could only stare at the ceiling and wonder what she was going to do. A moment later, her question was answered for her, as she grabbed the basin that lay next to her with both hands and belched, as sucker punch after punch was delivered, with both Sisters by her side this time, offering comfort... with a tinge of excitement showing in their faces.

Once this bout of nausea had run its course, Maria opened her eyes and saw a welcome cup of warm herbal tea left for her after she basically collapsed from exhaustion. Strangely, her stomach felt hungry again, and her senses began to pick up an aroma that almost did her in again... but then settled down as the wonderful warm liquid in her hands began to perform its magic as she added sip after sip until the cup was empty.

At least there will be something to bring up when my stomach begins to revolt again, Maria thought, as she allowed herself to close her eyes and dig deeper into the pillow that almost covered her head as if that would shut out the dread she felt about the unknowns that lie ahead. She needed to see a doctor... right away! She needed to know. *Who am I kidding?* She thought. *I am not able to have children. That is my punishment for sinning. I am not worthy to have a family,* she chided. Maria's thoughts turned back to that horrible time in her life when she first found out she was pregnant. Her mind replayed the nausea that hit her then as well... but she did not remember it being so rough on her. Surely, her mother would have picked up on that had she seen her daughter heaving more than once. But she didn't. She didn't even know I was there unless she needed me to work for her.

Maria remembers forcing herself to confront her sin and ask the village priest for forgiveness. She had timed her impromptu visit during one of her market trips to get food for the family. Father Morales was surprised to see her, but seeing the grief in her eyes and on her face, he quickly ushered her behind a curtain... and waited. Maria's hands began shaking again, reliving the same shakes she had as she prepared to tell all. All, except the part about her being pregnant. As Maria stepped from the booth, having received both forgiveness and instruction, she remembered feeling so much lighter. Her sins were forgiven once she followed the instruction by Father Morales to pray for others, light candles on their behalf, and pray to the Virgin Mary for forgiveness and to make her whole again. Then her stomach sank... almost reliving that experience again as she remembered going into an alleyway and throwing up her morning intake and then some. She realized there would be no forgiveness for her. She had failed to disclose all, and she couldn't force herself to look at the Virgin Mary statue at the altar of the church and plead for her forgiveness–she who had resisted the temptations of the flesh and was pure enough to enjoin the Holy Ghost in conceiving a child.

I am nothing like that woman! Maria remembers what she said to herself as she walked slowly back to her home prison many years ago. Her thoughts of her youth were too painful to bear. She hated that she had allowed herself to be fooled into pleasures of the flesh, as her mother called it. She deserved her punishment... But *how?* she wondered. *How am I pregnant now and still carry the punishment of God? There is no way I am with child...*

Mother! I am with you... Maria sat up with a jerk, sweat around her neck and chest causing a chill as she pushed out from under the covering that must have been put there by one of her angel Sisters while she slept. *Slept? Was it just a dream, that voice I heard? Calling out to me?*

The sound of a light rap on the closed door brought Maria to her feet, almost a little too fast as stars began gathering in her head as she opened the door and at the same time closed her eyes to get rid of her dizziness.

"What's wrong, Maria? Are you ok?" came the tender voice of her new friend, Carla. "Sister Medina has assigned me to be with you until you are feeling better," she spoke as she took Maria's hand and gently squeezed it, then led her to the wash basin and peered inside. "Ug," Clara let out in disgust, as a twelve-going-on-thirteen-year-old would do. But unusual for that age, this little girl made no further complaint as she picked up the basin and walked out the door, leaving Maria alone again.

The room grew even more silent as Maria waited for the return of her little caregiver. But she didn't have to wait long before the door burst open, and in flew the little angel, a basin of fresh water in her hands, a few drops still hanging on for dear life before they let go and slid down the slippery side of the basin to the floor beneath them.

"Maria, Maria, the doctor is here to see you," came the excited announcement from little Clara. "Sister Medina wants you to clean up and be ready to have the doctor inspect you," she said breathlessly, causing a smile to break across Maria's lips.

"Examine me, my little toad," came Marie's reply that drew a curious look. "Examine! He is going to examine me," explained Maria as she put both hands in the basin and drew cool water to her face. Clara was still looking at her, holding the towel, but just staring. "What is wrong, my dear?" Maria asked gently.

"No one has ever called me... a toad before, Clara responded... not really upset–just standing there a little dazed, still holding onto the towel.

"I am so sorry, Clara. I don't know where that came from. I meant you no disrespect. You are a lovely young girl, and I have grown very fond of you... and it just seemed natural to give you a playful name. I won't call you that again; I am sorry.

Before Clara could respond, a hard knock at the door preambles its swift opening to reveal Sister Medina... and another Sister behind her, also wearing a head covering, but her other outerwear was more... normal? "Maria, this is Sister Mora, our traveling convent Doctor. She is here to examine you and take some tests to make certain of your pregnancy...or illness, whichever condition you have," sporting a gentle, knowing smile.

Sister Mora offered her hand to Maria and joined her other hand over Maria's in a warm gesture that calmed Maria immediately. *Everything will be ok*, she thought to herself, *even if I am NOT pregnant.*

The exam was thorough, and Maria found herself completely comfortable with this stranger who had come to examine her. She was amazed at how easily she opened up her life to this woman, revealing her bitterness toward her mother and father for the circumstances she was raised in. For her mother taking her baby and keeping the truth from her for years, for the loss of her marriage from her indiscretions and lies. For the loss of her son. Maria had retreated into her own self-examination as the doctor asked her questions, completed her exam, opened the sealed pregnancy test kit she had kept in her bag, completed the test, and listened.

Doctor Mora said nothing now. She only listened as Maria concluded her story, turned her attention back to the present, and realized the resident doctor had also finished and was now just looking at her. "I am so sorry!" Maria gasped as she realized she had been spilling her guts for over an hour. "I... I didn't mean to take up all your time talking," Maria said, now feeling her face flush with embarrassment.

"Not to worry, señora, you needed that. It is therapeutic to talk, no? Sometimes, we hold in those feelings that only harm us... no one else even knows how we feel. It only hurts us... and it is not good for the child we carry, either!

Maria missed that last part of Dr. Mora's words at first. She merely nodded her head in agreement and closed her eyes, letting her words sink in. But suddenly her eyes flew open... "Wait... what did you say? What did you mean?" The questions shot out in rapid succession.

"I said, holding in our bitter feelings is not good for the baby you are carrying, my dear Mrs. Cervantes. You are going to have a baby!"

Maria just sat there, stunned into silence, not believing what she had just heard but unwilling to *not* believe it. "You mean I *am* pregnant? For real? I am going to have a...a baby?" she croaked as tears began to race down her cheeks. Sister Medina and Sister Torres reached for Maria simultaneously, laughing and crying while trying to find a part of her to hug.

Maria quickly put away her fear of being pregnant and having to face the uncertain future alone. She would continue searching for her Paulo so this new little sister... or brother, would have family for support. "I want to go to America!" Maria voiced out loud, drawing silence into the room. "I want to meet the parents of my Paulo, and perhaps they will know something about his whereabouts. And I want to meet them because we both have lost someone we love."

Dr. Mora closed the door behind her, giving Maria a list of things to do to ensure her baby would do well while growing in her stomach for the next eight months. She had advised Maria to make arrangements to have her baby in America so it could apply for dual citizenship if ever wanted.

Maria's excitement heightened as she packed her bag and began preparations to leave the convent. She had developed a love for these kind Sisters and would always be grateful to them for all they had done for her... and her family. She had the address of the Tone family in Utah, USA, and would need to start working on her travel arrangements as soon as she arrived home. With goodbyes and hugs shared with the Sisters and promises to send pictures of her baby, Maria let the big door she had come through only days before now close another chapter in her life while she began focusing on a new chapter and the days ahead.

Maria laid her head back on the headrest provided in the backseat of the cab that had been called for her. She thought about going to her mother's home first and sharing the good news... but her long-seated bitterness quickly took over and prevented her from even considering it. She would go to America, have her baby, find Paulo, and live a good life. She would need to apply for medical aid, but she knew the American healthcare system would not turn her away. She would have her baby in Utah... close to where Paulo's American parents live. Maybe she would even become an American.

Chapter Fifteen

PIRATES

Paulo never saw it coming. It was a mismatch–iron and steel against flesh. The hardened metal won easily, as Paulo only saw stars in his head before sprawling flat on the deck of Conquistador, blood spilling from his head wound and drawing swift attention from the deck boss as he knelt to check on his fallen deckhand. "Matey, are ye going to keep challenging the boom until it kills ye?" spat the big man leaning over Paulo, now applying a wet rag to the wooden deck that held the bleeding Paulo. Another hand bent down to appraise the boy's condition, tugging on his shoulder before receiving evidence Paulo was alive.

"He's ok," the skipper yelled above the roar of the sea around them, reaching the ears of about twenty men who stood in silence at their posts while awaiting the news of young Paulo's condition. He had become a favorite among the men, and they cared for him like a son, but that didn't stop them from treating him like an equal with equal responsibilities. In the twenty-three months he had been at sea with this crew, Paulo had also grown fond of his shipmates, even when they were hard on him, careful not to show him favoritism or softness. They seemed to sense that this boy had a mission in life to become someone special. They felt it when they were around him when he never let his disability become an excuse for lack of performance. Paulo began to regain consciousness and, without looking around, began flailing his arms and nearly knocked the deck boss on his back, only to be saved from embarrassment by a deckhand behind him.

"Whoa, Matey... don't ye be hitt'n at people... They might hit back," jeered the boss as he thumped Paulo on the shoulder while helping the boy to his feet. Cheers erupted from the crew, who didn't have the sense to return to work before receiving a stern rebuke. One of the men offered Paulo a cup of water while another placed a damp rag on the reddish mark on his skull.

"Ouch!" Paulo rang out, pulling off the rag and throwing it back at the well-intentioned man, causing instant laughter among the men still watching.

"Aw right, aw right men... back to work now, the fun is over!" Shot the deck boss. "Paulo, you need to be more careful," warned the ship's captain, Christofo Montague, making his way through the remaining onlookers.

"The crew needs a break, Skipper... We been at sea three weeks w'outa break," the deck boss complained. "The men..." but Captain Montague had already turned his attention elsewhere as the words from his deck boss were lost in the wind, now beginning to show some force. The bow of the El Conquistador began to disappear as each wave came at it harder and harder, eventually growing so large that the vessel was dwarfed, riding up and down the mighty swelling sea like a child's toy. There was no individual stability inside the ship unless the person was anchored in place, for the "floor" was wherever gravity and water turbulence had put it. In that state, they'd have prayed to Poseidon himself if they thought it would do any good.

There was no mercy in that November wind, no grace in the waves, only wrath and tempest. The air was thick with a briny mist, the deck awash with salty waves. The morning would either see them bobbing on calmer water or several leagues down with the fishes. Paulo prayed for the former. By the time the early morning sun' rays started to break just under the dark clouds that were beginning to lift from last night's storm, the deckhands on the El Conquistador were starting to breathe a sigh of relief, having ridden another bronco of a storm that seemed to be following their every move since their last port. Paulo had weathered them well, but with each storm, he grew increasingly impatient with himself and his circumstances.

Paulo had pledged to work as a deckhand for two years in exchange for his freedom and passage to an American port, but with the recent series of storms delaying their progress, he was growing impatient to fulfill the terms of his obligation. There were at least two ports to reach before their next scheduled dock off the coast of Florida. *At this rate, we won't reach American soil for another month or more*, complained Paulo to himself. But the life of a lowly deckhand on a merchant vessel did not leave much time for complaining, and certainly, there was no one to complain to. You did what was necessary... and everything was necessary!

"All hands on deck... CODE BLACK!!" came a cry from the lookout perch above. Code Black was a warning signal to the men to arm themselves and gather at the ship's center for instruction. The color black meant a "pirate ship" was spotted. Although the days of piracy on the open seas had been few since each country began controlling its water territories, a sailing vessel like the Conquistador was attractive prey to ruthless bands of convicts and foreigners with fast ships who saw an easy mark to take what they wanted. Captain Montague had learned the most frequented routes of the Pirates and tried to stay clear, but when such storms hit a sailing vessel as they had been plagued with lately, it was difficult not to veer off course and take days to resume their safe passage. Before the big ship could get to safety, they were spotted and now would need to defend themselves and their cargo.

"Paulo, get in the hold and stay there!" came the strict command of Captain Montague as he barked orders to his men, not stopping to explain or answer questions. But Paulo knew better than to disobey a captain's direct order, so he did as instructed despite feeling embarrassed from being ordered to withdraw from the fight he knew the rest of the crew would be facing shortly. Not that Paulo would be much help in hand-to-hand combat with a larger adult, but Paulo was smart and could use his brain to help protect himself.

Before he did as instructed by the captain, Paulo headed to the ammunition stronghold to arm himself. But he didn't count on Captain Montague working with the men passing out arms. One stern look Paulo's way told him he was fried... but then a slight upturn of the captain's mustache as Paulo reacted quickly to the offering in the captain's hand. "Do not fire this weapon unless you know you will die if you don't, Paulo. If we are overtaken, there are worse things than losing our merchandise," yelled Captain Montague over the noise of men around him in high adrenalin mode. "Now go!" With that warning and both hands clasped around the cold steel revolver, Paulo made his way around his crew members to a part of the ship the invading pirates would not likely find, feeling like a coward while his friends fought for their lives. A sudden jerk of the floor sent Paulo crashing into a solid wall and then to the floor–luckily, Paulo did not have his finger on the trigger.

We have been boarded, came an inner voice. Chills coursed through Paulo's veins as he stood up again, bracing himself but unable to walk to safety. He could not allow himself to hide from a fight like a child, no matter what consequences may follow such a move against the captain's orders. Paulo looked down at the small Smith & Wesson revolver in his hand and checked to see if he had any bullets loaded into its cylinder. He was lucky; the gun was fully loaded. Not wanting to be tossed again with a live weapon in his hand, Paulo looked for a safety of some sort–there was none!

Paulo then pulled back the hammer just a notch and found the safety... of sorts. He concluded that this would have to do before resuming his effort to climb out of the hull. What he heard next caused his knees to almost buckle. The bile in his stomach from the earlier skirmish with the iron rigging was now actively seeking an outlet.

Scuffling sounds from the deck and shots being fired stopped Paulo's progress up the stairs, causing him to instinctively duck, feeling very foolish for doing so.

Yelling and screaming and sounds of metal clanging, with frequent gunshots being fired, intensified as Paulo cautiously peeked his head out from his safe haven to only *gasp* at what he saw. Blood! Metal against metal. Man against man in mortal combat.

This was not just a robbery, Paulo thought to himself. *These men intend to take over the ship... and leave no prisoners!*

A new wave of fear hit Paulo so hard that he lost his grip on the ladder railing, sending him backward with such a jolt that there was nothing to do but fall. Luckily for him, he fell right on top of a stack of food cartons, breaking the otherwise serious connection with the ship's hull.

It took only a few seconds for Paulo to regain his bearings after the fall, and now he quickly scanned the hull's interior for provisions. That voice again. *Abandon Ship!* He needed to abandon the ship! Spotting some cheese and a small loaf of bread, which looked like it might have belonged to the cook's aide, Paulo stuffed the provisions inside his loose bandana and placed the contents inside his jacket. He picked up the revolver again and resumed his flight up to the main deck.

As Paulo cautiously made his way up the slippery steps to the cargo hold door, the drama playing above him was now in full view and almost made him freeze in place... but he knew it would only be a matter of time before he was discovered... So, with his hand gripping the small revolver in the right side pocket of his jacket, he slipped out of his protective cover and headed for the lifeboats, hoping to avoid having to use his gun to get there.

It became quickly obvious that Paulo's shipmates were outmanned, and what little resistance they offered was now wasted effort. The vessel was now under the control of the bandits, and Paulo sensed his life depended upon his next choice... to stay and fight or jump overboard and take his chances in the sea. He chose the latter. There was a small boat at the aft section of the ship that was used by his mates to do minor repairs to the exterior of the lower portion of the vessel and to remove scale build-up that can slow the ship's progress if not maintained regularly.

Paulo quickly put his plan into action and stealthily made his way aft toward the little boat's mooring. A strong hand grasped at Paulo's arm but was removed just as fast when a fellow shipmate decked the assailant with a solid punch to the jaw and yelled to Paulo to run. Paulo didn't need a second invitation but looked over his shoulder for a last appraisal of the situation... *It is only a matter of time*, he thought... and with that, he jumped into the small dingy and lowered himself as he had done hundreds of times before. Little did he know then that this dreaded activity relegated to the lowest man on the team hierarchy would, in fact, save him from further enslavement... or worse.

Lost in his thoughts Paulo was jolted back to the moment as the tiny boat hit the water with a thud. He quickly loosened the straps that held the vessel secure, took hold of each oar, and began to row, aiming for the dark side of the boat just in case he was spotted. He wasn't, but he was able to see in full view men struggling with one another, knives finding their target, and Captain Montague being secured while guns were being pointed at him... and fired!

It only took Paulo a few minutes to get his bearing from the stars above... and with all the strength he could muster, he leaned into each rowing stroke. As fast as he could row, his little boat was taking him away from this horrible scene.

Chapter Sixteen

MOBY

T he horrible scene of the ship's captain being shot, likely to death, replayed in Paulo's mind over and over again, providing plenty of fuel in the form of adrenaline to keep him rowing the tiny dinghy away from the burning ship without looking back.

An hour later, Paulo could no longer see the red and yellow glow signaling disaster upon the El Conquistador. He only hoped the US Coast Guard, who often patrolled these supposedly safe waters, would see the flames and come to investigate. Thoughts of them finding Paulo, a mere spec in these vast waters, frequently troubled him. Doubts that he would be found alive constantly assailed his mind. But there was this *voice* again that kept reminding him that failure was not an option. He must keep rowing.

Occasionally, Paulo's spirit was bolstered by brief intervals of being hopeful–with "brief" rather than "hopeful" being the operative word. Then reality would set in, and hope would once again become lost in the dark horizon before him.

Who am I kidding? Paulo thought. *I am so far away from the El Conquistador now that no one will find me. I have only a few days' provisions... and then I shall die.* But then the *voice* would insert just a glimmer of hope to be rescued with thoughts of being reunited with his American parents, causing him to continue rowing beyond his physical strength to do so, his mind becoming lost in the effort, and his intense focus taking his mind and senses off his surroundings.

The stars Paulo had focused on during the night had dimmed slowly until the sky was black. Paulo first became aware of the darkness enveloping him when he blinked, trying to clear his vision, having lost sight of the northern star, his compass. Allowing himself to drift for the first time in hours of rowing, Paulo took a small sip of the precious water he knew would have to sustain him. The sky before him was completely dark now, causing Paulo to look behind him in the direction he had come from and almost drop the jug of life when he saw lightning steaks illuminating massive forms in the sky.

STORM!!

Paulo's little dinghy boat was not large enough to withstand a fierce storm... but he looked for the first time inside the craft that might end up being his coffin to see if he might find supplies to help him ride out a storm. There was a rope! Twine... *even better!* He thought. *I may need to tie myself to the boat should things get dicey.* "Oh, yes, yes, yes, yes, yes!!" He fervently repeated out loud. There was a flare... Check – two flares! Paulo's hope of a rescue *soared* again.

It only took one look behind him to bring reality back into the boat again. But now he had hope in the form of two flares! Holding one flare in each hand, Paulo reasoned that he didn't dare use one this soon and risk being seen by the pirates who would surely kill him if he was discovered. Still, just having them improved his chances of rescue–also raising his spirits. He would just have to rely on faith to get him through. *Faith? Where did that come from?* Paulo wondered. Religion had not ever been a part of his make-up, despite the Sisterhood's efforts to convert him. He was still carrying such bitterness toward his birth mother... and that rancor had not lessened one bit despite the passage of sixteen years spent amongst those who prayed for him, even voicing their concern over his unwillingness to let go of what he could not change.

At the moment, however, Paulo felt fear start to well up inside him as he dared look over his shoulder as he rowed, alert to the streaks of light that penetrated the horizon and revealed those mountain-sized black shadows Paulo had seen before when he was protected by a large sea-worthy vessel capable of withstanding even the fiercest of storms. But this dinghy craft offered him no protection whatsoever, but it was light and would not sink, or so he had been told. *Have faith, Paulo.* There it was again.

Paulo unwound the heavy twine and secured one end through the metal eyelet on one side of the boat, slid the other to the opposite side, and wound the rest around his waist, using a seaman's knot he learned from his mates called the "Anchor Hitch," that would secure cargo much heavier than Paulo weighed. The knot could easily be released in case of an emergency. But He hoped the storm wouldn't get bad enough to overturn the boat, causing him to detach from his only source of protection against the elements and eventually die as his body gave out from trying to stay afloat, sealing his fate to become one with the sea and join his dead shipmates in Davy Jones locker.

Faith. There was that word again. *Why now, after all these years, am I thinking about faith?* Paulo mused. *What did Sister Morales say? Faith is a belief in that which was true but unseen. God is unseen, but some say His hand is in our lives...*

A distant sound jerked Paulo out of his thoughts. This was no time to lose sight of what was about to fall upon him, faith or no faith. He was in a boat alone, and it would be up to him to survive. And he did want to survive. The intermittent lightning flashes began to grow more intense as the storm continued to play catch-up with Paulo's small vessel, causing the tiny craft to follow the waves up and then down into their deep troughs after cresting them. Then, there was always another wave to climb steeply to its apex and down again. The risk of capsizing was foremost in his mind, and it was terrifying.

Paulo started to feel nauseous from the roller-coaster ride... but managed to hold his own as he prepared for the next assault... and the next, seemingly endless. The storm became his entire world; it would last forever and certainly outlast him. He hadn't fallen into a state of despair, but that was mostly because he was so busy trying to stay inside the boat, struggling to keep the bow pointed ahead of the storm as he did his best to row. Then, unexpectedly, on one of the return rides back up a small hill-sized wave, Paulo caught sight of several yellow lights just above the horizon. *A ship!* Paulo gasped.

And then it was gone.

"I know I saw lights," Paulo said out loud as he prepared for another coaster ride down into the watery valley and back up again... the waves gaining steam with each crescendo. As best he could, Paulo strained his eyes to catch a glimpse of the horizon before it disappeared again. He wondered whether he should shoot off one of his precious flares and risk alerting the pirate ship instead of a friendly one. But when his ride reached the apex of a large wave, Paulo could no longer see the ship's lights, causing him to release his hold on the flare gun. Something inside him caused Paulo to feel uneasy about using a flare. The risk was greater than the potential reward.

The distant light show that had grabbed Paulo's attention earlier was now close enough for him to see all too clearly the multicolored rays illuminating both sea and sky. Blackness filled the air until it penetrated with explosions of light that, until now, had seemed soundless due to the distance between Paulo and the storm. However, now, with each burst of light, there was an almost immediate explosion of thunder–followed by still another flash of lightning, each one adding to the other, causing Paulo's blood to freeze with fright as the explosions seemed to be striking within feet of the small metal craft. He had been overtaken!

Paulo grabbed one of the ends of the strap that tightened the life jacket he wore, feeling somehow less exposed with the vest tightened around him. Strangely, a mental picture came into his mind of Annette Tone holding him tightly with both arms as she whispered "I love you, Paulo," into his ear after the adoption papers were signed and he became their legal son. He hugged himself with both arms until the sinking feeling of the boat's quick descent caused him to regain his hold on the lifeline that provided him support. Rain now beat heavily on his face as he struggled to see into the black abyss that held him captive. Paulo did not want to die. He had so much to live for. His resolve took on new determination as he firmed up his hold and prepared for yet another plummet on the downside of a huge wave, down, down into blackness.

"Please, God, I have come this far not to die a lonely death. If you are there, God... now would be a great time to show me something!" Another wave washed over Paulo as he held on to his only means of survival. That in itself was a blessing, but Paulo could not yet see it as such. In fact, the storm that raged upon him was a blessing sent from God to preserve him, not end his life, for the lights he saw earlier were indeed those of a ship–the same pirate ship that took his sea family down was headed on the same course as Paulo, but it had been blown off its intended course, somewhat, by the heavy winds, rain, and severe lightening, that sent the pirate crew below the deck to their berths to wait out the storm, unable to see the tiny vessel and its single passenger that was headed in the same direction.

Somehow, the emotion of the night had consumed Paulo enough to drag him into unconsciousness, and he slept, unaware of the presence of unseen hands that kept him secured to the boat during the remainder of the storm.

Hours later, the little barge floated aimlessly like a piece of driftwood, foreign to its host, the sea... but alive and moving, nonetheless, grateful to have escaped the searing shrapnel from lightening bolts aimed at the sea and able to have protected its precious cargo to live another day. What's this? One eye fluttered open... then the other, sending mixed signals to the awakening cargo... *Am I alive or dead?* The thought began to form in Paulo's mind, still feeling the effects of being waterlogged for hours and hours. And now, the heat of the morning sun lit upon his face, telling him he was– a l i v e. – *"How,"* was the first question that popped into Paulo's mind upon realizing he was still alive. *"How did I survive?"* He wondered.

Raising himself up enough to see over the side of the craft, Paulo surveyed his surroundings, cautious to keep his head low enough in case he was not alone–but he was very much alone. Grateful to be alive, Paulo strained his eyes to the horizon surrounding him, but nothing but more blue sky and water. The sun was about a third of the way up for the day, causing Paulo's stomach to acknowledge that he had missed breakfast. He had come to enjoy breakfast on the ship after a couple of hours of early morning deck swabbing. But now, as he surveyed the squashed bread and chunks of dried meat he had hurriedly stuffed into his jacket before going overboard, he offered a silent prayer of thanks.

What is it with the thoughts of God and prayer? Paulo questioned himself as he opened the wrapping over the bread to find it surprisingly dry, considering his lengthy bath last night. A quick bite, followed by a chunk of meat, gave Paulo a sense of satisfaction and peace he had not felt in some time. *All would be well*, came an impression into his mind... causing a hint of a smile to Paulo's swollen lips and cheeks. He was beginning to enjoy the strange sense of reassurance from his pleas to God.

"He *did* deliver, didn't He?" Paulo answered, out loud, to his own question.

With two oars still strapped securely to the small barge, Paulo knew he must find shelter, or he would soon die out here on the open sea, so after another quick drink, he once again surveyed his surroundings and movement of the sun from a few minutes ago and with a direction in mind started rowing.

The afternoon passed quickly as Paulo got into the rhythm of the oars slicing through the calm sea, raising one oar and then another and then both in synch, pushing him forward to an unseen destination. *So this is what faith is like?* Paulo considered, occupying his mind while rowing. Working toward a goal that is worthwhile yet unseen? Believing in an unseen higher Power Who requires commitment and change of mortal nature in exchange for... Protection? Peace? Comfort?

"But the Comforter, which is the Holy Ghost, whom the Father will send in my name, he shall teach you all things, and bring all things to your remembrance, whatsoever I have said unto you," John 14:26

As Paulo lost himself in thoughts of his upbringing and those who had played an integral part in his life, he did not notice the large dorsal fin that had taken up position on the aft side of the boat, staying just beyond Paulo's range of vision. Sharks were plentiful in these waters, but Paulo had been taught by those who made their living on the seas to respect and not fear these warriors of the sea. A splash behind him jerked Paulo out of his trance as water drained from the cloudless blue sky onto Paulo's neck and shoulders. Turning quickly to his right... Nothing! And then, to his left.... a blue figure of a dolphin had raised its head and was in position acting like it was about to board the boat.

"Well, hello there!" Paulo welcomed, with a hint of what music remained in his voice. "Have you been sent from God to guide me to safety?" *Where did 'that' come from?* Paulo asked himself. As if the big fish understood Paulo's words... and thoughts, he brought himself upright out of the water and began dancing excitedly... or so it looked like dancing to Paulo. Racing to the bow of the craft, the beautifully colored fish acted in a way that Paulo interpreted to mean, *follow me!* But rather than follow those silly impressions that God had sent a fish to lead him to safety, Paulo stopped rowing and watched the big fish carry on without him.

I thought so, reasoned Paulo to himself. "You are nothing but a curious, playful, blue denizen of the sea!" he barked to the retreating figure. But Paulo's scolding words seemed to have no effect on his new companion, as the fish doubled back and rose excitedly out of the water again and danced ahead of Paulo as if again saying, *follow me!* So, without thinking much about it, Paulo once again grabbed the two oars and began rowing toward the fish, who now swam ahead, only looking back occasionally to assure itself that its charge was indeed still following.

Paulo had been rowing steadily for about two hours, and his muscles were complaining. Besides, all this energy output had caused his stomach also to complain... "Hey, uh, whatever your name is! Moby!! That's it, Moby! Or maybe Babe, as in the blue ox?" Paulo tossed this around while the fish-like mammal doubled back and began taunting him again with loud shrieks or whatever language it used. Paulo laughed to himself... "No, I think Moby works just fine for you, my big friend. Moby the Explorer!

Paulo pulled out another small chunk of dried beef and mixed it with a bite of bread and then a small swig from the water jug that was beginning to feel lighter... sending a chill of reality coursing through his veins and putting an end to the brief fun he was having. Moby had started moving forward, giving Paulo a sense of direction as he fixed his eyes on the dorsal fin ahead of him and again focused his energy on the task at hand–Survival.

The sun was now at its apex and dumping its rays upon Paulo with little mercy, except for the occasional stray cloud that drifted by, offering Paulo a brief reprieve. But the nights were such a pleasant change that Paulo found that he was much more suited to travel under the cloak of darkness and ceiling full of stars, with the northern star for his bearing, than sunny days with nothing to look at except that crazy fish who would not leave his side.

Paulo began a routine to preserve his strength and maximize his rowing capacity. His only hope of survival was to reach land, and by his earlier calculations, the port his ship was seeking was a three-day sail, or more like a week at sea for Paulo, even with a good current. And, of course, without a compass, he could miss his target and be lost at sea before he could recalculate his error. And he would die a lonely death, never having reached his potential as a human being.

But Paulo had Moby now... Moby! A gasp exploded from Paulo as he realized he had lost sight of Moby. Did the big fish find something that attracted him away? "Moby... where are you?" Paulo called out... only to be swallowed by the vast water space before him. "Where aa..are you?" Paulo sputtered, not noticing how quickly tears came, his eyes searching frantically across the horizon... coming up with nothing but emptiness. "Moby...! Moby...! Don't leave me now, Moby! Don't..."

Before Paulo could finish his sentence, a flash of light burst across his field of vision, almost knocking him out of his boat. And then it disappeared. "Moby! Was that you?" cried Paulo, now looking frantically toward the white splash he had just witnessed. Nothing but disappearing bubbles remained of the giant flash that had startled Paulo into almost falling overboard. Then, all was calm again.

Paulo waited, holding his breath to hopefully see his new friend again, but nothing came of it. The sea was again calm as the red sun descended into the horizon. Paulo knew he had to find land soon as his provisions would soon run out, and he would die of starvation, if not from exposure to the elements first... or in the jaws of some monster of the sea. And with the mention of a monster of the sea, a cold chill ran up Paulo's spine, sending goose pimples all up and down his arms and neck.

This is not a good sign, Paulo mused, looking carefully in all directions. And with both blistered hands back on the oars, Paulo pointed his craft toward the southern horizon and rowed until what seemed like hours had passed since Paulo had taken a break... but a quick look at his watch told him it had only been about 45 minutes. The sun had firmly set in for the night now, and the sea was as calm as he had ever seen it... *Almost like glass,* he described to himself.

Then he saw it! A figure on the horizon protruded up above the flat angle of the water, creating an illusion of a giant fin coursing through the water toward him. Another look woke Paulo from the illusion into stark reality... It was a fin! And he supposed that what remained underwater would reveal a monster shark!!! Paulo quickly removed both oars from their support and placed them into the boat. He could not lose his only means of survival, no matter what. And he hoped silently that the huge beast would not notice him, as his eyes locked onto the fin now appearing much closer as if projecting directly at Paulo.

Paulo thought about turning away from the intruder, but he knew his craft would be no match for this killer should it decide it wanted a boat for dinner... with whatever was in it as the main course. Paulo could do nothing but wait... And pray! *There it was again*, Paulo thought. Another invitation to pray. This time, he would follow the impression.

"Dear God in Heaven... if you can hear me, I really need Your help right now, so do you think you could make this shark or whatever it is bearing down on me go away? Or make me invisible? Or something?" There was no answer to Paulo's prayer as he watched in silence, helpless to do anything but... pray! And he did just that– again. Within minutes, the figure was now close enough for Paulo to unmistakably identify the shape and color of an enormous white shark, rarely seen in these waters, but here he was, and Paulo was about to meet him head-on, as neither form changed course as they neared an inevitable collision.

Paulo sat frozen in place, unable to do anything, say anything... He just sat and watched as his vocal cords constricted and tried to let out a yell, but nothing but dry heaves came out, leaving Paulo with his mouth open just before the big white took its first bite! What little daylight there was left was soon swallowed up by the huge form hurdling itself toward Paulo's boat until its mouth opened and revealed a bank of glittering white teeth... and then unexpectedly, "SLAM!" a blue projectile came out of nowhere and slammed itself into the side of the shark... followed by another, then another. Three forms in all pasted themselves onto the side of the attacking shark, causing it to lose focus on Paulo and reel instead in defense against the interfering blue warriors.

Paulo could not believe his eyes... "Moby? Three of you?" cried Paulo as he watched a scene unfold before him that would defy description. Three smaller blue dolphins had lured the big fish away, and now they were making sport of it as if the lumbering shark could not focus on them. Time after time, the smaller dolphins rammed into the monster shark until it had had enough... and swam away. The follow-up scene left Paulo even more shaken... but in a good way, as the three saviors lined up next to one another... almost shoulder to shoulder and in unison, they performed what Paulo would later describe as a dolphin "happy-dance," practically begging for a treat after a job well done.

Moby and his friends had saved his life, Paulo was certain of that. But why? And as if on cue, the three amigos back-flipped in a most amazing acrobatic display of agility and form, which caused Paulo to cheer and yell appreciation at the retreating forms as tears began to flood over his eyelids, down both cheeks and onto the floor of the boat. With both hands over his face, Paulo prayed. He prayed so long and so deeply that as the emotion of almost dying crushed over him, and the lack of sufficient nourishment drew out what little energy he had left... Paulo lay down, and without restraint, he slept.

Chapter Seventeen

RESCUE

L ight hit Paulo's face like a bolt of lightning, causing a disorientation of where he was and how long he had slept. But this light blinded him as he tried to shield his eyes against its penetrating rays, biting into his skull.

"Ahoy there!" came a loud, booming voice somewhere amongst the invading light.

"*God? Is this God speaking to me? Has He come to answer my prayer in person?*" Paulo questioned as he tried to make sense of what was happening.

"Ahoy in the boat!" Again, a thunderous voice spoke, now bringing Paulo up on one elbow to try and see through the curtain of light.

"Whwh.. Who are you?" Paulo managed to say, almost too weak now to speak above the roar of an engine. *Engine! I hear an engine!* Paulo said to himself. *This is not God... but maybe God sent them to save me*, he reflected. Just at that moment, the light diminished enough for Paulo to see the faint outline of a large boat... no, a cruiser... and the words USCG inscribed on the hull of the big craft now floating next to him.

"Grab the line we will throw to you and pull yourself to the side of the boat and climb up the ladder," came the next instruction. Paulo tried to move but found his legs unable to support his weight after several days on the water alone. But with encouragement coming from those above him, Paulo took hold of the line thrown to him and began to pull himself to his feet and up to the side of the boat. The heavy drag of the Coast Guard engine drowned out the voices from above shouting instructions to Paulo, who began to succumb to the weariness of his ordeal.

A man dressed in a wet suit yelled something to Paulo just before jumping into the swirling ocean and disappearing within the blackness below. Paulo kept hold of the support line and waited for the man to surface. A hand reached out of the water and grabbed the side of the dinghy, followed by a head and body.

"Let's get you aboard!" offered the rescuer. "How in the world did you get out here?" He continued.

"Pirates!" Paulo managed to get out. "Ship overtaken by pirates! All killed but me," Paulo added. "How did you find me?"

"You won't believe this... but a trio of dolphins intercepted our ship and raised such a ruckus that we stopped to watch. They kept walking across the water like a trio of dancers and had our entire crew out, taking pictures and clapping for them. We had never seen anything like it. They would go out a ways, and then it seemed like they would stop, return to the stern, and act up again. It was midshipman Nichols who said, 'They want us to follow them!' We all looked at him like he was crazy... but then they did it again, and we all said in unison... 'Follow them!' And then we saw this tiny blip on the radar that grew larger as we got closer. It was you," he said. "Those dolphins led us right here to you!" the rescuer now said with growing emotion in his voice.

"Hurry up down there!" came an urgent voice from above, causing the rescuer to snap out of his trance, reliving what seemed an improbable rescue.

"Let's go, kid..." as he fitted Paulo with a harness around his waist and secured it tightly before yelling into the air, "Hoist away!" Paulo was pulled out of his craft into the air in a flash, leaving the rescuer to check for any belongings left behind. What he found caused him to gasp. Under the only bench in the boat lay an empty jug and a white sack with what amounted to a bite-sized chunk of bread left uneaten. "How in the...?" the man uttered as he took one more look, secured his mask, and jumped backward into the frigid water–without a splash.

Paulo was met with several hands to help secure his arrival. Questions started flying almost immediately from the seamen until a large man sporting a row of gold braids on his cap appeared, causing the men surrounding Paulo to step to attention while making an opening for the ship's commander to enter.

"At ease!" snapped the tall, slender man sporting a grin. "What have we here?" the commander said, more as a declaration of surprise than a question. "You're just a boy!" he finished. "What is your name, boy? Do you speak English?" Paulo was almost too weak to answer, so he just nodded in agreement, then offered a very feeble reply...

"Paulo," he managed to utter.

"Commander!" came a voice from behind the men attending to Paulo. "The lad had no water left... and a mere morsel of bread. I've no idea how long he has been out there alone... but I would wager more than three days.

"Seven," came a weak reply. Been without water for two days. Bread... shared with the Dolphins!" A gasp of surprise burst from those closest to Paulo and could hear his weak reply, passing on the unbelievable news to those on the outer fringe.

"Well, that was a generous but stupid thing to do, my boy!" Exclaimed the commander. "But it probably saved your life. If it hadn't been for your Dolphin friends, we would never have paid any attention to the small blip on the radar they were leading us to."

"Aye matey...'twas those Dolphins who kicked up such a stir that alerted us to follow them," offered one of the men.

"They led us right to you!" came another.

Tears began to flow down Paulo's cheeks as the emotion of being rescued and now hearing how he was found totally broke the dam of what little resistance he had left. "Moby! It was Moby the blue dolphin and his friends," Paulo explained, expending what energy he had remaining to explain the miracle. He had been saved from sure death twice by these protectors of the sea... and by God, he heard himself say!

Paulo was wrapped in a thick blanket and given a small cup of water to drink. "Ease it in, mate, or it will come out faster than it went in!" offered one of the men attending Paulo. Another offered some warm broth with the same caution. Paulo was hesitant to close his eyes for fear this was all a dream, yet he savored the warmth of broth as it made its way to his empty stomach. *If this is a dream, may I never wake up!* He exclaimed to himself, fearing he was delusional and would soon open his eyes to the endless blue, watery grave from which he had spent the past seven days.

"More, please!" came a weak pleading, almost lost in the vast nothingness he was feeling.

"Here is another cup full, but take it easy," another voice said, placing the cup of warm liquid into Paulo's shaking hands, which he immediately raised to his mouth for another sip while his eyes finally closed, admitting to himself that this was indeed a dream, but one that came true. After finishing his second cup of broth, the commander gave orders to help Paulo to a bunk below where he could warm up and get some needed rest. He would question Paulo later. But for now, he needed to recover.

Paulo felt he was moving; *probably a storm coming in*, he thought, still not fully comprehending he had been rescued. Yet, a warmth came over him, and a sense of well-being followed. *So, if this is what death feels like... it isn't so bad,* Paulo thought to himself—and then there was blackness... until the dreams came—arms reached out to grab Paulo. He was running, searching for a place to hide, but there was nothing but white light around him. He felt totally exposed. His heart beat so loud that Paulo covered his ears, fearing whoever was chasing him would hear it. Two faces appeared. Paulo strained to see them, to recognize who they were. The woman was crying... Paulo recognized her immediately. Annette Tone! His adoptive Mother... and Richard Tone was holding his wife in the act of consoling her. They were crying for him!

Paulo cried out, "Mother Tone! I am alive! I am here!" he yelled, to no avail. No one could hear him. Hands were on him now. It was over. He would never see them again.

"Paulo! Young man, wake up! You are having a bad dream," came the voice behind the arms. Paulo's eyes flew open, and he stared right into the large brown eyes of Commander Hector Meade, who had his arms securely attached to both of Paulo's shoulders, trying to secure him without being punched in the process. Paulo had added some bulk to his frame during the two years at sea, and as a couple of the deckhands on his ship would attest, he does pack a punch.

"I, I'm sorry, sir... I must have been dreaming," explained Paulo, still a bit fuzzy in his head.

"That's ok, son... You sounded like you were lost and were calling out to, uh... someone."

"I have been lost," Paulo responded. "Actually, I was abandoned at birt h... raised in a Catholic convent until I was adopted by an American family a few years ago. But I was kidnapped on our way to America and forced into child labor for over a year before I... uh, before I was let go. I joined the El Conquistador as a deckmate two years ago in exchange for passage to America. We never made it. Pirates boarded our ship, and most of the crew, if not all, were killed trying to defend themselves and protect our cargo. I was down in the hold when they first boarded, and the shooting started. I stuck my head out, and what I saw convinced me there would be no survivors, so I grabbed some bread and a jug of water and made my way aft, where the dinghy was tied, threw myself in, and quickly lowered the boat into the water. I thought for certain I had been seen, as one of the pirates looked below and began preparing his gun to fire... but before he could get a shot off, one of ours hit him from behind, then giving me the signal to get away... which I did."

The commander did not say a word but only sat there, listening, as if he was mesmerized by Paulo's story of survival. "You were let go from a child labor ring?" Was the only thing the commander asked, somewhat incredulously. "No one is let go from those filthy snares until they are good and through with you, and then they sell what's left of you to work the streets as thieves and prostitutes."

Paulo thought about how or if he should answer the question more than he already had and decided to tell the truth to this man who had seemed so interested. "I set fire to the shop!" Paulo confessed. "During the confusion, I made my way to a farm where I took employment working the fields–until someone turned me in. I escaped again when the authorities raided our fields. A friend helped me find the El Conquistador, and I was hired to work the decks for two years. We were headed to port, where I would be let off to find my parents."

"Where do your parents live?" questioned the commander, now drawn into Paulo's story.

"Utah!" was the reply.

"Are they Mormon?" asked Commander Meade, now with raised eyebrows.

Paulo looked confused... before answering, "They are American!" which brought a wail of laughter from the commander.

"You don't even know what you got yourself into, do you, boy?"

Paulo blushed now, not knowing how to respond... but feeling anger starting to replace his embarrassment. "What do you mean, sir? My parents are wonderful people. I do not know what is... a Mormon? A knock on the cabin door caused both men to jump in surprise, breaking apart the heaviness that had settled in from the topic of discussion.

"Excuse me, Commander, sir. Do you still want to send word to the base that we picked up a refugee? Customs will want to be notified," asked the tall seaman standing at attention in the doorway.

Commander Meade didn't respond immediately as if giving it some thought before answering, "No! Do not notify base or customs at this point. I want to handle this myself," shot back the commander's reply, dismissing the seaman, who saluted again and took one step backward... and closed the door.

"Paulo, do you have any idea where your ship was located when the pirates hit it?" asked the commander. "We have been patrolling these waters for the last week on a tip that a rogue group of mercenaries were taking down merchant ships like butter on hot bread. Do you remember any significant landmarks or coordinates?"

Paulo explained about the storm that had saved him from certain capture and diverted the pirate ship to a different course. Paulo thought about what the plan was... He remembered the trawler was about three days from port, but he couldn't recall seeing anything but water from horizon to horizon. "For a brief time, I could see the pirate ship bearing down on me as if they knew exactly where I was. But then the storm came... and I saw them no more," Paulo recalled. "I was rowing south, hoping to reach port before my food or water ran out. I lasted seven days from when I first entered the water. And was about to give up... wh, when you found me." Paulo felt tears weld up in his eyes as he recalled his narrow escape from death. He was so close.

"Paulo, do you happen to have any identification on you that could substantiate your story? A passport, birth certificate, adoption papers?" asked the commander.

"As I told you, sir, I was kidnapped within feet of my adopted mother when I went to the restroom in the airplane terminal. I was grabbed from behind and had nothing with me but the clothes on my back. Mrs. Tone had everything."

"Well then, do you know which town in Utah they live in? Utah is a pretty big state with lots of small towns in it. Chances of finding them in a phone book would take a modern miracle. Like looking for a needle in a haystack!" the commander concluded. "Paulo, if I turn you over to the customs people, they will ship you back to Guatemala rather than keep you here. What was the plan of the boat people you were working for? Were they just going to drop you off in the water and let you swim ashore somewhere?"

Paulo felt the air escape from his chest as the pangs of defeat started to flush through him. He had come so far...so close, to now be sent back to what? Prison?

"I was given false identification papers," Paulo said with what little breath he had left.

Commander Meade's head snapped up at this revelation. "Where are they?" he questioned, now more interested than ever, hoping there might be a way to help this young man.

"I don't know... probably back at the boat. I didn't have much time to think about such things when the pirates hit us without warning," Paulo admitted.

"I understand, Paulo. Those things happen, and you certainly were not expecting to be drifting at sea in a dinghy. We'll think of something," A short rap at the door brought another young seaman carrying a tray of food.

"Excuse me, commander, but the men thought the young lad might be up for some real food now. That broth won't go far to give him enough strength to recover from what he's been through. Oh, and here are his belongings. Thought he might want the sack and jug as keepsakes," the sailor said, in almost a reverent tone.

As Paulo accepted the food tray, his eyes were drawn instead to an envelope wrapped in familiar faded plastic, his hands shaking as he reached for the envelope instead of the fruit and sandwich on the tray.

"The diver who secured you to the harness found this pouch stuck under the seat in the boat, along with the empty water jug and cloth sack of bread," answered the seaman as Paulo took the pouch and carefully inspected it while the blood in his face drained out, leaving his face an ashen white. Paulo's voice now started to tremble, which caused the commander to become alarmed and reach for a pillow for Paulo to lay back on, giving him support while he tried to gain control of his faculties.

"Paulo, are you ok?" questioned Commander Meade while holding the pillow against Paulo's back. "You look like you have seen a ghost!"

Paulo carefully opened the pouch and dried its contents with his napkin before handing them to the commander. "These are my papers!" Paulo said. "These are my false identification papers given to me by those who helped me escape on the El Conquistador! The papers that were left in my bunk!"

The silence that filled the room could have been sliced with a knife it was so thick. Not a word was spoken as Paulo just held out the papers to Commander Meade, who just sat there looking at them and then at Paulo and back again at these precious papers, without a word spoken.

"Will that be all, Commander, sir?" asked the seaman as he stood at attention while awaiting dismissal. "Yes," came the reply after a moment's hesitation. Commander Meade now held the missing documents in his hand and dared to examine them, looking first at the damp passport with a photo bearing a fair resemblance to his guest. The other document, a faded birth certificate, bore the name of Roberto Quinteros Jr.

"Ok, Roberto Quinteros Jr., welcome to America!"

Chapter Eighteen

THE CALL

"Hello, this is the Tone residence, Michael speaking," came the husky voice of 18-year-old Michael Tone, the oldest son of Richard and Annette Tone of Eden, Utah, a small suburb outside Salt Lake City, Utah.

"Hello... I would like to speak with Mrs. Annette Tone, please," came the shaky female voice on the other end of the line.

"I am sorry, she is not here. May I take a message, please?" The female caller did not wish to leave a message and promptly hung up, saying only... "I will call again."

Disappointed, Maria Cervantes hung up the phone that had connected her with the family who had adopted her son... and she would not speak to anyone but the woman who loved her son enough to want him as her own. She would call again, maybe later next time.

The back door opened and slammed shut, causing Michael Tone to cross the large living room floor and greet the three figures coming in from the garage, each carrying a brightly wrapped package that they quickly placed under the tree.

"It's about time! Did you guys bring anything home for dinner? I'm famished, and there isn't a thing in the fridge to eat! What's in the packages?" asked Michael, playing the part of a spoiled teenager to tease his parents... but frankly, spoiled he wasn't. The oldest of the Tone children had been so easy to raise as a first child that the Tones always kidded that he was born an adult into a child's body.

"Oh, someone called for you, mom. She didn't leave her name," Michael shouted over his shoulder as he ascended the stairs to his room. "I have mission prep class in thirty minutes," he added.

Annette Tone hurried to sort out the groceries and began preparing a sandwich for Michael to hold him over until dinner. She loved her son and did her best to spoil him, but he always took it in stride and remained very focused and humble. He seemed to know what he wanted from life as early as Annette could remember... and he has not allowed himself, or anyone else for that matter, to stand in his way. He stated early on that he would graduate high school with honors, graduate from church seminary after four years of attendance, attend one semester of college while waiting for his mission call to serve the Lord for two years somewhere in the world, and return home after his mission to finish college. Although Michael was a good-looking young man, standing 6′ 2″ tall, with sandy blond hair and blue eyes, just like his father, he had not dated any particular girl during his high school years, although his next-door neighbor, Torey McDonald, and Michael, had been fast friends ever since the McDonalds moved in five years ago.

"Hey, Mom, do you still have the car keys?" Michael shouted to the floor below him... as he bounded down the stairs two at a time, eyes searching for his mom's purse.

"I put them on the key rack in the hall, just like I always do!" responded Annette, playfully knowing that would get a rise from Michael.

"Sure! Just like you always do!" Michael chortled while fishing through his mother's purse for the keys. "Here they are... right where you said they would be, he laughed good-naturedly. And with keys firmly in hand, young Michael Richard Tone drove out of the garage and onto the icy road, only a couple miles from the meetinghouse where he met weekly for instruction on serving a mission for his church, The Church of Jesus Christ of Latter-day Saints. But Michael's legacy would change the very instant he

pulled out into the busy intersection. Thirty minutes after Michael left
with the car, Annette's cell phone rang. It was neighbor and fellow church
member Janet Faraway calling to alert Annette to the horrible scene she
had just seen up the street.

"Annette, is your van still at your house?" her voice sounding as if it was
under forced control. Annette paused before answering, remembering that
Michael had taken the van only minutes before.

"Uh, yes... I mean, no. Michael took it to mission prep a few minutes
ago. Why do you ask, Janie?" Air escaped from the caller's voice as she tried
to remain calm...

"Is Richard home, Annie?"

"Janie, you are scaring me! Why do you want to know if our van is here?
Has something happened to Richard?" Then, a thought pressed through
her mind that Michael had the van... now etched into her consciousness.
"Michael!" she screamed into the small smartphone. "Michael has the van,
Janie! Is there something wrong?" Fear smashing its way into her heart,
pushing aside the joy she had felt only minutes ago.

"There was an accident at the Hastings Road intersection, Annie. It
looked like one of the vehicles might have been your van. I don't know
for certain. The police and an ambulance had traffic rerouted, so I pulled
off the road to call you. I am heading your way now... Just be calm, Annie.
I don't know anything for certain. Maybe you should try Michael's cell
phone? Well, it's probably on silent anyway. Please send him a text. See you
in two." And without waiting for a response, Janet hung up and pulled
back onto the road, now filled with slow-moving vehicles.

Annette hit the red "End" on her phone and immediately pressed the
number 2. She held it long enough to connect to her husband's cell phone,
anxiously waiting for Richard to answer while looking outside for her
neighbor Janet's Toyota Forerunner. Richard picked up, and Janie arrived
at the same time.

"Richard, I am headed out the door to an accident that just happened
out on Hastings Road. Janie Faraway saw the accident and called me. She

says it looked like our van." There was a pause on the other end of the line as Annette opened the car door to see Janie's worried face before buckling up just in time to let her head relax into the soft leather seat as she now realized that Richard had not said anything in response to her call.

"Richard, are you still there?" Annette called out. "Yes, I'm here! Just waiting for you to get to the accident so you can see if it is our van," Richard offered hesitantly, not wanting to expose the fact that his heart was pounding loudly in fear of hearing the worst. Annette put the phone in her lap and closed her eyes to address her Heavenly Father in prayer, asking that her son be safe and would somehow be sitting with the other young men preparing for their missions. It was not to be.

Annette's hand involuntarily went to her mouth to stifle the scream that could not be silenced as Janet carefully descended the small hill that led to the accident scene below her, revealing the broken van that her son had been driving only minutes before. Richard was yelling her name, but Annette was stunned into silence now as Janet tried to find a place to park. The intersection was already secured, and cars were being routed away from the scene, but Janet was not about to leave her friend alone to face what appeared to be a serious accident involving her son.

Richard had already left work and started on the twenty-minute drive from his office to home, even before he heard his wife scream. He would arrive in less than ten minutes, but not before Annette had to face whatever lay before them alone.

Annette was first to exit the car almost before Janet could put it in Park, leaving her friend to catch up, slip her arm through Annette's, and hold tightly, offering physical and moral support against what may lie ahead. A policeman wearing a bright orange traffic vest saw the two women approaching fast and did not hesitate to raise his large hand to indicate to Annette and Janet that they should stop and not try to get past him. But Annette's sense of protecting her cub would have none of that as she pushed Janet into the waiting arms of the policeman and darted around him. Two paramedics were loading what appeared to be an injured person into the back of the ambulance. Annette reached them just as the two medics finished securing their patient and turned to see a wide-eyed woman about to jump through the opened doors.

"Hold on, lady, you can't go up there!" cried the medic closest to Annette, reaching out to grab her arm just in time to intercept her leap through the closing doors.

"My son!" Annette cried out, trying to get to the now-closed doors of the ambulance. "I am his mother!" she continued unable to make any progress through the big man restraining her. "I am sorry, mam, but you are not our patient's mother," said her captor, firmly. That is unless you are older than you look... Mr... uh, our patient is sixty years old," now commanding Annette's full attention.

"Sixty years old? Then... where is the driver of the van?" Annette asked while diverting her gaze back to the two crushed vehicles."

"The young man driving the van was put into the first ambulance," came a female voice from the second paramedic who had been listening to the exchange between her partner and Annette Tone. "He was badly hurt, and we needed to get him into surgery right away," she confided to Annette. "I am so sorry, but we must get going, Wil."

"Where did they take him? Where did they take my son?" Annette pleaded before the paramedics could drive away. "Salt Lake Regional," came the reply. And with that, the engine started as the siren began to wail, leaving Janet holding onto Annette as she felt her body begin to go limp.

"Annette!" came a frantic voice from behind the two women.

"Richard! Oh, Richard! they have taken Michael by ambulance to Salt Lake Regional!" Annette cried out as Richard took her into his arms. "We need to go quickly!"

Salt Lake Regional Hospital came into view as soon as Richard's sedan rounded the corner a block away. Annette guided Richard toward the lighted sign that read– Emergency–and spotted the two ambulances parked under the canopy in front of the entry doors. "There!" Annette pointed to an empty parking space and had her hand on the door latch before Richard could put the transmission in park.

"Annette, wait a moment before you storm in there," Richard spoke softly and as controlled as he could given the circumstances. "I think we should pray for strength before we go in there to face whatever may have happened to our son."

Annette's hand slipped off the door handle... and grasped Richards as her head bowed and eyes closed tightly as if to block out the reality of where they were and why. But a feeling of peace inched its way into her heart as she listened to her husband's words of appeal and pleading to an unseen God... who was not just a God, but also a loving Heavenly Father who was just as concerned about Michaels's condition as they were, maybe more so since He knew and loved Michael before they did.

After a moment of peace between husband and wife, a look of encouragement passed between them, and almost as if orchestrated, they both grabbed their respective door and opened it. Both doors opened simultaneously as Richard and Annette Tone left the familiar world they knew and crossed the threshold into the unfamiliar world of a major hospital system. They were not prepared for the scene that greeted them, nor for how raw their nerves were in fearful anticipation of learning how seriously their son was injured. Babies were crying; one man was holding a compress on his head that had bled through and was running down his arm, and another slumped in a wheelchair supported by a loved one rubbing her head.

"May I help you?" came a voice through the daze that had temporarily blinded the Tones as they stood surveying the scene before them.

"Oh, I'm sorry," Annette was first to respond to the pretty nurse sitting behind the counter at the check-in desk. "Our son was involved in a traffic accident, and I believe he was taken here by one of the ambulances parked out front." Annette noticed immediately the change in countenance from impatient demeanor to... what? Pity?

"Our son's name is Michael Tone," Richard broke in, noticing Annette's sudden hesitation as he quickly took hold of her hand and held on. "Is he alright? Can we see him?" Richard continued.

"Mr. and Mrs. Tone... let me see if Dr. Tahir is available to speak with you," offered the front desk nurse before she turned her back on the Tones and made a dash through the closing door to the ER patient area, leaving the Tones in shock at her abrupt departure. Seconds later, the door opened again, and a short man in light blue scrubs and a surgical mask now resting below his chin came walking through, looking directly at Richard.

"Mr. Tone?" he asked, not waiting for the answer before extending his hand. "Yes, and my wife, Annette," Richard offered. "Our son was..."

"Yes... would you both come with me, please?" Dr. Tahir did not look at Richard or Annette as he turned to lead the way, but they could feel from his demeanor that something was wrong... terribly wrong. Annette grasped her husband's hand tightly as they walked past the row of exam rooms, some closed, some open. But there was no sight of Michael as the trio reached the end of the examination rooms. Dr. Tahir hesitated momentarily as a nurse approached him with a file in her hand. She did not speak or smile. She just handed the file to Dr. Tahir and left. With the file in one hand, the Doctor opened a closed door with the other and invited the pair to enter. This was obviously not an exam room. Two plastic chairs and a couch adorned the small room with no windows. Dr. Tahir invited the Tones to sit on the couch while he pulled one of the plastic chairs up close to face them.

"Mr. and Mrs. Tone, your son was involved in a major traffic accident late this afternoon. He was brought to us by ambulance, but... unfortunately, he was not breathing when the EMTs brought him in. Annette screamed involuntarily before both hands reached her mouth.

"No! This is not possible," she cried. "Michael!"

Richard embraced her and looked at the Doctor in anticipation of more information.

"They did everything possible to get him breathing on the way here, Mrs. Tone, but your son..."

"Michael! His name is Michael!" Annette blurted between sobs.

Dr. Tahir grabbed a tissue and handed it to Annette. She did not accept it but kept her face buried in her husband's shirt, feeling his heart pounding against her cheek. Richard took the Kleenex still in the physician's hand and smiled a weak thank you as he applied it to Annette's cheeks and nose. She did not move.

"Michael... was severely injured in the accident; the oncoming car was going fast, apparently to reach the intersection while the yellow light was on. The camera shows that Michael was in the intersection a split second after the yellow light was off. He might have been anticipating the light would turn green as he was already in motion during the yellow phase," Dr. Tahir explained slowly, now speaking directly to Richard.

"Where is he?" questioned Richard, as he continued to hold a sobbing Annette in his arms, trying to keep his own composure intact.

"Michael is in the next room," Dr. Tahir said softly, making a point of calling him by name. "They are cleaning him up before the body, uh... before Michael is taken to the mortuary to prepare him for burial. You can follow up with them to make funeral arrangements. I am so sorry for the loss of your son."

"Can we see him now? I want to see my son, please!" Annette's painful cry of anguish came. "I want to see him now!"

"Yes, of course," submitting to a mother's broken heart. "And if you would care to discuss your feelings with clergy, we have a wonderful man of the cloth on staff here at the hospital. I can arrange..."

"That won't be necessary, Dr. Tahir, but thank you for the offer. I am certain our Bishop and home teachers have already been alerted and made aware of the accident. Michael was... is very well-known in the community and among his peers. This will be a tremendous shock to those who might question why a loving God would allow him to be taken so early in his life," explained Richard, still cradling Annette as tight as he could without it being too uncomfortable.

"Why... would He?" the Doctor asked slowly, eyes now searching Richard's as if seeking comfort of his own, causing Richard to raise his head to look into the Doctor's questioning eyes. "I see death all the time. It never gets easier, especially when a young man in the very prime of life is suddenly and tragically taken. I want to understand the purpose of such things because when our little Shaita was found dead at the bottom of our swimming pool two years ago, we have been unable to forgive ourselves, and it has pulled our marriage apart in the process."

It was Annette who spoke first, raising her head off Richard's chest as if being summoned to forget her own grief and focus on another's. "Michael is not dead, Dr. Tahir. Neither is... is it Shaita?" Dr. Tahir nodded and focused his eyes on Annette, begging for more.

"They are not dead or lost in some vast expanse. They live with other heavenly spirits who came to this earth to gain a mortal body, experience human feelings, learn, and grow from their experiences. Michael and Shaita have moved on past this 'second' estate to prepare for exaltation and the reunion of their resurrected body with the spirit that has always lived."

Dr. Tahir did not move his eyes from Annette's. "I do not comprehend what you just said, but I would like to understand," came his reply... a smile trying to break through his fixed lips. "But this is not about my problems or my family," admitted the Doctor.

"But it is, Dr. Tahir!" Annette said a little louder than she had intended. "We are all family... born from the same Heavenly Parents, the Parents of our spirits. We may have been born into different circumstances, but we were all together as one family in the beginning."

"Then why was Michael allowed to die before he could even begin to experience what this earth had to offer him? And my Shaita? She was but two years old when she was taken."

Annette looked at Richard as she prepared an answer, allowing her husband to join the discussion with Dr. Tahir and inviting him with her eyes.

"Dr. Tahir," Richard began. "Are you familiar with the Christian Old Testament scriptures?"

"Yes, I read from both the Old and New Testaments. I am Christian. My wife is as well," came the reply that caused both Tones to open their eyes wider. "That surprises you," he offered, not as a question but as a statement. "My wife and I... were looking for a living religion, and we have accepted Jesus Christ as our Savior. But when Shaita died, we could not find answers that explained why she died. We had tried hard to do the right things, live a good life, be generous to others. It was as if none of that mattered. She was gone! No explanation. No feelings of comfort. We... my wife and I, started blaming one another. Things spiraled down from there. We are... temporarily separated from one another."

"I am sorry to hear that," responded Richard, rubbing Annette's hand gently with his thumb. "I hope things come back together for you. When it comes right down to it, family is all that matters; it's all we have at the end."

"You are so kind to be concerned about me when it is you who just lost your son. How can you be so sure you will see your son again?"

It was Annette who responded first, again raising her head from the warmth of Richard's beating heart. "Because this earth life would be a waste if it were not so! The holy scriptures teach that before we came to earth, we lived as spirits. A loving Heavenly Father prepared this earth for us as He has other worlds, to gain an earthly body and to learn from our mistakes. This earth life is not the end... it is a beginning!" Annette smiled, looking directly at Dr. Tahir as she spoke.

"There is a foundational principle upon which this earthly experience was formed," Richard added, now taking his cue from Annette as the family scriptorian. "Do you remember in Genesis where the scriptures teach there was a family council held, and our earthly plan was announced?

Our elder brother Lucifer disagreed over the principle of agency... and took a third 'of the hosts of Heaven' with him. He did not want to risk losing even one of us to sin, so he convinced many of Heavenly Father's children that personal agency was too risky, and to revolt against Father. They were cast out to become Satan's minions, never to experience the joy... or pain, of having a physical body."

"Except through us when we sin," added Annette. "Both our children lost their lives to a tragic accident," Annette continued, wiping fresh tears away from her eyes with a tissue handed to her by Richard. "A product of earthly agency. No one was there from the other side to keep your daughter from falling in or to protect Michael from making an apparent mistake in judgment–if that was what caused the accident. Otherwise, God would be bound to protect everyone."

"But I have heard of miracles, where people have been saved from sure death, and no one knows how... or why," Dr. Tahir pressed, unwilling to let this go. "Why was not my child... and your boy saved from a terrible death?"

Annette steadied her gaze on Dr. Tahir, willing herself not to lose patience in light of her own grief. Here was a man who had been grieving for years and needed closure.

"Dr. Tahir, you profess to be a Christian. Is that correct?" The Doctor nodded without answering. "Do you remember reading about the night Christ left His disciples to pray in the garden?" Another affirmative nod followed." Do you remember why Christ went alone into the garden?" asked Annette.

"He went to pray!" came a weak response.

"He went to pray and was alone because He took upon himself the sins and mistakes of all mankind from the beginning of man's arrival on earth... to the end, whenever that is," joined Annette. "He has already paid for the pain you are experiencing. He knew this would happen, that you would suffer, so He went to the cross, willingly, and allowed Himself to be staked, and took upon Himself all those sins that were to be committed against us and paid the ultimate price for them, with His life as atonement. Our God is merciful and will provide a way for us to raise our children in the afterlife; of this, I am certain," Annette smiled as she stood to embrace another hurting soul. A moment of healing passed between the two as they connected through the joint pain of having lost someone very dear to them. *But if I depart, I will send the Comforter unto you – John 16:7*

"Thank you, Mrs. Tone... Mr. Tone!"

"It's Richard... and Annette," corrected Annette with a smile and another hug. "Do you think they have Michael cleaned up enough for us to see him now?"

"I will see," said Dr. Tahir as he turned to open the door, grabbing a white tissue from a box on the counter as he closed the door behind him, leaving Richard and Annette alone now to face their own grief. Richard's hand grasped Annette's as he closed his eyes and began to pray aloud, softly, expressing love for their Heavenly Father, His mercy, and for the brief years of enjoying this remarkable young man in their lives. It was not a prayer one might think a parent who had just lost a child would pray. It was full of gratitude, not despair, grief, accusation, or blame. It was spoken as one who completely understood life's purpose, however short.

A soft knock at the doorway announced the arrival of a nurse who had been sent to bring the Tones to see their son before the mortuary arrived to pick him up. It was a somber moment between the two, as reality once again loomed over them like a huge cloud of grey darkness. The entrance into reality was once again peppered with sounds of pain and concern as the couple was led out of the ER exam room area into another room, well-lit and cold. There on a gurney lay their son, covered only with a sheet, his face exposed.

"He looks like he is just asleep," offered Annette, placing her fingers over his forehead to straighten his hair as she often did. Dr. Tahir suddenly appeared at their side, joining the pair in his admiration of the body before them... returning to his role as a doctor.

"He is one good-looking boy!"

Richard nodded to acknowledge Dr. Tahir's comment, Annette's tears flowing freely down her face with no thought to wipe them off; her only thought focused on the son who lay still before her.

"Take as much time as you need," offered Dr. Tahir as he sensed the couple needed time alone with their son... and his pressing schedule drawing itself into his consciousness once again. "Just let the front desk nurse know you are leaving."

And with that, Dr. Tahir left their life as quickly as he had entered it, but not without reflecting on the words of other grieving parents. In considering their words and their tranquility even as they suffered their loss, he had seen that they were at peace with their son's death, although in deep pain for their loss. As he considered that, as well as the words they'd said to him, he realized he wasn't as gloomy as death usually made him feel. More than that, he felt better able to accept the loss of his daughter if it were part of a greater plan. The reasonableness of this concept caused him to decide to pray and to consider the words of Mr. and Mrs. Tone, and as he made this decision, a peace he had not felt in such a long time came to him. And, with that peace also came a renewed desire to hold, love, and console his wife in his arms.

"Where do you think he is at this moment, Richard? Is he with family? Is he here with us now?" Richard did not answer immediately, but after a moment to consider her softly spoken questions, he responded in like tone:

"Michael's earthly journey has ended, Annette. He has rejoined our family with such a welcome home celebration that I am surprised we cannot hear them," a smile began forming on his lips, exposing those high cheekbones that drew Annette to him the first time they met in the BYU cafeteria. She was carrying two trays of food, trying to juggle her purse, books, and trays by herself, when Richard came to the rescue, offering to take one of her trays, but not before making an eternal impression on Annette.

"Is it necessary to give his body a blessing?" Annette asked sincerely, bringing Richard back to reality. "I think it would be appropriate," Richard answered softly. "Do you remember when my father died unexpectedly while in the hospital from pneumonia? I felt impressed to bless his body because I didn't get a chance to bless his spirit at the end. His body has served him well. Please close the door a little so we are not on display, and I will give him a blessing."

Richard then placed both hands lightly upon the body before him and pronounced a beautiful blessing, mostly for Annette's benefit but also for her son Michael, who had lived well and had been such a blessing to her and the family. He, no doubt, would receive some "indication" that the blessing had taken place and receive added peace from being temporarily separated. Following Richard's blessing of their son, the couple made their way arm-in-arm to the front desk, where they alerted the duty nurse they were leaving, provided contact information, and stepped on the threshold of the sliding doorway, back into the cold and often harsh place called Earth, to face the reality of having just lost a son.

***

Paulo stood at the helm, watching carefully as the PT-100 made its way up the coastal waterway leading to the US Coast Guard base outside Pensacola, Florida; his heart was racing faster than the speed of the boat beneath him.

"Welcome to America, Paulo... er, Richardo!" Commander Meade said while placing his arm around Paulo's shoulder. "We still need to register you with customs, but I will walk through with you. It should be okay." Commander Meade was true to his word, and Richardo Quinteros Jr. entered the USA on a guest visa courtesy of the USCG.

***

The next few days following Michael Tone's death were a blur of activity for the Tone family, with overwrought emotions, visits from friends and neighbors, and, of course, the details of planning a funeral and burying their son. But when the darkness of night came at the end of each day, and the flurry of activity slowed and then stopped, the gap that was created in the lives of the parents and remaining siblings of Michael Tone came crashing in with almost mind-numbing loneliness and feelings of second-guessing themselves as parents. Had they been too loose with Michael in giving him access to the family car? Could they have done anything different to have prevented this tragedy in their lives?

And why Michael? He was such a good boy with a great future, creating his earthly legacy among mankind. Why would God take him now when he could do so much good? Knowing the answers to these questions and others like them did not keep the mortal side of the Tone family from feeling the persuasions of the natural man within them to want to blame... someone! But their upbringings countered those feelings with their belief that "all" experiences are meant to teach us, school our feelings, and help us grow in compassion, love, and charity toward others as we encounter trial after trial. Accidents happen. Lives are lost. Mortal beings are sometimes prematurely ushered to the other side. This right to be tempted, to fall, and to experience pain is what Mother Eve referred to as The Plan of Salvation when she and Adam forfeited their safe and secure life in the Garden of Eden for a life of pain and uncertainty... so that we might recognize the joy of a morning sunrise.

Chapter Nineteen

A VISITOR

Sunday afternoon following Michael's funeral brought continuous doorbell ringing / knocking announcements of well-meaning friends and neighbors... but the result was wearing thin on the Tone family, who longed to just be alone with their grief. But they understood the need for family and friends to grieve, as well as Michael's family. So when the doorbell rang just before darkness set in, Robert went to the door... unprepared for what was about to happen.

"Hello! I am sorry to intrude so late in the afternoon, but I just got off work and hoped someone would be home," the short, good-looking, and very pregnant Hispanic woman announced in broken but very understandable English. Robert did not recognize the woman who stood at the doorway, but he hadn't known everyone who had come to pay their respects today, so he did the most natural thing and invited her in. Annette came from the kitchen, wiping her hands on a towel, and was caught by surprise at the sight of a stranger Robert had invited to come in. Curiosity overcame concern as Annette walked past her husband, introduced herself to the woman, and invited her to sit in the parlor area just off the entry, where they had talked with most of the visitors that day.

The woman accepted the Tone's invitation and sat on one of the winged back chairs that faced the comfortable-looking sofa, where Annette sat first and was later joined by Richard. Their guest sat still for a moment, hands wringing one over the other as if she were nervous. Robert was the first to speak:

"We haven't met before, have we? Did you know Michael well?"

The woman's brow furrowed as if struggling to comprehend Robert's words, causing Annette to come to her aid. "Our son, Michael... did you know him from work?" As if her eyes had just opened, the woman fixed her gaze on the colorful plants and flowers that adorned the little room where they sat.

Too many to be decorations, the visitor thought to herself. *She said, "Did" I know her son, not "Do" I know her son,"* as the reality of what she had just stepped into came crashing through to her consciousness. "I am so sorry," she said after gaining control of herself. "I... Uh, came to talk about your *other* son, Paulo."

Annette and Richard were so emotionally burned out that neither could quickly process this unexpected visitor's words. "Other son? Paulo? *Paulo!*" burst Annette once the cloud on her mind cleared. "Our son, Paulo? How do you know Paulo?" Annette asked cautiously, peering deeply into the woman's eyes. The woman now stood...

"I am so sorry to have troubled you tonight. Perhaps I can come another time. I am afraid I have intruded!" Her eyes fixed upon one of the bouquets of flowers, trying to determine the reason for so many... as if there had been a funeral or something. Annette stepped close to the woman and grasped her hands...

"How do you know Paulo?" she pleaded in a soft but shaking voice, her remaining emotions now gone. The woman broke eye contact but spoke the words, "I am his mother! I mean his birth mother," she added. Then, seeing the startled looks on Richard and Annette's faces, she asked if she could sit back down to offer an explanation, sensing these people might not be able to stand the suspense of not understanding much longer. With Richard's arm around Annette's shoulders, he guided her back to the couch and said, before the woman started to explain, "Look Mrs..."

"Cervantes... Maria Cervantes. I was a young girl raised in a very strict household by parents who worked day and night to survive. I was impulsive and selfish and thought I could get back at my parents by sneaking out and running the streets. I was a foolish girl and allowed myself to be seduced by a rich boy who wanted nothing to do with me after he found out that I was pregnant. I planned to hide the birth of my child from everyone without any thought of the consequences. But my mother discovered my pregnancy, dragged me into town, and forced me to have an abortion. Except that the baby did not die, as I was told. He was taken from my womb and raised in a convent. I learned of this year's later. After I married and was unable to have children of our own, I had to tell my husband of my sin, and he left and never came back. My mother kept this from me until I could no longer stand it. I went to her and made her tell me where my son was. By the time I found the convent where he was raised, he had already been kidnapped.

"During my stay at the convent, I became very ill. The sisters were so patient and kind to me. I learned much about my son during this time, and I learned that my illness was... a pregnancy–a parting gift from my husband," she smiled awkwardly. "I decided that I had no life in my country, so I decided to come to America on a work visa and have my child here. I wanted to meet the parents of my son who loved him enough to try and give him a better life. I wanted to meet you!"

Maria's story penetrated a fragile emotional curtain within the Tones, and only seconds later, Annette and Richard clung to one another while allowing the emotions of losing two sons to bore into their souls. Annette explained through sobs that they had just buried their son Michael while almost simultaneously learning about losing their already lost son, Paulo, to kidnappers. Maria was invited to stay for dinner so the Tones could learn more about this remarkable woman who had learned from her mistakes. After losing her family, she chose not to be defined by her past but instead focus on creating a future for herself and her child. They learned that Maria had obtained an Associate Nursing degree while living in the city with her husband while he worked each day. When she discovered she was pregnant, she was drawn to the idea of leaving behind what remained of her family in hopes she could find a better life in America.

Maria applied for and received a work visa at the Salt Lake City Children's Hospital through the doctor at the convent who had diagnosed her as being pregnant. By no small coincidence, Dr. Claudia Mora had served on the hospital advisory board at SLCCH through a multi-country underprivileged children's effort sponsored by The Church of Jesus Christ of Latter-day Saints.

The evening ended way too soon for the Tones, who were emotionally spent but who had felt considerably refreshed over the sense of closeness they felt after getting to know Paulo's birth mother. They bid goodbye to Maria with a promise to come for Sunday dinner the following week.

Chapter Twenty

MISSIONARIES

T he blue sky over Paulo was covered quickly by a line of dark, ominous clouds moving in a straight line inland from the Atlantic Ocean in such a way that Paulo began looking for shelter from what was about to come. As a seaman, he had learned the patterns of clouds and knew how to recognize trouble... or at least the possibility of it. He had come to love cloud patterns and colors, but these clouds were streaming in way too fast. They would charge in, dump their load of rain, and be off. *This will be a quick storm*, he thought. Since leaving the security of the Coast Guard vessel, after being led past customs, Paulo had been handed an envelope containing cash donated by the men who had rescued him, as well as phone numbers of several who had offered to be a contact and reference as Paulo found his way in America.

Although his final destination would be Utah, Paulo felt he would like to see America before settling down into what he did not know. The child in him called out to explore and experience freedom before confining himself to society's rules and others' expectations. He did not know the family who had adopted him beyond the short visits he had had with them, and as much as he wanted to connect with them, he also wanted to experience America for a while as an unknown and on his terms. The familiar sensation of pelting rain against his face woke Paulo from his momentary lapse of forgetting about the clouds that had now positioned directly above him. Although used to being wet, Paulo never adjusted to the bone-chilling effects that lasted way past the storm.

Looking for shelter, Paulo spotted two businessmen huddled under the only awning that offered protection from the storm. *That's odd*, Paulo thought as he hurriedly walked toward them. *They are each holding onto a bicycle. Were they riding bikes in business suits?* Sliding in next to the two men, Paulo noticed they were young men, both about his age. They beckoned him to come in closer so his back was not exposed to the rain. Paulo gladly accepted, greeting the men with an awkward but friendly smile of his own... full of gratitude that he had found shelter from the passing storm.

"Hola!" came a familiar greeting from the husky, native-looking man... who extended his hand. "My name is Elder Lomu, from Tonga. Elder Wilkinson and I are missionaries from the Church of Jesus Christ of Latter-day Saints, sent here to Florida to rescue people from these nasty storms!" With a big laugh, he grabbed Paulo's hand and shook it vigorously, inviting his companion to do the same. "Elder Wilkinson is from Utah," the husky missionary offered while the other two men shook hands. "He isn't as friendly as me, but he's still a good man." And then he laughed, causing both his companion and new friend to join his laughter, although not as energetic, given the storm all around them.

Elder Wilkinson then spoke, pointing to his companion, who now was shaking the remaining water off his suit jacket. "We don't usually wear jackets when we are out meeting people on the streets, but we were on our way to a Zone Meeting to meet our new mission president, and full dress is required until he tells us otherwise!" Elder Wilkinson noticed Paulo's confused look and continued in Spanish. "We are missionaries with the Church of Jesus Christ of Latter-day Saints... or some refer to us as the 'Mormons' because of the Book of Mormon that is another witness of Jesus Christ."

"You are Mormons?" Paulo responded, thinking back to comments made by his sea rescuers about the possibility of his adoptive parents being

Mormons. "You are from Utah?" Paulo directed his question at Elder Wilkinson in flawless English... who responded with an energetic nod. "What's it like, please?" continued Paulo, acting curious but unwilling to reveal the root of his interest.

Before the Utah native could respond, his companion reminded him of their Zone Meeting starting shortly and asked Paulo for his name and how they might connect with him again. Caught off guard by the request for his name, Paulo hesitated momentarily before answering... "Roberto! My name is Roberto... Roberto Quinteros Jr.," he spat out three times as if the young men were deaf. "But you can call me...uh, Paulo... a name my Madre' called me. And... I do not know where you can contact me. I just arrived from my country and need to find a job and a place to stay."

The Elders looked at one another as if to question what to do with this new friend and how to help him. We know someone who might be able to help," came a reply from Elder Lomu. "Can you come with us now and meet our mission president? He is well connected and may have some ideas to help you get established." Paulo gave a short nod of agreement, which was all the two enthusiastic Elders needed... and they were off, with bikes in tow.

Rain clouds had moved further inland, leaving the local skies blue and clean again and creating a refreshing feeling of hope and promise within Paulo as he walked briskly, trying to keep up with these young men who were obviously used to walking. Rounding a corner from the main street hustle and bustle of retail traffic sat a rather large building with a fashionable steeple projecting upward. The grounds were immaculate, and the building was covered with red brick instead of the painted plaster he had seen on so many other buildings, with the name "The Church of Jesus Christ of Latter-day Saints" adorning the front of the building. The parking lot was spacious as if to indicate to the world that many worshipped here. But Paulo noticed only five cars parked in front... and several bicycles.

The elders quickly parked their bicycles and headed toward the front door, anticipating that the meeting had already started and they would have to apologize to the group and explain the delay in their arrival. Paulo followed in tow as the Elders opened the door and were greeted with strong male and female voices singing like angels, Paulo imagined, as he stopped the door from banging as it closed behind him.

"The spirit of God like a fire is burning, the latter day glory begins to come forth," came the united voices from what appeared to be a sanctuary of sorts, as the Elders quickly found an empty pew and slid in with their heads bowed as if they could will themselves to be invisible, glancing behind them to be sure their new charge was still in tow. As the song ended, hymn books were noisily placed into their holders as a Sister missionary stepped to the podium and bowed her head to pray.

"Our Father in heaven, hallowed be thy name and great be thy love for thy children," she began. Paulo found his eyes looking up at her, trying not to stare while everyone else had their heads bowed. She is beautiful! Paulo thought... quickly closing his eyes but opening them again as he anticipated she was finishing her prayer. She did not. "And let thy hand rest upon thy servants here in Florida that we might be led to the honest in heart who are searching for thy restored church and truths."

Paulo quickly closed his eyes again after stealing another glance at this young woman. Her long, dark, almost black hair fell over her face as she instinctively pushed one side back behind her ear, revealing the purity of her face and the bronze color of her skin. He thought she could be a model, opening his eyes quickly as she ended her prayer to catch another glimpse as she returned to her place with the others of this small congregation.

A kindly-looking man with graying hair above his ears stood and approached the podium, smiling directly...at Paulo. "Good morning!" He offered. Then, looking at Elder Lomu, he asked, "Do we have a new missionary I wasn't aware of, Elder?" Causing all heads to turn as if on cue to look directly at Paulo. He felt like running... but the instant his eyes locked onto hers, he froze in his seat. It was as if she was saying, don't go! But a strong hand grabbed Paulo's arm and almost lifted him out of his seat to stand next to Elder Lomu as he introduced Paulo to the others...

"This is our new friend, Roberto Quinteros. But he likes to be called Paulo."

"And Junior," added Elder Wilkinson from his safe seated position, cupping a hand over his mouth as if realizing his culpability by association.

"Hola, Robert Quinteros Jr...er Paulo," came a warm greeting from President Leonardo (Len) Ventura. "Elder Lomu, I bet there is a story I need to hear, isn't there?" With that, President Ventura turned to his First Assistant with instructions on what to teach the Elders while he spent a few minutes with Elders Lomu and Wilkinson and their guest.

At the back of the chapel, President Ventura extended his hand to Paulo and shook it vigorously as Elder Lomu again introduced his new friend to his mission President... who invited Paulo and the Elders into a small classroom just off the chapel so the Zone Meeting could continue without interruption, with both Elders talking at once, hoping the old adage, "a good defense starts with a good offense," proved to be more than just a catchy saying.

After a sketchy background of how the Elders met Paulo, along with some even *sketchier* background of how Paulo got there, President Ventura concluded the short meeting so he and the other two Elders could get back to their conference, surprising the two elders by inviting Paulo to join them for the day and he would see what he could do about finding him a place to stay... and maybe a job.

As the trio took their seats amidst stares from one dark-haired beauty wearing a name tag, Elder Lomu whispered, "That's the President's daughter. She is on a mission, too, which means she is off-limits... for at least another six months.

"What does that mean, *off limits*?" Paulo whispered.

"When you serve a mission, you don't date or mix with the opposite sex," replied Elder Lomu. "Our missions are for two years, but the Sisters are called for only eighteen months. Sister Ventura entered the mission field a year ago and will be finished about the same time her parents are released," he continued.

"Shush!" came a warning alert from the next row up... causing Elder Wilkinson to put a hand on his companion's shoulder and return his attention to the speaker, inviting his companion with an upward nod to do the same... provoking a smile from Paulo.

The first half of the Missionary Conference only lasted until 1 pm, at which time it was announced that lunch was available in the kitchen. There was no announcing twice as both Elder and Sister missionaries arose from their seats and, in a comfortable but steady fashion, moved as if choreographed into a single line forming from the kitchen out to the dining area/basketball gym/overflow seating area for Sunday services... and now lined with 8' long tables covered with white cloths and a single rose in a vase in the middle of each table. Paulo was steered ahead by Elder Lomu and placed between him and Elder Wilkinson in such a protective maneuver as to guard their "golden contact" from anyone even thinking of poaching him. That did not keep Paulo from searching with his eyes for the lovely Sister Ventura, whom he spotted almost instantly as a rose among many male thorns. Sister Ventura did not return his gaze but continued talking with her Sister companion and one of the Elders behind her, who was obviously trying to make points. She wasn't buying it and turned to look toward the line ahead of her and caught Paulo's stare.

Her brow wrinkled as she tried to process this young Gentile's interest. She was a dedicated missionary for her church. He wasn't even a member. End of story! And she turned away her gaze to... what? She had been locked into his dark brown eyes for way too long... longer than what was considered appropriate behavior for a Sister missionary. Yet, those eyes told her volumes about this young man who had "wandered" into this gathering. She saw pain and anguish... but she also recognized spirit and tenacity. And innocence. *I mean, who in their right mind would sit through hours of religious discussion without moving or showing his impatience?* She thought. Yet, she had observed him as being intent... and "interested?"

Sister Ventura shook her head as if trying to rid it of a bug or cobweb that had attached itself to her hair, causing a look of concern from her companion. "What?" snapped Sister Ventura, drawing a *funny face* look from her companion, to which both laughed after a good-natured poke by Sister Ventura as she reached for a bun to accept a hearty portion of lunch meats and companion fruits.

Paulo had not missed Sister Ventura's lingering look as if trying to read his mind. He smiled at the thought of her trying to read a mind as confused and torn as his–a mind that bore scars of betrayal and rejection from birth to loneliness and frustration as a youth, to finally getting a break and then tasting the bitter disappointment of separation and loss of a family who wanted him. Yes, his was not a perfect life at all, not even close... but somehow he had made it to America and, in time, would find his family, and maybe they would still want him. But he would not think of that now. He had found friends who were feeding him and held promise of introducing him to a place of employment so he could begin his new life and put behind him those disappointments that plagued him for most of his early years.

Nothing ever seemed to work out for Paulo... but that was about to change. Watching fifty or so hungry missionaries move through a stack of lunch meats, rolls, fruits, and, of course, cookies brought a smile of satisfaction to Paulo before he could even finish his plate of food. *They certainly feed these young people well!* Paulo thought to himself as he dared take another glance across the table and far to his left where the sister missionaries sat. She was engaged in storytelling and had the Sisters on either side of her gasping for air. Then, realizing they were drawing stares from the adult leadership who were also at the Sisters' table, they quickly bowed their heads and focused on their meal, shoulders still shaking un-controllably. *She has a sense of humor! Beauty and fun to be with... a great combination. Now, if she could only cook! What? What am I doing? I cannot even provide for my own needs, and I am eying the first pretty girl I see as if to make her my wife. No, Paulo... you are not even in her league, even if you could support a family. But... one day,* he thought resolutely, *I will deserve such a woman. I will!*

As if on cue, everyone started cleaning up the paper plates and cups around them and hauling them to the trash by the double doors leading to the drinking fountain in the hallway. Paulo grabbed his plate, and with intentions of filling up his cup with water, he spotted Sister Ventura gathering up her plate and those around her despite the smiling complaints by others that they could clean up their own plates. And Paulo saw an opportunity that he could not resist. In only four steps, Paulo had cut her off from her destination and said in as kindly of a tone as he could (in Spanish), "Not today, little flower... I will carry the load for you if you will please permit me?" Sister Ventura was taken aback by the act of such gentlemanly behavior, and at first, she held tightly to the stack of plates with one hand and grabbing the falling cups with the other, but realizing she was being spoken to in her native tongue by those delicious dark pair of eyes, she relaxed her grip and allowed the newcomer to have his way, accepting the *load* as he called it.

Sister Ventura loved hearing Paulo's words spoken with such tenderness. "Where did you learn such chivalry?" Sister Ventura asked while she picked up a fork dropped along the way to the trash.

"The Sisters in the Convent where I was raised insisted on teaching us how to speak English to help us be more attractive to adoptive parents. We were taught to treat others respectfully and never allow ourselves to be waited upon without doing our part to serve in return. I am merely returning the favor," Paulo said politely, with a slight gesture as if bowing to royalty. This act elicited an unexpected giggle from Sister Ventura, who responded without letting go of that giggle in her voice...

"But I have done nothing to serve you, silly boy," smiling broadly without drawing attention to her from the others that she was being flirted upon... and liked it.

"Oh, but you have, my Queen... My eyes have been served with slices of your beauty and wit all morning." Paulo retorted, his eyes remaining fixed on this royal lady.

"Elders and Sisters, please take your seats so we can begin the second part of our Conference," came a loud voice from the pulpit where one of the Assistants to the President stood patiently, seeking to restore the teaching spirit present before the lunch break. "President Ventura will now teach us for the remainder of our Conference," introduced the missionary.

Elder Lomu found Paulo standing with Sister Ventura over the trash can, just staring at one another before Elder Lomu broke the trance with, "Come on, you two... We are being summoned! And Sister Ventura, are you ever in trouble!" as she lifted her head to where her father was standing at the podium... his eyes affixed on the two of them.

"Elders and Sisters, the time has come for a hastening of the work," President Ventura announced from the pulpit, a little louder than he had intended. "The Lord has made technological advances available so that we might be better equipped to communicate our message to the world, thus harvesting the righteous souls earnestly seeking the truth. The First Presidency has authorized us to be one of the first missions to proselytize using iPads and computers to reach out and answer people's questions about the church." President Ventura then went into specifics as to how each of the Elders and Sisters would receive an iPad and specific instructions to guide them in learning how to enter online groups and to engage with people who have questions about the church. At the conclusion of his remarks, a video presentation followed to better enable the missionaries to maximize the use of these new tools.

Paulo was awestruck when a new video was played from one of the iPads to demonstrate its utility. The video was entitled "This is The Christ," and it told of the young life of Jesus Christ and how he set up His Church among the Jews, but they rejected Him. It portrayed Jesus as a religious leader, selecting fishermen unlearned in the Gospel to become the foundation of the Church. Paulo recognized several names of the chosen apostles, as they were also named for many different factions of the Catholic Church, as taught him by the Catholic Sisterhood.

The skies darkened in the film as it portrayed the events leading up to the Last Supper between Jesus Christ and His Apostles and their long walk to the Garden of Gethsemane where Jesus prayed to his Father and answered the call to be a Savior… by taking upon Himself the sins of all humanity, from the beginning to the end of creation. The film ended with the sun shining through the clouds and the message that the Lord's Church, with the same structure Christ had set up when He was on the earth, had been restored with a Prophet and twelve Apostles. These missionaries were sent to those who would watch this video to teach them the purpose of life and how to find their way back to Him through His restored Church.

Paulo just sat there… tears had quickly filled his eyes and overrun the banks meant to keep the tenderest of feelings from the world, but now gravity pulled them down his cheeks with no resistance. But then reality hit him, and he quickly wiped at them, unaware that President Ventura and his lovely missionary daughter had somehow been impressed to look at the young man just as he wiped at his face. Paulo could not define his feelings at that moment. He had never considered himself religious in the narrow meaning one would associate with themselves. This could have been because of the feelings of hate he carried for those who had brought him into this world in such a cruel manner and then tried to kill him. But he never doubted there was a God.

Paulo thought about his feelings toward God. At first, he blamed God in the same breath as he did his parents for bringing him into this world. But after his experiences over the years of being saved and warned and saved again, Paulo knew there was more to God than just a figurehead in the sky that we prayed to when things got tough. He was organized and had a plan for each of us that allowed us to experience pain but also joy. Paulo hadn't experienced much joy in his young life, but he could look back at his life and feel joy from overcoming his disabilities.

Paulo thought back to the little family who took him in when he was on the run after setting fire to the factory sweatshop. They gave him a place to work and recover from his captivity, and because of them, Paulo was able to learn the ways of the sea and become strong and capable. He learned so much in those two-plus years under the tutelage of kind-spirited and God-fearing seamen. And his body had healed in so many ways. This was where he had learned he had a natural talent for learning. He was like a sponge, picking up every tool the sea could teach him, ultimately saving his life as he survived long enough at sea to get rescued. He had been taught to prepare, and it was preparation that gave him sustenance during his time alone on the water. And, of course, he could never have been raised with such care and devotion with anyone else as he had been by the Sisters of the Convent... and Felicia, his best friend and mentor. So his life hadn't turned out so bad after all... at least to this point.

"Paulo! Come to, man! President Ventura has invited us to have dinner with him and his family tonight at the mission home. Can you believe that? Dinner at the mission home?" Came an excited reply from Elder Lomu. Paulo thought of mission homes he had heard of that cared for the homeless and forgotten. "Sure, as long as there is food, I'm in, uh... Elder Lomu," said Paulo, not quite as excited.

With the meeting over and everyone heading off to appointments, Elder Lomu arranged to have Paulo travel with President Ventura's family to the mission home while the Elders rode their bikes the few miles to join them. Paulo threw his backpack in the trunk of the nicely appointed sedan provided the mission for the President's use and opened the rear door only to see that it was empty. "Why don't you sit up here with me, young man, so we can get to know one another? No one else is coming with us, and the *others* have their own transportation, in case you were wondering," he said with a slight grin and "almost" a chuckle at the end.

Paulo quickly closed the backseat door, opened the front, and slid into the passenger side, not sure what was about to happen but full of anticipation to ride in such a beautiful car. "You better buckle up, Roberto," spoke

President Ventura as he placed the transmission in reverse and began to back out of his parking spot and into the heavy flow of end-of-day traffic. Paulo looked confused. He had no idea what President Ventura meant when he warned him to "buckle up!" He had never ridden in a car with seat belts in his twenty years. "You really don't know, do you?" President Ventura asked sincerely. Paulo nodded, saying that he did not know what that meant.

After showing Paulo where and how to "buckle up," El ' turned his attention to the road and carefully entered the slow stream of home-bound travelers. There was silence for maybe three or four minutes before President Ventura spoke, asking Paulo to tell him about himself and what he was doing on the streets to have met the missionaries. Paulo was sketchy in his explanation, not knowing how much to tell this man he had just met. He was fearful that his deception of who he was would be found out and that he would be sent home... or worse, sent to prison for falsifying documents... so he did not correct his host's use of his passport name. But his host did not pry; he merely listened as Paulo sketched out his background and plans for the future as best he could.

"I once thought I would come to America and learn to be a framer. I am pretty good with my hands, and I thought carpentry would be a good trade," Paulo summarized.

"But...?" Injected President Ventura with a hint of anticipation that caused him to wonder almost aloud... *This young man has expectations of himself that go beyond finding a job*, he thought to himself.

"But I would love to be a doctor," Paulo said without hesitation in his voice.

"A doctor?" came a surprised reply from President Ventura, causing Paulo to look out the window and gaze at the passing traffic while deep in thought.

"I am good with my hands... I think a surgeon would be a good fit for me." Paulo then told President Ventura about his experience assisting the ship physician in operating on one of the men because the three shipmates before Paulo volunteered had all passed out one at a time as the operation progressed. Paulo watched how the doctor stitched up one of the open wounds and then asked if he might try stitching up the shipmate's leg. With amazed looks from all surrounding their friend and shipmate, Paulo took hold of the needle and catgut used to stitch the wound and mirrored the doctor's stitch pattern flawlessly. From then on, Paulo was called to assist the Doc as his assistant.

This story amazed the President as he could only shake his head at such a story... but for some reason, this seasoned business executive from Utah, USA, did not doubt Paulo's story one bit. "I'll tell you something, Roberto..."

"Paulo! er... Senior... I am called Paulo by all who know me," corrected Paulo before he could stop what was coming out of his mouth.

"Oh, that's right, sorry!... Paulo, it is!" He said with a kind smile and a quick side glance as if to double-check to see if Paulo still had his seat belt on. "I was going to say that I am on the Advisory Board of the Primary Children's Hospital in Salt Lake City, Utah. Do you like children, Paulo?"

Paulo's mind was trying to process what this man was saying and couldn't get past the fact that he had already met two people from Utah, where he would ultimately end up. This brief silence from Paulo caused President Ventura to look over, curiosity on his face, at the silent young man next to him. Paulo, sensing he was being looked at, responded quickly without thinking again... "Oh yes, sir!... I was one once!" This brought a rousing bout of laughter from President Ventura, who paid Paulo a grand compliment...

"Not only is he a skilled surgeon's assistant... he has a sense of humor as well," complemented El ' out loud. The drive to the LDS Mission Home was so enjoyable that Paulo almost got lost in the beautiful scenery, tall buildings, and crowds of people moving along both sides of the street and sidewalks. President Ventura recognized that the young man had likely never been to such a modern city before and backed off from his intent to pursue his talk with Paulo about coming to Salt Lake City to learn more about becoming a doctor and just let him enjoy this new experience.

"President Ventura, what is it like living in Utah?" Paulo asked, not taking his eyes off the scenery unfolding outside the moving car.

"Well, I am prejudiced, I suppose," smiled President Ventura. I was born in the mountains of Utah, in a small rural area north of Salt Lake City called Logan. Growing up was like a fairy tale. My father farmed a small plot of land, mainly as a hobby... but we raised cows, chickens, and some hogs for food and worked the fields to grow food for the animals and veggies for our large family. My father was a teacher most of his life. He taught first at our high school as my older siblings and I grew up... and then he accepted a principal's position at a substantial high school near Salt Lake City. But my dad was one of those unique individuals who was not content with the status quo."

The puzzled look on Palo's face caused El ' to pause and explain what that word meant. "Status quo refers to being satisfied with where you are in life, with no real aspirations to move beyond. It is also used to describe where the masses reside. Most people get into a rut of familiarity and comfort with their job, marriage, and even their personal skill level, and never reach beyond."

"Then I am surely not status quo," said Paulo, almost a little too eagerly. "I mean to say I have always felt, even as a child with deformities and health issues, that I would become somebody. I don't mean to say that I am anyone special... but there is a drum beating within my heart that keeps me looking ahead–as if it were saying, *What's next*?" Paulo explained, still focused on the scenery.

"You would have enjoyed knowing my father, Rob... uh, Paulo. He was just like that, always asking what's next. Being a principal didn't satisfy his insatiable appetite to become all he could be. He became a writer and published several books over his remaining lifetime. He served as Bishop and Stake President for over fifteen years before being called to the Logan Temple Presidency."

"You sound very proud of him," remarked Paulo, looking at the driver now and leaning in as if afraid he would miss some vital part of this man's story about his father.

"About as proud as any son could be of a father. He instilled in me the desire to become all I *can* be so that I use this earthly experience for its intended purpose..."

"And what is that you speak of... the purpose of this earth life?" Paulo asked. "I, too, want to become someone special," he added with sincerity in his voice.

"From what I see, you are special, President Ventura complimented. "We each have been given gifts and talents before we came to earth that would help us become all that we can be, and then some... if we are willing," he continued. "This earth life is a proving ground for us to develop those gifts and talents we could not develop as spirit children living with Heavenly parents. What we do with those gifts is part of our earthly agency–a condition of earth life we fought for."

"We fought for?" Paulo asked, not comprehending the image of a spirit being able to fight or do anything else much more than just... float.

"Are you familiar with the Bible, Paulo?" Waiting for him to acknowledge, President Ventura went on, satisfied that he was. "In the Old Testament, we learn that there was a war in Heaven over our agency to choose, which resulted in one-third of Heavenly Father's spirit children being cast out of Heaven to follow their leader, who would become Satan. It was a struggle to preserve the right to fail... and to win by failing forward. But Satan would have life as we know it to be safe and secure, with no right or agency to act upon our own conscience, so that no one would fail, providing we all lived by his rules. You and I, Paulo, fought for the right to choose! The right to make mistakes. The right to learn from those mistakes. Satan would take that right from us so that no one would fail. But God's plan required someone to atone, or pay for our sins... with their own life. Satan said, "Choose me!" But he required us all to pay our devotions to him... giving Satan all the glory on earth. Your Elder Brother, Jesus Christ, stepped up and said, 'Here am I, send me! And all the glory on earth would be given to God, our Heavenly Father.' That is why, when we pray, either individually or as a group, we close our prayer, 'in the name of Jesus Christ,' but we address our prayer to our Heavenly Father at the beginning."

Paulo did not respond immediately, giving pause to President Ventura's teaching so Paulo could process the excellent principle he had just been taught. *Silence is not a bad thing when it gives the Angels and the Lord's spirit time to act*, thought the wise mission leader. And in this case the spirit was well received, as Paulo broke the silence with, "I believe what you have just taught me is true, President Ventura. It resonates well in my heart."

Paulo had lost track of his scenery watching during this experience with the spirit encompassing his entire being in such a way that he could actually see the scenes played out in his mind as his teacher explained to him the purpose of earth life and why we are here. He had attended Catechism at the Convent quite regularly as part of the condition of residency and had learned of God's plan to make us strong against the temptations of Satan, which usually meant so many candles to light, so many rosaries to recite... and confessions? Ah, yes, confessions...

Once a week, Father Ramos would come from the neighboring village fifty miles away and sequester himself in the confession booth for hours as the children and convent staff fasted and prayed for enlightenment for their sins and poor choices. When such enlightenment occurred, they could obtain almost immediate access to Father Ramos, who would, at the end of the day, join all in a bounteous feast before his driver returned to pick him up. Paulo was rarely in the mood to seek forgiveness. It was others who had sinned by bringing him into this miserable world anyway. How could he seek forgiveness for his sins when he was unwilling to forgive others of theirs?

President Ventura had reached the mission home entrance, and with the push of a button, two iron gates opened, allowing the sleek sedan carrying El ' and his guest to enter. Two young men in white shirts & ties came out of the house to greet their leader and acted surprised when

Paulo opened the passenger side door but welcomed him with a friendly handshake anyway. Paulo stood at the front of the vehicle as he watched the mission president greet his missionaries. *He really loved these young men,* Paulo thought, as he watched the way he conversed with them, apparently discussing matters that could not wait for him to get settled inside. Yet the President handled the interruption with patience and charm. Paulo liked this man.

Once the two white shirts were satisfied that their issues had been addressed, they turned toward the side entry door, with President Ventura in the lead. And then, as if he had just realized something was missing, he turned around to find Paulo still standing by the car with his backpack in hand. "Paulo, come on...!" he laughed, realizing he had forgotten his guest, who had a look of puzzlement on his face. Paulo quickly fell in behind the threesome and followed them into the patio area leading to this beautiful home's side entrance.

Paulo had never traveled any further than he could walk from the convent, so he was in awe of everything–the tall palm trees that seemed to be everywhere, lush grassy ponds, and exotic plants and colors he had never seen before. Houses in his country were tiny and poorly constructed. It seemed that every place he passed by was large and beautiful. *Everything they say about Americans being so wealthy is certainly true!* He thought, not noticing his wide smile reflecting at him from his window.

Chapter Twenty-One

EL PRESIDENTE'

The home occupied by El Presidente' was spacious and beautifully decorated as Paulo followed his host into what appeared to be a servant's quarters, with a washer and dryer on one side of the room, a sink between them, and an ironing board and many white shirts hung on a wire above it. There were jars of fruit lined on the counter, with fresh vegetables washed and ready to be cut up next to another sink where it looked like dinner was being prepared.

These people must have many servants! Paulo sighed. *Maybe I can secure a position of service here?* He thought. Paulo didn't realize he had fallen behind again while gazing at the "servant's quarters" and now lost sight of his host again. Voices were coming from his left, so he followed in that direction, entering a well-appointed and brightly lit kitchen and stepping right in front of a very attractive woman carrying a tray of food.

"Oops! So sorry, Señora, I was looking for El Presidente' Ventura," Paulo apologized immediately in his native tongue, trying to help steady the tray of delicious-looking meats and cheeses. The woman accepted Paulo's help with the tray and, without a second thought, asked him to bring the sliced pork roast, gravy, and sweet potatoes on the kitchen counter.

"And don't forget the condiments!" she added. Paulo just stood in place, his feet unable to move while he surveyed the spacious kitchen for the food list to bring...and condiments? He was spared further embarrassment when President Ventura came into the kitchen looking for him... and grabbed the tray of pork roast and sweet potatoes off the stove, and pointed to the bowl of gravy and salt, and pepper, with instruction to Paulo to "follow me, and don't get lost!" The dining room was filled with talking white shirts and colorful blouses, all seated around a very long table, with everyone talking and apparently no one listening... until Paulo entered the room. He almost dropped his load and ran from the house as the room turned deathly quiet, with all the talking shirts and blouses turning their attention toward him.

"Elders and Sisters, may I introduce you to our guest for lunch, Roberto Quintero Jr... or as he prefers to be called, Paulo!" And just then, the lovely Señora he had almost collided with came into the room, wiping her hands on her colorful apron, followed by... Her! Before Paulo could react to anything, the table of white shirts stood... as a man should when a woman enters the room.

"Paulo, may I present my beautiful wife, Courtney De Jesus Ventura... and my daughter, Sister Ventura, whom I believe you have already met! Paulo has just arrived from a three-year stint aboard a fishing vessel and is visiting America for the very first time," trying to explain the presence of his guest to mostly his wife. "He served as a surgeon's assistant to the vessel's medical team and was highly regarded," he exaggerated, drawing a curious look from Paulo. "He will be staying with us for a few days until other arrangements can be made," this time drawing more of a shocked look from Paulo. After a blessing on the food which was offered by one of the Assistants to the President, the President's wife was served first, and then plates of various dishes and sandwich fixings were passed around the long table, pausing for only a moment before the plate was snatched and moved on to the next person.

Paulo had been so well received by this group since meeting the Elders only a few hours ago, but nothing could have prepared him for such generosity and warmth he felt emanating from his host. *Elder Lomu and Elder Wilkinson...! Where are they?* Paulo thought as he helped himself to a spoonful of mashed potatoes as the bowl was passed to him. And no sooner had the thought of the Elders enter Paulo's mind than a noise from the opened front door reached his ears, followed by two hungry-looking coat-clad missionaries.

Elder Wilkinson apologized for being late, but they had to stop at the bike shop and pick up Elder Lomu's spare tire and red reflector that had been broken in the latest minor bike mishap. The two young men quickly found two more folding chairs and inserted themselves between two husky Elders, each offering a greeting but immediately returning to the delicious task before them. Paulo pretended to be focused solely on the feast before him but was actually more interested in feasting his eyes on the beautiful missionary, Sister Ventura, even though she paid him no mind. So, not wanting to appear forward, Paulo stole only quick glances at the beauty while in the act of helping himself to another portion of food. When dinner was over, and the Sisters came back into the dining room carrying generous helpings of peach cobbler smothered with vanilla ice cream, Sister Ventura made sure she was the one to serve Paulo his dessert... an act not missed by Paulo. Nothing was said between them, just a feeling that set Paulo's heart on fire.

Many hands made light work as the Elders teamed up to clear off the dining room table and wash the dishes as the Sister missionaries gathered around the piano in the living room and sang spiritual hymns and songs, capturing Paulo's interest and emotions. Paulo especially enjoyed the hymns that had rich harmony, with the sisters providing the high notes and the Elders bringing in the low. It was a beautiful end to a most interesting day. Then, President Ventura offered a few words of encouragement to the missionaries and called upon one of the sister missionaries to offer a prayer. *These Missionaries sure do pray a lot*, Paulo concluded.

Elders Wilkinson and Lomu stayed behind to see what President Ventura had on his mind for Paulo, feeling somewhat responsible for the young foreigner. President Ventura assured the duo that Paulo would be fine in his care and dismissed the pair to return to their apartment and press on...

and he would be in touch. With the noise level returning to a normal quiet, President Ventura invited his wife into his study to hear Paulo's story and to get her impressions of the young man. Paulo was asked if he felt ok sharing his story with Señora Ventura... and of course, he said yes. An hour later, the door to the study opened, and a teary-eyed Courtney Ventura returned to her duties as mission mother while her husband remained in the study with his guest.

The conversation between Paulo and Len Ventura had been frank, with Paulo feeling he could trust the man with his secret and not suffer the consequences. He was in the United States of America illegally, and he would need some help to get that straightened out. It appeared to Paulo that perhaps God had led him to this well-connected man for that reason, but for now, he was enjoying his new friends and the feeling that he was special and full of hope and promise. The full day and late hour finally caught up with Paulo as a hand gently shook his shoulder. "Paulo, you are exhausted. Let's find you a bunk so you can get some sleep," suggested Paulo's host. Paulo jerked awake, not even realizing he had dozed off. "I am sorry, Senior Ventura. I did not mean to..."

"You have had a long day, my friend. There will be time for more visiting tomorrow," Len assured as he led Paulo to a closed door and opened it. Paulo observed several rows of bunk beds inside, each three tiers high.

"Looks like you have your choice of beds, Paulo. We use this room for new missionaries when they are either getting ready to go home after two years of service and coming to the mission home for a final goodbye visit and meal. Or they are just arriving to begin their mission, and I get to know them for a couple of days before assigning them to a particular area," he explained. Paulo chose the first bunk he came to, dropped his backpack on the floor beside it, and turned to thank his host for his generosity in allowing him to stay tonight.

"Tomorrow, I must begin looking for a job so I can repay you, Senior," Paulo said weakly, pulling back the covers and grabbing the pillow to his chest at the same time.

El Presidente' smiled. "Breakfast is at 7 am," and closed the door behind him.

Paulo had no watch or any other way of telling what time it was, except that it was now light outside. *I couldn't have slept that fast*, he thought. He quickly dressed and opened the door to a quiet household. *Obviously, it was not yet 7 am*, he thought. Then he heard voices coming from down the hall.

"He is a very intelligent young man, Dr. Lu. He worked for three years on a fishing vessel and ended up assisting the ship Doctor whenever a surgical procedure was needed. He got pretty good and really loved to suture up," Len laughed into the receiver. "All I'm asking is that you give him a shot! No pun intended," laughing louder now. "I would like to see him take a couple of night classes at the U to see what aptitude he has for the sciences." Paulo had stopped right outside what appeared to be El Presidente's office and felt badly about eavesdropping on his conversation, even though it was unintentional. He heard some movement back toward the kitchen and turned to see if he could help fix breakfast, feeling a bit overwhelmed at his good fortune in finding a man who apparently believed in him enough to help him get established.

"Good morning, Señora Ventura. Is there something I can do to help with breakfast?" Paulo offered as he entered the kitchen and found his hostess scrambling some eggs. "That smells very good!" he said, pointing to the bacon she had added to another skillet.

"Paulo, good morning! Would you like to be in charge of the bacon and orange juice this morning while I get the bread toasted?" asked Courtney Ventura as she dashed from one side of the kitchen to another, giving directions to her mission office staff as they strode into the kitchen, one by one... looking first to Paulo and then back to their mission mom, as if expecting some explanation. When there was none, they just went about their business and helped set up for breakfast. Paulo joined in with breakfast preparation as if he was one of the staff and not a guest, which did not go unnoticed by Courtney Ventura, thinking to herself how such a boy with so many challenges in his life ended up with so many positives. *Maybe it has been the 'overcoming' of those challenges that made the difference for Paulo,* she thought?

Courtney Ventura had heard her husband teach the young missionaries that "*when* trial strikes, in whatever form or shape it takes, you will always have a choice on how you will respond! To some, trial will be their excuse when they quit. To others, trial will bring them closer to God. They will remain humble instead of angry, open their mind to impressions and inspiration from God instead of closing their mind, and choosing to make lemonade out of the sour lemons they are dealt. No matter what, you have a choice," He would emphasize.

"Señora, I have the bacon crispy and delicious," Paulo announced, enunciating the "delicious" part as if Courtney had made the bacon from scratch. After giving him directions on where to place the plate stacked high with bacon, Courtney went to the now-closed office door and announced, semi-softly, to her husband, "Breakfast is served!" but before she could take a step back towards the kitchen a hand flew out from behind the door, grabbed playfully at her arm, and coaxed her into his office, where they shared a rare moment of intimacy that was often lost amid the heavy responsibilities that accompanied their role(s) as mission mom and dad, church leader, and caregiver to one hundred twenty-five "older" teens serving their God as they were called to do for eighteen to twenty-four months.

President and Sister Ventura had been "called" to the Florida South Mission for a period of three years to provide leadership to the proselytizing efforts of the large number of missionary charges they would have responsibility over during their respective mission terms. Len Ventura, at fifty-four years of age, had risen to the top of corporate real estate but acted without hesitation when asked to lead a group of young men and women in search of new converts, performing acts of service and growing up in a hurry.

"Breakfast is being eaten! Prayer has been offered!" laughed two separate voices at the breakfast table… sending a message to President Ventura and his wife that they weren't fooling anyone with the door closed. And to hurry while there was still food on the table. Paulo, hesitant at first, filled his plate with a couple of pancakes, a scoop of scrambled eggs, and three pieces of bacon, smiling while he ate. After breakfast, Paulo and the two office staffers gathered up the plates while, after taking a phone call, President Ventura and his two assistants went behind closed doors. Paulo had hoped he would have time to discuss his phone call to Dr. Lu that he wasn't supposed to know anything about, but that would need to wait for El Presidente's timing. Right now, Paulo needed to be a role model of helpfulness where he could in exchange for the generosity being shown him.

These people have a full life, and yet they have included me, Paulo thought while finishing up drying the last dish and placing the damp towel back onto the rack to dry. He looked around and found himself alone in this spacious kitchen. He marveled at the beauty of the granite countertops and wondered what something like that would cost. At the Convent, he was used to wood countertops, and for the last three years aboard the ship, it was stainless steel. As Paulo's thoughts turned to home he wondered about the men he had come to know on the ship… and what happened to them. Some were no doubt dead. *What will happen to them after they die? What will happen to me?*

Chapter Twenty-Two

SISTER VENTURA

A slam of the door leading from the side entry to the house startled Paulo out of his wandering thoughts as he heard a female voice and then laughter... "Hello, anyone here? Did we miss breakfast? Asked one voice, somewhat familiar. "Are there any leftovers?" laughed another. Paulo remained at the kitchen counter, feeling as if he had been caught with his hand in the cookie jar or something, as two figures emerged from the back room into the kitchen with smiles on their faces and probably anticipating a free breakfast, but when they saw Paulo just standing there, the smile on one turned to confusion, and concern. But the smile on the other grew even brighter. "Hello, Senoritas! Good morning!" Paulo greeted, feeling like a fish out of water.

"Good morning!" managed the one Sister missionary while fishing around in the refrigerator for any leftovers.

"Third shelf, covered tin foil!" he disclosed... garnering a smile from Sister Ventura as she turned to join her companion. "And you probably would want to know where I hid the frosted cinnamon rolls?"

"Whaaat? You have cinnamon rolls? Where?" Both girls started rummaging around the kitchen like they were looking for a lost treasure.

"Well, not really... but those pancakes tasted just like the cinnamon rolls ol' Shakey-Jake used to whip up on special days on the ship," laughed Paulo.

"Ooooh, YOU!!! Cried Sister Ventura, throwing a hand towel at Paulo as if in disgust... but playful disgust.

"Ok, ok... to make it up to you, let me warm up these hot cakes and scrambled eggs." Paulo apologized. The girls sat down at the kitchen table as if they expected him to wait on them as punishment for his little prank. Kathryn Ventura, or Katie, as she liked to be called... when she wasn't on a mission, that is, stared at the Book of Mormon she had opened and read every morning as part of her breakfast ritual. Yet, her eyes were moving in whatever direction their server moved while preparing breakfast for the two sister missionaries. And before she could divert her eyes, Paulo cast a quick gaze at her... and their eyes locked, again feeling that familiar heat rising above his collar. "Uh, what are you reading, Sister Ventura?" Paulo asked, fabricating a reason he was caught staring at her.

"It's the Book of Mormon," Sister Ventura responded. "It's another testament of Jesus Christ. Have you not heard of it?" she asked playfully. Paulo held out his hand, waiting for Katie to surrender her read so he could inspect it–then looked at Katie Ventura with a smile, when she didn't immediately hand it to him. "What?" she asked.

Paulo was hesitant to reveal that his adoptive parents were LDS or the stories the ship's crew told him about the *cult*. "Is it true that men in your church have more than one wife?" Paulo asked, locking his eyes once again on the beautiful Katie Ventura as she put another bite of scrambled egg into her mouth.

"Oh yes!" Katie choked, wiping her mouth with a napkin. "My dad has at least three or four wives," she continued, causing a gasp from her companion and Paulo's eyes to widen with that revelation. "He keeps them hidden in the Salt Lake Temple!" she continued with her guise, enjoying the look of horror on Paulo's face a little too much and drawing a look of consternation from her companion. Paulo picked up on the look Katie's companion was giving her, and his mind slowly cleared, becoming aware that this mischievous wench of a missionary was leading him along. *Two could play this game*, he thought.

"I may be interested in joining your church," Paulo responded, looking as serious as he could–under the circumstances. "Is there any limit on how many wives one man can marry? I think three would be a good number to start with," he added, noting the flush beginning to crawl up Katie's face. "I am beginning to love America already!" He said, wringing his hands together as if he was about to open a Christmas present, with a sinister smile that betrayed his innocence. This put Katie over the top, and she responded by tossing the Book of Mormon in front of her right at Paulo, who skillfully caught the book and held it to his chest.

"Does this book hold the secret to how a man might win the heart of a woman?" he asked sincerely and, without blinking, stared right into Katie's eyes without so much of a hint of what he was thinking.

"Sister Ventura, do I need to remind you we have an appointment in thirty minutes and need to be on our way," Katie's companion broke in while gathering up the plates on the table.

"I will clean up your dishes, Senoritas. Be on your way. But, we shall have to finish this discussion, *mi belleza,* at another time," Paulo pressed while offering the hastily discarded Book of Mormon back to Sister Ventura. "You may need this when you deceive others into believing in your false doctrine of having wives locked up in a temple," he laughed, sending a sure message that he could give it back as easily as he could take it...

"He's a jerk! Let's go, or we'll be late!" Katie's companion said while pulling her arm toward the outside door. And in an instant, they were gone, and all was silent again. Paulo fumbled around in the kitchen for a few minutes but then had to admit the fair lady Ventura had smote him. The *off-limits* fair-lady Ventura, he finished, deciding that any further actions on his part to get to know this young woman would likely lead to misery for both of them. He had neither time nor money to support the courting of a future wife. And she... she was unavailable anyway! And that was that!

Chapter Twenty-Three

CHURCH

Turning his focus back to the here-and-now situation, Paulo found himself back at his bunk, thoughts of what he might do with his life moving now to the forefront. It seemed his life was destined always to be waiting on the actions of others. How was he to get into college anyway? He had no money and no means of support while he studied. His new friends had their own lives to lead, and from what he had seen, their lives were quite full with so many missionaries to account for. Len Ventura was on the phone more than he wasn't. His lovely wife had her hands full in the office, overseeing apartment inspections, caring for sick missionaries, and running a very busy household, never knowing who would be showing up for dinner.

Maybe I should just sneak out the back door! Paulo challenged his own resolve and finding it rather weak, actually. He was a bit surprised that he was so content to stay put and let things play out as they would. That was not his usual adventurous self. Still, with no money and no contacts or promise of a roof over his head, Paulo reasoned that God had seen fit to lead him to these people for a reason, and he should at least let things unfold naturally without making a roadblock where there was not one to begin with.

Paulo determined he should become a blessing rather than a curse or an additional load to worry about. He would immerse himself in helping his hosts wherever he might be needed. And before that thought had left his mind, a kindly female voice entered it. "Paulo, can you give me a hand with a few things this morning?" asked Courtney Ventura, already focused on tasks before her, hoping Paulo would become a solution to at least one of them.

"Si Señora Ventura, I am at your pleasure," Paulo said, drawing a smile from Courtney.

"What?" he cried, not knowing he was endearing himself to her with his innocence. The day went quickly, followed by the next and the next. Soon, it was Sunday before Courtney thought of asking Paulo if he had Sunday clothes. "Sunday clothes?" he questioned, showing his innocence again, this time not *totally* real. He would not be comfortable dressed as he had seen the young missionaries dress, with a white shirt and tie that seemed to be choking them. He had been wearing the same two shirts and long pants he had come with and managed to throw the dirty clothes into the washer when he heard someone else washing theirs, so he always appeared clean. But today was Sunday. And Courtney stood looking at Paulo with her mouth open as if she had just met him for the first time. Without a moment to spare, she turned on her heel and spun around to where she would be headed next, which would be her husband's closet.

Handing Paulo a white shirt and tie from Len's side of the closet, Courtney mumbled that she would explain later and hurried Paulo back to the bunk room to get changed. When he appeared minutes later with the tie in his hand... Courtney almost bent over in laughter–not at him, but again for his innocence. He had never worn a tie. What was she thinking as she did the best she could at tying his tie so that it didn't look like someone from the 1940's had tied it? President Ventura had gone ahead with his two Assistants, leaving his wife to bring Paulo and the neighbor lady, Mrs. Woodston from Illinois, with them to church. No one had asked Paulo if he wanted to come. It was just assumed that he would come, which pleased Paulo. He was a little surprised at how much he enjoyed being 'counted in' almost as a family member. *This must be what it feels like to be a member of a real family,* he dreamed, while listening to the constant chatter from neighbor Woodston and the responding "uh huh" from Mrs. Ventura. Paulo caught himself smiling... at what, he did not know. But for once in his life, he was experiencing contentment.

Paulo had not attended a church since he left the Convent years ago. He thought with all the rituals of the Catholic Sisterhood at the Convent, he would have sought out a Catholic Church when the ship set in at various ports, but he never did. But he was curious to see what these Latter-day Saints believed, so he let things ride... letting nature take its course.

And for now, the course was taking Paulo to church... and it didn't take long before the Ventura's sedan slowed and pulled into a crowded parking lot adjacent to a beautifully designed brick-faced building. *No cross on the steeple; that's odd,* thought Paulo. *I wonder if they believe in Jesus Christ?* He didn't have to wait long for his answer.

The service was about to start as Paulo entered the chapel area, which seemed completely full. But like Moses parting the Red Sea, a row in the center a short distance from the front made room for the trio. Then, a fourth joined them on the padded bench, squeezing them all in a little tight. It was El Presidente' with a huge smile for his wife when they locked eyes. A distinguished man with graying sides stood at what appeared to be a podium, and when the congregation quieted, he welcomed everyone and began the service.

The opening hymn was titled, "Jesus, the very thought of thee," and almost brought tears to Paulo's eyes. It set the tone for the prayer that followed, which was directed to the Savior's Heavenly Father. *Obviously, they worship both the Father 'and' the Son.* Paulo connected, apparently more at ease as his eyes opened and began to assess his surroundings... or was he looking to see if one sister missionary was present? He was sitting too far to the front to see more than the first four rows to his side and in front of him. She was not there.

Paulo was surprised to see the Lord's communion (sacrament) offered to those present by young boys dressed in white shirts and colorful ties of differing sizes but with a similar glow about them. There were Anglo, African American, and Latino cultures present, and what appeared to be a dark-skinned boy clothed in a very tasteful bamboo skirt, resembling youth from a Polynesian Island Paulo had seen on a television documentary... during one of the rare times the school children at the Convent were allowed to watch TV. The words of the sacrament prayers started with, "Oh God, The Eternal Father," as both the bread and water were blessed and passed to those wanting to renew their baptismal covenants, *or something to that effect*, Paulo thought.

The noise level in the chapel and the reception-like room connected with the chapel began to rise again with late-comers entering. This gave Paulo a reason to look behind him and quickly sweep across the back of the room—no sign of the beautiful Señorita. At the conclusion of the sacrament service, the conductor, who Paulo learned was the congregation's Bishop, rose and approached the podium, looking a little perplexed. But before he could explain, the side door to the chapel opened, and in blew two disheveled-looking young women, who immediately took the two remaining seats behind the podium, causing a look of relief on the face of the Bishop, which generated some soft laughter from the congregation. One of the young women was Sister Ventura; the other was her companion. Two youths, a boy and then a girl, spoke first, mostly reading their message, occasionally looking up and stealing a glance at their parents, and then quickly retreating back to the safety of the printed word.

Sister Peoples, Katie's companion, was up next. She spoke of her experience as a missionary and how wonderful it was to help people find the truth, considering the many interpretations of scripture out in the world. Her message was bright and happy, making Paulo feel better about her calling him a jerk the day before. A rest hymn, "Love at Home," was sung next. Paulo was taken in by this song and found himself humming along with the congregation even though he had never heard it before. Then Sister Ventura approached the podium, introduced herself, and, smiling at her mother and father, began to speak the words she had prepared. Paulo tried very hard to follow her talk so he could compliment her on it should he see her again, but he had to keep himself from drowning in those big dark eyes of hers as she seemed to connect with the congregation, not paying one bit of attention to Paulo.

Sister Ventura spoke of Christ being at the center of her faith and how, as a child, her parents taught her to *trust in the Lord with all thy doing*. She explained that as she has grown older, she has come to understand that trust extends to ALL her activities and involves asking the Lord for guidance, even for secular activities such as school and jobs. "I feel as though I have a link with my Savior, Jesus Christ," she continued... "as I try to live worthily to have the constant companionship of the Holy Spirit. It is that Spirit that connects me instantly to my Savior's influence, enabling me to drink of His wisdom and direction in my life."

Paulo found himself drawn into the speaker's kind manner in which she explained her relationship with God. He loved how comfortably she spoke of God as if He were her Father and not some iconic figure made of stone... or an unseen figure in space that one prayed to but never heard back from. *I have never heard from God*, Paulo thought to himself, feeling a pang of loneliness. But then another thought hit Paulo as Sister Ventura was winding up her talk, which countered the first. He had seen evidence of God. He remembered now... the impressions that prompted him saved him from his captors and then from the police, ultimately leading him to the family who gave him shelter and got him a passport and a job on a fishing vessel. And don't forget the impression that warned him to stow away some extra food and water... And what about his passport miraculously turning up in his boat after being rescued by the Coast Guard? And....

Before Paulo could add his fish tale to his list of evidence that God surely knew who he was and had a plan for him, Sister Ventura had finished her talk. The Bishop was now at the podium and, with tears in his eyes, thanked all who had participated in the service today. He reminded the young men to clean up the chapel before going to class so it would look clean and perfect for the ward who would be meeting next. The closing hymn and prayer came next, and at the sound of *Amen,* the congregation began to gather themselves and proceed to what Paulo thought was to the exit door... but then Courtney Ventura reached over to him and suggested he might like the Gospel Principles class, which is better suited for those just learning about the church.

And Paulo's spirit soared when she added, "I will see if Sister Peoples and Sister Ventura are going to stay so you will have someone in the class you would know," as she rushed to the front of the chapel to catch her daughter who was swarmed by several youth and others wanting to give their regards to her. Paulo did not miss the look of surprise on the face of Sister Ventura and the quick glance of her eyes his way as her mother spoke in her ear. She nodded, with what appeared to Paulo as reluctant acceptance of an assignment by her mother... but fell in step with her companion as the two missionaries motioned to Paulo to follow without saying a word. Sister Peoples pushed her companion in through the doorway of a small classroom just off the main foyer and waited for Paulo to catch up before entering herself, thus ensuring her companion was seated a comfortable distance away from Paulo. Paulo did not miss that action either. But instead of sitting next to Sister Peoples, Paulo chose another seat in the row behind her and Sister Ventura, giving him a perfect view of the beautiful Señorita missionary. And Sister Peoples did not miss that action, either.

Paulo sat silent as the class continued under the direction of the teacher, who spoke with a slight German accent. She proved to be quite interesting as she recounted the experience of Joseph Smith praying to know which sect he was to join... and then was rewarded with a personal visitation of both the Father and the Son. Paulo learned that Joseph Smith was told not to join any of them and spent several years waiting for God to give him more direction. Paulo thought it would have been so hard just to wait, but the teacher explained that sometimes we have to grow before God can use us to bless others.

Paulo was again caught up in the lesson's subject matter before a loud buzzer sounded, which he understood was to signal the end of class. He was surprised at how disappointed he was that it had ended so quickly. But, as everyone around him started talking, Paulo stood, walked to the front of the room, and stuck out his hand to the teacher to introduce himself and let her know how much he enjoyed the lesson. She, in turn, asked Paulo about himself and said she appreciated how he was into the lesson; even though he made no comments, she could tell he was absorbed into the learning atmosphere. Sister Ventura and Sister Peoples stood behind Paulo and simultaneously looked at one another–Sister Ventura raising one eyebrow as if to say, "Maybe we underestimated him?"

When Paulo finished his mutual appreciation discussion with the teacher, Sister Leopold, he started on his way out the door looking for the exit...but was met by President Ventura just coming down the hall, who greeted Paulo with open arms, asking how the class was and if he liked it? Before Paulo could answer, someone intercepted the mission President, and Paulo was again swept away by the stream of youth coming out of their classes and plugging up the hallways. Paulo could not see President Ventura any longer as he hugged the wall and waited for the congestion to clear.

A few minutes later, President Ventura reappeared at Paulo's side, apologizing for leaving him alone in the "hallway quagmire" of youth filtering their way to their various classes and chatting along the way in no particular hurry. Paulo just smiled at the President's description... thinking to himself how much he enjoyed the countenances of these young people compared to the kids at the convent school he lived with. Having family around you for support must be why these kids seem so... self-assured.

"Hola, Paulo!" came a familiar voice as the crowd of youth seemed to break into girls and boys, with President Ventura guiding Paulo into yet another doorway–this time into a larger room where the voice was coming from. Recognizing first the voice and then the two white shirts with name tags, Paulo embraced his missionary friends with handshakes and a half-hug shoulder bump. Paulo had seen the male youth greet one another in this manner and fit easily into this informal way of greeting his two friends. Paulo sat between the missionaries and was again introduced to those attending what Paulo picked up as a "Priesthood meeting." After what appeared to Paulo to be a meeting of reporting and announcements, a group of young males were dismissed... again causing what seemed to be a separation of ages into various classrooms. Paulo learned that the women members were following a similar procedure, with the young girls meeting with their female adult leaders and the eighteen-year-olds and up meeting in what was called Relief Society. The older adult men, along with President Ventura, left the larger group and gathered in a small room just across the hallway, Paulo observed.

These people seem to be very well organized... again thinking how often he had sat in catechism and morning prayer without moving for what felt like hours to a young boy who didn't want to be there in the first place. *I should have paid more attention when I had the opportunity to learn from those dedicated Sisters at the convent. They tried so hard and were so patient with me, but I refused to listen!* Paulo confessed to himself, feeling somewhat... humble?

As the smaller meeting progressed with what appeared to be a lively discussion about the evils of video gaming and other similar entertainment filling the lives of youth today, Paulo let his thoughts drift again–this time back to his rebellious years in the convent... and his best friend. He wondered if she was happy. He hoped she had been adopted, but he knew of her plans to join the convent if she wasn't.

A thought rushing through Paulo's mind almost caused him to fall off the chair, drawing looks from the missionaries and others. He sat up straight on the hard metal chair, feeling the pain of sitting for three hours starting to make its way into his ability to concentrate. But a thought of... his mother–came into his mind like a cold winter wind, causing him to feel chilled. Shaking his head, Paulo stood unexpectedly and went into the hallway where he could think. Why would thoughts about a mother he never knew come to mind so unexpectedly–and for what reason? She didn't want him, so why was he thinking about her now?

What is happening to me? Paulo questioned himself, now rubbing his head aggressively as if doing so would reveal the answer.

"Are you ok?" came a familiar voice from behind Paulo, causing his thoughts to scramble momentarily. "Uh, yes! I am ok," he lied. Sister Ventura was standing over the water cooler in the hallway leading to the foyer, wiping her mouth of the excess water from the fountain, when she spied Paulo rubbing his head. She knew her companion would not be happy if she were caught talking to a boy... alone! But he looked like he needed a friend... so she called out to him and then laughed inwardly at how he reacted to her voice. "You know, you need to improve on your lying skills," she teased, coming closer now, causing Paulo some discomfort. "You looked like you were deep in thought, Paulo. I'm sorry to have disturbed you," Paulo didn't move his gaze as she placed her hand on his arm, chills again rising in Paulo's chest, causing him a momentary loss of breath as he tried to respond but couldn't.

For a moment, Paulo felt as he did growing up... a speech impediment and shortness of breath caused him much anguish as a child, not to mention the shorter leg that he was born with and still caused him to limp when he walked. "I, uh... I am... dddoing ok," he stammered, embarrassed to even look at her.

"Paulo, let's go sit down in the foyer where my companion can find me when she is through teaching the young women," Sister Ventura offered sympathetically, still touching his arm but now guiding him to a couch where two children sat coloring, obviously waiting for a parent. As the newcomers joined the children on the couch, Sister Ventura greeted them, complimented them on their coloring skills, and then turned her attention toward Paulo, who had observed her people skills in action. *She will make a good mother*, he thought.

"Paulo, did you enjoy the services today?" Sister Ventura asked, looking him in the face, trying to connect with his eyes. "When I first saw you in the hall, it appeared as though you were stressed. Are you worried about something?" Paulo just sat still as if frozen in place, afraid to speak, afraid of what might come out. Paulo's pause was short-lived as he heard a voice saying:

"I was born to a mother who tried to kill me," said the voice without tremor or stutter. It was *his* voice! "I learned of this from a good friend who was 'assigned' to watch over me as I grew up in the Convent to keep me from being picked on, I suppose. We became best friends," his voice trailing off as if sending her a voice note across the seas. Sister Ventura's face did not reveal the heartbreak she felt inside that any mother could willingly take her child's life, no matter the stage of life.

"I have deep anger toward my mother and whoever my father is... uh, was," Paulo continued. "But I felt something different today. When the communion was administered, I watched those young men dressed in white shirts and ties, faces scrubbed clean," he smiled, chancing a quick glance into Sister Ventura's eyes, and almost lost his footing when he connected with her smile... and deep brown eyes, wide and searching. He continued... "Something was trying to get into my heart like it was trying to take control. The force was so powerful I almost wept. In fact, I did... a little," he confessed, head now bowed as before, unable to look at her.

"Was it a bad feeling, Paulo? Is that why you are stressed?"

"No, it was not bad–uncomfortable, maybe, but not bad." There was silence between them... Sister Ventura felt an impression to let him continue at his pace. She only hoped her companion would not break in and interrupt this good man's progress, experiencing what she knew to be the Lord's spirit and witnessing the power of forgiveness. When he did not continue, Sister Ventura was impressed to assist with another question:

"Have you ever heard of the atonement, Paulo?" Katie asked simply.

"Yes, of course. It was taught regularly during our religious classes and mass," Paulo responded. "A priest would come regularly to our school and encourage us to repent, and he would hear our confessions and give us certain penances to be forgiven. But I never felt clean... really clean after those confessions." He paused and then continued, noticing Sister Ventura's raised eyebrows... "Ok, I never went, but that is what others told me how they felt when they went. I was just always so mad at... everything–everyone! I could not bring myself to go."

"That's better," Sister Ventura complimented. "See, doesn't that feel better already? My dad once gave a lesson in our family home evening that I'll never forget," the young missionary confided. "It was about lying! He had this picture of a young boy, and each time he told a lie, no matter how serious, my dad put this ugly, snake-looking thing around the boy so that after a few lies, the boy was so covered with these snakes that he could barely be seen." She paused for a moment, hearing chatter coming down the hallway. "The point of the lesson," she continued while standing up, "was that every time we lie, we have to tell another to cover up the last lie until we are fully covered with lies... that feel like snakes!" She added.

"Hey, companion, where were you? I finished the lesson with the Young Women and..." Her voice trailed off as she saw who Sister Ventura had been talking to. Sister Ventura had a red blush rising from her neck to her forehead, and she could just imagine that everyone could see her red face.

"I'm sorry, companion, I was helping the girls, and then Brother Quinteros had a question about what he learned today in Priesthood... didn't you, Brother Quinteros?" Sister Ventura gritted out as if sending a message to Paulo.

"Oh...yes, yes, a question. I had a question about how two beautiful flowers in God's garden could..." And before he could finish his question, Sister Peoples let out a raspy "Oooh, let's go, companion, before he starts in again with that Latin sweet talk," and grabbing her companion by the hand, began leading her back down the hallway... but not before Katie Ventura looked over her shoulder and threw Paulo a smile that caused him to sit back down on the couch.

"We will continue our discussion another time, Brother Quinteros," she offered, now out of sight.

"Yes, we certainly will," was the soft reply. Paulo sat back on the padded couch, now finding himself in the grandstand observing the activity and chaos that signaled the end of the three-hour worship "block," as his friends called it. Yet, he would have thought at the end of such a long series of services and meetings that everyone would rush out to their cars and head for home, grateful to be finished... but that did not seem to be the case with these people. *They genuinely care for one another*, he thought, as he observed streams of people gathering in small groups, families gathering children, adult women huddled in conversation, men laughing and making plans for... another meeting? Paulo then heard a familiar male voice as President Ventura came around the corner and spotted him.

"There he is!" he announced to no one in particular. "Paulo, let's get a move-on... I smell dinner cooking," he laughed. "And if we are late for dinner at the mission home on Sunday's we will be eating Saturday night leftovers!" Again laughing and revealing a very good mood after such a long day.

Chapter Twenty-Four

FORGIVENESS

The drive back to the mission home went quicker than the ride to church, and before Paulo realized it, he was back at the Ventura mission home with bicycles strewn across the front lawn and backpacks in the hallway leading into the formal living room of the mission home. A mild roar of active chatter was building in the kitchen as missionary guests who had been invited to Sunday dinner at the mission home joined forces in preparation for the late afternoon meal, with the President's wife softly barking orders... bringing some semblance of a plan in action that might lead to a hearty meal. Paulo jumped right into the mix of missionaries preparing dinner, offering to cut and dice anything that required the use of a sharp knife. Soon, the table had been set, and extra chairs were found as everyone gathered around the big dining room table, not having to be asked twice. A blessing was offered on the meal, and soon the quiet chatter that had preceded the blessing was replaced with muffled mouths full of food asking for this and that, but mostly silent contemplation of how good the food tasted.

Paulo missed this time on the ship. It was a time when the men came together, and for a few minutes they could forget whatever burdened them. Most of the men were burdened over something. You didn't live and work on the sea because you enjoyed the salty air. These men were runners... every one of them running from something or someone!

"Paulo… Paulo, could you please pass the corn before you doze off again?" The voice of President Ventura roared amidst a chorus of laughter, bringing Paulo back to the here and now. Paulo took the jab good-naturedly and passed the corn while thinking to himself how comfortable he felt among these people. He would study their doctrine and see if he still felt as positive as he did now. *Why not become a Latter-day Saint?* He mused. *Why not?*

Dinner was not rushed, and casual talk carried on afterward… but rather than leave a mess for his gracious hosts to deal with, Paulo started "bussing" the table, first taking the empty dishes and used tableware from both sides of him to the kitchen sink where he began scraping off excess food and rinsing off the plates before he started placing them into the dishwasher. At first, no one at the table paid much attention, but as his intentions to bus the entire table by himself became clearer, several male egos kicked in, and soon, Paulo had competition. In no time, the kitchen was restored to its original condition as though a herd of hungry mouths had never been fed.

Before dessert had been served, the group was invited into the spacious living room to enjoy what they called a "fireside chat" without the fire. President Ventura took center stage and began discussing a second witness of Jesus Christ, in addition to the Bible. He held up a dark-colored paperback book as if this was the first time anyone had seen a copy of the Book of Mormon. "The way to Christ is through His scriptures," President Ventura began, with a little too much energy after the second helping of dinner was beginning to settle. He then held up another book in his other hand, similar in size but thicker. "The Bible speaks of two *sticks*, or rolls of parchment, as scripture was written during those days. The stick of Judah," he announced, holding up the Bible in one hand to exaggerate his point… "And the stick of Joseph," holding the Book of Mormon with the other hand.

"Much was lost during the many times the Bible was translated over hundreds of years. The Book of Mormon was restored to the earth during this last dispensation so that humanity would have... a second witness to the Bible."

"Excuse me, President Ventura," came a low voice from the corner of the room. "But what is it you speak of as the last dispensation, please?" Paulo asked politely, not intending to break the silence but amazed at his voice doing just that. All heads in the spacious living room turned to see who had asked the question, drawing frowns from some who were hoping for an early dismissal to the dessert table.

"Paulo, the scriptures teach that a dispensation is a period of time beginning with Adam and Eve when there was at least one prophet of God on the earth who had been called of God to dispense the gospel among the inhabitants of the earth. The scriptures teach that there are to be seven such periods throughout the life of this earth leading up to the time when Jesus Christ will reclaim the earth, that being the seventh, or final dispensation of the fullness of times," explained President Ventura.

Another missionary raised her hand and asked a question relating to the period of time after the Lord comes to reclaim the earth... which attracted Paulo's attention into wanting to know as well. It was explained that this period of one thousand years is called the Millennium... a time when Satan will be bound by the desires of the people to repent, leaving no heart for Satan to reside... and Jesus Christ will reign on the earth so that saving ordinances can be performed for those who have departed to the other side without their saving ordinances in place. Paulo looked a little dazed at where his innocent question about dispensation had ended up... Satan? Bound? One thousand years? Millennium? Really?

Someone moving in the kitchen easily drew Paulo's interest away from the discussion that now grew even more energetic as the young missionary dinner guests tried their individual best to stump their leader with questions of their own. Paulo excused himself with a slight nod to no one in particular and headed out to the kitchen. He had not seen her and her companion come in, but Sister Ventura and Sister Peoples had laid out two pies and were preparing slices with ice cream on the side, as Paulo caught Sister Ventura licking her finger after trying to balance a slice of apple pie on a knife while sliding it onto a plate. "I'll take that one," he said, pointing to the piece she had just nudged onto a plate with her thumb. "But smother it with ice cream so the germs get frozen," he laughed, causing an immediate flush to her face.

"Sister Ventura, do you have a spare copy of the Book of Mormon I could borrow?" Paulo asked between bites. "I have some reading I would like to do," he concluded while scooping a spoonful of ice cream into his mouth. "I love ice cream!" he declared, causing stifled laughter from both sister missionaries. Sister Peoples offered Paulo a book and then turned toward the group coming from the living room, grabbing a few extra plates and started filling them for the hungry crowd. Paulo took the book he had just received in one hand and deftly scooped another portion of ice cream onto his plate with the other... and escaped to his room without looking at anyone.

"I Nephi, having been born of goodly parents..." he began to read, pausing often to think about what he had just read. There was something about this book that drew him in. Before he knew it, the clock read 9:45 pm... He had been reading for almost three hours and barely noticed. He hadn't understood all he read, but the feelings within him were pleasant and encouraging. He felt good about what he read and wanted more.

The house was dark and quiet—all sounds of earlier activity and accompanying chatter were gone, replaced now with silent darkness, pierced lightly by illuminated night lights placed efficiently in areas that drew occasional night traffic... which was where Paulo was headed. Len Ventura's office door was closed, but Paulo could see the light streaming from under the door, signaling that the room was occupied... probably by his gracious host. Paulo rapped lightly on the door, holding his breath that he had not disturbed his host from something important. The door to Len Ventura's office opened immediately, revealing the intruder... with an apologetic smile on his face. "I am so sorry to have disturbed you, Señor, but your light was on, and I thought..." But before he could finish apologizing, Len grabbed his hand and pulled him into his office, leaving the door open.

"Paulo, please sit and tell me how your first Sunday among our congregation went. Did we exhaust you? Confuse you? Scare you?"

"Yes to all three questions, Senior, but all in a good way," he laughed good-naturedly, now evoking a smile from his host. "I was reading your Book of Mormon tonight." Thinking an explanation was necessary from the confused but pleased look on Len's face, he added quickly... "Uh, I borrowed a copy from Kat... I mean Sister Ventura. She found a spare copy for me to read. I have many questions," he added. Len allowed his missionary training to take over, now realizing he had unintentionally become not only a place of refuge for a fine young man in need of shelter but perhaps an actual investigator of the Church of Jesus Christ of Latter-day Saints. He leaned back in his chair, giving Paulo some space to reflect on the feelings of his heart. And reflect he did. It was as though he was making up for lost opportunities for confession with the Convent priest, Father Ramos.

"I find that I relate to several of the Book's characters," Paulo started. "But I was not born to goodly parents as this young Nephi proclaimed. I was a mistake! I was a burden. I was discarded like a piece of trash," Paulo spat, letting the deep-set hatred for his birth parents change his countenance to a darker mood... and causing Len to alter his course by leaning closer to him now, looking tenderly into Paulo's eyes, his instincts kicking into overdrive to help save this young man from the bitterness of unforgiveness that will canker a soul and often lead one into hell.

But, instead of saying anything, Len bit his tongue and just listened, allowing Paulo the opportunity to vent and bring to the surface his resentments, disappointments, and maybe even hatred for those who had wronged him in his life. Paulo did not hesitate. He recounted every instance in his life that had caused him pain. He had not forgiven, and as such, those many injustices committed against him had grown roots and were deep-set... affecting not only his current state of mind but any future chance he might have at gaining a relationship with the Holy Ghost who was the connection to God's glory and mercy.

Len was riveted on every word Paulo was saying, handing over tissues as emotions spilled over those time-tested banks of resistance, leading to change and forgiveness. On occasion, Len would acknowledge the feeling that time just seemed to stand still for this young man to dig deep and begin the process of repentance and forgiveness. There would be no holding back this night... he was witnessing the rebirth of a son of God that had been lost and now had been found. When Paulo slumped in his chair, eyes closed, and hands gripped tightly as if they were wrestling with one another, something happened that was so unexpected, so unplanned, so... necessary. President Len Ventura had risen and positioned himself behind the exhausted Paulo, who was so drained that his only sign of life was evidenced in the movement of his carotid artery beating steadily and causing the skin in his neck to visibly pulse.

Paulo did not notice Len leaving his chair beside him, but when hands were placed on his head, causing an immediate awakening and temporary jolt of adrenaline, Paulo at first tried to sit up and look behind him but quickly gave in to the overwhelming peace he felt when those hands laid on his head. Len's words were authoritative yet assuring and tender. He invoked God's blessing on Paulo with all the love and concern a father would give to a troubled son, rebuking Satan for his presence and opening Paulo's heart to forgiveness of parents who had made horrible choices that even in such extreme mistakes, there is forgiveness because of Jesus Christ's atonement, leaving *our* role only to forgive.

Paulo had never felt such love pouring into his injured soul, and he absorbed every word as it left Len's mouth, hearing as if in slow motion. Tears began to flow as Len's words of comfort, direction, and love found their way through to Paulo's cankered heart. Years of bitterness, personal hatred, and guilt came crumbling down, followed by heart-wrenching sobs of sorrow, regret, and... relief. Paulo was feeling the effects of Christ's atonement as his shoulders and chest continued their musical balance of heave and release–all the while, Len's hands remained lightly upon Paulo's head, with words of comfort and blessings adding spiritual mortar where there were once a broken and cankered heart.

After what seemed like hours to Paulo and bestowing upon him a physical sense of having been released from an ever-present burden, President Ventura's blessing came to a gentle conclusion, "In the name of our Savior, Jesus Christ, Amen!" Len's hands rested upon Paulo's shoulders before he returned to sit in the chair from which he had just come–waiting, not pushing for conversation.

A long few minutes of silence passed by the two men as they sat comfortably in silence, basking in God's grace and mercy for having sent His son to atone for the sins of all who would accept His gift, that all might be spared the spiritual death that sins unrepented of–and the lack of forgiveness of others–would surely have heaped upon humanity. Paulo continued to sit with his head bowed, eyes closed... but experiencing a feeling so overwhelming he could barely speak a whisper.

"What just happened?" Paulo asked softly, mostly to himself.

"You felt God's spirit, Paulo, testifying to you that forgiveness of others clears the way for the Lord to communicate with you. When we hold grudges and hatred for others, no matter the justification we feel, our spirit is cankered with those feelings and begins to weaken our spirit, making us vulnerable to Satan's voice and not so much to God's."

Paulo let that long explanation sink in a few seconds before asking another question: "How will I know that I have truly forgiven my mother? I don't even know who she is... or the man who got her pregnant," refusing to call him father.

"Well, the forgiveness part doesn't require any conditions to be effective, Paulo. It neither requires that you know them nor that they know you have forgiven them. Forgiveness is personal. God knows your heart, and he knows your intentions. If you have forgiven, He will send his spirit, as we both experienced. It was the spirit of God you felt, Paulo, confirming that God loves you and seeks a place in your heart. It is His way of communicating with His children," explained Len as he stood and began walking to his seat behind his desk. It was getting late, and Paulo still felt the effects of the emotional outpouring he had just experienced.

"I guess I had better let you finish up, Mr. Ventura," Paulo offered respectfully. "I have detained you long enough hearing my problems."

Len smiled and turned around to where Paulo was sitting, extending his hand and embracing Paulo in a spontaneous act of love. "You are a good man, Paulo Quintero. I hope you will consider having Elders Lomu and Wilkinson teach you about the Church. I know they would be very excited if you would accept my invitation. They could teach you right here in the mission home," President Ventura beamed.

Paulo smiled back at this man he was quickly learning to love—and answered affirmatively, without hesitation. "Yes, I would like that, El Presidente'"–Paulo beamed back. "I would like that very much," accepting another hug before saying goodnight and walking back to his room, feeling deep emotional exhaustion as he prepared to lay down, but instead, he just sat on the edge of his bunk and contemplated where his life was headed. Although he felt emotionally exhausted, he wanted to experience again that feeling of the spirit he had felt when Len had given him a blessing. He felt the connection of the Lord's spirit for the first time... and wanted more. He dropped to his knees... and waited. Thoughts came coursing through Paulo's mind—seeing himself as a young child when he first learned that not everyone was born into a family consisting of nuns, priests, and throwaways.

But Paulo's mind quickly focused on Felicia Torres, his best friend growing up. Felicia was always there for him... treating him like a big sister, even a mother at times. His heart warmed at the thought of her. Where was she now? Had she been adopted? She had been a lifesaver to him. Paulo's mind quickly checked through the list of nuns and teachers and administrators... even Priests, who had tried to talk him out of the bitterness he held for his mother... with no success, but they had at least tried, thus showing their love and concern for Paulo. It had only taken a few short days with his new friends before Paulo felt the full impact of the atonement and allowed himself to even consider forgiveness as an option. He felt a break in the dam that held the sweet coursing of forgiveness from reaching his heart... and he wanted more.

This *Len Ventura* possessed something the likes of which Paulo had never felt. When Len placed his hands on Paulo's head, he felt an almost instant submission to God... a humility that acknowledged a power greater than himself present in the room that night. And when he spoke, his words were like a healing ointment to Paulo's cankered soul, almost as if God himself was speaking through Len. It was an experience Paulo would not soon forget.

Paulo was not prepared for the next image that flashed into his mind. A woman... no, a young girl laying on a bed or something. Bright lights exposed the look of fear on her face. Two others were attending to her, trying to calm her, but she fought them, resisting. One of those present, a doctor perhaps, spoke, "It is too late–the child is coming! Just tell Maria her child is dead... and send him to the Convent. The Sisters will know what to do. Hurry!"

Paulo opened his eyes in shock. Maria? Had he just seen his mother fighting to keep him? She did not want to kill him as he had been led to believe, even though Felicia told him otherwise. He had seen it... or did he? What just happened? Paulo's emotional state at that point had no resistance left, and he lost all control. The dam had broken, and the healing ointment of God's love flowed evenly, fully, into Paulo's heart, causing the feelings of regret and hatred to be washed away, leaving in its stead an insatiable desire to grow, to smile... to live–and to love. He must find his mother. He must tell her she is forgiven. Jesus Christ had paid for her sin, asking only the price of full repentance... a broken heart and contrite spirit, Len had said. Paulo would need to do some more study on that one, but for now, he had felt God's love and forgiveness of his own sins and flaws and wanted the same for his mother.

Paulo did not remember when he fell asleep, only that he lay there for what seemed like hours after his emotional purging. His longing to find his mother weighed heavily on his mind, as he tried to craft a plan to find her. He had no idea where to start, notwithstanding he was in a foreign country and she was likely dead or living back where Paulo had just escaped from. There would be no returning to look for her. A thought came into Paulo's mind to "give it to God, He knows where she is." Paulo did not remember anything else after that... so that must have been when he sunk into a deep sleep, his conscious mind still thinking he must make a plan to obtain an education so he could earn enough money to return to his homeland and rescue his mother... and Felicia. And then it was morning!

Chapter Twenty-Five

BAPTISM

The next few days turned into weeks as Paulo prepared for his new life. The first order of business was to apply for a work visa and gain the necessary residence requirement for citizenship... with a legal name. This was harder than it would seem since Paulo had no papers other than the fake ID he came into this country with. So, it was decided, for the time being, to use the fake ID to establish legal residency. He could change the name to whatever suited him after he gained citizenship.

For the immediate future, Paulo would remain Roberto Quinteros Jr.

Paulo's next task was to establish residency in the United States in order to apply for naturalization and become a U.S. citizen. Len Ventura's very creative attorney was able to convince the USCIS that Paulo qualified as a 'refugee' during his three years aboard the Conquistador, allowing him to enroll in the U.S. Citizenship and Immigration Services (USCIS) work visa program and prepare to become a citizen of the United States of America.

Again, with the Ventura family's help and guidance... and some private tutoring from one Sister Katie Ventura, who by no small coincidence had graduated from Brigham Young University with a degree in American History Education, Paulo set out to become a citizen of the United States of America. Elders Wilkinson and Lomu came to the mission home each Sunday after church and taught Roberto Quinteros Jr. about the Church of Jesus Christ of Latter-day Saints. To say this weekly activity only drew a crowd would be an understatement. Extra places were added to the evening meal as Elders, Sisters, and private tutor Sister Ventura, who just happened to be in the neighborhood and hoped they would be welcome in support of Paulo. He had seriously become a hero of sorts to anyone who knew him and heard his story.

Because Paulo knew little to nothing about the LDS church, except for it being nicknamed the *Mormon Church* from the very beginning of its infancy due to the name of the Book of Mormon, the weekly sessions went slow, not to mention his private tutoring lessons about the birth and development of America. And, of course, *work!* Or, in this case, a lack of it. There was little time available for a job that required a typical eight-nine hour work day... and the Ventura's were so attached to this young man that they didn't want to throw him out to fend for himself and not accomplish his citizenship for whatever reason. So Paulo was given a job as President Ventura's private executive secretary, yard boy, and assistant mission cook to Courtney Ventura in exchange for room and board... and private tutoring by one Sister Katie Ventura. This arrangement pleased Paulo so much that he could not keep a smile off his face. "What?" He would say when someone would look at him as if to silently ask why the big smile.

Weeks flew by, and soon before he thought he was ready, Paulo opened his eyes for the tenth time that night, checking his watch to see what time it was... and turning over to catch a few more Z's, again satisfied that he had not slept through his watch alarm set for 6:00 am. Today, he would take his citizenship exam and hopefully pass it the first time so he wouldn't have to retake it and repeat this mind-numbing anticipation of becoming a U.S. citizen.

"Scripture study, Paulo!" whispered the alarm before the alarm. Paulo was hoping the Ventura's would call off their early morning scripture reading just one morning in deference to his need for a few more precious minutes of sleep, but that was not to be. Throwing the covers off his lean frame, Paulo jumped off the top bunk and landed firmly on both feet, raising both arms above his head as if to signal a triumphal dismount, as he had observed the Olympian gymnasts do. He was unaware that Len and Katie Ventura were standing in his doorway, smiling from ear to ear.

"What?" Paulo questioned as he hurriedly put on his robe and stuck both feet in slippers... his morning ritual for scripture study. With his left hand, he grabbed the favorite down comforter that Courtney had bought for him, especially for those cool coastal mornings. His right hand reached for the leather-bound Book of Mormon lying on the lower bunk, providing easy access to his copy of the scriptures they would be studying this morning.

Six A.M. signaled the same activity for each missionary team in the Florida Coastal Mission, so it was important that their leaders also follow the same procedure, preparing these dedicated missionaries for the Spirit to direct them to those who might be interested in their message of faith and hope. Paulo's life at sea had prepared him for early risings... and he enjoyed the feelings that came when he knelt in morning prayer with the Ventura's and whomever else might be staying overnight at the mission home—to begin the day and to invite the Spirit into their scripture reading. Today, there was a particular emphasis in both prayer and scripture for Paulo's need for a calm mind and recollection of the material he had been studying for that day.

Preparing for citizenship was nothing short of cramming an entire course of American History at the university into a Cliff's-Notes version of the class, hitting just the high points. But Paulo was capable... and ready. Following scripture study, breakfast, and hurriedly dressing, Paulo stood at the kitchen door to the garage, waiting for his ride. To say he was nervous would be an understatement. Where was the calm mind and confidence Len had prayed for? Paulo's resurgent worries began filling his mind with doubt as his faith started to weaken. Then, a gentle hand rested on his shoulder. "Everything is going to be just fine, Paulo. You are prepared—so give it up to the Lord. He wants us to succeed in this life... and I can't think of a greater blessing than to become a citizen of the country God helped bring his restored gospel to," Len consoled. "Besides, if you don't pass, we can always use that fake ID you brought with you!" he laughed, causing Paulo to join in and begin to feel just a little more confident with Len's encouragement.

Relief coursed through Paulo's body as he completed the last essay question on the exam and laid his pencil down, signaling he was finished well before the time allowed, as an immigration official quickly approached his desk and extended his hand to retrieve Paulo's work, indicating with his other hand the exit and waiting room where Len would be meeting him. Paulo could not use a phone to alert Len that he had finished early and expected he would have a good wait before he arrived... but there was Len, a big smile on his face when he saw Paulo. Len handed the phone to Paulo without saying a word.

"Hhh-hello?" Paulo spoke into the small phone and was treated to a chorus of cheers and shouts of congratulations from the other end, causing Paulo to tighten his lips and cheeks to the noise. Then his tears began to run down his face as he put the phone down and wept on Len's shoulder as the two embraced, without a word spoken between them. Although Paulo had not received his letter from the USCIS confirming a passing score, the party atmosphere awaiting his arrival back at the mission home was overwhelming to him... It was as though he was a returning war hero or something. Even Elders Wilkinson and Lomu were there, along with Sisters Peoples and Ventura. Although hugs were in order from everyone in celebration mode, Sister Ventura extended only her hand to Paulo, under the watchful eye of her companion, Sister Peoples, and congratulated her student for a job well done. Adding a whisper that only Paulo could hear. "Your hug will have to wait until I am released, Mr. Big Shot," Katie's smile revealing for the first time that she might have feelings for this young immigrant.

The following week was filled with activity at the mission home. It was release day for some missionaries, who came to the mission home for their final interview with their mission president. It was also an evening of debriefing with mission staff and confirming travel arrangements to and from the airport. And, of course, the legendary "last" meal, courtesy of Sister Ventura and her staff of one, with plenty of excited chatter from the missionaries thrown in.

After dinner, it was customary for the departing missionaries to participate in a farewell testimony meeting in the Ventura's living room. President Ventura spoke first, thanking and praising each missionary for fulfilling an honorable mission. He even had antidotes of each missionary that were mostly funny things that had happened during their mission.

How does he keep track of so many young men and get to know each one so well? Paulo mused, feeling so grateful he was building a relationship with this kind and generous man who had left his profitable and successful career and other worldly pursuits behind for three years to serve these young men and his church, selflessly and without pay.

The next day was again filled with a flurry of activity around the mission home, preparing for a new batch of missionaries just beginning their mission. Beds were prepared, restrooms cleaned, floors vacuumed, and tile cleaned. Grocery shopping at several stores yielded a van full of food and supplies. Paulo mainly assisted Sister Ventura, but occasionally he was called in by Len to go with one of the missionaries as his companion to run an errand in the Ventura's own vehicle, which was a modest Buick sedan, large enough to squeeze three in the backseat and one passenger, or two if one of the passengers was a child, or a skinny missionary.

Paulo loved the look of "eyes in the headlights" excitement radiating from the new missionaries as they entered the front door of the mission home, being welcomed by Sister Ventura and, of course, President Ventura's two assistant missionaries who would play a crucial role in assessing each young man's strengths and special abilities, which would be important in the decision of which area to assign them. President Ventura spent most of the day behind closed doors, interviewing each new missionary before assigning them an area and companion. When he finally opened his door, Paulo happened to still be in the kitchen and saw him stretch and yawn in the doorway. "I've got pie!" he called out, hoping he didn't draw a crowd with that declaration. Len came into the kitchen and sat on one of the bar stools at the counter.

"What flavor do you have, young man?" Len asked, with a tired smile on his face.

"Blueberry, with a side of vanilla ice cream, is my favorite," Paulo offered. "And the banana cream is a close second!"

"I'll try a small slice of both... and let you know which one I like best," Len directed, with a little more energy in his voice now, scooping some ice cream over the two pieces of pie on his plate.

Paulo stood across the counter from Len, who was enjoying the pie and ice cream treat, arms folded across his chest as he contemplated asking the question on his mind. When he couldn't keep it to himself any longer, he just blurted out: "What would I need to do to become a member of the Church of Jesus Christ of Latter-day Saints?" Len had just placed the last bite of banana cream pie on a spoon and into his mouth when Paulo's question almost caused him to choke on the contents, replaced with a huge smile as the contents found their destination before Len let out a "Yahoo" that would certainly bring to life the entire household.

"Please, sir... I may not qualify and would not want others to know until I am absolutely certain," Paulo quickly said in a hushed voice, putting his finger up to his mouth to hide the smile that had begun to form.

"What's wrong?' came an excited voice from behind the pair.

"I heard screaming...!" Came another, as several bodies came running to see what the commotion was about.

"Uh, this is the best blueberry and banana cream pie I have ever tasted!" Len quickly announced, placing another scoop of ice cream on his plate before Paulo added another small piece to his plate, both hiding smiles that were bursting to come out. Although Paulo had received the formal six pre-membership lessons about the Church from Elders Wilkinson and Lomu, they were under strict direction from President Ventura to not ask Paulo to be baptized but only to instruct and inform him about the

Church. He felt that Paulo needed to develop his own testimony without the heavy influence of the Church culture he was immersed in while living at the mission home. If Paulo was thinking about becoming a baptized member, he needed to come to that conclusion on his own.

And he did! Paulo wanted that brightness of hope he had heard others reflect on as they embraced the atonement and placed their sins upon the altar of forgiveness, accompanied by a broken heart and contrite spirit. Paulo had reached that point in his life that he was ready to let go of the hatred and guilt that had followed him–consumed him since his birth. He was ready to forsake those feelings in exchange for being washed clean in the waters of baptism, coming forth as a new child, clean and innocent, armed now with the sacrament of our Lord Jesus Christ to resolve future actions of the natural man that may influence choices in the future.

The journey Paulo was about to take would not be easy, given his past, but it could be done... would be done, with the help of Paulo's new constant companion, the Holy Ghost, and his active membership in the Church of Jesus Christ, both received the day he was baptized. When a son or daughter of our Creator enters the waters of baptism and takes upon himself the body and blood of our Savior, Jesus Christ, significant changes often happen in their lives to test their commitment to follow Him. One such change came to Paulo the very night he was baptized. Lying on his back on his top bunk, Paulo was alone with his thoughts about the day he just had, reliving the feeling of Elder Wilkinson's strength as he lowered Paulo gently beneath the font waters, completely immersed, and easily brought him forth out of the waters a clean and forgiven man. The very thought of that activated Paulo's empty tear ducts. There was nothing more to give. He had laid it all at the feet of his Lord and cried for what seemed like hours through the flurry of activity that followed.

Paulo had dressed after the baptism and came back into the small room completely filled with missionaries and the Ventura family, including one very nice-looking Sister missionary who had come up to Paulo and shook his hand, not the action he was hoping for, but he understood the code of conduct for missionaries. Had he seen that there was also something communicated in her eyes? Something that might mean more than just friendship, perhaps? Then it was gone! He didn't know whether he'd seen something real but unspoken or if his hopeful imagination had led him to see more than there was to see.

President Ventura gave an inspiring and emotional talk about our Savior's baptism... and his walk into the Garden of Gethsemane, where He took upon himself the sins of the world. He spoke of the Comforter who would come after Christ had died on the cross. He then said something that stirred Paulo's soul... "Brothers and sisters, we will now proceed with the confirmation of Church membership and the bestowing of the Gift of the Holy Ghost upon our newest Church member," announced President Ventura at the end of his short but powerful talk.

Paulo had been waiting for this moment ever since he had learned of the existence of a third member of the Godhead, joining God the Father and His Son, Jesus Christ. He had often felt promptings in his life, but he mostly dismissed those as coincidences or his body reacting to a particular event or something like that. He had no clear explanation of what those were until he met the missionaries. They seemed to have an answer for everything; he smiled. Today, Paulo would receive membership in the Church of Jesus Christ of Latter-day Saints and, as such, would be entitled to receive the "gift" of the constant companionship of the Holy Ghost. He did implant the significance of that blessing as a consistent compass in his life to keep him pointing true north in terms of how to keep himself from straying off the path to eternal life. Paulo would depend upon his new companion to warn him when he got too far to the edge. It would still be up to Paulo to self-correct under the sacred principle of applied agency, but at least he would be warned and know 'from whence this warning cometh.'

Paulo's thoughts returned to the here and now as several hands were placed lightly upon his head, and a single voice confirmed his membership in the Church and then pronounced upon him the Gift of the Holy Ghost. At that exact moment, Paulo's body began to shake from the flow of tears and the feeling of relief that coursed through him. He had been washed clean, preparing his tabernacle of clay to receive his new companion... and now he accepted his guest with open arms and an open heart.

Chapter Twenty-Six

I HOPE THEY CALL ME ON A MISSION

How does one describe the feeling that comes from a change in nature from a self-accusing, non-trusting, unbelieving, agnostic... to a happily, believing Christian, full of forgiveness and hope? Paulo embraced this change with all his heart. A brightness of hope radiating from his smile and demeanor left no doubt in anyone's mind when they looked at Paulo tonight; he had truly accepted God's grace and mercy in his life.

Paulo was famished as the emotion of the evening drained out of him, leaving a large appetite to be satisfied with finger foods and cookies. The support and love shown to him today were truly life-changing, and even now, Paulo almost had to pinch himself to be sure this wasn't just a dream, and he would wake up at any minute from a rough hand across his head by one of the supervisors at the factory, laughing at his wake-up call.

The drive back to the mission home gave Paulo time to reflect on this special day and how his *by-chance* connection with the Elders had changed his life for the better. Laying his head back and resting it comfortably upon the backseat headrest, Paulo's thoughts began to wander... eventually settling on his mother. He had forgiven her and now wanted to meet her in person and perhaps introduce the gospel to her if she hadn't found it already. In fact, Paulo was so excited about his own conversion and the remarkable change that had come into his life that he wanted to share his story with everyone he met.

Over the six months that followed, Paulo proved the change in his carnal nature was indeed real... not that he was anywhere near perfect, but his heart had softened toward others, and he began seeing those he met truly as a brother or sister, leading him to introduce the gospel to them. Almost every week Paulo was bringing someone to the mission home to be taught the gospel. His enthusiasm had affected the entire mission, as Paulo was going on splits with the missionaries almost nightly when he wasn't joining in on the lessons to his own investigators.

Paulo was enjoying his new life so much that he didn't think it possible to get any better, which may explain his surprised look when one of his investigators caught him totally unprepared for an answer, "So Paulo, why aren't you one of these missionaries with a name badge on?" Serving a mission had entered Paulo's mind a time or two since he had become a member of the Church, but with so many changes in his life, he couldn't comprehend what that meant in terms of another life change, not to mention how he would support himself since missionaries are not paid to serve. So, he usually dismissed those thoughts as quickly as they came. But for some reason, this time, he didn't.

One evening, as Paulo came into the kitchen for a late-night snack before retiring, he was surprised to find the Ventura's sitting at the counter, each with a cup of hot chocolate. "How did your discussion go, Paulo?" asked Len without looking up as he raised the cup to his lips. Paulo sat down beside the President while smiling broadly...

"It went very well," he responded. "The Spirit was so strong tonight, I could hardly keep my eyes off Elder Lomu as he challenged the Knight family to pray about the teachings they had received. Brother Knight was the first to respond; with tears in his eyes, he said... *Yes, I will pray, but only for confirmation of what I have already felt!*

"I thought Elder Lomu was going to jump up and hug him, he was so excited," Paulo laughed, causing both Len and Courtney to do the same. "But he waited until after the lesson, and we were leaving to do that," causing another round of happy laughter, knowing Elder Lomu's nature to hug everyone, even some he wasn't permitted to hug.

"Am I too old to go on a mission?" The silence that seemed to suspend Paulo's question in mid-air was knocked out of the park by a squeal of delight from Courtney, who jumped off the bar stool she had been sitting on and threw her arms around Paulo, causing both a look of pleasant shock and profound joy on Len's face, as he tried to maintain some manner of control over just a question.

"Courtney! The young man just asked a question," Len chided. Then, looking at Paulo, who was visibly enjoying the hugs he was receiving, Len responded with... "Paulo, being twenty-one does not disqualify you from serving a mission, although you would certainly be one of the older missionaries," his answer brought a smile to Paulo's face as Courtney composed herself and returned to her stool after tousling Paulo's hair in a playful gesture.

"He's not old... he's still a kid at heart with so much life yet to experience," Courtney played.

"Paulo, are you thinking of serving a mission," Len asked in a more serious tone, glancing at Courtney with a "my turn" look.

"Well, I have been thinking about it," Paulo responded. I understand that I need to be a member of the Church a whole year... and qualify to receive my temple endowment, although I am not sure what that means," Paulo confessed. "And there is the matter of savings. I don't have much, but I did manage to save my 'slave wages,' as the men called them, after our ship was boarded by pirates and I was directed by the "voice" to jump ship. But I would be eager to get a job... besides helping out here, of course!"

Len squeezed Courtney's hand... "Paulo... I think I can speak for Courtney when I tell you not to worry about the money for a mission. Our daughter Katie will finish her mission in six months, and our ancestral mission fund will be available to make up the difference in what you need for your mission. Isn't that right, Court?"

"Wait a minute," Paulo squeezed out, almost breathless. "I can't let you pay for my mission! You have done so much for me already," argued Paulo. "I will get a job and work nights to earn my mission money. I have to do this!"

And he did.

Working nights at Burger Barn and sleeping four hours until morning prayer and scripture study with the Ventura's reminded Paulo of his days... and nights aboard the Conquistador–no clock to remind him that he missed a night of sleep. And here he was doing it all over again, but this time, he had an end goal in mind, and if losing some sleep was the price... then he was willing to pay it. He was going to be a missionary.

Hours turned into days, and days turned into months, as Paulo worked nonstop to prepare himself financially and spiritually to become a full-time missionary for the Church of Jesus Christ of Latter-day Saints, assigned to serve somewhere in the world for twenty-four months. When the day came to celebrate the end of Katie Ventura's missionary service, only then did Paulo raise his head from under his almost inhuman schedule. Although he did his best to avoid working on Sundays, he usually had difficulty sitting through the 3-hour block of services that started at 8 am without his head weaving and bobbing. But this Sunday would be different... it was Sister Katie Ventura's last Sunday of her mission, and she was one of the speakers.

Paulo finished up at the Berger Barn a little early to return to the mission home, get cleaned up, and make it to church for the sacrament portion of the service. He loved the inner peace he felt during the most reverent portion of the meeting as the bread and water were blessed and passed to those in attendance, giving each the opportunity to reflect on that week's choices... celebrating the good ones and repenting of those not so good. The Ventura's and several missionaries were sitting front and center when Paulo entered the chapel, greeted by a chorus of voices singing the opening hymn... "Welcome, Welcome, Sabbath Morning..." Len spotted Paulo first and motioned to a space left open next to him, with Courtney on his other side. As Paulo tried to be as inconspicuous as possible, making his way to the front of the chapel, his quick glance upwards to those seated on the rostrum told him he had not been successful. A generous smile from one of the speakers almost melted his heart right there, as did her eyes riveted on his. It did not go unnoticed by her mission president, either... covering what appeared to be a smile of his own.

The topic the Bishopric chose for that particular service was 'Love At Home'... and each speaker contributed their thoughts on the subject, which kept Paulo's attention away from staring at the concluding speaker, who had yet to speak. Finally, the choir sang the intermediate hymn, and Sister Katie Ventura was introduced as the concluding speaker. The Bishop then called Sister Ventura to stand by him while he expressed his love and appreciation for her tremendous help to his ward in serving both members and non-members.

With tears in her eyes, Katie stood, but a little unsteady, feeling somewhat alone now in trying to compose her thoughts after her Bishop had just broadsided her with such kind remarks. Paulo felt the urge to walk up and stand by her, giving her the support to carry on... But one look from her mission president would surely have turned him to stone before he could have taken even one step toward her... so he settled back down, searching her face with his eyes to let her know he was there for her. But she did not return the hidden gesture and only looked up with a quick smile at the congregation before giving her thoughts on the topic.

"I, too, was raised by goodly parents," she began, immersing Paulo in a dream of what it would be like to raise a family like the Ventura's, with the lovely Katie Ventura as their mother. Paulo must have had a smile plastered on his face during her entire talk because when Sacrament Meeting was over and after what seemed like an endless line of ward members anxious to say their goodbyes, she was first to speak when he extended his hand to congratulate her.

"Paulo, what was up with the plastered smile all through my talk?" she teased. "Every time I dared look at my parents during my talk about family, there you were with that big smile. You almost caused me to lose my train of thought!" As she good-naturedly punched him in the chest with her other hand, then realizing she was still holding on to his with the other, as though shocked, she released it immediately. Awkward!

Back at the mission home, the Ventura's were busily preparing to send their daughter home, and Paulo was hoping to steal a few minutes alone with her before she retired for the night. Len was behind closed doors with his daughter for most of the afternoon, completing her end-of-mission interview and dealing with arrangements to bring her home and prepare for when she enters Brigham Young University. But Sunday dinner would provide the opportune time to talk to her while Paulo worked steadily to prepare salad condiments.

While he worked in the kitchen, Paulo 'kept an eye out' to search for any sign of Sister Ventura. His hopes were dashed as Courtney Ventura announced dinner was ready, and bodies started appearing out of the woodwork without any sign of Katie. "Did someone tell Sister Ventura dinner is ready?" Asked Paulo to no one in particular.

"She isn't coming until later," offered Courtney. "She and Sister Peoples had two appointments this evening to say goodbye to the special investigators she didn't get to see baptized." Paulo didn't realize his groan could be heard so easily... until Courtney answered with her own question. "Are you wanting to visit with Sister Ventura about something, Paulo?" Paulo didn't know whether or not to confide in Courtney, but he felt he needed to know if he had an ally in her, or not.

"Uh, yes... I was hoping to have a few minutes with her, a...alone, if possible?"

"Well, she is still on her mission, Paulo... and being alone with a good-looking young man might not be the best way to finish her mission," Courtney teased. "But let's see what time she gets in, and maybe she will want some ice cream," trying to muffle a laugh. And with that, Paulo returned to cleaning up the kitchen, his thoughts clearly not on his work. *What would he say to her? Did he dare express his interest? She was a missionary, for goodness sake! But would he ever see her again? Would she even be interested in writing him while he served on his mission?*

"You have been drying that glass for almost ten minutes, Elder Quinteros!" came a familiar female voice just before a wadded-up napkin hit Paulo... coming from somewhere behind him, but the thrower was well hidden in case there was retaliation.

"If you hadn't been "partying" all night, I might have saved you some chunky monkey ice cream," Paulo accused, which elicited a surprised and happy smile.

"Well, then, I guess I will just go to bed instead," shot back her smiling reply. Paulo turned around to find Katie standing at the back door, watching him with interest.

"Well, maybe I could dig up some extra Chunky," he offered before opening the refrigerator to retrieve the designated peace offering. "But it will cost you!" Paulo teased back. Katie took her seat at the counter while Paulo prepared the treat for both of them to enjoy.

"You want bananas and whipped cream on yours?" Paulo asked with a smile.

"And extra chocolate syrup," came her reply as she pushed her bowl back toward Paulo, who now held a plastic container of chocolate syrup over the approaching bowl... But at the last minute Paulo pointed the container toward Katie... and squeezed. A dark liquid stream shot outward and landed between Katie's chin and lower lip, causing a reaction of disbelief and temporary shock, before she grabbed the spray can of whipped cream and let a stream fly toward Paulo, catching him squarely between the eyes. And laughter erupted... as the two battle-scarred warriors just stood there, gawking at one another.

"What is going on in here," came an authoritative voice from the garage door. "What are you two, uh... misfits, doing in here, alone!" boomed President Ventura in the most mission president's voice he could muster given the sight before him. "You two get this kitchen cleaned up... and yourselves, too. And Sister Ventura, to my office as soon as your part in this little war is cleaned up," Len barked, covering his smile with the towel he picked up and threw at the pair, landing nowhere close to his target.

"Nice shot, Dad..." the laughter continued behind him as Len walked back into his office... and closed the door behind him.

What do you say to a woman you just covered with dark chocolate, but you want your only chance to be alone with her to leave an unforgettable impression? Paulo quickly thought.

Katie retrieved the ill-thrown towel her father contributed and wiped at her face and blouse before reaching across the counter to wipe the cream from her opponent's face. "You make quite the lasting impression, Mr. Quinteros," Katie whispered, looking right into his dark eyes, causing them to start twitching involuntarily. "What's the matter, young man? Did I cause you to feel guilty for ruining a poor girl's favorite blouse?"

Oh, how he wanted to jump over the counter that separated them and hold her in his arms, but he could only smile. "Yes, guilty as charged, Seester Ventura," he joked, not moving his eyes from being locked onto hers. After a period of awkward silence, it was Katie who spoke first.

"So what did you want to talk with me about? My mom texted me that you wanted a few minutes before I finished packing. Did you have something on your mind? Or did you just want to sweep me off my feet by covering me in chocolate?" Now laughing.

Sweep her off her feet? Does she feel something for me? Paulo dared think. "I, uh, wanted to... I was hoping..."

"Yes?" she asked, not wanting to make this easy for him, and still locked into those dark eyes of his." Are you going to ask me to the prom because that is exactly what you look and sound like?" she again pestered.

"What is a.. prom?" Paulo responded, clearly now off target. Before Katie could wipe the exasperated look off her face, Paulo gained his composure and dove in... "I have feelings for you, Katie Ventura, and I know this is not an appropriate time to express them or to ask if you have feelings for me but I was hoping you could find time to write me while I am away serving my mission and then maybe when I return if you are not already dating someone or even if you are maybe I could come visit you and your family?" He rattled.

"Sister Ventura!" A voice from El Presidente's office boomed. "I would like to go to bed at some point... Do you think you could tear yourself away from cleaning up the kitchen and come to my office?" President Ventura called from the now-open door to his office, startling both his daughter and the hired butler.

"Yes!" Katie whispered without taking her eyes off his. And then she was gone.

***

Four months later... "Elder Roberto Quinteros Jr... You have been called to serve a mission for the Church of Jesus Christ of Latter-day Saints to labor for twenty-four months in the Spanish-speaking Salt Lake City, Utah, City Center Mission."

"City Center Spanish mission? No way?" shouted the excited female voice on the other end of the phone held to Paulo's ear by his shoulder while he stirred the eggs and poured them into the frying pan, adding a small cup of green chili, black pepper, and a dash of salt to the mixture before returning his attention to the cheery voice of Katie Ventura on the other end.

"Do you know how special that mission is, Paulo? No one from the States gets called to that mission! You work Temple Square, referrals from the First Presidency and Q12, AND the MTC!! You also teach the new missionaries going out to foreign-speaking missions," Katie announced, her excited voice continuing to crescendo.

"Frankly, I am a little disappointed," Paulo confided, his voice taking on a more serious tone. "I was so sure with my ties to my homeland that

I would be sent there... so I could find my birth mother," his voice now trailing off. "But I am happy to be going to Utah–to be closer to... uh, those beautiful Wasatch mountains," he lied, eliciting a giggle from the other end of the phone, but also lost in conflicted thought over whether or not he should try to find his adopted parents before he arrives in Utah. And whether or not to confide in Katie to ask for her help locating them. But he jumped in, anyway...

"Katie, can I confide in you about something–without worrying that you will tell your parents–until I am ready?" he asked sincerely.

"Of course, Paulo! What is it?"

"I lied about how I came to this country! I mean, not about how I arrived, but why I arrived," he finished.

"Go ahead," Katie said cautiously after taking a deep breath.

"I was actually adopted by a family from Utah while I was still at the Orphanage. But before they could bring me to the States, I was kidnapped and forced to work in a child labor factory." Paulo let the silence grow between them, so Katie had a little time to process what he was saying. "I never did say how I had come to be working on the merchant ship that sea pirates attacked... but to escape the labor factory, I set fire to the building and used the confusion to provide cover while I and a few others escaped. I found my way to a farm where the foreman and his daughter took me in as a farm hand, but when the Federales came to the camp on a tip from someone that I was there, I had to run. The farmer had a connection with the skipper on the Conquistador, and a fake passport was made in exchange for my service aboard the boat for three years, at which time I would be dropped into this country." Paulo let out a breath and continued...

"Katie, I never expected to find the Church, your family... you, and so I put off trying to locate the family who adopted me until I had a chance to see for myself what America was all about, without seeing it the way my new family may have wanted me to see it. It turned out to be the best decision I ever made," he confided. There was still silence on the other end... so Paulo decided to get to the point of asking for her help. "Katie, would you be willing to help me try to find my family," he asked bluntly. "I don't know anything about them, their place of residence, or even who they are. Or if they would even want me in their life after all these years of thinking I was lost."

"What are their names?" Were the first words Katie spoke since Paulo started talking, but bringing much relief to Paulo.

"Tone!" he quickly responded. "Richard and Annette Tone, Utah, USA."

"And they are members of the Church?" Katie asked.

"I think so, Katie. That part of my life was such a confusing blur that I only remember sketchy information at best. But I do remember their names," he confided. "And the way Annette Tone looked at me–like she believed in me, even loved me, without knowing what a selfish and angry boy I was."

"I can believe it," Katie spoke softly into the phone, her words almost paralyzing Paulo's ability to communicate. It wasn't *what* she said as much as the way she said it... and her almost breathless tone. But Paulo knew he could not move in that direction... not yet, anyway.

"Then you will help me, sweet Katie?" It was as close to love-sounding words he dared utter for fear he may change his mind about leaving her alone in the great state of Utah without him by her side to protect her. "If I can find them and they still want me, I would love to see them when I arrive at the mission home. I don't officially report until the 28th of next month," he informed her. "That would give us almost a month. I could arrive a day or so early, and maybe you could pick me up and..."

"Or maybe not, Paulo!" she interrupted. I promised my parents I would not see you again until after your mission. Let's just see if we can find the Tone family who adopted you and make contact before you report," she concluded. "It would be easier that way." Paulo finally agreed to delay his arrival at the Salt Lake City airport one day early, giving him a full day in case Katie did locate the Tones and could arrange a meeting. The fact that she and her parents had spoken about him and were concerned enough that she would not see him alone before he reported for his mission did not go unnoticed.

She "does" have feelings for me, he thought to himself after hanging up. *And her parents know it and haven't kicked me out into the streets! A promising sign,* he concluded, feeling good about his chances that she might wait for him to return home from his mission... wherever *home* might be then.

***

It only took Katie Ventura one phone call using her father's connection to the First Presidency to confirm that Richard and Annette Tone were indeed church members. Their address in Pineview, Utah, was a rural P.O. Box, but she now had a phone number. However, how to inform these unsuspecting people that the son they had adopted almost eight years ago was still alive, had found his way into the USA, had joined the church, and was headed to the City Center mission and wanted to see them before he reported... might just be too much for them to handle.

Maybe they adopted a whole baseball team of boys and had no more room for Paulo, not that he would depend upon them for anything given the way her parents felt about him, Katie imagined. But she was pretty sure Paul Quinteros Jr. would remain in her life one way or another after his mission. But only time... and Heavenly Father's will would tell what their future might be together. *For goodness sake, I haven't even kissed the boy, and I'm planning a marriage?* she chastised herself.

Katie's next phone call was to her father. She needed guidance on how to approach the Tones about Paulo wanting to see them. Her father would be either very happy or quite disappointed that Paulo had a family. She figured she might as well find out.

Chapter Twenty-Seven

THEY DID!

Annette Tone did not recognize the number on the caller ID brightly displayed on the house phone screen. She rarely answered the house phone because most people she knew used her cellphone number... and the number was an out-of-state prefix. She decided to let it ring and walked back to the microwave oven where she had placed a stick of butter to soften in anticipation of being blended with the other cookie ingredients for her visiting teaching appointments that afternoon; she had no time for spam sales calls.

"Mrs. Tone, my name is Katie Ventura. My father, Len Ventura, is President of the Florida South Mission of the LDS Church. I understand you and your husband are members? What I am calling about is too sensitive to leave you a message. Please call me back as quickly as you can. It is about your son." Then, as if reminded to clarify which son she had—in case she had others... "Your son, Paulo!"

Finishing up her last pan of chocolate chip cookies, Annette Tone made a call to her visit teaching companion, Jamie Laughton, to let her know as soon as this final batch of cookies cooled enough to be put on a plate, she would be ready to go make their scheduled visits before her two girls burst through the front door, home from school. Then, after putting her cell phone down, Annette picked up the house phone to see if the last unidentified caller left a message. He had. Except it wasn't a 'his' voice.

Annette's hand almost dropped the receiver as her knees bent, threatening to give way under the dead weight the unexpected mention of Paulo's name added to her now small frame. She had become very sickly after the death of her son Michael–and the loss of Paulo almost finished her–but the knock on her door that day, two years ago, that brought Maria Cervantes into her life... and now, her newly-born son, Matias... gave her new purpose and hope again, as she and Richard helped Maria become established, and assisted, on occasion, with care for her new son.

The Tone's two young daughters, Halie and Heidi, only two years apart, now at nine and eleven years old, respectively, loved little Matias like the brother they once had. He had been sent to her family as a tender mercy from a loving Heavenly Father who knew of the hole that had been created in the hearts of the Tone family over the loss of Michael... and, of course, over the loss of the son they never had–Paulo.

Shaky hands kept Annette from writing legibly, as she had to back up the message three times to get all the phone numbers right that were spoken into the phone by the caller. A million questions riddled Annette's mind, but she practiced the deep breathing exercises her doctor had prescribed during those nights. The dark envelope of anxiety enveloped her without mercy. She could do this. No matter what, this person had information on her son, and she was going to hear it. The phone rang once, twice... and a third time before the phone picked up and a female voice answered.

"Hello, this is Katie," the voice answered with a steady tone, giving Annette a measure of control herself until she tried to speak. Nothing came out.

"Hello, this is Katie Ventura! Who Is calling, please?" she persisted.

"Mm.. My name is Anne-ette Tone, she stammered, almost sounding like a drunk person. Katie spoke next, sensitive to how hard this would be to hopefully avoid the woman passing out right over the phone.

"Mrs. Tone, I want you to please find a chair by the phone and tell me when you are sitting down," Katie instructed. "Is there someone there with you who can help you in case you faint?" She asked.

"No, I am alone, but I am sitting down now. Who are you, and how do you know our son?" The fact that she referred to Paulo as "our son" gave a positive rise to Katie's hopes that this family had not moved on. He still had a place in their heart–in their home.

"Mrs. Tone, I am the daughter of a mission president in the South Florida mission of the Church. Are you LDS?" she inquired.

"Yes, both my husband and I were born into the church as were our thr... two children," she corrected.

Katie continued, "I was serving as a missionary in the same mission as my father and mother when two of our elder missionaries brought a young man to our zone conference. He said his name was Roberto Quinteros Jr. Does that name mean anything to you?" She continued, sounding a bit like a cross-examination attorney.

"No! I don't know that person, nor have I heard the name before. What does this have to do with our son?" Annette pressed, now beginning to feel a little irritated with the caller.

Katie responded, "Once we got better acquainted with this young man, he felt safe confiding to us that his *real* name was actually Paulo, with no last name because he was deserted at birth and raised in a catholic orphanage." Katie stopped there to listen for a response on the other end, but there was none. So she continued..."May I call you Sister Tone?" Katie asked, still treading softly.

"Yes," Sister Tone answered.

"Sister Tone, do you have a son named Paulo?"

"We did," she responded flatly, still not connecting with the caller. "He was stolen from us before we could take him home to the States," she continued as if reliving that horrible period of her life.

"Sister Tone, maybe we should meet in person when your husband is home? Or maybe I will call back and speak to you both about this first. Will he be home tonight?" Katie asked, feeling Sister Tone had zoned out on her, and she was impressed to stop before moving further. "What time may I call back when Brother Tone is home?" Katie pressed again. Annette and

Katie agreed they should talk again when Richard was home after seven o'clock that night. Katie did not want this to drag out. Paulo was either their son or he wasn't. The sooner they found out, the better.

At seven o'clock, the Tone phone rang, and this time, it was quickly answered by a strong male voice. "Hello, this is Richard Tone. Who is calling, please?"

He did not sound happy, Katie thought before answering.

"My name is Katie Ventura, Brother Tone," she began. "I just returned from the Florida South mission where my father, Leonard Ventura, is mission president. As I told your wife, a young man about eighteen years of age at the time was brought to a missionary meeting and introduced to us as Roberto Quinteros Jr. The short story is that he and my father became friends, and after a time, the young man admitted he had entered the United States on a false passport. His real name was Paulo, and he had been raised in a Catholic orphanage but was kidnapped by child laborers and sold to a labor factory until he escaped by setting fire to the place. He spent three years on a fishing vessel earning his way to the U.S. but was attacked by sea pirates and almost lost his life with the others, but was saved by... well, I better let him tell you that part."

Without a breath, Katie continued, afraid Brother Tone would hang up on her. "I just learned that Paulo was actually adopted by a family from Utah by the name of Tone. It was on their way back to Utah that Paulo was kidnapped. Paulo asked me to make contact with you to see if you are his adoptive parents."

"Wait a minute, young lady... " came an exasperated reply. "Are you trying to tell me that our son Paulo just wandered into your meeting and has been in this country for over a year without trying to find us or letting us know he was safe? And he now has sent you to tell us he is ready to come home? Am I correct in my understanding, Miss Ventura?"

Katie could tell by the sound of Brother Tone's voice that this was not going to end well. She couldn't blame him, really. But none of this was

Paulo's fault... and why this man was acting so upset instead of welcoming home a lost son just didn't make sense to her.

"Mr. Tone..." If he wanted to get all formal with her, she could return the action. "What is it that you don't understand here? I call to let you know that your missing son has been found and has joined your church on his own and is preparing to serve a mission, and you act like I just invited you to an Amway meeting or something. What is up with you?"

There was a pause on the other end of the line, but Katie could hear him take a deep breath..."Two years ago, our oldest son Michael was killed in an automobile accident shortly after we returned from Argentina without Paulo. We lost two sons within days of one another, Miss Ventura. I don't know what you are up to... or what you expect to gain with this story. Do you want money? Am I now to wire money to this Paulo's account so he can serve a mission?' Is this a scam, Miss Ventura?"

Katie's heart had heard enough. This family had lost so much that they failed to recognize what she was saying. They had lost all hope, and that resulted in their minds closing to any possibility that their son had returned to them. To them, he was dead.

"I'm sorry to have bothered you, Mr. Tone..." Katie concluded in defeat. "And for your losses. Your son will be entering the Provo MTC on November 28th, exactly twenty-eight days from now. And you will not see him for two more years, if ever at all. Goodbye." Katie could understand a family needing time to grieve after the loss of a son... even two sons. But this man's unwillingness to even consider the possibility that one of his sons might still be alive and... not just alive, but here in the States... and, a member of their church... and about to become a missionary?

I gave them too much! Katie chastised herself after hanging up the receiver. *Of course they didn't believe her. Of course! Who would believe such a fairy tale? Now what do I do? I botched this one... really good,* continued the second-guessing tar and feathers! *What do I tell Paulo? This will break his heart.*

Richard Tone just stood there with the receiver still in his hand, paralyzed over what he had just heard, unwilling to allow himself even the slightest ray of hope that his lost adopted son... their son, was not only alive but had come to the States? *Not possible,* he countered. *Or is it?*

What if? What if this was 'not' a prank extortion call at all? Do I even dare check out this Ventura hoax attempt? Could Annette survive such a breakdown should this play out as an attempt to extort? Richard did not say a word to Annette but went to his study and knelt by the side of the small two-person couch he used mainly for Sunday naps while preparing for the following week's Sunday School lesson. The solitude this small room afforded him was also his portal to God. He would seek his Heavenly Father's help to understand how he should handle this. And Maria... Richard's heart almost stopped beating at the thought of Maria Cervantes and her son, Matias. How would they react to this revelation if true? It was just too much to comprehend! Richard couldn't even get the words out before his suspicious nature took over and closed his mind to the possibility.

Richard tried praying again after taking a deep breath. "My dear Heavenly Father..." he began. When Richard concluded his prayer for direction, which had mostly been pleadings to protect his family from further heartbreak, his Amen was followed by–nothing! At least not in his mind. But his heart felt something. He would call the Missionary Department in Salt Lake and inquire if there was really a Ventura mission president. He would do that much and no more!

Annette's non-inquiring gaze sent chills through Richard's heart as he came into the kitchen where his wife was pouring hot chocolate for the girls, who were busily chatting between themselves about some dumb TV program they had been watching and were now trying to beat the other at reciting funny lines of the show.

"Girls, isn't it about time for bed?" Richard said before pretending to steal one of the cups of chocolate from Heidi, the oldest daughter.

"Dad!" Heidi protested. "Mom!" she threatened before Richard slid the cup back to her in mock defeat. The big guns had been called, and there was no way he was going to get away with his plan to steal and plunder, except that one look at Annette told him she had returned to that hole in her heart where she spent so many months trying to repair after returning home without Paulo.

"Kiddos, let's drink up and have family prayer so mom and I can have some parent time," Richard said with a weak smile, hoping the girls would not play their usual hard-to-put-to-bed routine on him tonight. He was just too emotionally weak from his encounter with Miss Ventura. But as in answer to prayer, both girls hopped off the bar stools almost as in a choreographed sequence and ran into the family room, where they knelt at the big couch, leaving Richard almost speechless as he extended his hand for Annette to join him for prayer. Absently, she accepted his hand and let him guide her into the family room.

Chapter Twenty-Eight

QUESTIONS

"Good morning, missionary department... this is Sister Richards speaking. How may I help you?" came the pleasant female voice from Richard's cell phone held to his ear with his shoulder, his favorite multi-tasking exhibition that drove Annette crazy when she rode with him, especially after Michaels's accident.

"Good morning, Sister Richards; my name is Richard Tone. I was wondering if I could speak to someone about the mission president assigned to the Florida South mission?" Richard asked politely, feeling anything but polite at the moment.

After a brief pause, Sister Richards answered: "That would be Brother Harmon. One moment, and I will connect you!" And then there was silence.

"Perry Harmon! How may I help you?" Came the declaration on the line, causing Richard to lose his breath for fear of what lie ahead. He wished he could hang up right then and not have to deal with the answer about confirming or denying the validity of Miss Ventura's information.

"Brother Harmon, my name is Richard Tone," he began... and then repeated the information Katie gave him.

"Yes, President Leonard Ventura is the mission president of the Florida South mission!" Came the answer after a brief moment of search. "Actually... he and Sister Ventura will be released in about four months from now," he added. "Is that all you needed?"

"Actually, no... I mean, do you happen to have information on arriving missionaries to the MTC? We have a, uh, a relative who is supposed to be entering the missionary training center on the 28th of this month and... "

"No, you will need to call the MTC for that information, Brother Tone. I don't get into arrivals of new missionaries, in general. Is he called to the Florida South mission? Maybe I could help..."

And before he could finish, Richard ended the call with a polite. "No, thank you, Brother Richards, you have been helpful enough!"

So there was a Leonard Ventura in the Florida South mission, and Richard began processing out loud: Step one checks out, but how can I verify there is a new missionary named Paulo "something" when I don't even know his last name? Would he be using his birth mother's name? Or our name? Of course... he has a name, it is Tone, Paulo Tone. Finding the MTC phone number in Provo, Utah, was a piece of cake, but it was the wait time until a live human being answered that was the challenge. Richard could only imagine the hundreds of calls that flood through the switchboard at the MTC every minute of every day. And here he was, swept up with trying to find someone who would take their time to answer his question–his extremely important question.

"Hello, thank you for calling the Provo Missionary Training Center. If you speak English please press one," came the automated response. Richard did as he was instructed and waited. There was no ringtone... only silence. *Why wouldn't they at least put on calming music?* He wondered. *At least the Tabernacle Choir!*

Richard had had enough silence and was about to hang up when a voice answered. "Thank you for calling the Provo Missionary Training Center. If you are calling to check on a particular missionary, please press one now." Richard pressed the number 1 and waited in silence. Then a surprise, a real voice!

"Good morning, this is Sister Beckham speaking; how may I help you!"

Yay! A live human, non-recorded voice, Richard almost thought out loud. "Uh, good morning, Sister Beckham, I am calling to check on one particular missionary," Richard spoke into the receiver in his best-controlled voice. "And what would be the name of that fine missionary?" Sister Beckham asked in a very pleasing and still patient voice.

"His name... well, I think his name is Paulo; either Cervantes or Tone," Richard answered, very unsure of himself. Again silence.

"I am sorry, but there is currently no missionary with that name serving in the Provo MTC. Are you certain of the name? Asked Sister Beckham. "And are you sure he is here now?" she continued to pry, hoping for more information.

"No, he doesn't report until the 28th of this month," Richard responded quickly.

"Well, we wouldn't have him on our roster yet. You will need to check with his Bishop for that information... Or call back on the 27th. We should have him on our roster by then," she concluded... and courteously ended the call.

Richard sat silently, hoping for some sort of revelation or direction on what to do next. He had treated the caller very poorly IF it wasn't an extortion scheme. And he did learn that there is a Florida South mission president by the name of Ventura. Maybe he should start there? Confirm with the mission president that he does have a returned missionary daughter, and ask if he knows a Paulo Tone or Cervantes. A quick Google search for the Florida South Mission Home phone number gave him what he wanted, and he wasted no more time calling it.

"Hello, Florida South Mission Home; this is Elder Jackson speaking," answered a male voice with a deep southern drawl.

"Hello, I was calling for President Ventura?" Richard said, almost as a question.

"He is not here, presently," came the confirmation. *It was true! Or was it?* Richard thought. "Can you tell me if President Ventura has a daughter named Katie?" Richard inquired, trying to appear nonchalant but holding his breath.

"Well, can I have you speak to Sister Ventura about that? I would rather she answer questions about her family than me," the Elder wisely said. And in a matter of minutes, Courtney Ventura was on the phone.

"Sister Ventura, I am sorry to trouble you, but I am trying to confirm a phone call to my home last night from a young woman named Katie Ventura. She claimed to be your daughter," Richard spoke... again in a practiced and controlled tone, or as controlled as he could make it. Richard could feel the tension in the woman's voice when she responded to his question.

"Why would my daughter be calling your home, Mr....?"

"She called with some wild story that a young boy we adopted years ago had somehow survived a sea pirate attack and miraculously made his way to America, was converted by LDS missionaries, and is entering the Provo MTC as a Church missionary on the 28th of this month. Sister Ventura, is any of this unbelievable story true?"

Courtney could barely hear the last words spoken by the caller before her mind started spinning– about the exact same time the man introduced himself as Paulo's adoptive parent. "Elder Jackson, would you please use another line and call my husband? Tell him to please call me immediately!" Courtney directed to the office missionary while muffling her voice with her hand over the receiver. She then returned back to the caller, who seemed to be patiently waiting for her confirmation, denial... or explanation.

"You are Paulo's fath.. adoptive father?" Courtney corrected in a questioning tone that revealed complete surprise.

"I don't know, Sister! That is what I am calling to find out!" Richard's tone of voice now rose to match his lack of patience–as another piece of the puzzle seemed to be confirmed. This was the caller's mother, or at least she has a daughter named Katie. And she obviously knows a young man named Paulo. "Did this Paulo just wander in off the streets, and you took him in and converted him so that he wanted nothing to do with his real parents, Sister Ventura?" Richard now becoming almost accusing and on the belligerent side of rude.

But Courtney De Jesus Ventura would not accept this man's rude behavior any longer, and after taking a deep breath, she let him know he had just entered deep water with no life jacket on, in a sea full of sharks. Plus, a few choice words in a Latino language Richard had no idea of their meaning and had no desire to find out. And then she hung up, leaving Richard with the sound of a dull dial tone in his right ear!

"Sister Ventura, line two! It's the President," announced Elder Jackson with his southern twang a little more controlled after what he and the entire household had just heard from Sister Ventura. And the only sound in response was a door slamming shut.

"Len, is there something you have not told me about Paulo... and his *chosen* name? Was he adopted by an American family from Utah? And he did not tell us?" Her voice rising with each question.

"Court... I only just learned this myself," Len began in defense. "Apparently, he called Katie and told her the story of how he was kidnapped, and he asked her to see if she could find his parents. And you know Katie... but to her credit, she called me this morning and asked my advice. I have not had time to tell you."

"But why didn't he call the parents, Len? They must have been sick thinking he was sold to a child labor factory or worse!" Courtney added, her voice still in high pitch.

"He wanted to experience freedom, sweetheart. He wanted to see America for himself *before* he submitted himself to parents he didn't know. He did not plan on *not* calling them; he just got carried away into our culture and life—and, well, you know how we feel about him."

"Well, I just met one of the Parents, Len... and it did not go very well," Courtney retorted. I guess I should have just waited until you finished up your meeting to let you know he had called... but his attitude got under my skin, and I just flew into him," she recounted.

"Whoa, Nelly! What? Who? Paulo?" Len stammered, his mind unable to connect his thoughts.

"Len, it was a Richard Tone who called. He said he was Paulo's adopted father. Apparently, Katie called his wife and him last night... and things did not go well. He was on the phone this morning calling everyone remotely connected to Paulo, trying to determine if Katie was part of a scammer group or something."

"Scammer group? What in heaven's name is he talking about?" Len questioned. "What did Katie say to him that would give him the idea that Paulo was trying to extort money? What is wrong with people today, always thinking everyone is out to get them?"

"I don't know enough about the Tones to come to any conclusions about them, Len, but he certainly came on to me like I was at fault for Paulo being taken. Something is up with that family. I can feel it!" Courtney expressed.

"Well, do we tell Paulo things did not go well, or do we hold off and not dash his hopes for a reunion before his mission?" Len mused.

"We could tell him we couldn't connect with them because I certainly did 'not' connect with him!" Courtney added, infusing a little humor into the drama.

"No, I am thinking we should come clean and prepare him to face his mistake in not trying to at least let his family know he was alive," Len proposed. "I would hope by the end of his mission, they will come around to accepting him. He made a very selfish mistake by not contacting them, but you have to give the young man some slack in judgment when you consider where he started and how far he has come.

"Paulo did not get to know the Tones before he was adopted, so for him to feel the need to contact them when he was growing into his own here at the mission home would not have likely even been on his mind. I think he felt he had time and had no guilt feelings about the expectations of a family who thought he was dead," Len concluded, still processing his own feelings about how to resolve the drama that had now settled over his family unintentionally.

"Katie did her part by letting the Tones know their son was safe. If they want to play the injured card and miss seeing their son off on his mission, then that is their choice. But one I believe they will live to regret," Courtney added.

Richard volleyed back with, "In any case, if we let on how the Tones feel about Paulo's decision to not let them know he was alive, without any real connection to the Tones yet, I am afraid Paulo will cut them out of his life for good, Courtney. I don't believe that would be a good thing for the Tones or for Paulo. Unless you have been blind to the growing connection between our daughter and this young man, it is entirely possible we may find ourselves future in-laws rather than surrogate parents," Len informed, leaving the door open for Courtney to comment... but she only opened her mouth, and nothing came out.

"Sister Ventura, I believe Katie is on line one," announced Elder Jackson through the closed door.

"Len, it's Katie on the other line; I better take this," and with that, she promised to call him back after speaking with their daughter. "Hello Kat! You sure did stir up a hornet's nest," Courtney dug right to the core.

"Mother, Paulo's parents lost their other son in a tragic auto accident a few days after returning from losing Paulo," Katie shot back with a torpedo of her own. Neither woman said anything, both trying to make sense of what to do with this new revelation.

"We need to get your father on the line," Courtney blurted... as she put Katie on hold and called Len, who answered on the first ring.

"Katie, I have your father on the line with us. Please tell him what you just told me about the Tone's other son?" Courtney asked.

"Hello, Father, I understand I created quite the stir," Katie said, not meaning to sound flippant. "But before you chew me out or something, you need to know that the Tones lost their only son to a tragic auto accident only days after their return home from losing Paulo," she said quickly.

"Lenard, I told you they were not acting rational... and I was right," Courtney pronounced. "That family is dealing with the heartbreak of losing two sons. No wonder they are full of suspicion and anger."

Len was silent for a few seconds but then offered, "Well, this does shed some light, doesn't it? At least why the man wanted to put Katie in jail for trying to scam him and then blindsided her mom for stealing their son and converting him to the Church. It does make more sense now that he would act the part of a bereaved and despairing father mourning the sudden loss of two children," Len calculated. "I suppose we should at least tell Paulo about the death of the Tone's other son," Len continued. "But do we tell him not to contact the Tones, given their anger? Would he be better off leaving for his mission with no hurt inside him when he learns how distraught the Tones are over his choice not to contact them?"

"Len, I think we need Heavenly Father's wisdom in deciding what to do," Courtney offered. "I just do not feel capable of making that decision," she added.

"Where is Paulo now," Len asked, trying to put a plan into motion.

"He is with Elder Wilkinson teaching the third discussion to Brother and Sister Wong and their kids," Courtney provided. "You were gone when Elder Wilkinson called and said he needed Paulo. He isn't expected back until later tonight."

Knowing they each needed further reflection and prayer on handling this situation so it didn't affect Paulo's decision to go on a mission, each on the call hung up with an open invitation to call with any answer received. Len promised to be home soon so he and Courtney could pray together. After a rare dinner by themselves, Len and Courtney retired to Len's office to sort out their feelings. Len did not immediately drop to his knees, as Courtney did, causing her to open her eyes and look up at him, now sitting on the small couch. She didn't have to wait long before Len explained his thoughts.

"Jesus Christ offered to pay for the sins of mankind because of the natural man within each of us," Len started. "The natural man was placed inside each of us not by Satan but by God himself," Len explained. "Without the urges built inside us, we wouldn't have children, eat when we are hungry, or sleep when we are tired. And it is the combination of the natural man inside us and the principle of *Agency* entitling us to choose our actions–when and if to control them–that we grow and learn how to become respectable human beings," Len continued, causing Courtney to wonder now where her husband was going with all this. He wasn't teaching her a principle she wasn't already familiar with, but she now recognized this familiar pattern as his way of processing even deeper thoughts.

"And the Atonement was meant to cover both the sinner and the one who was sinned against," Len's voice now gaining life as he finally reached the point where he was beginning to receive some clarity in asking for Heavenly Father's help.

"I see where you are going with this, Hon," Courtney added. "It is not just Paulo who is expected to learn from poor choices made in life, but those affected by his actions are also expected to learn how to forgive. In other words, the Savior of all, Jesus Christ, already paid for the poor choice Paulo made..." And before she could finish her thought, Len finished it for her...

"And He also paid for the hurt and anger felt by the injured party so that they would not need to be burdened with carrying that hurt all their lives," Len finished.

"Unforgiven acts against us, whether intended or not, if carried and fed long enough, can turn into hatred," Courtney expressed, reflecting on a time in her own life as a teen when she was treated poorly by others in her school and how her reaction had affected her school work and even her prayers and scripture study. She had actually drifted away from the church for a time because of how she was treated.

"And hatred, if allowed to remain with us, will affect our life; maybe even change the course of our life," Len said. "We need to pray not only for Paulo..."

"But also for the Tone family," Courtney completed as she returned to her knees–now joined by her husband–offering a silent prayer to Heavenly Father about how grateful she was to have married this man.

Both Len and Courtney took turns vocally expressing their concerns about how to handle the situation with Paulo and the Tone family, followed by a period of silent reflection while still on their knees in supplication.

Courtney was first to raise her head, signaling she had completed her prayer, followed almost simultaneously by Len, who leaned over and kissed his wife, tenderly but firmly. "I love you, Mrs. Ventura," and repeated the kiss.

By the time Paulo returned that evening, Len, Courtney, and Katie had each come to the same conclusion after Len shared his thoughts on the atonement again with Katie by phone. Katie wished she could be there, but she knew her parents would handle this as best they knew how.

Len was the first to hear Paulo come through the garage side door closest to his office, where he waited. "Paulo, do you have a moment you could visit with Courtney and me?"

Paulo set his backpack on the floor outside the President's office. "Sure, President Ventura, what can I do for you?" Paulo asked while loosening his tie. Courtney was not far off when she heard the door slam and immediately went to Len's office. Len motioned to Paulo to sit on the couch as he came around from behind the desk to join him, but when Courtney entered, he pulled one of his office chairs around to face the sofa instead. Paulo stood as soon as Courtney entered and reached out to give her a hug, as he always did when he first saw her or went to bed. He had grown to love her as much as he had ever wanted to love– a mother. She had filled that role for him and had done a marvelous job. Len asked about the teaching discussion Paulo and Elder Wilkinson had been on that night, and both Len and Courtney sat back in awe of how far this young man had come in his understanding of gospel principles since deciding to go on a mission.

When Paulo slowed, and it was apparent he wanted to know what else the Ventura's had on their minds, Len began by teaching the same principle of the atonement he had shared with his wife and daughter. It was a powerful concept and widely misunderstood by Christians and theologians alike. But Paulo grasped it on the first try, probably because he did not have the depth of understanding that years and years of study might have overshadowed.

"If my adopted parents do not forgive me of the pain and anguish I may have caused them by being careless and allowing myself to be kidnapped, then that will be their choice, but I am to love them anyway! Is that what you are saying, President?" Paulo's voice now taking on a hint of defensiveness, but preferring to remain as a missionary being taught a religious principle rather than a friend being lectured to by another friend.

"Yes, that is right, Paulo... but only part of the principle–the agency of choice. The other part is that the atonement covers both the sinner and the injured, offering divine power to heal wounds. Although a significant component of the repentance process of the *sinner* is restitution, if possible–a similarly important piece of the principle of the atonement on the part of the *injured* is forgiveness, often a very challenging state of being to let go of anger, to forgive, and to accept the mercy of our Lord in healing the heart of the victim as well as removing the sin committed by the offender... should they repent. This is the full scope of the atonement, to be found clean... clean of guilt, clean of unforgiveness, grudges, and hatred so that we could be considered worthy to enter God's presence, either connected with the spirit while an earthly mortal or in person as a deceased being." Len still felt he needed a bit more explanation of this very important principle.

"Paulo, do you remember the scripture reference you learned about the condition of entering into God's kingdom?" Len probed."

"Sure... 'No unclean thing can dwell with God!'- 1 Nephi 10:21," Paulo quoted, almost effortlessly.

"So, if one holds anger inside from the actions of another against them, are they as guilty as the person who committed the action against them?" Len asked.

"Sounds like you setting me up for something, President Ventura. Are you?" Questioned Paulo in a humble persona that Courtney found most endearing.

"Your adopted parents lost their oldest son in a car accident about the same time you ended up missing," Len stated, flatly... letting that revelation hang in space for Paulo to consider.

"Your parents are distraught, Paulo," Courtney stated. "They aren't thinking clearly right now."

"You met my parents?" Paulo questioned.

"Well, not officially, but I have spoken to Richard Tone by phone," Courtney shared.

"And..?" Paulo inquired, anxious to know more.

"Well... they are distraught!" Richard stated, drawing a direct stare from Courtney in response to Len stealing her caption.

"So they are mad at me!" It wasn't a question.

"Paulo, I wouldn't say they are mad at you. They are heartbroken from the loss of two sons, and that can take a toll on anyone's emotional reserves," Len tried to explain, but looking at Courtney for some help.

"Paulo, nothing makes sense to the Tones right now," Courtney offered. "We planted the seed that you are ok... and that you joined their church on your own. And that you are preparing to serve a mission. That is more news about someone you loved and thought you had lost than anyone should have to face. I think you should just be grateful that they know, and that is one less thing in your life right now that you don't need to face before you leave for two years."

"Courtney's right, Paulo. Celebrate the little victories when you can," Len said.

"I suppose!" Paulo resigned himself. "I suppose if they are there on the 27th, then I might have a chance to reconnect with them, and if they don't show, then they will have two years to think about it, and so will I."

Courtney stood and reached Paulo in two steps, wrapping her arms around his neck and holding him tightly, motioning to Len to come and join them... and the group hug brought laughter back into the household.

Chapter Twenty-Nine

REUNION

The next few weeks around the mission home were quiet, with no transfers or new missionaries departing or arriving. This allowed the Ventura's to focus on preparing Paulo for his mission, finishing up with mission prep class, scheduling his temple endowment session once his membership hit 365 days and one minute, and, of course, continuing his almost daily splits with the local missionaries, who had elevated Paulo to celebrity status. The day Paulo was to fly to Salt Lake City, Len came into Paulo's room for a last set of instructions... only to find him sitting on the side of his bed, his hands supporting his head and deep in thought. "Paulo, may I speak with you for a moment?" Len asked, knowing he had just interrupted.

"Sure, what's up?" Paulo asked, slowly raising his head.

"Two years is a long time," he started. "You need to know how much Courtney and I have come to love you, like a son we never had–and how proud we are of who you have become," Len expressed, tears now forming and no resistance capable of holding them back. "Whatever happens while you are away–on your mission–with Katie, that is... please know that Courtney and I will always stand ready to help you toward your goal of becoming the best surgeon in the state of Utah if that is what you choose to do with your life upon your release."

***

The scene at Miami International Airport was filled with tear-filled joy for this young man who had come into their lives eighteen months ago. Leonard Ventura had been to this airport many times since the beginning of his and Courtney's mission, but he did not remember crying when any of his missionaries returned to their homeland; sad to see them go, yes, but no tears shed. Today, however, it was different. Surrounded by missionaries and ward members alike, Elder Roberto Quinteros was about to embark on the most amazing journey of his imperfect life as a (two-year) full-time missionary for the Church of Jesus Christ of Latter-day Saints.

Palo stood tall as those touched by this young man's decision to change gathered around him, seeking one last touch, hug, or handshake... knowing it would likely be the last. When the last boarding group had been called, Paulo could not delay any longer, now drawing dagger-like looks from the airline personnel who were on a tight schedule to get everyone on board and into the air on time. Paulo gave one last round of hugs before pulling away and handing the gate steward his boarding pass. One final look over his shoulder as he entered the jetway revealed Courtney Ventura being wrapped in the arms of her husband, who was dabbing his white handkerchief over his own eyes. Two years would come and go... and Paulo knew they would be waiting for him, at least to be his friend, if not a future son-in-law.

The flight into Salt Lake City International took eight long hours. Still, it being Paulo's first-ever flight, he had the time of his life exploring every moving part and service of the plane, much to the enjoyment and some dismay of the passengers and crew around him. He did not forget for one minute who he was and who he was now working for; thus, copies of the Book of Mormon were handed out, along with several pass-along cards with the beautiful photo of the Salt Lake Temple on the front and website information on how to become an eternal family.

Paulo's heartbeat quickened as he felt the airplane begin to descend, never having felt that sensation before. However, the traveler seated next to him was a self-appointed plane tour guide who kept Paulo from jumping out of his seat every time the plane hit some turbulence. Paulo did not experience complete relaxation until the wheels touched the tarmac, and the rear thrust began to slow the aircraft down. And he was not prepared for the energy that burst from passenger seats the minute the engines shut down and the all-clear indicator sounded. So he just sat there, enjoying every minute, every sound, and every face, until his seat companion motioned to Paulo that it was time to go.

Paulo's heart nearly beat through his chest in anticipation of seeing Katie again as he walked quickly from the plane's rear to the front, where the two pilots and crew said goodbye to the passengers. Paulo briefly took his mind off Katie for the opportunity to hand each a pass-along card with his soon-to-be-famous smile tearing down walls of rejection and warm thank-you handshakes. After all, he was on duty as a missionary. At least two other suit-clad missionaries had been on board the plane, but when Paulo reached the waiting area, it was as though a famous celebrity had just landed. Several clusters of admirers grouped together began chanting names of "Elder Johnson, Elder Cameron..." and Paulo couldn't distinguish the other name.

Hand-held posters with WELCOME HOME written on them adorned the waiting area, with kids jumping up and down when they sighted their target, almost blocking the passengers from getting through. Paulo was practically lost in the moment as he coasted to the side and just took it all in until his trusty seat companion pushed him from behind with "Keep the line moving" and "See what you have to look forward to, Elder?"

As Paulo and his seat companion shook hands and Paulo invited him to Temple Square, where he would be serving for much of his mission, Paulo's eye caught a familiar face... and it wasn't Katie's. Standing arm in arm with two young girls beside them were Richard and Annette Tone. Already crying the minute she laid eyes on Paulo, Annette broke free of her husband's arm and actually ran the short distance to her son and into his welcome embrace, amid mixed tears of apology and happiness... soon joined by Richard and the girls, as Richard introduced first Halie, then Heidi, followed by more hugs. It was amazing to Paulo how warmly this family welcomed him with exchanges of "Please forgive me, I'm so sorry" and "I can't believe how much you have grown!"

The Tone family reunion was soon joined by a silver-haired man in a business suit and a similarly dressed woman... both with missionary name tags, except his read "President." Richard had been talking with the man and his companion before Annette burst into Paulo's waiting arms through the front line of proper decorum.

"Elder Quinteros, welcome to Salt Lake City!" President Vaughn L. Dunn introduced himself and then his wife as the Mission President and Companion, of the Salt Lake City Center Mission. Paulo extended his hand, but his left hand was still intertwined with Annette's. She was unwilling to part from the boy she connected with so many years ago.

"Elder Quinteros, I usually don't meet our new City Center missionaries until after their week at the MTC, but when I heard you were coming in early and may not have a place to stay, Sister Dunn and I wanted to see if you might want to bunk over at the mission home?" Richard was the first to speak up, catching Annette a split second behind.

"Would it be acceptable, President Dunn, if Elder Quinteros stayed at our home this evening? He is our son... and we promise to have him at the Provo MTC by 11:00 am tomorrow, and well rested." Richard asked with emotion.

"And well fed!" Annette added, smiling broadly as Halie and Heidi chimed in with their favorite place to be "well fed!" With approval given, the Tones and Paulo headed to the baggage claim after President and Sister Dunn excused themselves to tend to another matter at the mission home.

The girls walked on each side of their dad, arm in arm, with Richard still carrying Paulo's backpack and Annette holding tightly to Paulo's right arm, not allowing anyone to come between them again. There was no mistaking the surreal feelings that passed between the three as they walked in silence, consumed with thoughts of a similar walk together in a foreign airport over five years ago.

"I never thought we would see you again," Annette whispered without emotion. Paulo only nodded his head in affirmation. He did not know the words that would heal a broken heart.

"I am so sorry... about your, uh, son." he tried. "I did not know." Annette squeezed his hand, now intertwined with his, communicating she understood.

"It was tragic," Annette whispered, not wanting the shadow that remained in her heart over the loss of her son to cloud this brief reunion with this fine young man. "But we are doing better now," flashing that broad smile once again and almost melting Paulo's heart, as his thoughts returned to that day at the orphanage when he first caught Annette staring at him and then flashing her broad smile.

"Girls stay off the carousel!" Richard barked as the sisters chased one another and laughed loudly, annoying an older couple waiting for their own luggage. "Sorry!" Richard acknowledged to the couple, who returned a weak smile. Richard vowed to himself not to let his view of life get cankered, and tolerance for others weakened as he grew older. He recognized that trait in his parents as they had aged.

The carousel started rolling as baggage began to appear off the chute right in front of the Tone family, eliciting Richard's pumped fist of triumph. "We picked the right chute for once!" he shouted, drawing another irritated look from the older couple and laughter from his wife. A large bag came off the chute next as the older couple moved to stop it from disappearing into the crowd that lined the carousel... but without success.

"Is that your bag?" Paulo asked, moving to retrieve it before receiving confirmation. Richard also caught the other end, and the two pulled it off the carousel to the waiting couple, who now had broad smiles.

"No, that's our bag over there!" the man pointed... drawing a jab from his wife.

"Oh Karl, stop it!" the man's wife commanded, with laughter in her voice. "Yes, this is our elephant! Thank you so much young man," glancing at his missionary badge. "Coming or going?" She asked.

"Both!" Paulo exclaimed... drawing laughter from Richard and Annette. Paulo enjoyed talking to the older couple and learned they had just returned from a cruise, celebrating their 50th wedding anniversary.

"Have you been married for all eternity?" Paulo asked sincerely.

"Well, it sometimes feels like it's been for an eternity," the older man joked, drawing a friendly punch from his wife. Paulo took that as a no, so he proceeded to pull out a pass-along card with a picture of the Salt Lake Temple on it and wrote his name and cell phone number while his new friends looked on.

"I would love to give you a personal tour of this beautiful temple grounds where marriage relationships can be sealed for time and for eternity," Paulo invited. "Please call me in about two weeks, and I will be trained and ready to go," Paulo said as he handed the pass-along card to the man, but his wife took it out of his hand and stuck it safely in her purse.

"I will keep the card, young man, or you'll never see us again if Karl has it," drawing laughter from the Tones and Paulo. Paulo then spotted his bag just coming out of the chute and finished up shaking hands with his new friends and sprinted over to the moving carousel where he grabbed a corner of the bag and pulled. After doing an eye check to be certain he had the right bag, Paulo hefted the bag onto the floor and joined the girls walking behind Richard and Annette as they headed to the exit door, Annette not willing to take her focus off Paulo for one minute as she sent him a high five hand slap for being such a good missionary.

"You are going to be an amazing missionary, Paulo. That was great what you did back there," Annette complimented, feeling the rise in Paulo's self-esteem over her acknowledgment. The afternoon was quickly drawing to a close, and soon it would be time for dinner, or later, by the time the Tones drove over the mountain to their home in Pineview, a quaint little community of mostly gentlemen farmers and family, nestled in a Garden of Eden atmosphere with dark green fields and towering snowcapped mountains as a backdrop. They so wanted to show Paulo the home he would come home to after his mission, but it would be pitch dark by the time they ate and then drove over the mountain. So Richard called an audible, after returning to the car to the jeers of "We're hungry, dad! Can't we eat in Salt Lake?"

"Ok, I have a surprise!" Richard announced, bringing a hushed atmosphere to the car as if a balloon filled to the max was about to burst. "We are going to eat in Salt Lake!"

"That's no surprise, Dad," Heidi offered flatly.

"Wait! I didn't finish," Richard interrupted, laying his hand on Heidi's... "And we are also having a *sleepover* in Salt Lake!"

"Yay!" As a chorus of glee shot upward from the girls and Annette. Paulo just smiled from ear to ear, watching these two new sisters of his become so happy over this news.

"What about our pajamas?" Heidi asked.

"And our toothbrushes!" Halie added.

"Mom took care of all that, just in case," Richard revealed, squeezing Annette's hand for her 'prior planning prevents poor performance' wisdom.

"We only have tonight to spend with your new brother," Annette choked. "We have a lot of catching up to do," she said, casting her eyes to the young man sitting between his two sisters in the back seat.

The Salt Lake Downtown Marriott was a favorite stay for the Tones when they wanted to celebrate a special occasion. Its close proximity to Temple Square, retail shops, and restaurants made this an easy choice. They would enjoy a late night with Paulo, sleep in late, and have breakfast delivered right to their room while they dressed and got ready for the drive to Provo to deliver their missionary to the front steps of the MTC by noon. Richard and Annette had made the decision not to tell Paulo about his birth mother, who now lived in Salt Lake City and worked for the SLC

Children's Hospital. After much prayer they decided not to tell his birth mother either–of his arrival and serving a mission almost on her doorstep.

Richard had spent an hour on the phone with Len Ventura and was cautioned very wisely to move slowly. "The changes in Paulo have been dramatic when you think about how far he has come," Len stated. "But he is like a newborn colt with strong but shaky legs that just need some exercise and growth to stabilize. This mission is exactly what he needs to set in place the future greatness and legacy of Elder Roberto Quinteros Jr.!" The name selection was discussed between the two men, and Richard understood the circumstances and timing. For now, his son would need to remain Elder Quinteros.

"I want to hear every experience you had after you were captured," Annette asked first once they were situated in their two-room hotel suite. The girls would share one of two king-sized beds in the parent's room to give Paulo his own room where a 60″ flat screen TV commanded center stage, normally. But for now, it was Paulo who had everyone's attention as he quietly and humbly recounted how he was captured and removed from the airport to work with other children in a sweat factory. He had the girls on the edge of their seats as he relived for them the night leading up to the sea pirates boarding the ship and the miracle of his fake passport somehow ending up in the sack of food he grabbed at the last minute before launching his dinghy off the side of the ship. It was Annette who first started blowing her nose and dabbing at her eyes, while Paulo described the scene he witnessed as he fled into the darkness created by the ship's shadow. But when Paulo told how God sent him Moby the exploring dolphin just as he thought he was done for, even Richard reached for the tissue.

As hard as they tried, first Halie... then Heidi lost the battle of exhaustion, and Richard took them one by one into their own bed, leaving Richard and Annette alone with Paulo, who now turned the tables as soon as Richard came back into the room.

"Please tell me about Michael," Paulo asked sincerely. "Please tell me how it happened and how you kept from being angry at God over this."

Annette stared down at her intertwined hands for some space of time before answering honestly. "I didn't win that battle, Paulo! I was angry–very angry! Losing not one but two sons in a matter of a few weeks from one another was more than I could bear." Richard began rubbing Annette's back as if trying to remind her not to open the door to what really brought her back from shutting out God from her life. The day Maria Cervantes knocked on her door and the subsequent birth of little Matias brought life and hope back into Annette's broken heart. She understood Richard's subtle hint and responded in a whisper:

"Oh Paulo, tonight is your night. Let's save that memory for another time," Annette pleaded without fooling Paulo one bit. He knew there was more to her resistance than a consideration for his night, as she tried to portray. But he let it go, a memory for another day. Richard wanted to hear of Paulo's conversion stemming from his chance meeting with the missionaries... and Annette wanted to hear if this girl "Katie" was a girlfriend or just a girl friend? Their questions were successful in drawing Paulo away from discussions that might lead to his mother.

Before they knew it, the night had silently turned into morning, and as if on cue, all three felt the tug of gravity on their eyelids. "Well, if we don't call it a night, this young Elder will be sleeping through his first day as a missionary," Richard managed a laugh, drawing agreement from Annette. Paulo, however, had something to say before this special night ended.

"If it hadn't been for you..." as his gaze lovingly fell upon Annette's already tear-filled eyes, "I would never have found my way home. What I went through to get here has made me who I am today. I had so much baggage on my shoulders when you first met me at the orphanage–so many unresolved anger issues, so many . . . that coming to America at that time just may have been the worst thing I could have done."

Paulo was beginning to reach for a tissue when Annette handed him one instead. "As weird as it sounds, if I had not been kidnapped, I would never have learned what God's voice sounds like. If I had not spent hard times learning how to work aboard the fishing trawler, I might not have developed the work ethic I need to be a good missionary and a doctor. And had I not been on the brink of death, alone on the raging sea, I may have never been stretched in such a way that helped me understand the meaning of no excuses–no limits." Annette reached out her hand to grasp Paulo's, but instead, Paulo rose to embrace her, tenderly. And then he went to Richard, offering a slightly awkward man-hug with a part-handshake and part-shoulder bump. Annette just giggled inwardly at the sight of her Richard and her Paulo starting that walk of bonding that would one day develop into a solid father-son relationship that she knew both men desired.

The healing process of a broken heart is a delicate dance between forgiveness and a willingness to forget, thus the old adage to "forgive and forget." If one is out of balance, the dance may result in prolonged agony to the broken heart.

Such has been the case for this grieving mother and father.

Tonight, the dance would begin a miraculous restoration of hope for Richard and Annette Tone. A son had been returned to them as if resurrected from the dead. Another son's mortal body lay in a coffin beneath the surface of the earth, awaiting resurrection, his spirit now residing temporarily among other spirit sons and daughters of God, preparing for the reunion of their perfected mortal body. There would be a call for more dances along the way, but for tonight, this was a *good* dance, and the mending of hearts had begun.

The sound of laughter reached Paulo's senses, followed by a rush of anticipation for what lay ahead. Once his head cleared, Paulo recognized the young voices as Halie and Heidi, peeking around the now slightly opened door to his room. "Time to get up, sleepyhead," Heidi giggled before slamming the door. Muffled laughter carried through, even though it was now closed completely. Paulo found himself grinning despite the few hours he was actually asleep. Thoughts of last night's activities and talk ran through his mind, releasing some of the tightness in his stomach from the realization of what was about to happen today. He wondered if this is how the consecrated Sisterhood of the Sacred Hearts Convent felt the night before dedicating their entire life to serving others. His dedication of time was so small in quantity by comparison but no less accepted by his Heavenly Father as a significant personal sacrifice.

Paulo would soon enter the Provo Temple with the other missionaries who had also pledged themselves to God's higher law of service and conduct, a pledge of faith that would affect the rest of his life, a promise known and referred to as the endowment. It was truly a gift to make such covenants with God, and although he would be free to live a normal life outside the temple, he was no less consecrated to a life of virtue and service.

As Paulo laid his head back down on the pillow, enjoying this brief reflection of how his imperfect life had become so perfect, another presence attacked his heart–the face of Katie Ventura. His heart began to ache as he thought of not seeing her again for two long years. He would have to trust God and put her care into His hands. Maybe, just maybe, she would still be there for him when he returned. Perhaps she would help him find his birth mother so he could beg forgiveness for the anger he had carried toward her for so long.

"Paulo, we are going to be late for the mission home if you don't drag yourself out of that bed and come eat your cold pancakes!" called out the two sisters in practiced almost-unison from the room next door, followed by laughter and slamming the door again, jarring Paulo out of his dream-state. Paulo slowly climbed out of the bed that folded into the couch and made his way to the restroom, grimacing when he saw himself in the mirror. His dark hair was still a little long for mission standards and had taken on a newly worsened countenance after only a few hours of sleep. He would have to fix that after breakfast, but for now, he was being summoned. Paulo first exposed his hand, his arm, a foot, and his leg through the partially opened doorway and then jumped in with a loud "whoot" to practically scare the living daylights out of the girls, who screamed and started throwing pillows at the stranger in the doorway.

"Stranger-danger! Stranger-danger," the girls chanted as Paulo tried to make his way into their room, where a tray of food atop a hotel cart lay waiting, the enticing smells of freshly cooked bacon and eggs, surrounded by pancakes and fruit, attacking the five empty stomachs that waited impatiently to be fed.

"Help me push this cart back into your room, Paulo, so we have a place to sit while we eat," asked Richard, pointing to the other end of the rolling food cart. Paulo quickly did as he was asked, and, within minutes, the family prayer had been offere,d and forks began to fly toward open mouths.

"There is just something special about being served breakfast in bed," Annette quipped, drawing a side glance from Richard and laughter from the girls and Paulo. Little was said after the initial merriment was over, the cart pushed out into the hallway much lighter than when it had arrived, and the reality of the long drive ahead of them to deliver the missionary son they had bonded with so quickly as a family. The girls were hungry for a big brother to help heal the wounds that remained after the tragic loss of their beloved brother, Michael... and Paulo was a willing replacement, bringing his own brand of eccentric humor and personality to the family.

Paulo's contributions to his new family were especially welcome when exposing his innocent misunderstandings of American customs and persona. This family would miss Paulo–although just a short driving distance to his area of labor, parents and family were not encouraged to have any contact with their missionary other than letters, phone calls, and Skype on special occasions such as Mother's Day, Christmas, and the missionary's birthday–so that they could focus on the Lord's work exclusively for the short duration of their mission. With Annette and Richard in the front seat, Paulo and the girls sat buckled comfortably next to one another as Richard's Lexus powered south on I-15 toward Provo. There was little chatter as each occupant was lost in their own thoughts.

Annette was first to speak after what seemed like an hour of driving–by handing an envelope to Paulo.

"I wrote down our email addresses as well as our home mailing address. Please take time during your P-Days to write us and let us know how you are doing and where they have you working?" Paulo accepted the envelope but noticed it was thicker than a standard letter and proceeded to open it, only to find several twenty-dollar bills stuck neatly inside the paper containing the Tone's contact info.

"My email address is on that too, isn't it, Mom?" Heidi asked, watching Paulo open the letter and give Annette a perplexing look as he fingered the bills.

"It's not as much as it looks, Paulo; just use it for emergencies," Annette smiled, turning her eyes to look out the window to avoid Paulo's frown. "Brother Ventura told us how independent you are about allowing anyone to help, but it's just for emergencies. You can return it if you never need it," she finished, sealing the deal as Paulo folded up the envelope and stuck it in his suit jacket, mouthing "Thank You" to Annette as the Lexus slowed down to turn into the Missionary Training Center.

"We're here! We're here!" Halie yelled excitedly from the back seat. "Look at all the missionaries!" Heidi pointed ahead of them. The missionary drop-off point was clogged with family and friends saying their goodbyes as Richard pulled his Lexus into one of the lines.

"I'm glad we got here early," Richard said sarcastically but with a good-natured sense of humor. As Paulo watched in amazement the throng of people ahead of them, his eyes started to play tricks on him–He thought he saw Katie.

"Katie Ventura?" he mumbled in surprise... then she was gone, swallowed up in the crowded entry leading to the 'Missionaries Only' entrance sign. "Not possible!" he thought out loud.

"Did you see someone you know, Paulo?" Annette asked, looking out across the crowded concourse as Richard finally brought the Lexus to a stop and pulled to the curb.

"I think we better unload you here and walk the rest of the way, Paulo," Richard suggested, looking at the wall of cars and suits ahead. "Looks like everyone had the same idea and arrived early," he added, with a tight laugh.

With Paulo's luggage unloaded, Annette stood by him with her arm through his. "Do you mind if we walk you to the door, Elder Quinteros?" she asked, tears beginning to form as she lovingly tightened her grip on her son.

Richard grabbed the handle of Paulo's suitcase and began walking toward the point of entry, followed by Paulo, arm in arm, with Annette on one side and Heidi and Halie on the other. Paulo couldn't stop smiling over the feeling that he was loved as the Tone group made their way along... before Paulo stopped dead in his tracks.

"Katie? Katie Ventura?" Paulo yelled... breaking loose from Annette and the girls and moving toward a young woman who had turned around at the sound of her name above the chatter of the crowd around her. She had been standing near the drop-off doorway but had her back to Paulo, expecting him to come from the front as the other missionaries had. At the sound of her name, Katie turned around... and liked what she saw!

"Katie!" Paulo called out again as he drew nearer. Oh, how he had missed this young lady.

"Elder Quinteros, remember who you are!" came a warning voice from behind him, drawing Paulo up short before he followed through with his emotions to give sister Ventura more than a friendly missionary handshake, drawing a laugh... and a touch of disappointment from his intended target.

"What... What are you doing here?" Paulo asked breathlessly as he came up short of taking Katie in his arms.

"I thought you needed a good send-off," she pretended... "But it looks like you brought your own harem," pointing to Annette and the girls coming up quickly behind him.

"Uh, Annette... and girls, I want you to meet Katie Ventura. She is the daughter of the Ventura family who took me in when I arrived in Florida,"

Paulo tried to explain, drawing an awkward look from Katie on one end and Annette on the other.

"Nice to meet you, Katie," Annette recovered enough to say, extending her hand... and feeling a bit guilty for pretending she didn't know who she was. Richard and the girls came up behind carrying the luggage and were likewise introduced, but before Richard could fit his size eleven shoe in his mouth, Annette grabbed his arm and suggested they secure a place in line with Elder Quinteros's luggage, thus giving Paulo a few precious minutes alone with Miss Ventura.

Paulo stood awkwardly for a moment, trying to grasp what had just happened... but recovered quickly. "You look great!" he started, causing a slight blush up Katie's neck.

"Thank you. So do you, Pau... Elder Quinteros," she corrected.

"I really appreciate you coming to see me off," Paulo said warmly, causing more blush. "Will you write to me?" he asked directly. Katie quickly handed him an envelope, smiling with pleasure.

"Of course, Paulo," she whispered as she leaned closer. "Here is my first one," she said, extending her hand in a most appropriate missionary handshake. "I hope you will not have time to write back, being so busy teaching discussions and all," she half-joked.

"Katie, I meant what I said when you left your mission..."

A loud "Elder Quinteros!" Rang from a husky voice behind them.

"As did I!" Katie said a little louder than needed, for he had not moved one step. "You have to go, Elder!" she laughed as she took his arm and guided him toward the voice.

"Will you wait for me, Katie Ventura?" He practically pled, drawing another response from the husky voice... but all he heard above the noise of the crowd–was, *Yes!*

Chapter Thirty

FORGIVENESS

*E*ighteen months later

Paulo hadn't received a letter from Katie Ventura in three months, although he hadn't exactly been consistent in writing her, either. His mission had turned out to be more than any young man could expect, being assigned to the First Presidency referral follow-up detail with a select group of City Center missionaries assigned to Temple Square during most of each Monday - Friday, but also handling any teaching and follow-up assignments coming directly from the First Presidency and Quorum of the Twelve Apostles.

The holiday season was just beginning, with Thanksgiving and Christmas around the corner... bringing with them the excitement of Christmas lights and daily performances at Temple Square, drawing throngs of visitors to the City Center. Paulo began to sense the end of his mission while strolling... or chumming, as some of the missionaries referred to the assignment just to mingle and be friendly, hoping to be asked a question and then be guided by the spirit, always inviting the visitor to receive a free copy of the Book of Mormon, usually delivered by two local missionaries.

Paulo had been assigned to leadership in the little core of specialty missionaries and often spoke directly to the General Authorities of the Church when they had requested some special handling of a referral. He loved this close association and the fact that he, the least knowledgeable in gospel scripture and protocol, was selected to serve such great men and their wives–who were also likely to call him with details of someone who had just expressed interest in the church and wanted to know more. And they loved hearing Paulo tell his conversion story, which was another much-requested assignment given to Paulo almost every Sunday evening at an organized stake or ward fireside in the Salt Lake basin area.

It was only one week before Thanksgiving as Paulo strolled the busy Temple Square grounds amid the background sounds of The Tabernacle Choir at Temple Square and occasional soft announcements that the Choir and Orchestra would be giving a free concert at the outdoor stage area near the historic Tabernacle building. Paulo had been assigned to monitor any 2-way radio chatter during the performance, so he just wandered through the crowd, earpiece dangling from his right ear.

"Elder Quinteros, what's your 20?" pierced a voice through Paulo's radio earpiece. Paulo pushed a small button attached to his shirt, but hidden under his tie... and answered back.

"I just left the tabernacle, and I'm headed to the pioneer family statue near the south entrance," Paulo responded.

"Negative on that, leader one... I have a message from Sister Q Ten to have you call her ASAP. She is on her cell phone, waiting for your call.

Paulo immediately found a secluded spot behind a clump of bushes and made his call to Sister Clara Redlands, the wife of newly called Apostle Glenn Redlands, a native of Salt Lake City and tenth in the line of apostle seniority. She picked up on the first ring.

"Elder Quinteros, thank you so much for calling," Sister Redlands said excitedly. "I met the sweetest nurse today at the Primary Children's Hospital while accompanying two General Primary Board sisters on their visits. She was assigned to us while we visited some seriously ill children, and I was so impressed with her tender but efficient manner. We just seemed to connect, and before I knew it, our conversation turned to the Church. She is a single mother with a young son and only came to this country from

Guatemala a few years ago... and has already learned the English language so well."

Sister Redlands' voice gained both volume and speed now as she added... "She seemed genuinely interested in hearing about the gospel, and since you speak her native language, I want you and your companion to handle this one yourselves. And I would love to attend some of the discussions, if that would be ok?" she asked as if she needed his permission.

"Of course, Sister Redlands, I would be excited to meet this nurse friend of yours and teach her the gospel," Paulo responded, trying to match the energy in her voice. "Would you please send her contact information to my phone so I can get right on this?" Paulo asked into the cell phone. "Maybe she and her son would like to come to Temple Square for her first lesson?" Paulo shared a thought. "I bet she and her son would love the lesson about the Savior taught here on Temple Square, where the spirit of light is so strong this time of year," Paulo added.

"Yes, yes, I am certain she would love that, Elder. Would you please call her tonight and arrange it?" Sister Redlands asked, her voice so excited Paulo had concerns she might blow a circuit or something.

"Yes, of course!" Elder Quinteros agreed and ended the call. Closing up after such an amazing night left the "S-Squad," as they were often referred to, totally exhausted. Paulo's group of missionaries began returning to the visitor's center, waiting for the LDS security detail to arrive and take over, so Paulo had a few minutes to contemplate the beautiful replica of "The Christus," which was such an imposing sight when one first entered the spacious building on Temple Square. Paulo looked at his watch - It read 9:00 pm. He realized it might be a little late to call someone and set up a meeting, but he did promise Sister Redlands he would get right on it! He dug for his phone out of his pocket and checked his messages; there was one from Clara Redlands, with a name–Maria Cervantes–and a phone number and address. *She doesn't live that far from here,* Paulo thought to himself. *And close to the Children's Hospital where she works. I had better put in a call so I can report back to Sister Redlands,* he reasoned.

Paulo put in the phone number of Sister Redland's contact and hit Send–and waited. "Hola - Uh, hello," a female voice answered.

"Good evening. Is this Maria Cervantes?" Elder Quinteros asked, sounding tentative for calling so late and possibly waking her up if she worked night shift hours like most Children's Hospital nurses did. Paulo had been invited to teach nurses; mostly young and single, and knew of their exacting work schedules. No wonder they were single, he had often considered.

"Yes, this is Maria," she answered.

"Ms. Cervantes, this is Elder Quinteros from the Church of Jesus Christ of Latter-day Saints. Am I calling too late?" Paulo asked cautiously.

"No... No, I just walked in a few minutes ago from work," she said, somewhat hesitantly.

"I spoke with a new friend of yours, Mrs. Clara Redlands, this evening, and she mentioned she had met you at the Children's Hospital and was very impressed," began the Elder. "She asked me to invite you to learn about our church. Would you like to come to Temple Square and allow us to show you more about the Church?" There was silence on the other end for just a moment while Maria processed the connection. Once she did, the countenance in her voice lit up.

"I really enjoyed meeting Mrs. Redlands. She made me laugh," came the reply, causing Paulo some surprise. "I would love to learn more about her church."

Paulo and Maria chatted for a few minutes longer before setting a time for the following week to meet at the visitor's center on Temple Square. Once off the phone, Paulo sent a text message to Clara Redlands' cell phone, confirming he had contacted her referral and advised her when the meeting at Temple Square would be. The following Tuesday at six o'clock in the afternoon, Paulo and his companion, Elder Ringal from Alberta, Canada, entered the massive entryway to the Temple Square Visitors Center, pausing for a moment to allow the Savior's presence in the form of the imposing Christus figure to set the stage for the new investigator coming to meet them.

It had been almost nineteen months since Paulo had been dropped off at the MTC in Provo, Utah, by his adopted parents–but it felt like an eternity since hearing the one word that provided a brightness of hope to his heart *and* his future: *YES!* But, for now, his thoughts would focus on following the Lord's guidance in teaching this friend of an apostle's wife. He hoped she would be receptive to the spirit and that he would have a favorable report to give. And with that thought, the front door opened right on the hour... and who but Sister Redlands, accompanied by a short, good-looking woman he guessed to be in her mid-thirties... with a little boy holding hands with both women, entered the visitor's center, only to stop mid-way in and pause to look past the two Elders waiting for them.

"Oh my!" Maria gasped, placing her free hand up to her mouth. "Is this... a statue of Jesus?"

"After He was resurrected, Maria," finished Clara Redland. Nothing else was said for a full minute while Maria and her son Matias stood in awe ... as other people entered the beautiful building and navigated around the trio by an Apostle security officer assigned to the Apostle's wives whenever they were out in public. When Paulo sensed the little group had absorbed the magnificence of the Christus, he moved to greet them, extending his hand to welcome Sister Redland... and then to Maria.

"I am Elder Quinteros," Paulo said as he extended his hand to Maria. "And this is my companion, Elder Ringal, from Alberta, Canada, ay?" letting out a childish laugh as if everyone understood his reference to the Canadian use of "ay" instead of the American "huh?"... drawing a scowl from his companion. "Sorry!" he blushed.

"And who is this young man with you, Mrs. Cervantes?" Elder Ringal inquired, trying to overcome the poor start. Matias was then introduced as Maria's son, as he attempted to hide behind his mother, still peering up at the imposing Christos figure above them.

"Hi Matias... welcome to Temple Square!" Paulo said with a formal greeting before kneeling down to shake Matias' hand to make him feel more welcome.

After a brief introduction to the guided tour, Elder Quinteros pointed toward a lighted mural of Joseph Smith as a young boy on his knees in front of two heavenly beings, about two feet in the air above the kneeling Joseph. "In the year 1820, a fourteen-year-old boy named Joseph Smith wanted to know which church he should join, there being a spiritual revival underway in his region at that time," he began...

"One day, young Joseph was reading in the fifth Epistle of James: '*If anyone lacks wisdom, let him ask of God and it shall be given him,*'" Paulo quoted, and then Elder Ringal, as if on cue, took the lead explaining the events leading up to the young boy Prophet's visitation by the Father and Son. As the two elders paused at each mural, causing them to come to life one at a time, with explanations following, Paulo could not take his eyes off Maria. There was something about her that drew him in. She was at least twenty years older than he, but he felt a strange attraction to her that sometimes caused him to lose his place in the tour, drawing looks again from Clara Redland.

The tour was ending way too soon for Paulo's wishes, and he and little Matias really hit it off. When it was Elder Ringal's turn to introduce the next mural, Paulo beckoned the little boy to leave his mother and join him as he walked over to where a pair of Sister missionaries were standing so Paulo could introduce Matias to them, causing a red blush to darken the young boy's naturally tanned face, which Paulo loved seeing because he then knew Matias felt something radiating from the faces of the Sister missionaries.

Paulo kept a close eye on how Elder Ringal was doing with Maria and Sister Redland, and as soon as the explanation ended and the trio moved to the next lighted mural, Paulo moved to where he could resume the dialogue, and Elder Ringal followed Matias back over to where the Sister missionaries were standing... and so it went up to the last mural depicting Christ's appearance to the Nephites.

"When Jesus Christ died on the cross, He was placed in a burial tomb from which He escaped. The angel who appeared to those who found the empty tomb declared that '*He was risen,*' and the three days following His crucifixion, Christ appeared to a select group of people right here in the Western Hemisphere and showed them also the marks on His hands and feet where the nails were driven," Paulo instructed, explaining the activity portrayed in the beautiful scene before them.

"It is the beautiful act of the atonement that brings comfort and peace to the afflicted and forgiveness of the afflicter. Jesus Christ took upon himself not only the sins of all humanity but also the grudges and hurts caused by others toward us," Paulo continued. "He carries our burdens when we are overwhelmed and sends the Comforter–the Holy Spirit, to speak peace to our soul..." adding that part with shakiness in his voice.

"I, uh... I can speak of this peace personally. I was deserted by my birth mother and left at an orphanage to be cared for. I grew up with no love for whoever was my birth mother!" The volume in his voice gained both heat and sharpness. "But Christ saved me time and time again–from myself and the evil forces that tried to take me, and I found my way to this country, and that is where I found the true meaning of the atonement and what it can do for you."

"Where are you from?" Maria asked, looking deeply into Paulo's eyes as if searching, trying to explain... something. A feeling?

"Far away," Paulo smiled. "On a distant planet...!" he continued, causing Clara Redland to playfully punch him in the arm and then recoil as if she just realized what she had done, provoking a reaction from Paulo, just as funny.

As if on cue, Elder Ringal and Matias rejoined the tour, ready to continue. "Hey, here comes the little man," Paulo said in an attempt to break the awkward trance Maria was in. "And Matias, too!" He joked while stifling a chuckle... returned by Elder Ringals' forced "Ha, Ha!"

Outside the visitors center, the late autumn air enveloped the little group as they huddled together to make plans for another session.

"We could meet at my apartment," Maria offered. "It isn't big or fancy at all, but it is warm," she shuddered, wrapping herself with her arms and opening them just long enough to pull Matias into her embrace to keep him warm. A date and time were arranged for the next meeting, along with an invite to attend church... and the Elders bid the ladies and Matias goodbye, causing a bit of an attitude between Matias, who didn't want to leave the Elders... and the Sister missionaries, of whom he had grown very fond. But after drawing a promise of hot chocolate and whipped cream from his mother, Matias swallowed his tears and managed a smile and a cute little wave to the Sister missionaries while taking his mom's hand and exchanging high-fives with the Elders before they headed back to their car and to their apartment to make phone calls to the S-Squad elders, checking on their progress for the evening.

The following week, Elders Quinteros and Ringal bundled up to head over to their appointment with Maria Cervantes and Matias–and had just closed the door to their apartment when Elder Quinteros's cell phone buzzed in his pocket. "Hello, this is Elder Quinteros," Paulo answered, not recognizing the caller ID.

"Elder Quinteros, this is Maria Cervantes. I am so glad I caught you. You haven't left for our meeting yet, have you?" she asked, with too much emotion for something not to be up.

"Yes, we are just leaving, Maria. Is there something wrong?" he asked, meeting Elder Ringal's searching eyes.

"Yes! My Matias is not feeling well. His temperature started to spike about two hours ago and is still rising. I have tried everything, but it is still rising. I am afraid I may need to take him to Emergency–and will have to call off our meeting tonight," Maria explained.

"Maria, what if Elder Ringal and I come over anyway and help you with Matias?" Elder Quinteros petitioned. "My companion and I hold the priesthood, and we can help with that fever," he assured.

"You hold the priesthood?" she questioned. "You are a... a priest?"

"No... well, yes... No! Not the type you are thinking," Paulo quickly corrected. "We hold the authority to act for Jesus Christ. The same authority Jesus gave His apostle Peter," Elder Ringal yelled over Paulo's shoulder, causing Paulo to wave him off and motion to start the car while he tried to calm Maria and convince her to let them come by to help. Elder Ringal drove while Paulo explained to Maria how the laying on of hands by one who held the authority of God to perform healings could help Matias.

"Before Christ was crucified, He laid His hands on the Twelve Apostles' heads, one by one, and gave them the authority to act in His name. That authority included the power to perform miracles–even heal the sick as Christ had done. At first, the apostles were hesitant about using this power," Paulo said, trying to keep Maria on the phone while they drove. "But Christ told them it was their lack of faith that prevented the miracle–they had the authority."

Elder Ringal signaled to Paulo that they were just around the corner. "Maria, we are here! We will be right up," Paulo announced as he and Elder Ringal made their way to Maria's apartment on the first floor and knocked. Maria opened the door almost immediately and let in the anxious missionaries.

"Thank you so much for coming," Maria greeted, maintaining a warm but weak smile. "I hope he isn't contagious. I would hate to see you infected," she added, leading the Elders to his room.

"We'll be fine," Paulo said from behind Maria. He didn't see the corners of her mouth break upward in appreciation. She had already grown quite fond of these boys, especially Paulo, and felt their devotion to their callings as missionaries. She hoped they could help her son.

"Wow, he is hot!" Paulo exclaimed, placing the back of his hand on Matias' forehead and noticing that he did not open his eyes.

"Maria, this is not magic. It is going to take the faith of each of us to heal Matias, but I believe it is the will of Heavenly Father that we anoint him and heal him. I feel that as plainly as I have felt anything in my life," Paulo assured. "I know this is what Heavenly Father would have us do!"

Elder Ringal removed a small vial containing consecrated oil and placed a small drop on the crown of Matias' head, followed by a hands-on anointing ordinance. Paulo then joined his hands—with his companion's... and sealed the anointing, followed by a beautiful prayer of faith and healing. Elder Quinteros felt impressed to bless Matias that his body would call upon reserves sent by God to bring his temperature under control and heal the cause of his infirmities. When Paulo opened his eyes, they focused on Maria, whose eyes were also moist.

"Thank you, Elders! I'm sure my baby will be fine now," Maria said, looking at both Elders and then back at her son, who had just turned over and again closed his eyes. "I already called in to work and took a personal day tomorrow, just in case," Maria smiled, looking at the Elders with a slight hint of questioning in her eyes.

"Mommy, can I have something to drink?" Came a weak voice from the bedroom.

"That's a good sign, already!" Maria grinned as she excused herself, leaving the elders to themselves. While Maria was attending to Matias, Paulo looked around the tiny but comfortable living room for a space to set up for the discussion with Maria when the doorbell rang, drawing Maria out of Matias' bedroom with a big smile plastered broadly on her face. "His temperature is headed down," she announced as she opened the door to greet Clara Redlands and her husband. Elder Ringal gasped as he focused on the male form entering the home.

"Elder Redlands!" the young missionaries welcomed, almost in unison.

"I hope we won't distract from your discussion tonight, Elders?" the tall apostle asked, extending his hand to Paulo and his companion.

"We'll just sit and listen," added Clara, responding to Maria's invitation to sit beside her on the couch.

Once everyone was seated, Paulo asked Maria to offer a prayer to invite the Lord's spirit to this discussion. She hesitated, responding that she had not prayed for many years. Her religious affiliation did not encourage personal prayer but rather that she attend mass whenever possible and take communion. Paulo offered to help her, but she declined, suggesting that one of the Redlands would be more... qualified. Sister Redlands quickly volunteered to offer the prayer.

Paulo started the discussion by asking Maria what she felt while visiting the Visitors Center at Temple Square. "I felt a tightness in my chest," she answered honestly. " I was quite nervous at first, but the tightness relaxed as we progressed along the murals... especially the one showing Jesus Christ appearing to the... uh!"

"Nephites!" Elder Quinteros helped. "Jesus appeared to the Nephites, following His resurrection."

"But it was what you said about the atonement–about forgiveness, that truly warmed my heart. I believed what you were saying. And I believe it now," Maria said, tears beginning to form in her eyes. "And I believe you were sent to Matias and me from God," she added. Then, addressing the Redlands: "The Elders blessed my Matias tonight. He was sick, but they healed him."

The discussion with Maria lasted forty-five minutes and covered more doctrinal information about the members of the Godhead... and baptism, being the first ordinance of the gospel. "I have need of baptism," Maria said without provocation. "I have much to repent of, Elder Quinteros. I am afraid I deceived my husband, and he left me. He doesn't even know he is a father. There is much more to tell, yet I want to be baptized. I have need of baptism!" And tears began to fall–from everyone.

Clara Redlands surrounded her friend with loving arms, whispering consolation to her. Elder Redlands stood and motioned to the Elders to follow him outside, leaving Maria in the care of his wife. There would be future discussions with the Elders, but none so dramatic as the one where Maria Cervantes requested baptism... punctuated with the beautiful blessing–healing of her son, Matias.

Thanksgiving week was full of meal appointments and crowds of visitors at Temple Square, but nothing like the day after Thanksgiving and the lighting of Christmas lights on the Temple Square grounds. With nightly live musical performances from a variety of artists to draw even more visitors to the Square, Elder Quinteros had no trouble keeping his mind off his release date as a full-time missionary. But thoughts of Katie Ventura still plagued his mind when he had a few seconds to dwell on things other than missionary work.

One evening, Paulo's heart almost jumped out of his chest when he spotted a "Katie-twin" at the Square, almost completely covered in the arms of some husky BYU jacket-wearing young man. Paulo broke rank and headed to the couple but quickly changed course when her face came up for air, and he realized it was not Katie. Experiences with Katie sightings were rare but when they did happen Paulo's quick responses scared him. *What am I going to do if she did not wait for me? And worse yet, what if she is engaged... Or married?*

Paulo realized how quickly he could get distracted when thoughts of Katie came to mind. Perhaps her disconnect from him months ago was a blessing in disguise so he could focus on his mission. He had come so far with God's help and guidance; where was the faith he had built and cultivated that Heavenly Father always had his back? Such talks to himself became more frequent as Christmas approached, and longing for family and future unknowns scratched at his resolve to put such feelings behind him until his official release in sixty-seven days–but who's counting? Paulo would laugh at himself.

Maria had chosen Christmas Eve to be baptized. She and Matias had become regular attendees at the Sunnyside Ward, located close to the Primary Children's Hospital and the University of Utah, and had been adopted by many of the young families who attended there. Each time Paulo and his companion visited the Ward with Maria and Matias, he was reminded of Katie. And thoughts of whether or not he had a future with her rose in his mind and heart.

"I'm planning to be baptized into the Church of Jesus Christ of Latter-day Saints on Christmas Eve," Maria announced over the phone the Monday before Christmas Eve.

"Maria, that is wonderful!" exclaimed Annette Tone into the receiver on the other end. "I told Richard you would make a great member of the Church and that we should send the missionaries, but we tend to get mired in our own lives, I guess," Annette's voice trailed off... "When is the date so we can get it on our calendar?"

"On Christmas Eve!" Maria said again... this time exclaiming a little more than the last. "Can you and Richard come?" Maria pleaded. "The Elders say I need to ask someone to speak at my baptism. I was thinking Richard might be willing to do it?"

"I can't speak for Richard," Annette said, politely... but my guess is he would be happy to do it," she finished. "And I would be happy to watch Matias while you are baptized. By the way, who is baptizing you?" Annette asked casually. "One of the Elders will baptize, and one will do the conforming, whatever that is," Maria answered, drawing a chuckle from Annette.

"It's confirming! You will be confirmed a member of the Church," Annette clarified, smiling to herself.

"Maria," Annette said softly. "Richard and I are so proud of you!" There were only sobs on the other end of line. "Are you happy?" Annette asked... searching. "Yes, I believe so. I... uh, my husband... I do miss him so!" Maria confessed, in between sobs. "I wish I had someone to share this with."

"You have us, Maria! And Matias," Annette assured.

After a brief pause, and the sound of a nose being cleared, Maria apologized for being so emotional. "It must be the Christmas season," she mused out loud, followed by a chuckle.

"What's so funny?" Annette asked, managing a chuckle herself. "I was just thinking how strange life can be," Maria shared. "If my husband had not left me, I would never come to America. I would never have met you and Richard... and probably never found the Church."

Then, just as quickly, "Goodnight, Annette, and please tell Richard 'Thank You' for me! And please arrive a little early so you can meet the Elders and Sister Redlands... and maybe Elder Redlands."

"You have an apostle coming to your baptism? How?" Annette asked incredulously. "Long story!" Maria answered before saying goodbye and grabbing another tissue to contain the tears that followed.

As Elder Quinteros and his companion drove into the spacious parking lot on Christmas Eve, it was evident that Maria and Matias were well thought of... The parking lot was almost full on one side of the building. "Wow!" Elder Ringal exclaimed. "Are all these cars here for us?" he asked. "Not for us, Elder... for Maria!"

"That's what I meant," Ringal corrected. The Elders were met by the ward mission leader in the hallway leading to the crowded Relief Society room where the doors to the font stood open... and waiting.

"You are here! Awesome crowd, ay?" came the excited greeting. "Which one of you will baptize and which one confirm?" asked the mission leader, looking first at Paulo and then his companion... and back at Paulo again, drawing a smile from Paulo.

"I will baptize! And my companion will confirm," came the reply, causing the mission leader to write down their names etched into the black and white name badges attached to their shirt pockets.

"Follow me, Elder, and I will show you where to get dressed into your whites," instructed the mission leader as he turned and motioned to a side door.

Richard and Annette were just entering the building as the Elders dispersed and continued down the hallway to an open door–a location that typically ends at the Relief Society room in pretty much every LDS chapel built. They were early, as directed by Maria, but it was obvious that Maria was very well supported by her Ward family, with most of the young families attending with their small children.

Annette looked for Matias and found him playing peacefully with a girl about his age, sitting next to her mother in the row directly behind Maria.

They were sharing crayons, and each held a coloring book that kept them occupied.

"Looks like things are under control," Richard said warmly, placing his arm at the curve of Annette's back and gently guiding her to the back of the room where the only empty seats were on the last row. "Since we don't have anyone behind us, we can stand when Maria is baptized and see her through the mirrors in the back of the font," Richard said softly, leaning in toward Annette's ear. "I guess the scripture passage... the last shall be first applies to us," Richard said, smiling, remembering his wife's prodding to drive a little faster so they were not late for the baptism.

People were still filing into the room, causing the ward leader in charge to begin looking for more chairs. Annette heard a little rustle among those in attendance, with Elder and Sister Redlands' names scattered around the room as the Apostle and his wife tried to sneak in unnoticed. But who did go unnoticed, at least by those in the back of the room, was the dark-haired figure who came out of the dressing room from the opposite side, dressed in white, and sat beside Maria. After the brief rumbling among those in the room to find a place for the Redlands to sit, the mission leader finally stood with his back in front of the open font and welcomed everyone to the baptism of Maria Cervantes. An opening song followed, along with a prayer.

"Brothers and Sisters, we are so blessed to have Apostle and Sister Redlands with us this evening," offered the mission leader, not absolutely certain how to proceed with the program preceding the baptism, so he called an audible and asked Elder Redland to say a few words, "followed by Maria's friend 'Richard Tone,' who will speak on the principle of baptism."

Paulo's head shot upward, expressing confusion and surprise as he looked around the room in search of his adopted parents, without success in locating them before Elder Redlands started speaking. Paulo turned his attention back to the Apostle, now standing in front of the font, and gazing into the crowd as he gathered his thoughts.

What a blessing it was for Maria to have the Redlands as friends, thought Paulo... but how did his parents know Maria?

Elder Redlands only spoke for a few minutes before closing his remarks with his powerful testimony that included the need for all to be baptized by the proper authority and that the Elder who will baptize Maria does, in fact, hold the same priesthood given to Peter, James, and John, by Jesus Christ, himself. "This same authority has been restored to the earth today. That is my testimony," the Apostle concluded and returned to his seat as Richard Tone stood and walked to the front of the room and turned to address the group but instead stopped dead in his tracks when he locked eyes with the dark-haired man sitting next to his friend, Maria.

Questions - confusion - happiness - all crowded into Paulo's head as his adopted father stammered at first and then regained his composure with, "I don't know how you follow the incredible spirit brought into this room by an Apostle of the Lord," Richard began. "But if anyone deserves the full-time companionship of the Holy Ghost, it is Maria Cervantes," as he let the spirit direct the remainder of his thoughts.

Following Richard's remarks and before Paulo could get an explanation from Maria, Paulo heard his name called to proceed with the baptism of Sister Cervantes. As Paulo stood and helped Maria to her feet, and turning to look over his shoulder at the crowd, he spotted a pair of eyes that needed no introduction, as smiles were exchanged between them, causing Paulo not to see the feet of a little boy sitting across the aisle from him, and nearly tripped, which would have had Paulo entering the font head first. Instead, it was like he had two unseen hands on him, steadying his balance so that he recovered quickly, and... after drawing a few snickers from those sitting on the first two rows, Paulo made his way to the opposite end of the font steps and waited for Maria to come from the ladies side, not missing a chance to search again for Annette Tone, as if she could provide an explanation to why she and Richard were at the baptism.

Maria appeared in her white baptismal jumpsuit, with rolled-up pant legs, holding on to the step railing like it would disappear right before her.

And her eyes... they were glistening from wetness as tears overran their lid-banks and rolled down her cheeks, with no effort made to wipe them dry.

Elder Quinteros met Maria at the bottom of the font steps and looked into her eyes as he led her into the water. A feeling unlike anything he had ever felt before with other baptisms he performed now coursed through his veins. There is always a tender connection between the Elders and those they are privileged to baptize, but this was different. This was deeper—like there was... history?

When Maria was positioned properly, Elder Quinteros raised his right hand to the square and began reciting the words of the baptismal ordinance just before immersing Maria in the water—symbolizing the death and burial of Jesus Christ—and then brought her out of the water, symbolizing the resurrection of Christ—rising from the dead to new life, as the reality of her *new life* began to unfold.

"Thank you so much, Elder Quinteros," Maria managed to say through the water dripping from her face—before offering an appropriate hug to her baptizer. Maria began to shiver from both the excitement of what had just happened and from the water now evaporating from her torso as she took Paulo's hand to assist her back to the familiar step railing and into a large white towel held by Annette Tone, who, with an arm around the shivering Maria, guided her back to the dressing room to prepare for the next part of the baptismal ordinance.

Paulo, however, was still standing waist deep in the water, stunned over what he had just felt, and stuck with the impression that had invaded his mind... that Maria Cervantes was his mother. Shaking his head to rid himself of the silly thought that had him still standing in the font, Paulo opened his eyes to peer into those same searching eyes of Annette Tone.

"Paulo!" Her pleading eyes left no doubt that the impression he had just received was more than an impression—it was reality. "How?" Is all that could come out before tears exploded like two balloons releasing their contents.

After quickly regaining his composure, Paulo removed himself from the font and turned to walk back into the men's dressing room... but before he could open the door, Annette had reached him, now standing with her back to those seated behind them.

"She came to this country after her husband... not your father, left her when she confided to him that she had a son," Annette said in a hushed but steady voice. "He was so broken-hearted over her keeping that a secret from him before they were married that he left... and never came home. Paulo... you must give Maria a chance to explain." Annette pleaded, with Richard now by her side, holding her back for fear she would try to follow Paulo into the men's dressing room.

"There is more to this story that needs to be told," Annette pleaded as Paulo opened the door to the dressing room and walked inside without saying a word or looking back. Annette looked to Richard to do something, but he just shrugged.

"I don't have the relationship with Paulo you do, Annette. Just give the young man some time to digest what just happened. After all...he didn't think he even had a mother, let alone one he had been teaching the gospel to," Richard said, sounding very much like he didn't believe it himself.

"Richard, we don't have the luxury of waiting! Paulo is in shock. In just a few minutes he is expected to face a woman he was raised to believe had tried to kill him. Without telling him that was a lie perpetuated by the school to keep Paulo from searching out his mother, he is liable to... who knows what he is liable to do?" Annette pleaded. "I don't care if this is the men's dressing room... I'm going after my son!"

Paulo was not hard to find. He sat alone in the men's restroom, still wearing wet clothes. "Richard you had better let the Ward leaders know we are going to have to delay the confirmation a while, why I try to work this out," Annette whispered, before making her presence known to Paulo.

"Yes, I agree," Richard complied... And I will try to hold off the confirmation for now, but we also have to think of Maria."

Annette had no one else in her mind but Paulo at this moment. She had to tell him the truth, poor timing or not, now placing her hand on Paulo's shoulder. "Paulo, please listen to me before you make a huge mistake," Annette pleaded. This brought Paulo's head up, revealing the anger in his eyes.

"What mistake? Is she my mother? The one who wanted me dead rather than try to raise me? Or the mistake you made when you adopted a broken-winged little kid...?"

"Paulo, we didn't make a mistake by adopting you," Annette started. "And it was by a miracle that Maria came to this country and somehow found us after her husband left her. She was pregnant with Matias and came to us for help. None of us knew you were even alive. She dug the info out of her mother about where you were taken and raised. It was there... at the Convent that she discovered she was pregnant."

With the mention of the Convent, Paulo raised his head for the first time. Annette picked up on this instantly and continued with her explanation. "Your friend Sister Torres cared for Maria while she stayed at the Convent!"

"Felicia! Maria met Felicia?" Paulo asked excitedly. "You said, Sister Torres?"

"Yes Paulo, Maria can tell you all about it. Your friend is a nun," she smiled... then suggested to Paulo that he dress quickly, and she would continue to brief him on everything she knew.

"Why didn't you tell me this? You knew Maria was my birth mother, and you withheld that from me? Why?" Paulo now retreated into the locker area to dress, giving Annette only a sharp glance over his shoulder.

"Because it would only have served to make you more bitter and perhaps keep you from serving a successful mission." Annette countered. "What good would it have done if you would have known that Maria was a single mother living near you? How would that have made you feel? Would you have had enough maturity before your mission to do the right thing?"

"The right thing? And what is the right thing, Mother Tone? To just forgive and forget?"

Annette almost yelled. "Yes, that is exactly the right thing to do, Paulo," not backing down one bit, but simultaneously allowing a tear to roll down her cheek, an emotion unleashed when Paulo referred to her as *mother* Tone!

"Maria has made mistakes! Richard and I have both made mistakes! And I suppose even you have made mistakes, Paulo. But look at the growth in her! She has joined the Church. Her sins have been removed and absorbed by Jesus Christ as part of the Atonement. Are you going to *not* forgive her when your Savior has?"

"Does she know?" Paulo asked, now from behind one of the dressing partitions.

"I don't believe she does know, Paulo. She knows we adopted her son, that is all," Annette responded.

"What do you suggest I do?" Paulo asked, now standing before Annette, fully dressed, missionary badge and all. He looked like his old, amazingly handsome self again.

"Let's go welcome her into the Church!" Annette offered. "And join your companion in confirming her a member of Christ's Church. She needs her 'Elder Quinteros' right now more than she needs to face who he is," she wisely added. "There will be time to hear her story and time for her to hear yours."

"You are a wise woman, Mother Tone. And I am blessed to have become your son," Paulo said, enjoying a much-needed embrace with his mother... then the two of them walked back into the Relief Society room where Sister Maria Cervantes awaited the presence of the slow-dressing Elder Paul Quinteros, and broke into a huge smile of relief when she saw him walk out of the men's dressing room. The fact that Annette Tone was close behind Paulo as he returned to the smaller gathering only served to confuse Maria more... but that thought was quickly lost in the moment as she was invited to sit in a chair at the front of the room as a circle of men, each holding the priesthood, surrounded her and gently laid their hands upon her head... as the constant companionship of the Holy Ghost was bestowed by Elder Ringal, along with membership in the Church of Jesus Christ of Latter-day Saints, confirmed.

Maria was then swallowed up by those who had participated in the ordinance, as well as little Matias running to her, yelling, "Mommy, I want to be baptized too!" Matias announced, drawing laughter from those still in the room. As customary, those participating in the ordinance... Elders Ringal, Quinteros, and Redlands... along with Maria's Bishop and the ward mission leader, each took turns congratulating the newest member of the Church with handshakes and hugs. When it became Paulo's turn, he hesitated slightly before offering his hand. But Maria didn't hesitate to grab it and press the young Elder into a hug, sending laughter into the room again. Paulo leaned into Maria's hug, amazed that he felt no animosity or regret towards this woman who he had just learned was his birth mother, but instead feeling a pang of his own guilt from harboring such ill feelings against someone he had never met, or toward anyone for that matter.

Tears began to gather in Paulo's eyes and then burst over the dam that held them, down his cheeks and onto the shoulder of his birth mother. This was not a fairytale story that had brought him to this point. His beginnings were filled with drama and pain. But here, in the arms of the one who had conceived him, Paulo felt a "sweetness" that can only come from experiencing the atonement of Jesus Christ and complete forgiveness of another.

Only time would tell just how close birth mother and son would become, but for now, this was a start—a chance for redemption by one... and an opportunity for forgiveness by another.

Jesus Christ had already paid for Maria's sins, but Maria had to make future choices that would define her life moving forward and not let past mistakes control her future. And by the way she held on to Elder Quinteros and received a group hug from his family... with laughter spilling out into the room, she would not be letting go anytime soon.

Paulo had learned along the roadway of his imperfect life that there was no such thing as a "perfect" life, with no hills, twists, or turns to face. He had come to understand the words his dear Felicia had tried to teach him as he left her sitting in the convent courtyard so many years ago:

"Hills are for climbing, Paulo," she had whispered to him.

We are here (on earth) to be tested, tried, and refined. Like steel, we, too, are formed and purified and made spiritually and emotionally stronger with each hill we are called upon to climb. And no matter the outcome as compared to the standards of success set by mortal man, the God of this world has put in play His own mission statement upon which to judge success:

"And this is my work and my glory to bring to pass the immortality and eternal life of man." -Moses 3:19 (Pearl of Great Price)

Heavenly Father's supreme plan is for each of His children to return to the God who loves them, having experienced life, successfully, by "overcoming the natural man within each of us," and having developed faith in God as their creator. He sent His son, Jesus Christ, to absorb those pangs of guilt, the successes of the natural man giving in to temptations of the flesh, and grievous, even heinous, crimes of passion and pre-meditation in exchange for a broken heart and contrite spirit of true repentance. Paulo had learned to trust those impressions that had become stronger as faith in his Creator became more personal and sought after. God had reached out to him, as He will do to each of us... but we must knock first, trusting in God's timing and wisdom for the answer.

Sometimes, trial–as well as faith, must precede the miracle in order to hear and accept the answer when it comes. Sometimes, our faith must be tested first in order to accept God's plan for us when it is time. The underlying love from our Father in Heaven is that He loves us and wants only what is best for us so that we might experience all that life has to offer... while at the same time becoming all that we can be–for *we* are His work and His glory.

Epilogue

"**M**y mission was one of the many highlights of my life...so far," a mature-looking young man spoke from the podium, looking out over the congregation spilling over into the second overflow. A friend of mine at the Convent where I grew up once gave me some wise counsel, but I did not understand it at the time. She said: '*Hills are for climbing, Paulo!*' It was such a simple statement, but I did not comprehend its meaning at first. But looking back in time, I can now see how wise she was," Paulo continued while reaching for a tissue.

"She was trying to tell me that life wasn't going to be easy outside the walls of the Convent and to not look at ups and downs and twists and turns as bad for you. Life isn't going to be perfect, my Brothers and Sisters," he continued. "In fact, it's going to be anything *but* perfect. Yet, it is the imperfect part of our lives that will have the greatest impact upon our preparation for life after death... and life with God in His kingdom, experiencing His glory."

Paulo let out a huge sigh of relief as he came to the end of his talk to his home ward congregation, as is customary for returned missionaries–but his eyes could not be restrained from darting from one smiling face to another as he spoke... searching–until finally holding steady upon one radiant smile. A smile that would hold his heart forever.

Afterword

Author's Personal Message: Paulo (aka Paul Quinteros-Tone) had found his way to the road which would lead him safely home. Unwanted at birth, this young man fought against the turmoil of life without giving in. He did not live a perfect life, but he learned how to do more than survive in an imperfect world–he *thrived...* without being *of* the world–by partaking of the blessings offered through the atonement of our Savior, Jesus Christ.

We, too, resonate with many parts of Paulo's imperfect life. We, too, have held back from forgiving those who have wronged us. And we, too, have wronged others without seeking forgiveness. But there is a way to clear the slate and discover the road that leads to happiness, as young Paulo did. It starts with desire–a desire to change, so sincere that it can bring you into a condition often taught by Jesus Christ... that of a broken heart and contrite spirit–a condition of humility leading to repentance, enabling you to *seek forgiveness* from those you have wronged, and a willingness to make right what you can... a condition enabling you to *forgive* those who have trespassed against you (the Lord's Prayer).

Forgiveness is not always an easy process. Sometimes, it takes time and effort to completely recover from what occurred to hurt you. But if you can look at forgiveness as obtaining one more Christlike attribute, it may become easier because you can visually see yourself changing for the better.

Even when you strive to seek forgiveness for the wrongs you *may* have committed to another, it sometimes takes a broken heart and contrite spirit to overcome the pride to admit a mistake or the fear of rejection that may result from your attempts at resolution. In either case, *attempting* to seek forgiveness is a step forward in removing the heavy burden of carrying guilt or sorrow for being human. You are mortal and will undoubtedly make mistakes. The key to mortality is to *learn* from your mistakes and try not to repeat them.

Seeking forgiveness from another does not always carry a happy ending. There are two wills that must align for complete forgiveness to take place in both persons affected. Agency is still alive and well, even when someone who has offended you knocks on your door to seek forgiveness. You still have agency to let them in or not. If you are the one seeking forgiveness and no one answers, then you now have the opportunity to add one or more Christlike attributes to your ever-growing list. Take, for example, the attribute of *Empathy*.

A person exercises empathy when attempting to understand the actions and needs of another by removing judgment and replacing it with fairness and love. When you try to see the actions of another through their eyes (point of view) and come to recognize *their* humanity for making mistakes as well as your own and *forgive* them for exercising that humanity in the process, then you are on the road to claiming for yourself the atonement of Jesus Christ. Loving another, in spite of their weaknesses and choices is truly a Christlike attribute.

I have learned that choice plays a huge role in forgiveness. No matter the response by the injured to your request for forgiveness it is your choice to either continue carrying the burden or to see yourself as Jesus Christ sees you–one who has sinned against another, has reached the condition of a broken heart and contrite spirit for doing so, sought restitution, asked to be forgiven, and has accepted the right of the injured to either forgive or carry the burden of unforgiveness, themselves. It is then *your* responsibility to forgive yourself so that you may open new vistas of personal opportunities to grow from that experience.

The words, "I'm sorry!" Contain such powerful "potential" for moving mountains in our lives, if spoken sincerely and genuinely.

Compassion is another Christlike attribute to be learned from unforgiveness. Is it not a sign of compassion when we feel the pain of someone else's suffering... and then act to help alleviate it? Can you feel the pain of someone who holds a grudge against you? Can you let them know you are sorry for whatever it was that injured them and that you will do whatever you can to help them recover from their injury?

My dear brothers and sisters in Christ, please begin your quest today to find your road back into *His* grace, that you may discover for yourself the *sweetness* that can come from true forgiveness, as one who has been injured or one who may have injured another... forgiveness is indeed the Bread of Life.

-Charles P. Malone

About the Author

Charles Patrick ("Chuck") Malone was raised in Holbrook, Arizona... a small northern AZ town much like Mayberry, the fictional hometown of Sheriff Andy and Deputy Barney. Depending on who was calling him, he was known as Charles (mostly by his mother), Charley, Chuck, Moose, Gus, and sometimes other names that shouldn't be printed. His unique writing style was in hibernation well beyond his formal education in Holbrook schools, Arizona State University, and Arizona State College (now Northern AZ University), finally coming to life at one of the author's darkest moments while unemployed for two years and fighting his daughter's cancer at the same time.

Chuck (as the author prefers to be called) was guided to answer an ad placed by a regional magazine for a copywriter, which led to using his developed skill of writing real estate contracts–to impress the editor of the magazine into giving him his first writing assignment–leading to his first published photo (front cover) and lead article. This immediate success as a writer gave Chuck the self-confidence to develop his writing style further, approaching a subject with clarity and expression, sprinkled with humor–with just a touch of mischievousness. This "side gig" has earned him copywriting success with many published articles... with such titles as "Decluttering! An Eternal Perspective" and "Dutch Oven Cooking and the Plan of Happiness."

Awarded "Prison Volunteer of the Year" by the Arizona Department of Corrections, Chuck uses his experiences gained from having a front-row seat to the atonement–by serving in prison ministry for five years... and as a Sealer in the Gilbert, AZ Temple and Stake Patriarch–to skillfully guide the reader into the eye of trial to taste the "Sweetness" of the Savior's embrace and to do more than endure trial... but to *Win.*

An active Arizona real estate broker for over fifty-three years, beginning in 1971, Chuck continues to serve his new and longtime clients, placing him among the top producers of the company's licensees, and still finds time to cheer on his seventeen perfect grandchildren from five incredible adult children and their spouses–and stay married to the love of his life, Linda, for fifty-seven years... and counting.

The author has written his many published articles and four full-length books on his iPad (fifth in process) at the local fitness gym while on the treadmill/elliptical/stationary bike, with only one slightly embarrassing fall. He loves public speaking, probably a result of the "fall," and has been a paid motivational speaker in the field of business development and entrepreneurship for many years–back in the day.

Most of Chuck's early book writings were taken directly from his personal experiences, and his third self-published book, "Winning Thru Trial," uses *7 Winning Ways* Chuck developed (from Heavenly inspiration–He takes no credit) to not only endure his many trials but to thrive and "win" from them.

Chuck has discovered his love for writing fiction novels, weaving in faith-based principles taught by Christ. He loves to see his characters change once they embrace the spiritual giant within themselves and accomplish greatness as a disciple of Christ. Through his characters, Chuck inspires his readers to raise the bar of spiritual influence in their own lives.

You can find Chuck on YouTube – Facebook – Instagram – and Twitter... and on the WWW at Facebook.com/ijustwriteit, and Amazon.com /books (search for Charles P. Malone), and his business website: gilberta zhomestoday.com. He loves to speak at family gatherings, empty nesters, church, and special events... He promises not to fall off the podium but will occasionally "drop the mic" when expressing his love for and testimony of Jesus Christ.

You can also "hear" Chuck on Spotify.com reading his first published book, "The Sweetness of Trial," at https:://podcasters.spotify.com/pod/show/charles-p-malone and also on Apple Podcasts... Just search for "The Sweetness of Trial" Book Reading and Commentary.

Chuck loves to hear from his readers and listeners at cmijustwriteit@gmail.com or on Facebook at facebook.com/ijustwriteit/ or his personal Facebook page at facebook.com/chuck.malone. His Instagram page is: instagram.com/chuck.malonejkrealty.

And all the hard work and time spent in writing and self-publishing really pays off when you leave a detailed review on Amazon .com/books that lets Chuck know his book or podcast made your day just a little brighter or gave you just a little more encouragement to become better. Now that's payback!! Thank you so much!

www.ingramcontent.com/pod-product-compliance
Lightning Source LLC
Chambersburg PA
CBHW070544260626
47161CB00002B/496